# Me Cheeta

# Me Cheeta

## My Life in Hollywood

An Imprint of HarperCollinsPublishers

If you would like to make a donation to the
C.H.E.E.T.A. Primate Sanctuary, please visit
http://www.cheetathechimp.org

HarperCollins books may be purchased for educational,
business, or sales promotional use. For information, please write:
Special Markets Department, HarperCollins Publishers,
10 East 53rd Street, New York, NY 10022.

Originally published in a slightly different format in Great Britain
in 2008 by Fourth Estate.

FIRST EDITION

Library of Congress Cataloging-in-Publication Data
is available upon request.

ISBN: 978-0-06-164742-0

09  10  11  12  13  DIX/QWF  10  9  8  7  6  5  4  3  2  1

*To D*

"A movie star is not quite a human being."
—MARLENE DIETRICH

# Contents

# CONTENTS

# Note to the Reader

Dearest humans,

So, it's a perfect day in Palm Springs, California, and here I am—actor, artist, African, American, ape and now author—flat out on the chaise by the pool, looking back over this autobiography of mine. Flipping through it more than reading it, to be honest: the whole Lifetime Achievement idea of an autobiography makes me a little nervous. The—what's the word?—the valedictory aspect to it. I'm in fine health, I'm producing some of the best paintings of my career, I'm in no obvious danger of being killed, but I've seen it happen too many times to too many of my fellow greats. The book comes out, and next thing you know, they've disappeared.

Or, as Johnny once told me, "Soon as they start calling you an Immortal, you start worrying about dying."

I think *Sports Illustrated* had recently made Johnny one of their "Fifty Greatest Immortal Sportspersons" or something like that. This was an evening in the early eighties at his lovely home overlooking the Pacific in Playa Mimosa, Acapulco. He had health issues at the time and people couldn't stop giving him Lifetime Achievement awards. They came at him like diagnoses. And even Johnny Weissmuller, who was so unfailingly upbeat and so reliably delighted by trophies, who'd been inducted into so many Halls of Fame and festooned with so many honors over the years, was finding it difficult to feel any joy about his new Immortal status. After all, it wasn't like it was any kind of a guarantee. He and I both knew for a fact that several "Immortals" we'd once palled around with were now dead. "Past a certain point in your life it's all awards," he added, "for things you can't remember doing."

Well, over the last few years I've started to notice similar, vaguely ominous, signs around *me*. I'm not a superstitious creature, but on the Palm Canyon Drive "Walk of Stars," just around the corner from here, they've already got a star with my name on it, between two guys I've never heard of. There's a campaign brewing to get me a proper star on the real Walk of Fame—at 6541 Hollywood Boulevard, no doubt, between Johnny and Maureen O'Sullivan. The ideal jungle family together again, and rid of the Boy at last. So any day now I expect the arrival of a slab of wet concrete and a delegation from Sid Grauman's Chinese Theater asking for my handprints, though they'll have to live without a signature. (Roy Rogers, I'm pretty sure, signed Trigger's name for him beside the pair of hoofprints that Trigs left, and I think it was the same arrangement with Gene Autry and Champion, the other Wonder Horse. But in truth, if Grauman's does decide they want my handprints, I'd be pretty surprised if Johnny was there to do the same for me. Anyway. Most of the time I don't even think about it.)

So it's my hope, dear reader, that you'll think of this book as more of a hello than a goodbye. If anything, my real worry is that it's somewhat premature.

My original title was *My Story So Far*, as a sort of charm against the idea that it represented a final statement. But unfortunately Donny Osmond had already used that, along with a whole pack of athletes and childhood-abuse survivors. Then I decided that *My*

*Life So Far* would do equally well, but Jane Fonda had bagged it. And let's face it, in the context of Jane's life, the title sounds like a threat. So I figured that, what the hell, I'd plump for *My Life*. Simple and classic and modest—and, I came to realize, already taken dozens of times. As was *My Story*. Also *My Autobiography*, to my irritation by Charlie Chaplin, so that was out. It's bad enough that people think any of my routines owe anything to the bewilderingly overrated Chaplin, shallowest of the great silent clowns. (*Motion Picture Herald*, March 1942: "The chimp Cheta [*sic*] is well handled and provides pic with some decent laughs via antics that almost make you think of Chaplin." For that "almost," a small round of ironic applause!) Furthermore, *The Story of My Life* also turned out to be gone. Similarly *My Life Story* and *In My Life*. And *My Lives*. And *My Lives and Loves*. Likewise, as I soon found when attempting to branch out, *My Life in Film*, *A Life in Film*, *My Life in Movies*, *A Life in Movies*, *My Life in Art* and *My Life in Pictures* (unbelievably that goddamned Chaplin had snaffled that one too).

Despairing somewhat, I thought it might be terrifically daring to begin something with "*American . . .*" or "*Hollywood . . .*" before discovering that *everything* begins "*American . . .*" or "*Hollywood. . . .*" *Cheeta Speaks* came to me as a revelation while I was dozing in this very chair, as did the realization that another great clown, Harpo Marx, had used it up.

Switching tack, I cast around for something a little more descriptive of my story: *Wonderful Life* seemed just about perfect for the five minutes I thought it was mine. Ditto *Survivor*, *A Survivor's Story*, *Memoirs of a Survivor* and the one I really wanted most, *From Tragedy to Triumph*. It turned out that there are whole libraries of books called *From Tragedy to Triumph*. And not a single one called *From Triumph to Tragedy*, I noticed, as if human life only ever proceeded in the one direction, at least in autobiography.

These were meant to be the first words of my literary career. Those humans who thought the very idea of my writing an autobiography was laughable would have been thoroughly confirmed by the sight of me struggling through a series of sleepless afternoons, incapable of producing so much as a single letter. Maybe they were right—actors should stick to acting. My respect for writers, whom I'd silently sneered at throughout my career when presented with another psychologically incoherent script for Tarzan or Jane or me, went through the roof.

Writing was *hard*! It seemed like there had just been too many human lives, and words were no longer capable of coping with them. Words were wearing thin with all those human lives using them up, and always the same lives, moving confidently away from tragedy toward triumph. Who could possibly, I thought, want another memoir by *anyone*? Let alone yet another ex–movie star's reminiscences? How presumptuous to assume that a celebrity's hoary old Hollywood war stories could be of interest to anyone but himself!

At this low ebb, my dear old friend the utterly inimitable Kate Hepburn came to the rescue. Kate had had no such difficulties with the title for her own autobiography. What was the subject? Me, Kate had decided. "A book all about me, by me. I see no reason why it shouldn't be called *Me*. What d'you want me to call it, *You*?" Now, Kate has her Connecticutian sense of entitlement, which helps her march unblushingly up to anything she wants and take it, but I couldn't accept that she had permanently vacuumed up the title *Me*. What about the rest of us? Enough—surely somebody else could call their book *Me* as well as Kate Hepburn, or "Katharine of Arrogance," as she was rather unfairly known during the time we were closest. So, after nearly a month of work, I had my beginning. *Me*. I even had a perfect vision of the cover, which the publishers will mess with over my dead body: *Me*, and then my name in a different font, and that terrific photo which . . . well, you've already seen it for yourself. Left to right—Barrymore, Gilbert, Bogie, Bacall with the ice creams, me, Garbo doing the rabbit ears behind my head and I think that's Ethel Merman's drink I've just knocked over. Don't I look *young*?

I was delighted with this breakthrough—who says chimpanzees have no business writing memoirs?—though keenly aware that unless I managed to up my rate from an average of one letter a fortnight, the whole project might turn out to be a bit of a long haul. In fact, the next two words—the dedication—represented a moderate acceleration in that they took only three weeks of agonized wrestling.

I took a break and returned to my painting—a series of nostalgic jungle-scapes that hardly stretched me. I wanted some time to reassess. What was I writing this book for? The ostensible reason was the one proposed by my dear friend and housemate Don, in partnership with Dr. Jane Goodall, the charming and still attractive (though frequently wrongheaded) English naturalist. That is, I would use the story of my life to help their campaign against the cruelties perpetrated on chimpanzees and other animals in the name of screen entertainment. Of course, I love Don and respect the eminent and attractive Dr. Goodall, and will certainly do what I can to assist No Reel Apes, as the campaign is snappily known. But it seemed to me that something about this conception of *Me* was still preventing me from getting at the story I really wanted to tell. The second ostensible reason—to make damn sure that the Internet Movie Database gets its facts right once and for all—ditto. So what was the story I *really* wanted to write?

Returning to my text, which remained stalled at a word count of three, I attempted to press on into the acknowledgments section, the part writers often refer to as "the hardest page of the book." Or actors do, anyway. And here I had my inspiration: I was lolling in my tire, where I do most of my best thinking, struggling with those tricky little questions of who to put in, who would have to be left out, how to make each message of gratitude sound personal and different, who ought to come first and, more importantly, last, when I realized that it was pointless trying to pick out individuals. Without Hollywood, without humanity as a whole, I wouldn't be here to write these words. Without you I'd literally be nothing. The whole *book* ought be an acknowledgments section!

*This* was the book I wanted to write. No matter how dark the subject or how painful the memories, no matter how tough times occasionally became, no matter how appalling and oafish the behavior of certain people—such as Esther Williams, Errol Flynn, "Red" Skelton, "Duke" Wayne, Maureen O'Sullivan, Brenda Joyce—I would write without bitterness, name-calling or score-settling. I would celebrate what has been a lucky, lucky life, and try to find the good in all those tremendous characters it has been my privilege to know. This would be a book written in gratitude to and with love for your whole species, and for everything you have done for animals and for me. A thank-you. A book of love.

And having made this decision I found that the whole thing just came tumbling out. *You* are my reason for writing this book, all of you, and Johnny, and of course the fact I've learned over seventy years of survival in movies and theater: that if your profile ever dips below a certain level in this industry, you're as good as dead.

Humanity, I salute you!

Cheeta
Palm Springs, 2008

# PART 1

# 1
# Inimitable Rex!

On my last day in motion pictures I found myself at the top of a monkey-puzzle tree in England, helping to settle a wager between that marvelous light comedian and wit Rex Harrison and his wife, the actress Rachel Roberts, and thinking, This is gonna look great in the obituaries, isn't it? Fell out of a fucking *tree*.

This was in '66, during a day off from filming my supposed comeback picture, Fox's disastrous megaflop *Doctor Dolittle*, with Dickie Attenborough and Rex. We were on the grounds of some stately home in the charming village of Castle Combe in County Wiltshire, some time after a heavy lunch.

Rex was convinced that the tree would puzzle me. Rachel thought I'd be able to work it out. Arriving at the terms of the bet had not been easy. How exactly was I to demonstrate my mastery of this cryptic plant?

"You ought to let it start at the top, and then it's got an incentive to climb down," said Lady Combe. Servants were ordered to fetch a ladder. She was delighted at the success of her party. "This *is* exciting. Is it always so much fun with you film folk?"

"Now then, Cheeta," said Rachel, holding a pack of cigarettes very close to my face. "You see these Player's? They'll be waiting at the bottom for you. You understand? Yummy cigarettes. Don't you dare let me down."

"Darling, I've just had rather a splendid idea," said Rex. "Why don't we forget the money? If the monkey makes it you can sleep with Burton, if he'll have you, and if it doesn't, then I can divorce you but you have to promise not to kill yourself."

"Getting nervous, Rex?"

"*Au contraire*, my sweet. Let's call it two thousand."

"Oh dear," said Lady Combe. "Is something the matter?"

"Yes," said Rex. "Your cellar is atrocious."

Rex and I had had a number of differences on the set, but nothing you wouldn't expect to see between a couple of stars pushing a script in different directions. Far from being the coward and sadist Rachel frequently described him as, Rex was, somewhere beneath the caustic exterior he had designed to conceal his vulnerabilities, a good man and a very special human being. Nonetheless I'd been upset to have every one of my off-the-cuff contributions vetoed. This interminable "Talk to the Animals" song had already taken us a week. Perhaps I was a little rusty—I hadn't worked in movies for almost twenty years—but Rex had nixed every one of the backflips or handstands I'd been trying to liven it up with. So I was pretty keen to get this tree climbed. Plus I wanted the cigarettes—and, anyway, I wasn't about to be outwitted by a *tree*.

But the French call them "monkey's despair." From a distance, each limb had appeared invitingly fuzzy, furred like a pipe cleaner or the interior of Rex's arteries, but as soon as I grasped one I discovered that the thing was made entirely out of horrible spiky triangular leaves, more like *scales* than leaves. Unfortunately, Rachel had already ordered the ladder to be removed and I could do nothing but cling to the crown of the tree, slapping my head with one

4

hand and communicating via some screaming, which required little translation, that I was perfectly happy to let Rex have the money.

"Don't make such a fuss, Cheeta! It's just getting adjusted," Rachel assured the little crowd, as I tried cautiously to inch down that torture chamber of a tree for her. But it really was impossible. The French were right. The English name had led me to believe that the tree would be no more than some mildly diverting brain-teaser, the chimpanzee equivalent of the Sunday crossword—but this was a puzzle only in the sense that being violently assaulted by a plant is, yeah, a somewhat puzzling experience. Fucking typical English understatement.

"I rather think," Rex commented, "you owe me two thousand pounds."

"Don't go off half-cocked, darling, like you always do. . . . It's only been up there a minute."

Jesus, was that all?

"Don't be absurd, you drunken bitch. It's stuck."

"You're not welching me out of this one, Rexy-boy," I heard Rachel say. "I never expected it to start climbing right away. You just hold your damn horses."

"Now, Rachel, *please,* it's perfectly clear the poor animal's in distress," I heard another voice interject. Oh, great: Dickie. "The pair of you should be ashamed. Lady Combe, can we please please *please* get that ladder back up? This is quite frightful!"

"You touch that ladder, Lady Whatsyourface," Rex said, "and I promise you, there'll be tears before bedtime. Nobody touch that bloody ladder! My pathetic shell of a wife is making a point. Dickie, do piss off and stop blubbering."

"Thank you, darling," said Rachel.

"You're welcome, darling," said Rex.

They weren't all that much fun to be around, Rex and Rachel, it does have to be said. I'd never liked the goddamn English anyway, with their razor-wire elocution, their total lack of humor and their godawful pedantic spelling. I clung on, cheeping in distress and swaying eighty feet above the ground. This had all begun a week ago, as we were embarking on Rex's endless song, which I don't think he believed in any longer. He regularly punctuated "Talk to the Animals" with violent outbursts of animal-related abuse. He was failing to cope with the toupée-munching goat, the parrot that kept shouting "Cut," and the general incompetence of the inexperienced English animals, and he was beginning to take it out on me. "I don't mind the bloody ducks and the sheep," he'd complained after we'd abandoned shooting for the day again, "so much as this *monkey* trying to upstage me all the time."

This was distressing to hear. I'd been lucky to get the job after two decades of stage work and it was important to keep my co-star happy. I accepted Rachel's half-offered cigarette and demonstrated one of my old standbys, the amusingly raffish side-of-mouth exhalation. But Rex was unappeased.

"And now it's pinching your fags," he said, "or did you do that deliberately? Is it that time of the afternoon already?"

"What an absolutely irresistible charmer you are, my sweet," said Rachel. "I was just thinking how much it resembled you, though it's still got all its own hair, hasn't it? I expect it can still get it up, too."

From this point on, Rachel began to refer to me as Little Rexy— "Ooh, look! Little Rexy's smelling his own poo!"—and would then make references to my superior intellect, charm, personal appearance, talent, virility and odor, which of course were the last things the universally despised, impotent, alcoholic, cruel, vain, brittle, snobbish and mephitic but still, under that carapace of protective acerbity, very gentle and insecure human being Rex needed to have rubbed in.

Meanwhile, he was oscillating between this rather threatening fantasy of buttonholing various exotic creatures on obscure subjects and straightforward abuse of animals. "If this unspeakable fucking shit of a goat touches my hairpiece again, I'll rip its throat out," he'd say in his inimitably crusty manner, and then he'd be off again, wearing his "gentle" face, with his unlikely plan to set up a multispecies *salon*—

> I'd expatiate on Plato with a platypus
> On sex I would talk man to manta ray
> I'd discuss dialectical materialism with a micro-organism
> I'd enquire of an echidna if Picasso were passé . . .

and on and on. I mean, this song of Rex's was endless—

> Oh, how I yearn to yack with yaks in Yakkish
> Or interrogate a fruit bat about Freud
> I'd like to natter with some gnats in Gnattish
> I'd harangue orang-utans about the Void . . .

Ostensibly a beautiful dream, it missed the point. Nothing needs to be said. There is no need for humanity to put its love for animals into words, no need for further explanation or apology. We understand each other perfectly. And besides, Rex's idea raised the nightmarish possibility of animals having to participate in the sort of "sophisticated" discussions the unbelievable Chaplin used to host in Beverly Hills, with unfortunate fauna being hounded for their opinions on the latest Eugene O'Neill, etc. Jesus, that poor fruit bat,

I thought. If Rex got onto Freud, he'd be there all night, hearing about how bizarre it was that so many of Rex's girlfriends had killed themselves, or tried to: I saw Rex touring the remaining forests of the planet agonizing to unwary wildebeests at the water hole about, for instance, his failure to call an ambulance when his lover Carole Landis killed herself with Seconal because he wanted to keep the affair quiet. Then turning on some warthogs and screaming that they were shits who didn't have half the money or talent he did. I could hear him now (nobody could get the song out of their heads) below me: "Oh silly little clever little monkey / You're going to plummet to your death in just a tick / tum-ti-tum-ti-tum, stick it up your bum / tah-ti-tah-ti-uh . . . ick, ick, uh . . ." Sadi-*stic*?

Belatedly I understood the full horror of the situation. It had been my co-star Rex who had made the suggestion that I accompany the other leads to Combe Hall. It was he who had floated the swattable second serve of a notion to Rachel that "If the monkey's so much cleverer than I am, then surely it should be able to climb that tree. . . ."

Or was I being paranoid? Ask Carole Landis if I was being paranoid. Oh, what larks!

I heard Dickie sniveling eighty feet below ("This is all very *upsetting!*") and Rex cleverly setting up his mentally ill wife to take the blame ("Satisfied, darling? Shall we bring it down yet?"). I swayed above them all on the boneless branches that bit my hands and feet and looked out over the pretty fields of County Wiltshire. I watched the shadows of low, flat-bottomed clouds pass across the rain-spoiled wheat, like paranoid fantasies through Veronica Lake's vodka-sodden mind, and saw them dissolve into a gray mass, becoming a black line at the horizon, reminding me of an unfortunate snake I once knew. England—where chimps meant *tea*. Somewhere out there was Jane, if she was still alive, tough as old boots, crow-footed but trim, and ferocious about the rent. Maybe Lady Combe *was* Jane? And Boy, too, who'd ended up in England. He was probably somewhere across the fields—a part-time film producer with his hand between the thighs of the filly he was taking down to see Ma in the MG.

I once knew a man who did talk to the animals. All he'd ever needed was a single word.

Well, in attempting to inch closer to the trunk where the branches were thicker, I jabbed my palm, lost my grip, tried again and grasped nothing. I fell. Ho-hum. Death. I had no business being here anyway. You hear a lot of crap on the Discovery Channel these days about animals making a comeback. Take it from me: don't bother, you can't ever come back. It was a terrible movie and I wasn't any good in it. I descended and bumped into my first ever memory on the way: Stroheim! Hadn't thought about him in years!

I carried on plummeting through the tree's interior and, though I had no say in it, my fall was broken by several instinctive grabs, not so painful at that speed. It must have looked pretty good, I imagine, as I looped in three or four swings through the branches to land on my feet—ta-dah!—next to the pack of Player's. The audience in the garden was startled into the first real applause I'd heard in a long time. I, of course, looked nonchalant and helped myself to a cigarette. What do you think about that, Rex?

He looked like a guy who'd just lost two thousand "quid," to utilize a little Limey-speak. But he was only a weakling and a bully and a near-murderer, scumbag, self-pitier, miser, liar, ass and oaf on the outside—who isn't? Somewhere on the inside there was a decent human being. Oh, all right: Rex Harrison was an absolutely irredeemable cunt who tried to murder me—but still, you have to try to forgive people, no matter what. Otherwise we'd be back in the jungle.

I forgive you, Rex.

Anyway, I was unsurprised and quite relieved when I found out that evening that they didn't need me any longer. Rex had had a word. And that, folks, was the end of that.

# 2
# Early Memories

Once upon a time in a land far, far away . . . or pretty far away, anyway. It's eighteen hours even if you get a direct flight from Vegas. And there's nothing much there now anyway, except some farms and red mud. Don Google-Earthed it. Once upon a time I was a little prince in a magic kingdom. I can't remember anything before my memory of Stroheim, as if that was the thing that shook my consciousness awake. He fell out of a fig tree chasing after a blue-tailed monkey. *Thump* went Stroheim, and I was off and running, once upon a time—but let me tell this straight, dearest humans. You must know how it ends. . . .

There was Mama and me and my sister, and we lived in the forest below an escarpment with about twenty others, whose names I guess I'll have to change. I slept high up in a nest of leaves that Mama would prepare in the crook of a branch, with Victoria curled around me and Mama around her. In the mornings Mama would take us across the stream to fish for termites. Victoria would ride on her back and I would cling underneath. The water was cold and fast-flowing and pressed against me as we crossed but I always felt safe. And when we climbed into the trees and moved through the canopy, Victoria would climb behind us on her own, following Mama's soft hoots.

When we got to the termite mounds, Mama would strip a twig and insert it into one of the holes, leaving it in long enough for the termites to clamp their mandibles onto it. You were supposed either to crunch them off one by one or slide them through your mouth in one go, or just mop them up with the back of your wrist. You've seen it on National Geographic. Me and Victoria were too young for termites and I liked it very much when she copied Mama and groomed me, or held me up by one leg to dangle upside down.

What else did I like? Figs, moonfruit, a big yellowy-green fruit that fizzed when you ate it, passionflower buds, Victoria, Mama, holding on to Mama's hair to ride her, being suckled by Mama, playing with Frederick, Tyrone and Deanna, the taste of the leaves that Mama would chew into a little sponge to dab up fresh rainwater, the flashing orange on the heads of the turacos, dreams of the escarpment and, most of all, rain dances. I didn't like termites, palm nuts, the faces of baboons, the tree that had killed Clara, the smell of the python we chased after, Marilyn, whom Mama had to fight, young males charging at Mama if we were on our own, nightmares, the mewling of leopards, Stroheim.

You've never seen a rain dance, have you? They were us at our best. For hours beforehand you'd feel the electricity building in the air. You'd climb up into the lower canopy to escape the humidity, and it would slither up the trunk behind you. So you'd climb higher, until finally you'd be perched in the topmost branches, high over the rest of the forest, panting and sticky with moisture, too tired even to reach for one of those fizzing yellowy-green fruits whose name, dammit, escapes me.

From across the forest you'd hear the low coughs given out by other tree climbers. No birds. No insects. Only our low, muffled coughs, echoless in the wet air. Then the first pant-hoots: the long low hoots, the shorter higher breaths. Mama and the others in our tree would respond with their own hoots, counting themselves in, and then the pants would climb higher, flowering into screams, and the screams would link into a continuous long chorus, and as the rain began to leak a few drops Mama would start pounding on the trunk, shaking the branches, like she was trying to wake the tree up too, and you could hear us all through the forest, drumming up the storm. And over it all, our alpha, Kirk, summoning us to gather for the dance.

We'd climb down from our tree and follow his call through the forest. In my memory it's always dusk as we spot Kirk, walking upright at the top of a long-grassed ridge and howling in the approaching rain, looking terrifying up close, twenty times my own size. He seems to be coaxing the thunder toward us, reeling it in. The other grown-ups, like Cary and Archie, are quieter but also tranced and visibly shaking. The thunder swings through the upper canopy, approaching in huge, looping leaps until finally it's upon us, above us, all over us, and the air suddenly turns into rain.

The mothers clear themselves and us children away into the sloe trees to watch. We're absolutely rapt. Kirk, illuminated by lightning, charges down the ridge at an astonishing speed. Then Cary, who's clever, discovers that rocks can be made to bounce up and smack satisfyingly into the foliage. Cary can always do certain things Kirk can't. Archie is smaller than the others and finds a branch to whack against a tree trunk, leaving a series of white scars. They are our heroes, and Victoria and I are too enthralled by it all to eat our sloes. And soon, as it always is, the wicked thunder is faced down and slinks off, cowed by our vigor, sent on its way with a kick by the youngsters, like Stroheim and Spence, who are pelting down the charge route in imitation of Kirk. The rain falls as applause and we drink it up. Mama and Victoria and I share out sloes between us.

I love rain dances. When I grow up, I think, I'm going to be in them.

We were the only ones in the forest who made art or fashioned tools, the only ones who cooperated, the ones with the most sophisticated and highly evolved culture. We thought there was nobody like us. And our queen was Mama. My mother was the queen of the world.

She was extraordinarily beautiful, and not only in her children's eyes. I know now how to describe her coat: it was the color of Coca-Cola refracted through ice, a deep black with an accent of copper, and yet there was also, especially when she sparkled with rain, a faint blue nimbus around her as if she were coolly on fire. Broad-backed and not tall, she had a low center of gravity and huge hands and feet, which meant that even the way she moved was serene. Her eyes were direct and emitted a soothing amber light. She'd lost only a few teeth and the tatter in one of her ears she wore kind of rak-ishly, a concession to imperfection, like the abscess on her upper lip. Kirk held sway over us, but it was Mama who shored him up, calmed Cary and the other rivals, did the grooming and reconcil-ing and generally stopped everyone from killing each other.

Forgive the boasting, but it's true: she was respected and loved where Kirk was merely feared. It was Mama to whom both Kirk and Cary came screaming for reassurance. She was always two steps ahead. She could figure out how a squabble between Cary and Archie over Marilyn would lead to Veronica being battered by Kirk. She gave Marilyn a real dressing-down when she ate Veronica's baby, Jayne. We even used to visit with Stroheim's crippled mother, Ethel, since Mama realized it would do the nervous Stroheim good if his mother could move up a little in the hierarchy. She endured the beatings she had to take with grace and was pretty handy in a ruckus. She was so beautiful, so smart; she was so *young*.

I remember riding her on our patrols, led by Kirk across the stream and through the ravine guarded by Clara's tree, six or seven of us in single file through the deep grass—so deep only I, sitting on Mama's back, could see above the blades—and down again into the forest of moonfruits and figs where our territory overlapped with that of the hostiles who roamed the other side of the escarpment. We would fall silent, grinning nervously, and I'd feel my mother's hair bristle scratchily erect beneath me. Here, the thrashing of a branch might mean a baboon or a battle. I've never seen a hostile properly—I find it difficult to believe in them. Hostiles to me are black blobs who answer our calls from the ridge on the horizon. We listen an enormous silence into existence. Above us white-faced monkeys pitter-patter through the canopy; turacos flash their orange crests. Now there's something in the silence. Everyone touches each other. We're all here. Phew! Keep calm, everyone: we certainly do seem to need to give each other a hell of a lot of reassurance all the time. Everyone OK? And immediately there's a pant-hoot from ahead of us and a tree quivers and a male hostile drops to the ground with a crack of branches.

We panic. Kirk and Cary are on their feet and hooting. I find myself squashed into Mama's back as Spence and Stroheim scurry behind her, frantically embracing each other, her, me, anything. If only Kirk had a stick or some rock or something! But it's all right. It's all right. It's not a hostile, only old Alfred, who used to roam with us and now lives on the other side of the escarpment. We never do meet hostiles. Still, you can't be too careful.

But I remember this incident because Stroheim, his nerves too taut, came barreling out from behind the shelter of Mama's legs, screaming, and caught Alfred with a kick on the side of the head just as he was turning his back to be groomed. Everybody else panicked again, but Mama was there first, to sink her teeth into Stroheim's arm and hustle him away from the maelstrom he'd nearly created. Give her an awkward social situation and she always blossomed. She was the one who coaxed the sulking Stroheim down from his tree to join in the general grooming session everybody felt the need of after all that. It was Mama who kissed and cradled him, nuzzled the wound (not serious) in his arm and meticulously picked over every inch of his back as if in search of what it is in some that makes their every cell crave dominance.

His problem was that he just couldn't act to save his life. Ricocheting downward between the branches of the fig tree as that blue-tailed monkey scampered away, poor old Stroheim was already, before he hit the ground, composing his features into an expression of wholly unconvincing unconcern. Breaking his ribs? Sure, that was what he'd been *meaning* to do—potential alphas liked nothing better!

Nothing that he did convinced. Whenever the big lummox did manage to catch a blue-tailed monkey he was somehow never able to keep it in the mêlées that ensued, and his supposedly indifferent saunter toward the empty fruit trees was heartbreaking to see. And acting was so very important, so central to everything we did, because of the hierarchy. Acting big, acting injured to save yourself from worse, acting unconcerned to avoid conflict, acting yourself into a credible rage. Stroheim hadn't played enough as an infant because Ethel's withered leg isolated her—but he was huge for his age. He had no confidence; he had an excess of confidence. He didn't know who he was supposed to be. Since human beings have both a mother and a "father," you should be able to imagine it easily enough. How, if the two things that made you are constantly fighting, it can just rip you apart.

But we only had mothers, who would build us nests from leaves, and soothe us when we whimpered in our sleep, dreaming of the bird that was red, blue, green and gold at the same time, or of the escarpment, where I always imagined there was a paradise of figs, tended by wiser, gentler apes than us. Our mothers woke us by blowing in our faces. They were always with us, only abandoning us for a moment to climb an awkward tree and shake down fruit for us. I can remember waiting and waiting in the grass for what must in fact have been only a minute while Mama shook away at the branches of the tree above me, and how, out of the canopy, came dropping one of those fizzy yellowy-green fruits . . . whose name now drops from an obscure branch of memory into my beautiful home here in Palm Springs, gently rotating as it falls. Wild custard apples.

I was a little prince, whose mama was the queen of the world, and then everything changed.

In '39 or something, I remember being at this theme party in Marion Davies's beach hut—you could have fitted a beach inside it—with Nigel Bruce, the English actor you'll remember as Basil Rathbone's sidekick, an excessively slow-witted Dr. Watson. The theme was Movie Stars. Wallace Beery had come as Rudolph Valentino. Joan Crawford had come as Shirley Temple. Shirley Temple had come as Joan Crawford. Gloria Swanson had come as Gloria Swanson. W. C. Fields had come as Rex the Wonder Horse. Rex hadn't been invited. Champion the Wonder Horse had come as Rin Tin Tin. Nobody had come as Charles Foster Kane. And Nigel Bruce, who was a friend of Johnny's and had arranged to borrow me from MGM, had come as Tarzan. He wore a loose pinkish body stocking on which were printed leopard-skin shorts. Nigel was an absolute brick and had furnished me with a cigar so that if anyone asked he could tell them I'd come as Groucho Marx. I strained at Nigel's hand, convinced I was bound to see Johnny somewhere in the ballroom. I swore I saw him, thought I saw him again, caught a glimpse of bare flesh and leather that turned out to be a Red Indian, and then saw him *again* . . .

It was just a pity for Nigel and for my misused heart that Melvyn Douglas, Walter Pidgeon, George Axelrod, Louis Calhern, F. Scott Fitzgerald, at least two of the Hearst sons and Myrna Loy had all come as the King of the Jungle. Some were in body stockings with the seams showing, some stripped down to impressively authentic loincloths: all of them (apart from Fitzgerald, who had accidentally left his in a cloakroom) accompanied by leashed chimpanzees, mostly borrowed from Hearst's zoo at San Simeon. And meanwhile, Johnny was nowhere to be seen. But then again, how was I to know what to look for? He might have been blacked up as Al Jolson or masked as the Phantom of the goddamn Opera.

And everywhere I looked the two of us were bound together in mythic partnership, *solemnized* as a couple, and in reality I hadn't seen him for over six months . . . but another time. It's not the point of the story—please forgive the digression, the point is that the unifying theme behind all of Marion's beach-hut parties was Drunken Sex. I ended that night in one of the little cabañas that were dotted around the grounds, watching my new friends Ronald Colman, Paulette Goddard, Hedy Lamarr, Harry F. Gerguson, a.k.a. "Prince Michael Alexandrovich Obolensky Romanoff" of Romanoff's restaurant, and about half a dozen other very special but not so famous human beings copulate *en masse* and thinking, *Bonobos*. They're like a bunch of fucking bonobos.

I was gloomily perched on a Louis XIV dressing table, which had doubtless once stood in the Palace of Versailles, yawning into my bottle of Canadian Club while my colleagues toiled through their biological necessities at inordinate length, when I became aware that a note was missing from that alluring olfactory chord of urine, vomit, fungal infection, menstrual blood and sweat that characterizes any human gathering. Not one of the six or seven women was ovulating. It wasn't necessary, I brooded, for dear Paulette to remove Paul Henreid's phallus from her mouth, which still sported its packing-tape Charlie Chaplin mustache, and for her to hiss over her shoulder at the laboring Colman, "Don't fucking get me pregnant, Ronnie, OK? Come on my ass."

How I envied them, these humans who, like bonobos, didn't confine sex to the times when conception could happen. That, I suddenly saw, made all the difference in the world. How happy they looked! How easy and gay the scene was! How much fun—no matter how comically, almost endearingly, protracted. (Not to boast, but I used to pride myself on never taking longer than fifteen seconds over a female's pleasure, managing on several memorable occasions, with sparkling technique and due consideration for my partner, to get it down to less than two or three.) There in my bourbon fog on the Louis XIV table I was wondering why the hell it couldn't have been like that for us. Why did it all have to be hierarchy, and possessiveness, and blood and shoving?

I guess love has its mysteries. Thanks to good old National Geographic and Discovery, which we have on pre-select in the den, I've puzzled out a few things I didn't know then. At the time I didn't have a clue why, when Mama began to swell, everything turned into such a circus. Why it was impossible for the three of us to go anywhere without a wake of screaming males, their hair up like iron filings, bipedaling around in a delirium of insecurity and violence? When Mama was actually mating with Kirk, Cary, Lon, Archie, Stroheim, Spence, Mel or Tom—those were the relatively quiet interludes, lasting for a good ten seconds at a time. But the rest of the time we just walked in a forest of out-thrust penises, which was always one misplaced gaze away from going up in flames. We tiptoed gingerly through a minefield of erections.

The tension between Cary and Kirk was a constant scream in our nerves. And every flare-up had to be followed by the long reconciliations we needed, reconciliations that increasingly ended in fresh fights that had to be reconciled. Everyone was either fighting or reconciling all the time. (We used to have some neighbors like that in Palm Springs until, thank Christ, she got some therapy and kicked him out.) Spence had had a finger broken by Cary, who had a wound in his shoulder from Kirk, who was carrying a fractured ankle after a tangle with Lon and Cary. And Mama couldn't help because she was the flashpoint. Her sumptuously taut vaginal swelling, twice the size of her head, was a blazing beacon of division. When Mama presented for young Spence, Kirk clamped Spence's foot between his teeth and hurled him away with a wrench that ripped off a toe. He outranked him, so fair enough, I guess.

Around the time that Mama's swelling was approaching its height, Cary killed a pair of colobus monkeys, and with the others occupied by the feast, Mama slipped away with us down to the stream to drink. Archie knuckled out of the trees with a greeting of quiet pant-grunts and Mama, he and Victoria groomed each other for a while; then Archie crossed the stream, shaking a branch to make us follow. Mama swung me onto her and we set off behind him: I lay straddled on her back, looking out for the many-colored bird or marmosets or turacos in the canopy. Victoria knuckled along quietly after us, holding a termite stick she'd made out of a msuba twig, and Archie led the way, impatiently shaking branches at us if we lagged behind.

There were fig trees below us, and Mama and Victoria were tired, but when we tried to turn back, he came hoot-screaming and charging out of the shadows, and I tumbled off Mama's back as she went sprawling under his impact. He grabbed her by the leg and dragged her down the slope, kicking and pummeling her, then stalked back past us with his hair bristling and sat down, waiting for her to stop screaming and come to him, which she did. She had to: she had us to look after, you see. He apologized with kisses and caresses, and groomed her for a while before we set off again. This was the beginning of what National Geographic refers to as a "consortship period." Discovery calls it "Honeymoon in the Trees"!

Where did Archie take us? Over the hills and far away. Past the place where we'd met Alfred, through strange forests of moss-covered trees to the higher ground beside the escarpment, where the clouds clung and little groups of banded mongooses scurried around, carrying frogs in their mouths. We nested in a giant msuba beside a termite mound, and Archie kissed Mama's wounds and groomed her and apologized for hours and mated her again and again. Next day Mama and Archie took Victoria and me termite fishing, and as a special treat Archie showed me how to make a termite-fishing stick.

Mama hardly played with us because Archie was all over her, and if we tugged at her fur while she was being penetrated, she'd distractedly wave us off to play elsewhere. Victoria taught me how to climb, but I missed Tyrone and our tumbling games and groomings. Archie, on the other hand, was having a ball—constantly either guzzling termites, in his horrible lip-smacking way, or mating. I tried a bit of mongoose and didn't like it. It rained all the fucking time.

I remember, too, one evening near the end of the honeymoon, how we were surprised by the cries of a strange animal from far, far away. The distant hoots of the hostiles had died away at dusk, and then came these other cries—sudden barks, or cracks, like sharp thunderclaps. Little sequences of these long-echoing thunderclaps, out of a stormless sky, far away but loud. Crack, crack, crack. Crack-crack. In six months, I'd be sucking on a Lucky Strike and making prank phone calls in a bar on the Lower East Side of Manhattan. So. What happened was this.

We were on our way back to our old territory when we came across Kirk, lounging between the roots of a msuba in a shaft of sunlight that illuminated a haze of golden flies. He'd been stuffing himself with passionfruit and his front was matted with juice and seeds. And then I saw the white bars of his ribs and all the turmoil in there and understood that the seeds were flies and the juice was Kirk's blood. Archie darted toward him, then away, and Mama barked feverishly at the air and pounded the earth on all fours. Victoria raced back and forth, blindly, very fast, cheeping, and I realized that something very bad was happening. Archie darted up to Kirk in his cloud of flies, lifted his hand and let it drop. He recoiled and did it again and Kirk's hand did nothing—and still I didn't really make the connection that he was dead, like a bushpig or a blue-tailed monkey could be dead. It was too hard to grasp: Kirk, our heroic rain-dancer, our thunder-conquering king!

We moved on, quickly, without grooming, and Mama's hair wouldn't stop bristling beneath me. Death was sticking to us. I became frightened because I thought I'd done something very wrong and was going to be punished for it. It hadn't been me, I wanted Mama to understand. It was a leopard—or maybe he'd fallen out of a tree, like Stroheim! We crossed the stream back to where we'd been when Mama's swelling started, and the feeling of Death forded the water with us. It climbed up among the empty nests of our old roosting tree and slept beside us too, and woke with us in the night to the echo of more of those far-distant cracks, louder in the blackness, and when morning came, slow and white and wet, we saw another adult male, whose name I didn't know, caught in a tangle of branches high above, gnawed by the baboons or leopard that had left him where he was hanging and much more dead than Kirk.

Even Victoria and I knew it then, I think. What else could have done this if not the hostiles? All we knew about hostiles was that they were hostile. In fact, it was absolutely typical hostile behavior, if you thought about it. Mama climbed to the crown of a custard-apple tree and pant-hooted in four directions, but got no answer: the whole forest seemed to be teeming with death. At a fast trot she led us up one of the deep-grassed ridges that spoked off from the escarpment and gave a view of the canopy below but there were no black blobs moving in the treetops, no chains of dots leaving a wake through the long-grassed slopes; neither friends nor enemies. High up we climbed, toward the escarpment, into the tatters of mist that beaded our coats, and then, where the ridge finally flattened and was reabsorbed by the forest of the escarpment, at last we heard a long, low hoot from ahead, and though Archie bristled, I recognized the voice as Spence's.

Poor Spence was limping. Fucking hostiles, I remember thinking (my translation). He gave another weak hoot and tried to move toward us out of the trees and down the ridge, but wasn't really able to. He whimpered and tried to lift his arm to show us, and Mama set me down in the tall grass and scampered up toward him, followed, after a nervous grin, by Archie. Victoria pitter-pattered after them, through the skeins of mist that scudded over the ridge. Mama paused, and held out a hand to her, and as she caught up, and the three of them got to the edge of the trees, Spence suddenly disappeared from sight and the hostiles came screaming out of the long grass toward them.

Archie was engulfed in a tide of bristling black and that was the last I saw of him. I never saw Victoria again; the last I remember of my sister is the sight of her catching up to Mama. I fled back down the ridge the way we'd come, suddenly capable of running, and when I fell, I looked back up the ridge and saw Mama running toward me, and a couple of hostiles—except they weren't hostiles, of course, but Cary, who once carried me down from a msuba tree, and Spence, who used to feed me bits of moonfruit—running shoulder to shoulder with her. She fell, or was tripped, and then Cary was stamping on her, and others were catching up. From the tall grass I watched her try to rise. But Cary and Spence and Tom were on her—all my fathers were on her, screaming with hatred, with outrage. Stroheim nipped in and out, capering with excitement, but I didn't see him strike. It didn't even occur to me to try to rescue her. I just took off down the side of the ridge where the slope was so steep I could almost fall down it into the upper canopy of the trees below.

I blundered through a maze into the lower canopy, where I was hidden, and blundered on until I had to stop and rest in a little cradle of branches. After a while, there didn't seem to be much reason to go anywhere; Mama was my only home, and she would find me if she could. So I didn't move, except once to get some leaves when the cradle began to hurt. I breathed and slept and didn't grow hungry, and let the rain fall on me as it fell on everything else.

What happened to us, dearest humans, was nothing special. I suppose Cary must have staged a coup against old Kirk, and then against his two other main rivals. But who cares? It was just politics. Sooner or later, every creature that lives in a forest has to learn that there's only the hierarchy and alphadom and the constant dance of death. From the termites to the turacos to the marmosets and pythons, from the mongooses to the leopards and the apes, every one of us, every second of every day, was simply trying to pass on its death to another. Even the bushpigs at their mothers' teats, stealing milk from their brothers and sisters, and the trees and the grasses too. Everything that lived, murdered. We were meant to be the best of all creatures, the paragon of the animals, and we also were mired in it. I watched the turacos around me stab the caterpillars and kept thinking there had to be something—one thing—that wasn't hostile to its bones. But everything was steeped in death: all creatures great and small.

I stayed in my tree for what seemed a long time; a day and a night, and a day, and another night, and another day. I heard the turacos' chicks screaming for their caterpillars; I watched the many-colored bird alight and fly off and wondered whether I might become a bird now that I meant never to go to ground again. I heard hooting and barking close by; glazedly I watched Cary make the leap from the foliage of the sloe tree next to me; I saw the way the branch gave as he landed; I saw the turacos and the orioles scatter, the butterflies explode, and the streams of ants not minding; and I watched him prise open the ribcage of the tree toward where I lay cradled. And only when he was almost upon me did I realize I wasn't reconciled to it: I didn't want to die. To my surprise, I wanted to survive.

There was no chance that I could outclimb Cary: I waited until my own branch was quivering with his weight, and then dropped back down into what I had once thought was my own little princedom. Then I was running again on rubbery legs, and I thought the worst that could happen was that I'd be chased off and could maybe find Mama or Victoria before the leopards got me. But I saw that closer to me than Cary, and even more frightening, was Stroheim. He was almost *hopping* with exultation at the way his world had suddenly become a whole lot simpler. Big dumb Stroheim, who later, by the way, went on to a nothing-much career in Hollywood. In fact, MGM used to loan him out to RKO, where he'd occasionally crop up in tenth-rate B's, bull-necked, horse-faced and bald, staring into the camera with a kind of George Raft aura. If you just wanted an ape to sit there and not bump into the furniture, then he could do a job for you. He was no worse than a stuffed one, you could say that much: he *breathed* perfectly convincingly. Sorry, I digress. Where was I? Of course—about to be murdered by an extra. I veered down a slope, fell, felt Stroheim's fingers missing my heels and then catching them, and then, as we skated over a slippery slick of leaves, he was on top of me and then horribly around me and Cary was skidding into us as we both fell together. So it was in a ball of enemies—a sort of writhing bolus like you see snakes make—that I died and began to ascend to heaven.

I was shot up toward the canopy, toward the sky. I rose faster than you can fall. I understood that I would become a bird—it all made sense. A many-colored bird was what you became when you died. And then we sagged to a halt and hung, the three of us, still tangled in our ball of hatred, denied entry to the next stage of life.

About a foot from my face I saw an ape, white-faced, complexly coated, smiling. This, I would later discover, was Mr. Tony Gentry, whose funeral in Barstow, California, 1982, would be such a solemn affair that I ended up playing a few of my favorite atonal noodles (not *yet* available on CD, but there are plans) on the organ to cheer everyone up a bit.

"Got three!" shouted the ape. "Three of them, having a little play together!"

Humanity. Thank God for you.

We were lowered to the ground, separated, and gently ushered into wooden cubes. Kind hands urged us inside our chambers; gentle voices urged us to eat. I saw old friends in other chambers—my old playmates Frederick and little Tyrone. And others: the innocent and the guilty alike. I was pretty sure we were still alive, though it did seem equally likely that we were all dead and in another world. But I didn't see Mama, or Victoria.

Two mind-bendingly peculiar days later, we were sitting in a monsoon in a town that Don's pretty sure used to be called Kigoma, an old West African term that translates as "Salvation."

# 3
# Sailing Away!

When I think back to my last day in Africa, I can't help but remember something Maureen O'Sullivan said to me at the very beginning of my career. "There, there, Cheeta. The hurt will die down. It has to. Otherwise none of us could stand life!"

Maureen's rather breezily delivered comment, by the way, was an attempt, some fifty minutes into *Tarzan and His Mate*, to offer consolation on the death of my on-screen mother. My on-screen mother who had just been impaled on the horn of a stampeding rhinoceros *while saving Jane's life*! She said it briskly, in her trademark singsong, which made it seem as if she was cheering me up after a surprise omission from the varsity lacrosse team rather than helping me come to terms with a bereavement she herself had caused. I'm getting off the point but if Maureen's daughter, Mia Farrow, had been fatally gored while saving *my* life, I'd have gone straight to her with an apology that I'd at least have tried to make sound sincere. (Though—dare one say it—that would have been one hell of a popular rhino in Hollywood.)

But that was Maureen all over, I'm afraid. She couldn't even *act* affection for animals although, to be perfectly honest and give the harmless old trout her due, it was probably just me she disliked.

To be completely, *completely* honest, I don't think she ever recovered from the downgrading implied by that title. Not *Tarzan and Jane*, you'll note, or *Tarzan and His Wife*, but *Tarzan and His Mate*. That is, a buddy movie built around the electric chemistry of the Weissmuller-Cheeta double act. A bitter pill for Maureen to swallow, that title, but there, there, my dear, the hurt will die down. Actually, had she and I ever been able to communicate, that's exactly what I would have told her when she was, yet again, sobbing and swearing at me after I'd gotten in another good nip to her flank—"There, there, Maureen. The hurt will die down!" See how she'd have liked *that* for consolation while she was wailing at the crew to fetch her Band-Aids and iodine!

Forgive me, I really am getting off the point. For the record, Maureen and I certainly had our ups and downs, I won't deny it. But there has always been a strong professional respect between us, and I think we both cherish our relationship, which has always been the healthier for a bit of teasing.

My point is: those are wise words, no matter how poorly delivered by however atrocious an actress. *The hurt will die down. It has to. Otherwise none of us could stand life.* And never mind that when the hurt doesn't die down, you have to go ahead and stand it all the same. What Jane said remains true—call it Jane's Law. Pain has its own long-term interests at heart. Like a virus too smart to kill off its host, it ebbs, dies down and, to our own great surprise, we live through it. Just as, for instance, my dear friend Ronnie Colman lived through his hideous wreck of a divorce from Thelma Raye and went on to marry my colleague Benita Hume, a more than adequate Cousin Rita in *Tarzan Escapes*. Or, in fact, just as Benita herself lived through that dreadful period after poor Ronnie's lungs killed him: she picked herself up from the floor and married George Sanders. Or, indeed, just as George in his turn lived through it when bone cancer killed his poor beloved Benita. Lived through it, that is, until of course he eventually *couldn't* stand it any longer and killed himself in a fishing village near Barcelona on a spring day in 1972, leaving behind a note calling the world a "cesspool." Sorry, not a good example. Jane's Law does have these occasional tragic exceptions.

Anyway, that last day, sitting in a monsoon on the dock at Kigoma, I was frighteningly underweight and probably still in shock. A nagging voice kept telling me I wasn't out of the woods yet. But I could already feel my grief and pain beginning to die down. I was younger and less vulnerable then. I had an immigrant's resources. I was damn well going to live through it.

It wasn't just that we'd been rescued, though that was, of course, a miracle in itself. There was also the astonishing care that was taken during our rehabilitation, which I like to think was due to Irving Thalberg's legendary attention to detail. We had no way of knowing this at the time, but on the dock that day in Kigoma there was a collection of apes, monkeys and other creatures that MGM scouts had selected from among literally millions of hopefuls to play in Metro pictures. We were "part of the family" now, as Louis B. Mayer liked to say of everyone from the carpenters to Norma Shearer, valuable assets to be cosseted and packed in cotton wool. Hence the tiny protective crates in which we found ourselves snugly ensconced on the quayside. We were housed in pairs, each of us safe inside our own ingenious little slatted wooden shelters, where the raging alphas could never get at us. It was typical of the Metro touch. Once you were in with Metro, you were in. You had everything you could have asked for.

So there was Tyrone and me together, Frederick and little Deanna in the next crate. Stroheim and Spence, the wannabe-alphas, were in their own individual shelters, thankfully out of sight. Cary I didn't see. Tyrone and I lounged through the afternoon, secure for the moment, stuffed with strange fruit, protected from the downpour and our enemies.

Throughout that weird and disorienting day, other animals that had been chosen by MGM were set down around us in their own personal shelters. It was absolutely ingenious, an incredible system. Packed in tight were a pair of leopards, dozens of baboons, spider monkeys, blue- and red-tailed monkeys, bushpigs, mongooses. There was a sudden moldy stink of snake, and I realized that a python had been set down on top of Tyrone and me. But because of our shelters, none of us needed to come into conflict. It was as if you'd taken the jungle and poured all the death out of it. Here, by the jetties on the Zimbugu River, in the human settlement of Kigoma, I saw for the first time a forest live cheek by jowl in peace together, thanks to the intervention of Irving Thalberg, Prince of Hollywood.

Gorged on exotic fruit, Tyrone and I occupied ourselves in trying to throw the leftovers through the slats of our shelter at the leopard, which was pacing around in its own shelter next to us. He was closer than we'd ever seen a leopard before, but he seemed not to notice whenever a scrap struck his flanks. We displayed at him for a while, but he was oblivious to us. We groomed nervously, and toward dusk the rain slackened and a bank of released scents rose from us all like mist—the must of the snakes, the musk of the monkeys, the loam smell of the bushpigs, and other odors that were as indescribable to us as new colors.

With all these smells, we were excited into sound, and up went the hoots and barks. There was Spence's voice, then Frederick's. There were growls and grunts and whistles, the call-and-response of the turacos, the squeakings of the marmosets, the hypersonic trilling of the snakes, or whatever the hell it is they do, and there were other voices I'd never heard before and couldn't possibly describe to you. I realized that there were hundreds upon hundreds of us in our shelters here in Kigoma. Maybe the whole forest was being evacuated! Maybe every last one of us down to the termites had, in Thalberg's eyes, potential star quality!

And at that moment, as we all celebrated ourselves, the sinking sun shot a sideways gleam across us and illuminated a shining wall standing upright in the river—what I later learned was the 420-ton, 215-foot freighter SS *Forest Lawn*. Anyway, with the freighter lit up on the river like that, it seemed, to my ears at least, as if our chorus of voices formed one great ironic cheer of utter relief to be getting the hell out of Africa.

And that's my last memory of the place, pretty much, because soon afterward I fell asleep and when I woke up it wasn't there anymore and never came back, for which deliverance I owe every human being on this planet a drink.

Not all of us went on to be stars, or anything more than extras, but I can say with some pride and great fondness that *Forest Lawn* carried probably the biggest concentration of simian, avian and pachydermatous acting talent that has ever been assembled. For years afterward you'd come across elephants, antelopes or zebras you recognized from *Forest Lawn*, dumb animals that had quite forgotten where they came from. Elephants—let me tell you definitively—forget. But I remember it all perfectly.

The primary purpose of the place seemed to be as a rehabilitation center. It appeared the humans recognized how traumatized most of the animals were by their experiences in the jungle because we were all subjected to a lengthy period of complete rest and relaxation. This consisted of almost permanent darkness, coupled with a total lack of potentially distressing or dangerous social interaction, and strictly no exercise. Indeed, many of the animals required such intensive therapy that they adhered to this routine throughout the whole of their stay on *Forest Lawn*. We were encouraged to sleep and, soothed by the constant low hum and initially rather uncanny gentle rocking, also to unwind in general and let our shattered nerves repair. You could actually feel the tension drain out of you. Tyrone and I spent virtually the whole of our time snoozing in one another's arms.

At regular intervals there was an explosion of stark light as a rescuer interrupted our twenty-hour naps with a fresh bucket of exotic fruit. I would take the chance to look around and do a who's who of our party. There were various birds stacked up in little boxes not much bigger than my head, a delicious assortment of edible monkeys, some equally delicious-looking bushpigs, a fat and hairy chimp with a black face and a gentle expression, a number of pythons taking the weight off, six or seven other chimps and a charcoal-gray snake that I instinctively feared. Stroheim and Spence were both displaying and hooting like idiots—I didn't respond; like, get with the program, we're here to relax. "Here you go, boys," our kind rescuer would say, poking bits of fruit through the slats of our shelters. "Here you go, you poor little fucked-up lonely little hairy fucking bastards."

To be honest, what changed everything for me on *Forest Lawn* was a fruit—a fruit that will forever therefore be associated for me with humans—the banana. My first banana! I remember thinking, Why don't *we* eat these? Why didn't we have *these* in the forest? I had a similar feeling years later, sipping my first properly mixed martini in Chasen's—a pulse of surprise that it was legal. Same as my first snort of cocaine off Constance Bennett's breasts. The flesh: firm with a kind of memory of a snap to it, but melting as you held it in your mouth. This is the banana, not Connie's breasts. The skin: a sensationally chewy contrast, with the added bonus of a chompable fibrous stalk to round it all off. I'm still talking about the banana here. The flavor: like a *cleverer* flavor than any other fruit. The size: the perfect shape for a single lateral mouthful.

My second banana was, I'm ashamed to say, supposed to be Tyrone's, but he, like many of the other chimps, had become so lethargic on the *Forest Lawn* discipline of constant sleep and catered meals that he hardly even stirred when the rescuer brought the fruit around.

We developed a routine, this rescuer and I, whereby I'd cling to the slats of our shelter as he approached and make grabs at his bucket. "You're a little fucking Dillinger, aintcha, you little smart-ass sonofabitch?" he'd croon, as I rummaged through the bucket in search of the bananas. Sometimes he would hold up other fruits for me—a custard apple, a fig, half an orange—and wait for my reaction before he handed over the only thing I wasn't silent with disapproval at. On other occasions he'd hold out his two hands, a fruit distending each fist differently, and allow me to peel open one set of fingers—the *banana*, thanks very much. Then *four* figs on the floor outside the *left* of the shelter versus *one* banana on the floor outside the—banana, thanks. (All this, by the way, accompanied by a background track of impatient screaming from Stroheim, who had, I noticed, progressed in the meantime to the dizzy heights of the dominant male in an environment of one.) Finally, a whole bunch of bananas was wafted at me, withdrawn and set down out of reach near the charcoal-gray snake. Tricky, but whatever was necessary, I'd do it. At long last I was managing to put on some weight, even though the increasing difficulty of obtaining my bananas was starting to give me a headache.

The human showed me a small, intricately glittering object and opened the front of the shelter, all the while making reassuring noises: "All right, you goddamn little fucking Edison, you little Greenwich fucking Village fucking pointy-head, work this one out." He slowly placed the intricate object on the floor to the other side of the custard apples, within reach. I understood that if I were to choose the custard apples, I would be denied the glittering thing. I got that. What the glittering thing had to do with bananas was anyone's guess.

Again he fixed his eyes on me, picked up the glittering thing and opened the shelter's front. Then he slowly replaced the glittering thing and waited, all the time staring at me and muttering kindly, "You're not so fucking smart after fucking all, are ya, H. L. fucking Mencken?" I didn't have the faintest whiff of an idea what was going on—I'm a comedian, not an intellectual, never claimed to be one—but once more, holding my gaze, he picked up the glittering thing and opened the shelter and I thought, No, don't know, but since it's open . . . and I whipped through the opening in the shelter between his legs and bounded toward the bananas. The ashen snake showed its startled pale underside as I veered past it, pouching the loot. I could hear the human coming fast behind me, shouting violently over the screeches of Stroheim and Spence, so I scooted with my bananas up a sort of vertical sequence of branches and kept going toward where the light was coming from. My disused legs seemed about as sturdy as a pair of termite-fishing sticks and one of my hands was full of bananas so I nearly fell, hauling with one arm only on the glossy branches, but I kept hoisting. myself up, and eventually knuckled out, limping, into a somewhat bewildering landscape.

For a moment I thought I'd come out of the wrong opening— the one marked "Not Your Life"— and almost backed quietly out, as if I'd inadvertently walked in on Jack Warner banging a secretary (which I have done). For a start, *where was everything*? Why was I standing in the middle of a windy gray plain? How come the rehabilitation center didn't open onto a gentle prospect of fruiting fig trees and termite mounds, as I'd half suspected it did? It took me a moment to grasp that we were in the middle of a huge, swiftly flowing river, that the world was circular like the moon, that what I needed above all was to get back to my shelter. But, much as Gary Cooper always appeared to be profoundly in touch with the nuances of existence while what was actually passing through his head was "food, sex, sleep," what I thought then was "bananas, safety, up!"

I clambered up a handily narrow treelike thing and found a place to cling with my legs so that I had both hands free, for the eating of bananas. Down below me I could see scores of huge shelters containing leopards and various other unnameable and mind-boggling megafauna—the first elephants, rhinos, hippos, lions, zebras and giraffes I'd ever seen. Now, the Discovery Channel becomes reliably breathy and awestruck whenever it approaches the subject of "the visitor's first glimpse of the animals who make their home here, on these teeming, majestic plains." Imagine how overwhelming that "first glimpse" might be with all of them seen at once in a single panoramic view. On top of that, all around, the gray water was rushing by us uninterrupted as far as I could see. There were no banks! I wondered if Kigoma and the forest had simply been *flooded*, and that what we had here was a small number of humans who had collected as many other life-forms as possible on a kind of floating platform with a view to starting afresh when the waters receded. Was everyone else dead? Were we the Saved? Was this the reason that, as I had noticed, all of us chimpanzees were *children*? It seemed too insane an idea to be plausible, so I dismissed it and concentrated instead on eating half a dozen bananas, while various humans called up at me, "Hey, cheat! Come on down, you damn cheat!" Eventually I allowed myself to be coaxed down and recaptured. They were offering more bananas as bait, you see.

# 4
# America Ahoy!

Janos, or Johann, Weissmuller was seven months old when he made the same trip, on the SS *Rotterdam* out of Holland to New York in February 1905 (in steerage, though, not in MGM luxury). So he was too young to experience crossing the Atlantic in the way I did. I got to know that ocean in March 1932, with Tony Gentry and Captain Mannicher and Gabe DiMarco and Earl and Julius and the rest of the guys. It was a great time. Humans, it turned out, were on the whole a delight.

Tony, or "Mr. Gentry," was the kind one with the sprightly alpha air and the spiffy line of white skin down the center of his sleek head. The lopsided one with long, mournful ears and the bubbles of flesh in the crooks of his nostrils was Captain Mannicher, and so on and so forth. It wasn't hard to pick things up. "Whiskey!" meant if you went to the other side of *Forest Lawn*, opened a number of doors, retrieved a bottle and brought it back to Mr. Gentry, you got a banana. "Get my hat" or "Smokes, please" meant . . . well, you follow—there were a lot of banana-based interactions between Mr. Gentry and me.

By now I was consuming so many bananas that I had taken to imitating the humans and using the stalk to unfurl the skin petal by petal. You missed the chewiness but discarding the skin enabled you to get through them quicker. "Come on, kid, you're going to Hollywood," Mr. Gentry would say, as he worked on another task with me. "You ain't gonna meet Dietrich if you can't fetch her a smoke. You want the banana, do it again."

"Elephants" meant taking a bucket of water from Mr. Gentry and climbing up the shelters onto the backs of the bristly giants and sluicing them down. "Giraffes" meant carrying armful after armful of hay up to a kind of bier on a pole and avoiding being licked on the way by the creature's hideous two-foot-long blue-black mouth-tentacle, or "tongue." "A key" was an intricate glittering thing. "Somersault," "Do it again" and "Again" all meant performing the backflip I was so adept at. "Hold Number Four" was where I'd come from; "the Atlantic" was the river without banks we were crossing to get to "America," which was where all the humans lived. "Cheats" or "Cheatster" or "The Cheater" was me.

"Bluffing or packing" was simple enough. The humans sat around displaying fans, like male turacos in courtship, made up of prettily colored cards. The longest display, again like turacos, was rewarded with "chips." When Mr. Gentry said something like "It's my notion that you ain't packing nothing, Earl," or "He's bluffing, Cheats," it was my job to circle the table while the others showed me their fans. Mr. Gentry would ask me, "Bluffing or packing?" with a raised forefinger. Whichever word he lowered the forefinger on, I had learned through a long afternoon of withheld bananas, I was at that moment to display wildly, and he would make his call based on the Cheatster's "advice." As far as I could tell, bananas seemed to be allocated on a completely unreadable basis for this task.

Of course, I didn't have any idea of what was going on most of the time. I was a very young chimpanzee and had only just started to read human beings. But frankly, I hadn't had any idea of what was going on in the forest either. It wasn't any *more* confusing being on *Forest Lawn,* and at least I was hanging out with a higher consciousness, and who doesn't want to do that? Death seemed very distant among the humans. Also, I was struck by how deeply they seemed to love animals. And a further plus was that I was eating more bananas than possibly any other chimpanzee on earth. Whatever *Forest Lawn* was, I liked it!

The only problem was that with my fetching and carrying Mr. Gentry's cigarettes and whiskey all the time, and my smoking and drinking "imitations" at the card displays (they weren't imitations, I *was* smoking and drinking) proving so popular, everybody else decided that they wanted a chimp familiar too. Earl, my banana-denier, was the first to follow where Mr. Gentry had led, and one day I was surprised to see Frederick scuttling across the "deck" with one of Earl's dirty brown cigarillos between his lips.

Frederick was a nervous little chimp and spent most of his time huddled inside Earl's shirt, puffing on a cigarillo so that it seemed Earl's chest hair was constantly on fire during the card displays. He couldn't do backflips or feed the giraffes but he could smoke, that kid, and drink, and of course the *Forest Lawn* rehab program, with its fierce commitment to relaxing us, encouraged him to do both to his heart's content. But when another of the bluffing or packing boys sat down to the game with his own chimpanzee helper (a stranger to me, and the first of many "Bonzos" that I would come to know over the years), anxiety kindled inside me. I was beginning to notice just how imitative human behavior was. If Mr. Gentry or Captain Mannicher burst out laughing, betas like Earl, Julius or DiMarco would immediately follow suit. I could see where all this was heading.

Sure enough, the next day Stroheim was squatting beside Julius on top of the wheelhouse, engaged in some lesson requiring a large

amount of bananas. I could see that Julius was having a little difficulty with him, since Stroheim kept breaking off to pant-hoot at
the elephants, which were obviously causing him distress, but all
afternoon Julius kept him at it. I stayed downwind of them and
tried to put them out of my mind, tumbling with Bonzo in the
giraffes' mound of straw and generally keeping my head down. But
bluffing or packing came around all the same, with the humans in
a state of high hilarity. Mr. Gentry and me, Earl and Frederick, Baxter and young Bonzo, Captain Mannicher, DiMarco and, making a
grand entrance, wiry little Julius with—like the big dog the small
man tends toward—the bulky Stroheim.

"Gentlemen, I would like to introduce to you *my* assistant,
Dempsey," said Julius (*Dempsey?*), "who will be cutting the pack for
us tonight. Some cards, please, for Dempsey."

Cutting a "deck" (I know, very tricky) of bluffing or packing
cards was something Mr. Gentry had been helping me master. But
cards are terribly difficult for a young chimpanzee to manipulate,
and my attempts at cutting had never elicited the full banana of approval from Mr. Gentry. There was room for improvement, to be
honest—I either dropped or ate them. As the oldest chimp on *Forest Lawn*, Stroheim could be expected to make a better job of things
requiring more developed motor control—that must have been
Julius's thinking—but it never came to that.

Stroheim was staring at me with his muddy brown eyes and his
hair erect, making a series of threatening pant-grunts. He ripped
his hand out of Julius's and thumped up onto the table with a
heavy, hollow *ber-bang*, hooting at me in an aggressive four-square
posture—arms out, knuckles down, ready to spring. I abandoned
to him the banana I was peeling and scampered around the back of
Mr. Gentry, who stood up, making a rucksack of me. Bonzo and
Frederick had scattered, squealing but ignored by Stroheim, who

was still bristling and pant-grunting at me even though he was now in possession of both my banana and the cigarette I'd left burning on the table. We were straight back in the jungle.

"Are we playing cards or having a tea party?" Captain Mannicher asked, reasonably enough. "Get it out of here, Julius. And the rest of them. Put 'em back in their cages and we can get on with our game." Stroheim had retracted himself into a sullen bundle and was puffing gloomily on my cigarette as if savoring the shift in mood. "And Cheats as well, Tony. Enough. We're gonna have some serious poker tonight."

So we were all trooped back into Hold Number Four. I didn't mind it as much as you might think—I'd been wondering about the safety of my shelter ever since I'd seen Stroheim gibbering around the wheelhouse roof that afternoon. Without shelters there *was* no rehabilitation program. The program's key principle—not to be constantly threatened by death (a *good* principle: mark me down as a "pro")—was dependent on them. After the light and the wind of the Atlantic, the hold seemed black with dreams and comforting thick smells: feces, urine, rotting fruit.

"Hardly the goddamned Ritz down here, is it?" said Julius, admiringly.

"Smells like the, uh, the Tijuana Hilton," said Baxter, "but with better room service," which confirmed my suspicions that we were indeed recipients of some special treatment on *Forest Lawn*.

Earl peeled off with Bonzo and Frederick, and Julius hit a little cluster of moonfruit-like globes on a stand (whose sudden light stirred up a fluster of cheeps and squeaks from those expecting dinner). He and Baxter were leading the banana-clutching Stroheim and me back toward our shelters—and I thought, We'll be back in our shelters in a second anyway, and what can he do while there are two humans here? *That's* my *goddamned banana*! and I jinked sideways and plucked it—ha!—from Stroheim's grasp.

Unfortunately, my momentum carried me into Julius's legs, and in catching his balance, his hand separated from Stroheim's, freeing him. Stroheim swiveled, ducked Julius's grab and—he had this way of instantaneously converting his sullenness to ferocity—charged shrieking into me, catching me and clutching hard so that we spun over painfully into the side of a shelter. For a moment I was winded, and then, dropping the banana in the hope that that'd be enough for him, I skittered out of reach and doubled back toward the humans. I figured they were my best option. But Earl and Julius were backing away from me with expressions I had not yet seen on human faces, and I had time to think, *Surely* between the pair of you, you can handle him—and don't forget, guys, it was my banana in the first place, before they started to shout.

Down from its busted shelter flowed the charcoal-gray snake. It decanted itself, horrible in its ease of motion, raised its head from the ground, flashing its paler underside, and bared its mouth.

The inside of its mouth was *black*. It wasn't the black of a chimp, or a crow, or a panther—it was infinitely more intense. It was what you'd arrive at when you got to the end of black. You just looked at it and thought: Death. That's Death.

"It's the fucking *mamba*, Earl," Julius said, "the *fucking mamba*!"

The snake moved with a quite hideous rapidity toward Stroheim, who was hoisting himself up the outside of a stack of shelters. It strained after him, five, six feet vertically upward, then fell sideways and magicked itself into the darkness behind a stand of lights.

When I think about it I sometimes wonder whether Louis Mayer was in fact right and that Thalberg *was* losing it. There was simply no chance that that snake could have handled an MGM family-oriented or comedy role. Warner's could have used it, perhaps. TV, sure, but not opposite Deanna Durbin. What had Thalberg been thinking in offering it a slot on *Forest Lawn*? The snake was like poor old Anna Sten (remember her?)—everybody in Hollywood, apart from Sam Goldwyn himself, knew it just wasn't going to happen for her. Or it might have been that Tony Gentry had simply picked the snake up hoping for a straight-to-zoo sale. Whatever the reason for its presence on *Forest Lawn*, with the mamba's escape the whole noble premise of the rehabilitation center collapsed. You try to make it out of the jungle and the jungle comes with you. Death was still here, shelters or not.

And, in a sort of chain reaction, the serenity of *Forest Lawn* exploded. Captain Mannicher was furious and used his hand against Julius. It was the first blow I had ever seen between humans. "We're six hours out of New York!" he shouted. "Don't give me this shit! Who the fuck do you think is liable? The longshoremen? They're not even going to think about unloading the cargo! My men aren't going to touch it. Don't fucking tell me it was damaged in transit! This is your fucking liability. Your fucking problem!"

Mr. Gentry was behind Captain Mannicher, trying to groom him down from his display. "Pete, come on, this isn't helping us. . . ."

"Don't tell me what's helping, Gentry. I've got a million and a half dollars' worth of cargo that the Port Authority's not gonna let me unload until you find this fucking thing and I am gonna— listen to me—I'm gonna fucking *close you down* if it harms anybody on board this vessel." It was fear-based aggression, I could see. And he hadn't even seen the fucking thing yet!

I would like, by the way, to make the point again that it was actually *my banana in the first place*, not Stroheim's, and in that sense it was all *his* fault. It was not easy to communicate this at the time.

"I'm not suggesting that anyone involved with the freight

company or the ship look for the mamba. Quite the contrary," Mr. Gentry said, with calming gestures of submission. "This is a highly aggressive, deadly animal. No antivenom has been developed for it. It'll be disoriented by its surroundings, which may mean it's less aggressive, or it may not. But I and my men will do the searching. In the meantime, I suggest that you keep on all the lights we have and gather the crew here on the top deck."

"Rats, Tony," said Earl.

"Yeah, I know. It'll feed on rats, Captain, given its 'druthers. Tell the men to stay clear of places where rodents might be found—the giraffes' straw, the bulkheads, the binnacles, you know better than me. OK, Earl, come on, not your fault. Let's go."

"Don't let the fucking lions out," Mannicher said in farewell. "Never afuckingain, Gentry. And take fucking Bonzo with you!"

"This animal is safer where you are, Captain. The mamba won't have any difficulty entering the cages in the hold and getting after the stock. In fact, that's where we're starting. So let's just all keep our heads and we'll solve this." Mr. Gentry was very white where Mannicher was red. "And it's not Bonzo, Captain," he said, "it's Cheater."

A very special human being, Mr. Tony Gentry.

All that evening I stayed in the wheelhouse with Captain Mannicher and various other extremely anxious humans. As the night wore on they relaxed somewhat, having little else to do except display cards and drink whiskey. DiMarco was volunteered to travel with a number of others to the galley and return with something to eat, and by the time they came back, unscathed, the humans were again laughing and conversing in that reassuring way of theirs. "Skipper, a specialty of my country: *linguine alla nero*," said DiMarco, laughing and lifting the lid from one of his silver dishes and dangling a handful of writhing black strands in front of Captain Mannicher. All the men displayed and wept with laughter. There was something terribly strange and not very human about them at that moment, as if they had gone slightly mad.

Not able to stand any more of it, I knuckled outside with a couple of bananas and gingerly dropped down to the deck, keeping an eye out for the death-snake. Away across the Atlantic, I noticed that some of the stars had formed themselves into a thick cluster in a way I'd never seen before, all crushed together like a broken-up moon.

Day came slowly. Mr. Gentry, Earl and Julius came up on deck for coffee and descended into the holds again. Nobody had any news of the death-snake. But now I saw that, where the star-cluster had been, there was a solid gray mass, high and steep like the escarpment in the forest. It didn't move, and when I looked again a while later, it still hadn't moved. It was, surely, the other bank of the river!

Captain Mannicher and members of the crew began to walk cautiously around the deck now, each of them holding a long piece of wood, scouring the planking with their gazes. I shuffled over and held out an arm to DiMarco, and he allowed me up into the crook of his elbow. "All your fuckin' fault, kid," he muttered soothingly. "We're stuck here until we kill it or it kills us. You *bad* chimp. No America for you." I was very grateful for the consolation, the human touch.

We moved slowly around *Forest Lawn* while the gray mass stayed where it was and I suddenly noticed that DiMarco was unaware that the death-snake, blacker in daylight, was pouring itself out of the grille of a bent-over kind of funnel thing about ten yards ahead of us. It noticed us, though. Opening its terrible, terrible black mouth again it slid toward us, veered away toward Mannicher ("It's the—the—the fucking *thing*!" he managed to get out) and held its position, switching its head from side to side as if uncertain whether to go for the captain or DiMarco and me, scenting the air with its tongue. It didn't look disoriented by its surroundings at all.

It looked like it was spoiling for a fight and simply couldn't decide which opponent was nearest.

So there was America and there was me. And between us, Death. We were the nearest. DiMarco was slow to see it, and by the time he did, it was gathering speed across the gap. They're *fast*, black mambas, you'll remember from Discovery, and they like to strike high. Two or three feet of its body was raised above the ground as it rippled over the planking. "Oh, Jesus," breathed DiMarco, because he could see that any chance of outrunning the thing had already gone in the previous second. He must also have seen the awful black of the inside of its mouth. And it flowed up into the air, four, five feet off the ground and still rising as it struck, and we were suddenly tumbling down on the deck with the heavy body of the snake whipping over us.

It was one of my fucking discarded banana skins that DiMarco had stepped on, we later worked out. It had taken his legs from under him just at the moment of the mamba's strike.

Captain Mannicher and the crew ran over to the snake as it sprawled, somewhat surprised, or as surprised as a snake can ever look, and momentarily vulnerable. A couple of them managed to jam its head down against the deck with their wooden sticks and, with a long knife, Mannicher decapitated it.

And still the snake's head and half a foot of its body continued to slither on toward him, and we watched it, pleading with it to die so that we could go to America.

It did. But to this day, I retain a loathing for two things in particular. (Three, if you count Mickey Rooney.) I fear snakes. And I cannot stand the taste of bananas.

That was April 9, 1933: my official date of birth, if you look at the website. The day of my arrival on American soil. As is almost traditional in these cases, my name was misspelled at Immigration.

# 5

# Big Apple!

I'll always have a soft spot in my already well-tenderized heart for New York, and not only because it's generally agreed that some of my very best work, including the now classic "hotel-room sequence," can be found in *Tarzan's New York Adventure* (1942). The last of the truly great Tarzan pictures, *New York Adventure* was built around the simple but brilliant conceit of getting the Boy out of the goddamn way (he'd been kidnapped, or something). Without Johnny Sheffield there to muddy everything up, the central Tarzan-Cheeta-Jane relationship was free to return to its original clarity. I like to think I managed to make a reasonable job of the opportunity.

I don't know whether I'd go so far as the *New York Times* reviewer—"Cheta (*sic*) the chimpanzee who well-nigh steals the picture runs amok in a swank hotel boudoir, shakes hands with astonished clerks, causes havoc with hatcheck girls, babbles over telephones and even makes wisecracks nearly as intelligible as Tarzan's. . . . More than anyone, the monkey turns the Tarzans' excursion into a rambunctious simian romp"—but the truth behind that "picture-stealing" performance, and the real reason I quote from that review, was that I was simply playing from life. The famous nightclub sequence with the hatcheck girls? That was for real. All I had to do was dredge up my memories of a little spree I'd had in Lower Manhattan, the summer of 1933. By then I'd already spent several months in New York. Rehab. But right from the get-go America seemed to me to be some sort of paradise.

The morning we docked was spent overseeing the unloading of the stock into smaller mobile rehab units. I was touched to see how delighted the longshoremen along the pier were at the sight of the rescued animals, crowding around the shelters, offering bits of food and cigarettes, calling and waving. If not quite on the same scale as, say, Gloria Swanson's reception on her return from Paris, with crowds strewing gardenias and roses in the path of America's Sweetheart (while she secretly nursed a near-suicidal guilt over the child she'd just aborted in order to stay on top), *Forest Lawn* nonetheless received a welcome that, I think, would have satisfied even my old friend the great MGM publicist Howard Strickling. It was a very moving moment, and confirmed everything I'd suspected about humans—they were the happiest damn things I'd ever seen in my life. And they *loved* animals.

"Sonofabitch, this goddamn Depression," Mr. Gentry muttered inexplicably, as the longshoremen maneuvered the shelters around. Christ, I thought, if they're like this when they're *depressed* . . . "Soon as Earl gets this lot sent off to Trefflich's you know what I'm gonna do, DiMarco?"

"You're gonna quit with the poisonous snakes."

"I might do that. And I might take a walk down to the corner of Fulton and Church where I hear a little place called the White Rose Tavern has opened for business. And I suggest we make a Noble Experiment on our first legal drinks in the United States of America."

"We takin' the Cheater, boss?"

"The Cheater of Death? Sure we are. Gentlemen, I propose we embark on a little stroll."

Which was what Julius, DiMarco, Mr. Gentry and I did. Now, I don't know whether or not April 1933 was some sort of an economic peak in American history—I'm an entertainer, not a historian, never claimed to be one—but it seemed to me like you humans must have been going through a quite mind-boggling period of success. Over the course of that first awestruck walk I saw lines of men and women patiently attending huge vats of steaming soup, not shoving or fighting for it as we'd have done, but respectfully observing a hierarchy that extended back down the street for hundreds upon hundreds of humans. They also had a miraculous system of circular receptacles on the trails beside the streets, into which humans would toss scraps of food for other humans to discover and relish. Even in the gutters there could be found pieces of exotic fruits, which I saw several humans scoop up and savor! New York wasn't, good grief, a "jungle," as it's so often described—the forest, now *that* was a jungle, with its everyday infanticide and cannibalism. There were no leopards, no snakes here, "Nothing to fear but fear itself!" was the boast I would keep hearing. And I thought I began to understand why *Forest Lawn* had been refused entry to America while the death-snake was still at large. This land was a haven dedicated to freedom from Death. The whole damn place was a rehabilitation center!

Any remaining anxieties I might have been harboring about being separated from the other chimps were overwhelmed by the storm of sense-impressions of Lower Manhattan, and the bewildering fact that every second person on the street seemed to *know my name*: "Hey, Cheeta!," "Where's Tarzan, bud?," "You're in the wrong jungle, Cheeta!" Either that or they called out, "Kong! Hey, Kong! You takin' that thing up the Empire State, mister?" It was a case of mistaken identity, perhaps. Perhaps I'd somehow been here before. I mean, *what was going on*? My head swam with it all—the humans crowding around smiling at me and shaking my hand, the stacked towers of shelters that hinted at the promise of unimaginable fruits should you clamber to their crowns, the glossy black shelters on wheels that sped by and kept the humans penned in on the "sidewalks . . ."

It was a sort of prophecy in a way, my unforgettable procession down the sidewalks of Manhattan seventy-odd years ago, shaking hands and grinning at people who knew my name. I was a nobody; I was a novelty; I wasn't who they thought I was. And nowadays when they *do* know who I am—it's exactly the same. There's the scrutiny, the handshake, the "Hey, Cheeta, how's Tarzan, buddy?," the *pause*. . . . If you want to know what being famous feels like, what it means—and I speak as perhaps the most famous animal alive today—then picture a human and a chimpanzee facing each other in awkward silence, with nothing to be said, the faint inanity of the interaction stealing over both of them. That's what fame is.

Anyway, we stepped off the sidewalk and descended some stairs into a cavernous shelter. I'm not ashamed to admit I was already salivating at the prospect of this "legal" booze in the White Rose Tavern when my nose caught a thick whiff of leopard, with topnotes of monkey. No, not topnotes, I thought, as we entered the tavern, a great smoggy stench of monkey.

Mr. Gentry greeted a rather solemn young man in shirtsleeves and striped tie—the Son, I was later to learn, in "Henry Trefflich & Son: Animal Importers"—and was soon laughing with him about the mamba; DiMarco was doing pratfalls to illustrate. I could see Earl and several other men at the far end of a corridor wrangling a shelter onto a cart inside which Frederick was hopping and whining; I could see the wire mesh of shelters through which delicate little monkey-fingers curled. My heart sank. Quite obviously this wasn't a "tavern" but some kind of further rehab center.

"And this is him, Henry, got him half trained already—the Cheater. The Cheater of Death," said Mr. Gentry, unfurling me from his leg, which I'd quietly coiled myself around. He held me out to the pale young man. "Cheats, let me introduce to you the son of a friend of mine—Henry Trefflich the Younger."

I sensed something unnatural or false in his gesture. It made me nervous and I scooted away from Trefflich back behind my protector's leg.

"We'll get acquainted later over a banana or two," Trefflich said to me, threateningly. "But he needs a new name. Got a couple of Cheetas upstairs already."

"Hell, they're on a different order, ain't they? You can't be changing the Cheatster's name," said DiMarco. "Cheatster saved my life, man."

"Well, maybe not, if he's going with the L.A. order. I don't know how much more stock MGM are after. But you wouldn't believe what's happening with the private buyers here. Dad says we sold more chimps in 'thirty-two than the last ten years together. You know for why? It's that great lummox Weissmuller. The ladies go crazy for him. It's, uh . . . subliminal. They want Tarzan—they end up buyin' a chimp."

As Trefflich talked, I felt Mr. Gentry's hand trying to detach my arm from his leg and I clung tighter, but I was just a kid, with a kid's sinews, and there was another force in the room beyond Mr. Gentry's strength, a gravity that was pulling me away from him and toward Trefflich.

"Dammit, Tony, you got yourself a friend there," Trefflich said.

"Yeah. I'm going to miss you, little feller," Mr. Gentry said, his clawing fingers continuing to insist. He went on talking to Tref-flich. "Me and the boys've been up all night snake-hunting. . . ." Their nerves were shredded after the mamba, he said, and they needed to take the weight off for an hour or two before coming back to do the paperwork. "Come on, Cheats, off now."

My grip finally went and Trefflich advanced with both arms out to shovel me up into his clasp, so I gave him a warning shriek and bit him as hard as I could on the side of his wrist. To no effect whatsoever, except to send a vibrating pain up the roots of my teeth, and a sharper, thinner hurt into the roof of my mouth. I *knew* they'd have some kind of magic protection. By the time the shock had subsided, Trefflich had hold of the back of my neck and I felt very strongly that I had somehow passed to the other side of the room.

"Half trained, Tony?" Trefflich said. My teeth were still jangling horribly, and I thought there was a cut in my soft palate. I jigged up and down in an attempt to shake the pain. "Exactly which is the half you got trained, huh? Chrissakes, look at that! Look at the toothmarks he's left in the metal."

Around his wrist was a band of dense, shiny material in the middle of which a white, glassed-over circle displayed—oh, this is gonna take forever: his watchband. I'd bitten his steel, chain-link watchband. And I wonder sometimes just how much the gentleness of my character was formed by that little lesson in the pointlessness of violence. It's a rare chimp who has bitten so few humans as I have over the years. Or so many famous actresses, come to think of it.

"Stop jigging, kid, I can scarcely write," Trefflich was saying. "Oh four oh nine three three, uh . . . little . . . *Jiggs*, brand-new U.S. citizen."

Mr. Gentry approached me as I squirmed in Trefflich's grasp. That exquisitely straight white line of scalp down the center of his glossy brown head somehow imbued him with an aura of rectitude that made you trust him. He stroked the side of my head and made shushing noises. "We'll be right back, Cheats, OK? You're in good hands here. Wait a minute, uh, DiMarco, you got any smokes?" Di-Marco held out the pack of Luckys he liked to wedge between bicep and rolled shirtsleeve, and flourishing the pack, Mr. Gentry disappeared down the passageway that led out of the room. "OK, Henry, you can let him go now," he said, when he returned. "Watch this. Smokes, Cheats, go get me my smokes!"

Well, for pity's sake, you had them just a minute ago, I thought. But I desperately wanted to please him, to do something for him that would bind him to me, so I scampered off down the passageway between the caged galleries of monkeys, looking for the Luckys. There they were, in plain sight on top of a bucket of sand. I grasped them and loped back between the dumb gray monkeys, not in any expectation of a banana or an orange, but only of pleasing him.

When I got back to the room there was nobody in it but Trefflich, and it was another sixteen years before I saw Tony Gentry again.

So it was that the kaleidoscope of America dwindled to a shelter in another rehab center. Of course I was grateful, and impressed by the sheer number of animals who had been rescued, but I wasn't altogether convinced that I was in any need of *further* rehabilitation.

I was sharing my shelter with Bonzo and a couple of other males the same age as us, but there wasn't much cause for interaction. Trefflich's was like *Forest Lawn* in that most of us slumbered through our days, roused only by the internal alarm of our hunger going off and the light traversing the room. It grew more and more difficult to hold anything in mind other than breakfast and dinner. Our muscles whispered at us about things they recalled doing, but only very faintly. Our dreams became incoherent and naggingly repetitious. Every once in a while we'd stir our stumps for a gallivant around the shelter, or while away an hour or so with a good long groom. . . .

Please, dear reader, please don't for a second think that I'm not grateful. Each second of my life is a record-breaking triumph that I owe to you, to human protection and intervention. In me, the shelter system has magnificent proof of its efficacy and I salute the ambition of the whole project. By the time Trefflich's heart killed him in 1978 he had been involved in the rehabilitation of around 1,450,000 monkeys, mainly rhesus macaques. Nearly one and a half million macaques had either passed through Fulton Street or been helped in their resettlement by a single man! I suppose the only tragedy was that he didn't live to complete his work. So much more remains to be done, and one trusts that many millions more macaques will benefit from his work. But I was a foolish little thing in '33, and I'm sorry to have to admit, I began to feel the whole process of rehabilitation weigh a little heavy on me.

If I squeezed my head against the mesh at one corner of our shelter I could see a section of window where the sky mooched from gray to white. This was the corner the others would vacate when I approached, where I had banked up straw for myself so I could look out and dream about America. Out there were the sidewalks with humans who knew your name, the rolling shelters and the great towers, and Tony Gentry sitting in the White Rose Tavern with a fan of cards. I had no idea whether the other animals feared or yearned for the other side of the mesh; maybe it was just me who'd been corrupted by the energy of America on my walk through Manhattan. But I thought I could read messages of sorrow in the toes of the macaques where they gripped the wire, in their sudden maniacal pacing and the listlessness of their unceasing masturbation.

Several times a day Trefflich would enter our gallery of shelters and remove one of us for a short period. Only once or twice was it a chimp, and never a macaque. Most often it was one of the parakeets, or one of the many little ratlike things that snuffled around in transparent shelters, twitching their flamboyantly excessive ears from time to time but never doing anything else. Nearly always the parakeets and big-eared rat-things came back, but occasionally, I noticed, they didn't, and I wondered about the fate of these non-returnees. Had they completed their rehabilitation? In which case, what had happened to them? Were they just cast back into the jungle and left to take their chances? I couldn't really see the big-eared rat-things having that much fun back in the jungle: I'd have eaten one myself. And this thought made me nervous. There were pythons and leopards in Trefflich's rehab center and they'd have to be eating something. And if the parakeets were python food, wasn't it possible that the same thing applied to us? What the hell was all this rehabilitation *for*? What was the *point* of animals?

Time passed. We slept and masturbated and nothing happened, except that I became more and more obsessed by these profound philosophical questions, as unanswerable as the mesh of our shelters was unbreachable. I was compulsively bashing my head against them as usual one morning when another occurred to me. Why was Trefflich's helper struggling with one of the macaques in the shelter opposite us? These shelters of ours, I should explain, had an outer and an inner section. When Trefflich or his boy came to remove our excrement (what did they want with it? Why were they harvesting it?) we would be hustled into the inner section behind a second door, and I now saw that this particular macaque had trapped itself in the mesh. Its paw had gone right through the diamond of wire, trapping its wrist, and the boy was having to shove hard at the door to squeeze the now-screaming monkey's pinky-gray fingers back through. But as he did so, he simultaneously swung the door back onto himself—it banged painfully against his head and a dozen macaques scampered out past him and into the space between the shelters. Hello, I thought.

They're not stupid, rhesus monkeys. I believe they share something like 92 percent of their DNA with chimpanzees. They may be inscrutable and standoffish, and hardly pleasant to look at, with their pale ginger fur and pleasureless frowns—I could never see Johnny's fourth wife, Beryl, without being reminded of a macaque—but they get things done. In a group, they have an almost insect-like singleness of will. Thick as thieves, they consulted briefly in a knot, then scattered themselves across the room, working on the bolts of the outer doors of the other macaque shelters. Of course, the door of the room itself was closed, and I doubted they would have the smarts to get that open, but I applauded and pant-hooted in excitement anyway. You go, macaques! And, you know, wasn't it a pretty clever tactic to go for the other doors in the first place, so that Trefflich's boy would be outnumbered?

Now that the macaque shelters were springing open, a little delegation *had* in fact scampered over to the main door. Second by second Trefflich's boy's day was getting worse. He stopped trying to chase the macaques and instead took out a set of keys with which, I suppose, he meant to double-lock the remaining shelters. And at that moment my feelings about rehabilitation came clear to me. I *hated* it. I suddenly needed to get the hell out of there very badly—not to go anywhere in particular, only to, Christ, only to be *free*. And then a little ginger ball sprang onto the door of our shelter and flipped the bolts.

Panicking parakeets fluttered through the air as we evaded Trefflich's boy and knuckled into the maelstrom of macaques. Big-eared rats were hopping among them, looking flummoxed, and some busy little critters twitched their high-held tails. I shouldered my way through the monkeys to the door, which was a breeze. I'd worked out harder doors on *Forest Lawn*. A swivel knob and an outward push and the stairwell lay open to us. But beyond this door, I knew, there would be others. There'd be a whole succession of doors, and Trefflich, and other impossibilities. Instinct told me all this in a moment, as macaques eddied around me and down the stairs. Instinct told me too: always escape upward.

For a second I vacillated, looked around to see Bonzo and our shelter-mates, and Tyrone (my heart brimmed at his face) and various others behind me, and then I pelted upward into the dark of the stairwell, not in fear so much as pure joy. The door at the top yielded to a push and we opened out onto an escarpment. All around were the territaries of the humans and beautiful, beautiful, climbable America.

I do love Palm Springs. You've got the cool, dry air from the desert coming down from the mountains, a low crime rate, half a dozen championship-quality golf courses that Don can drive me around while he hacks away. Impeccably liberal, pro-animal, pro-environment views are standard among the humans you meet. But you wouldn't want to be young here. There's nothing to climb. It's a flat, bungaloid city. Whereas New York is the greatest climbing city in the world. I'd advise any young ape looking to break into the entertainment business to find a human backer living privately in New York. You may not make it—and you certainly won't if Don and the No Reel Apes campaigners get their way—but you'll have a better time clambering around the place, especially if you live on a block with an old-style iron fire escape like the one that invitingly ushered us down the back of Trefflich's building.

Down we all swung like a waterfall, six or seven chimps and twenty or so macaques. We hit the streets with a certain simian swagger, I like to think, if a little scrambled by the question of what to do with our freedom. It wasn't as if we had a plan to return to Africa, raise children and retire. What to do? What does any organism *ever* do, except survive?

The rolling shelters in the street slowed themselves so their occupants could gawk at us, and the braver macaques vaulted up onto them. I saw Tyrone hesitate, then rush into the crash of the rolling shelters but I couldn't make myself follow: with their glossy depths of glazed black, their frictionlessness, their somehow angry speed, they reminded me of the mamba.

I took off down the sidewalk. Possibly I had some mad idea that I would run into Mr. Gentry, and we could parade regally together through Manhattan again, I don't know. But I saw immediately how much things were changed simply by the absence of his hand from mine. No human called my name or sauntered up to slap palms now. Instead they stooped to grab at me or tried to corral me with the long cloth-covered sticks many of them carried. By baring my teeth and shrieking, I managed to clear a path through a cluster of them. But it was clear that I couldn't survive long on the sidewalk and I ducked into a gap that opened up in the wall to my right.

My luck was good. I scuttled low past an old man in a booth and through a pair of doors (what is it with you and your addiction to *doors*?) and found myself in a cavernous dark room. Having nothing else to do, I rested there for a few minutes, thinking of Mama and Victoria. The silvery light coming in a beam from a window at one end of the room was the color of the forest under a full moon. I thought of the three of us curled together in a nest of leaves; it had been a long time since I'd seen that light, and it calmed me. There was a whole rectangle of it illuminating the room, and when the light brightened for a moment, I was shocked at the number of humans scattered throughout the gloom. They were all facing away from me and the shifting moonlight was so soothing that I felt no urge to leave.

After a while I began to decipher the shapes within the light up on the wall. Real humans formed, snapped away and re-formed. And once I'd deciphered the humans, the sound in the room became their speech. It was exactly like a dream, I thought, all chopped up and shuffled, and then it hit me that that was what it *was*, a dream, dreamed onto the wall by the silver-haloed heads in front of me.

After a few minutes the dream-story became intelligible to me. The humans were hunting for a female lost in a forest. Something wicked had stolen her. But in order to rescue her, her friends had to defeat various predators. The humans watching in their seats screamed at the succession of predators that Jack and Carl and the rest had to battle with in order to get to Ann.

At this point things went a little crazy. Ann, who turned out to be a tiny little creature no bigger than a termite grub, had been stolen by a *chimpanzee*. Jack and Carl rescued her and the chimp lumbered after them, only to be captured himself. I have to say, my attention was flagging a little, but when Jack and Carl turned out to have a ship rather similar to *Forest Lawn*, I sat up again. And when the chimp's name was revealed to be *Kong*, as in all that "Hey, Kong!" I'd experienced on my first day in Manhattan, I thought, *I know this dream*. They're going to take him to New York, right? And so it happened! Now, hold on. Don't tell me he's going to escape from his rehab center. . . .

As Kong busted out of the miniature rehabilitation unit and

went in search of Ann again, I found I was scarcely breathing, so strong was my desire that my dream-brother should win out, should survive this ordeal. By now the humans in the room were screaming pretty much continuously. Kong retrieved Ann and started to seek some place of refuge. *Up*, I was thinking, *safety is up*. Come on, old Kong, you know that, get *up* somewhere! And, god-dammit, he did, in a fantastically enjoyable clambering sequence that culminated with him surveying New York from the escarpment at the summit of its topmost tower, Ann cradled in his palm, tiny and vulnerable but very beautiful: the sweetest little human being in the world, in Kong's protection.

What a finish. The most amazing, inspiring dream imaginable. I felt tremendously happy and proud of Kong for a second before I sensed human fingers scrabbling at my arm and there was the old guy I'd sneaked past at the door suddenly ahold of me. A flash of my teeth loosened his grip enough for me to free myself and I blundered off through the blackness, smashing into invisible objects in my way. I heard the old fellow barreling along behind, so followed my instincts: up, and toward the light from the window.

Luckily for me, there were little staggered ledges I was able to use to scramble up the wall that led to the shaft of light. Having gained the bottom shelf of the window, I hoisted myself into what turned out be a cramped little room almost entirely filled by a fat young human lounging in a chair. A piercing shaft of very white light emitted by the machine behind him half blinded me, but I tried to display at him as frighteningly as I could. I needed to get him out of the way of the door he was blocking. And my display seemed to work fine, except that the panicking fat boy could do no more than flail and flounder in his chair, still in my way, so I displayed more angrily, waving both hands wildly above my head, bristling my fur and shrieking. At that point I heard an upsurge in the screams of the dreaming humans below.

I glanced behind me to see the twilit room transformed. Screaming humans were stampeding headlong toward its edges. It was the sort of chaos you might see when you ambush a family of bushpigs. Hugely and blackly above it, blotting out nearly all of the dream, was the silhouette of a colossal ape, its fur bristling. Kong, my brother! I gestured at him in excitement, and you won't believe me, he saw and gestured straight back! The poor humans were desperately emptying the room, vaulting over their seats in terror to escape the thing—and who knows where Kong went because, when the room was finally emptied and I dropped back down into it, he seemed to have melted back into the dream, which read, simply, "The End," and then went blank. I guessed that it figured: with none of the dreamers left, the dream was over.

There was nothing for me to do but pick over the rather large amount of extremely appetizing nuts and delicious little morsels of something that was sometimes salty and sometimes sweet that were lying spilled on the floor. Having eaten pretty much all I could find, I sauntered out into the darkening New York evening, feeling fifty feet tall.

What the hell had I got to lose? If they caught me, they caught me—there was no glory in scampering abjectly around in search of hiding places. I felt intoxicated by Kong's example. After all, there was no need to fear *humans*!

In this new expansive mood, I strolled down the comparatively empty sidewalk, looking for action. A rambunctious simian romp, that was what I was after. The first place that looked promising was some kind of food store where I picked up a couple of sticks of something with a hideous rind and a sensational inside. I don't think they even saw me. The next joint I left with a couple of hats and a cigarette case—but no matches, alas, so I dumped the case with the hats. I boosted an armful of oranges from a sidewalk display and spent a diverting five minutes tossing them at passersby from a striped canopy that jutted out of a tower.

For a while it was pretty good fun snatching sticks off of old males and females, until a plan took shape in my head. What I needed was a *drink*. Yeah, a drink, a smoke, and a game of bluffing and packing. I'd noticed places all over where the smell of booze was alluringly heavy, and it was easy enough to slip into one.

Rendered invisible by the head-high shelf of tobacco smoke, I was able to reconnoiter the joint without being noticed. All along one side of the room there was a raised counter at which humans sat. Behind this was a glittering wall of whiskey, inaccessible but reachable. I swung up onto one of the high wooden chairs and then onto the counter, where I was distracted from my goal by an unattended half-drunk glass of what I recognized with joy was Scotch. Here's mud in your eye, as Mannicher used to say.

"Hey, Jimmy! Like a refill for my friend here. Smoke?" asked a human standing behind me, offering me an already burning Lucky.

I took it, and you know, it's a pity more animals don't smoke. It's one thing that Don, who's a great guy in nearly every respect and who loves me more dearly than anything in the world, just doesn't get. There's been a blanket ban on smoking inside the Casa de Cheeta for the seventeen years I've been there. The last officially sanctioned cigar was out on the deck on, I think, April 9, 1998. And then you catch a glimpse of George Burns or Jack Nicholson on *Entertainment Weekly* and you could weep, because nobody has any damn idea how hard it is for a world-famous chimpanzee, noted in *Guinness World Records* for his astounding longevity and health, to shoplift cigarettes in historic Palm Springs.

So far this year I've managed to snatch one pack, containing six cigarettes, from the handbag of an apologetic post-grad zoologist whom Don refused to allow to light up even in the garden, and a single forgotten or abandoned Camel Light from an ashtray outside the doors of the Desert Regional Medical Center Hospice. I ought to try getting them smuggled in disguised as toothpaste, like Joe Cotten in *Citizen Kane*.

And finding them is just the beginning. They then have to be concealed at the back of the herbaceous border behind the pool, and when Don's lit the stove for coffee but has, for some reason, left the kitchen, I have to make it to the shrubbery, disinter one, run across the lawn and into the kitchen, get it lit (never easy when you're not inhaling) and beat it back out to the cage, where I can hunch my back to the Sanctuary and, goddamn it, smoke, never forgetting to bury the butt. There've been some close shaves but I'm pretty sure no real suspicions have been aroused.

I'm getting distracted. What Don can never know is how many, many times I've charmed a reaction out of an indifferent or unwelcoming human by plucking a cigarette from between their fingers and taking a good toke. To convert Bette Davis from a "Puh-lease, this is a restaurant not a freak-show" to the hostess of a riotously memorable evening at Sardi's is not an easy trick, and would have been an impossible one without a cigarette. A smoke broke the ice between me and an initially hostile Bogart, for instance. A smoke set me and Gary Cooper up for life. Sharing a fat stogie with a member of a different species—what better way to forget, for a moment at least, what Charlie Chaplin once described, with his unerring knack for perfectly inane pseudo-poetry, as "man's cosmic loneliness"?

It needed that Lucky in the New York bar to get the evening under way, an evening that ended with me sinking Repeal Specials (legal lager and a shot of Canadian bourbon) with Benny, Red, Kreindl, Hal, Crelinkovitch, Tall George and the rest, hanging upside down from the ceiling fan and catching the coasters they skimmed up at me. What else? There was that bowl of indescribably delicious nuts (I loved American food, I was finding) I won for a rolling sequence of backflips—and I also seem to remember pant-hooting for quite some time down a shiny black thing that contained a succession of miniature but angrily squeaking voices called "wives."

I learned more about acting in that bar, I believe, than under a dozen different trainers at MGM and RKO. I think most serious actors will tell you they learned nine-tenths of their craft from life and stole the other tenth. Or the other way around if you're Mickey Rooney. Acting classes? They're OK—but you either got it or you ain't. And all you really have to do is watch and copy. That's all. When the boys applauded the end of another Repeal Special I just clapped 'em back and they loved me for it. And when they grinned . . . That bar was the place where I first developed my fail-safe standby: the double lip-flip. A human grins at you, you give him a look, then flip your upper and lower lips back to reveal your pink gums in imitation of their cushiony pink mouths. I might possibly have overused that one over the years, but it's still funnier than anything Red Skelton ever did. The boys loved it when I lip-flipped, awarding me a new name for it: "Louis."

The evening broke up with a slight altercation between Benny and Kreindl, which I sensed had much to do with the privilege of my further company. "You take Louis to flop at Turney's, he's gonna ask for something, you mushhead. It's gotta be worth twenty, thirty bucks to someone and Turney ain't having a slice.

Who found it in the first place, huh? We did, and we're gonna keep what's coming to us."

This was Benny, I think, and he was the one who took my hand. By now the city was dark, with lonely pools of light splashed here and there across the sidewalks, but I was still joyful at life, and full of nuts and Repeal Specials, and couldn't stop jolting and tugging at Benny's grip, trying to shake him out of his human plod. All the feeling of that very first parade through the streets with Tony Gentry was in me—if I can make it here, I remember thinking, I can make it anywhere!—and too happy to hold it in, I pulled away when Benny was trying to reset his grip, saw a wall of tempting handholds and ledges and set off up it.

I was Kong the Mighty, scaling the summits of New York. I was also unprecedentedly drunk. But inspired in a Harold Lloyd–ish fashion. By traversing a number of ledges I managed to find myself at a vertical section of simple jutting stones, which led me up toward a metal box, from which a wire ran across to the other side of the street. Beneath me, Benny had stopped yelling quietly at me and started yelling loudly as I shimmied toward the wire, which gave off a buzzing hum. Every chimp has a feeling in his hands that's hard to explain, that itches for a good branch, or a vine with just the right kind of give, and that wire looked as if it had just the right kind of sag to it.

Terrific fellow by the way, Harold Lloyd, quite unlike Chaplin. A demi-ape. Harold had a nine-hole golf course on the grounds of Greenacres, the mansion he'd had built in Beverly Hills, where the fast set was always welcome to swing by for a few holes. But it was really an eight-hole course, with a specially constructed fake ninth. From the tee it looked like an almost insultingly easy, ideally flat green, with the pin dead center. A seven-iron, no sweat. It was, however, an algae-mantled pond, into which, especially if you were playing as the light began to fail, perfect drive after perfect drive would inexplicably disappear. Now that was funny. That was *fun*, with golfers striding angrily up to the green and sinking into it themselves, and Harold's wife, a frail, beautiful thing called Mildred Davis, mixing martinis on the terrace behind.

Great times, although less so for Mid, of course, who'd suffered terribly with drink and depression ever since dear old Harold had forcibly halted her screen career in a funk of jealous paranoia at the possibility of being overshadowed. But you can't keep judging someone for destroying their wife, least of all when they have such beautiful, apelike grace and a highly amusing golf hole, and Harold will remain for me one of the greats, whatever time has done to most of his *oeuvre*.

As for that wire, well, Kong the Mighty was about to demonstrate his incredible prowess on it when a human head suddenly emerged from the wall a foot in front of me. "Shut the fuck up, you bum!" he shouted down at Benny, and disappeared back into the wall. I thought, *Mmm, nice handholds*, forgot about the wire, shimmied up the window's surround, and carried on up another vertical stripe of stones. It kept telling you to climb, the city. That was what it was saying: *Climb me*. And looking down from the plateau at the summit of that tower, I saw what I had perhaps been looking for all along in this leafless, treeless, greenless place—a rectangle of dark forest inlaid among the lights. I felt the gravity of home, stronger than all of America, and took the fast route down a fire escape, across a wide street and into the trees, pant-hooting with delight. Who knew? There might be chimps roosting in the branches— Tyrone, or Bonzo, or bushpigs scuffling through the long grass. The forest was sparse, sure, and the undergrowth was thin, but what did it matter when you could take a running jump up a tree trunk and loop from branch to branch? So I swung my way through a sequence of trees until I was too exhausted to bother breaking off the branches I'd have needed for a nest, and fell asleep, drunkenly and dream-lessly.

And woke in pain on the ground with a human hand around my throat. There was dirt in my mouth and a heavy weight on my back pinning me down. I instinctively thought: Trefflich. Something was slipped around my head and I was flipped onto my back, bringing into view the sight of a couple of humans looking down at me from an early morning sky. Neither was Trefflich, of course—they had none of his well-fed sleekness. I made an attempt to flee but a choking pain in my neck stopped me. In a panic, I turned and rushed at the man who held me on the "tether" (as I would come to know it in Hollywood) and he beat me away with a length of stick. Raising his arm higher, he hit me again, and then a third time. I was dizzy with the surprise of it as much as the pain, and scrambled away as far as the tether allowed.

"Shit, don't bust it up," the second human said. "If you bust it up too bad, they might not take it back, Pops." Both of them had the same thin beards and large eyes, but the second was very much younger than the first.

"Yeah. I don't want to bust it up but I ain't getting bitten, is all."

"You bust its head, they'll say it was us when we bring it in and we get nuthin'. "

I was whimpering at the end of the twine, keeping an eye on the older man's stick.

"What're you talking about, son? We ain't bringin' it in. Zoo ain't got no money to pay you for bringin' them in an absconder. This is good meat. Stewin' meat. Chinese eat monkey stew on a reg'lar basis."

"I ain't eatin' no monkey. That's cannibalism, near enough."

"It ain't cannibalism. Ain't no different from a squirrel or a pigeon once you got its throat cut and the fur off."

"Or a nigger baby, Pops. I just ain't eatin' no monkey. Zoo's gotta give a reward if you return their property."

Chafing at the end of the tether, I was trying to rid myself of the twine around my neck by backflipping it off me. Down came the stick across my raised arm again. I screamed and, without thinking, did something you may have seen me do a number of times on screen. It may even be the first picture you have of me in your head. I leaped toward Pops and wrapped my arms around him, where he could no longer get at me with his stick. It's the first action all chimps work out with their trainers, pretty much. When you see the chimp jump up into those human arms and cling there like a baby being comforted, sometimes it's love and sometimes it's the memory of fear. It's very hard to tell them apart.

"Come on now, Pops. You can't eat this monkey," the younger man said. "It's picked you for a pal. You ain't been hugged like that in a time."

Pops was trying to unpick my grasp from around his shoulders but I was too tightly wound around him, and it took his son to yank me off. I came loose and the old man threw the twine away from him.

"Take it back to the zoo, then, but you won't get a nickel out of them. Just breaks my heart to see a workin' man starvin' and a bunch of monkeys and lions eatin' like kings. It's fucked up, when a beast eats better'n a man."

"You see it do those flips? This is a trained animal, Pops, has to be worth a dollar to somebody." But the old man had turned away in disgust, and I wasn't sorry to see him go.

So the young man led me on my length of twine through the forest as the light strengthened, and I saw that what had seemed a pretty lush jungle at night was actually hard-worked land, dotted with clusters of rickety shelters where tattered children were playing and older humans lolled. Much of the grass had been ripped up and was now mud in which little lines of plants were growing unenthusiastically. Every tree had been brutalized and was missing half of its limbs. It was somehow dispiriting, neither forest nor city, a mess.

On we went, through the half-made shelters and mud, the tether digging into my skin, my arms throbbing from the blows and a hangover, of heavy alcohol and heavier fear, settling in me. We approached the zoo, and there were a dozen wire-mesh shelters in a line, most of them empty. In one, a pair of white parrots roosted. A few other animals were slumbering in corners. The whole place had an air of being semi-abandoned. The young man and I waited for maybe an hour, but nobody showed up, and in the end he must have figured there was no reward for him there. So he looped the tether through the mesh and walked away.

I could easily have untangled that tether and gotten out of there, but the truth is that New York seemed too dangerous to go through again. Another day of it would kill you. Great for an adventure, maybe, but it wouldn't be long before you'd be found dead at the base of one of those high-scraping towers. Not everybody got away with it like Kong had.

After a while, a guy shambled up to the shelters and unlocked the gate. I whimpered at him, and before sundown Trefflich was around to collect a very chastened chimpanzee from the empty shelter where I'd been happy to be led. And by the time we finally left New York for California, every single one of the escapees had been returned to its cage, to use the more usual term, at Henry Trefflich & Son's.

# 6
# Big Break!

I remember that over the entrance to MGM's Central Casting Office on Western Avenue, just outside the lot at Culver City, there used to be a sign that read, "Do NOT try to become an actor! For every ONE we employ we turn away a THOUSAND."

I guess they knew that too many people becoming actors would eventually damage their business. For the movies to work, they needed large numbers of people who weren't stars to do the actual watching. Hence the violent "Keep Out!" sign, which was, however, completely useless. Like a "Do not throw objects into the animals' cages" notice, it was almost touchingly unrealistic about human nature. The lines beneath it were comprised of humans who considered odds of a thousand to one to be really rather tempting: the sign had quadrupled the line.

Nowadays, of course, the problem has become critical. How *can* you stem the tidal wave of Americans who want to become famous actors? I don't know what the answer is. Bigger, more violent signs? To continue enlarging the number of things humans can act in? The only feasible long-term solution to your pandemic is, I suppose, in each individual's hands: don't try to become a famous actor. And who's going to go for that? The YouTubers? You can't change your nature, can you? You can't stop.

In the Golden Age, however, things were very different. Actors formed only a tiny minority of the population, so maybe some of the studios' scare tactics did pay off. Certainly for an animal, there were powerful disincentives. . . .

Our journey from the east took a week and a half of almost intolerably cramped intensive rehab. In the thirties and forties, most MGM employees traveling out to the coast from New York would take a sleeping compartment on board the 20th Century Limited, which departed Grand Central at six in the evening. Before the passengers woke the next morning, the sleeping cars were tacked onto the Santa Fe Chief in Chicago, and two whole days later they'd be in Union Station, L.A. Very civilized. But for us there was just a long period of darkness, semiconsciousness, tasteless fruit left to rot in our dungy straw, and a herky-jerky rhythm that didn't soothe like the rocking of *Forest Lawn*.

And for me, perhaps for the other escapees too, there were bad dreams on the journey: I dreamed I was climbing one of the towers of Manhattan, and that the old man from the city-forest was climbing after me, trying to swat me with his stick so that I fell. As I dropped through the sky I looked into the shelters in the sides of the tower and saw humans displaying wrathfully at each other, or embracing each other, or giving smiles that were really grimaces of fear—a multitude of humans who seemed to contain just as much violence as we chimpanzees did.

Whenever the vibrating motion and noise of the sleeping compartment ceased, we would all wake and cry out nervously to each other in the sudden stillness to check that we still existed. I could distinguish Bonzo and Frederick and Tyrone among the different calls, and I thought at those times that you could hear the residue of troubled dreams in most of our voices but I don't know, maybe it was just me . . . maybe it was just me who was fretting about whether humans were really the answer after all. So the world spun under us and we traveled west toward the Dream Factories.

We were unloaded, reloaded, unloaded again. For the first time since *Forest Lawn* we smelled leopard, rhinoceros, lion and musty python (those things sure do reek), and heard turacos sending out relays of warning. And I thought I understood at last—our rehabilitation was over. It came to me like an epiphany. This was surely the reason we'd been deprived of the touch of each other, of the comfort of mutual grooming, or those kisses of reassurance that meant so much to us. We'd been deprived of it so that we would cherish each other now we were finally considered ready to return to the forest! So that we—and I guessed this included the rehabilitated leopards and snakes—would do it *right* this time. The humans had helped us see the error of our foolish ways, and now it was up to us to make the most of our second chance!

But when the slats of my shelter were broken down, they merely revealed another of those landscapes like the docks at Kigoma, another transit camp for animals, which I was beginning to know all too well. Another shelter, Tyrone and I cast together once again, another reconnoiter around its eight corners, turning up nothing. I knew the drill by now: the insufficient straw, the diamond mesh. We could see a brick pillar, a stretch of wall, and a fraction of one of the leopards' shelters. And then, suddenly, the dividing partition between us and the next shelter along was thrumming with the aftershock of a heavy impact, and there, bipedaling around his shelter, his hair bristling up like the Bride of Frankenstein's, was Stroheim.

Always a pleasure . . . a little bit heavier than the last time, but that was to be expected. What was shocking about Stroheim was his head. He'd always had this rather noticeable central part between his two wings of hair, which were long and lay sideways. He used to look like a human schoolboy, furious at having been patted on his just-combed brow. Now this central part had become a barren desert. As I watched him display, I saw his familiar old gesture of dropping both hands onto his head and fiddling at the edges of the bald patch, plucking at the remaining hairs there. With full weight of shoulder, he crashed his slab-hands against the partition again, barking at me to show off his teeth, but still, though I feared him, I couldn't quite bring myself ever to believe in Stroheim. He subsided, and hating myself for my gratitude to my godawful shelter, I turned away and began the long process of grooming poor shy little Tyrone down from his shock.

Stroheim's hair-pulling business worried me. Was it anything to do with this new rehab center? There was a general air of low morale around the place, as if even the best efforts of the program could not prevent the animals turning in on themselves. Certainly our shelter was on the snug side, and the leopard opposite seemed completely sunk in despair. But there were humans who occasionally toured our shelters and at least they were diverting to look at as they observed us, doubtless assessing our recovery.

Always, for some reason, these humans were accompanied by children, who offered us morsels of delicious American food through the mesh. To my surprise, they demonstrated a better grasp of the prevailing realities than the adults, who frequently attempted to interfere with these vital nutritional supplements. But the children's actions made sense to me. They dispensed supplements to those animals that showed the most vitality—in other words, those who seemed most worth assisting. So the chimpanzees did well compared to those whom the program was failing, those whom you knew were alive only after long scrutiny of their ribcages, which slowly gained and lost faint stripes of shadow if you peered closely enough into the tangled straw. Unreconstructed jungle violence, which Stroheim demonstrated, went unrewarded by supplements. It all made sense.

And this extra human food was crucial. Something had happened to the quantity of fruit we were getting; it was radically less than what we had been used to at Trefflich's. By the time the twice-daily ritual of winning supplements from our human coaches came around, you were ravenous. There were two of them to about fifteen of us, and every mouthful of food they deigned to grant you was a complete fucking performance. And it wasn't at all like *Forest Lawn* and its cheerful abundance: you got a single, bright little bean hardly worth the chewing each time you did something the human liked. The little beans were highly addictive, however, and you were so hungry you'd chow down on as many as were offered.

So when Tyrone and I were led out of our shelters on tethers into the courtyard, we were already desperate to please. Each of the coaches carried a short length of smooth stick—"the broom handle," or "ugly-stick"—with which they threatened to beat us if we failed to imitate them. They went at us two at a time. And for me, seeing the coach raise the ugly-stick above his head brought back memories of the gaunt old man from the New York forest and I couldn't suppress a pleading grimace of fear.

"That's right, gimme a smile. Gimme a great big Gable grin, Jiggs. That's good."

But Tyrone was confused by the ugly-stick and was beaten heavily before he could produce the fear-grimace on order. It took only a single hard blow across my back to understand that a leap of faked love into the coach's arms was required, and here again Tyrone suffered badly when he bit the human's shoulder. I'd come close to biting my own coach, but the memory of Trefflich's watch held me back.

There was no joy in the coach's face, no love in his voice—he was a relentless man, he bored it into you. He lessened the world, made it hard even to think of what there was outside the corridor of actions he'd laid down for you. Oh, yeah—pain, that was what was outside that corridor. So after you'd clapped for him, and kissed him, and "laughed" for him, donned a hat and drunk a glass of water, then gone and fetched the little tan notebook in which he wrote notes at the end of the session, you were left with the feeling that there was really nothing between you—a foretaste of that emptiness all actors, all auditionees, know. The one time I felt emboldened enough to fish a cigarette from the pack in his chest pocket, I got a couple of cracks from the ugly-stick. I was only fooling around. But there was no love in the man, only dull, inexpressive alphadom.

Mornings and evenings, this routine on the tethers. Almost the worst of it was hearing the others taking their beatings. With my experience on *Forest Lawn*, I'd been fortunate. It seemed, I don't know, somehow *natural* for me to do a triple-backflip-handclap-double-lip-flip-and-grin. You didn't even need to ask me. Not so for the rest, and they got the brunt of it. Bonzo was hopeless; he was continually bewildered into mistakes by his fear. When we returned to the shelter I'd try to reassure him with strokes and grooming, but after a short time he'd slink away into his corner and slump motionless for hours.

Frederick was good: he'd picked up plenty of coaching on *Forest Lawn* and was quick with the fetching. And there were two or three other apes who were awarded full rations of colored beans. Being older, Stroheim was less moldable. For this reason I think they cut him more slack. Certainly we rarely heard him scream, and when he knuckled back into the shelter he never seemed cowed and was soon displaying away boneheadedly in his own little fiefdom. I didn't rise to it. I was slipping into the lassitude of the program. We all were.

Life shrank to hunger and the ugly-stick, the pulsing pain of your bruises and masturbation. Dimly you'd see the children who visited your shelter recoil, but you couldn't stop yourself hunting for a little pang of pleasure in your misery. We were all at it, ten, fifteen, twenty times a day, and each time I vowed it would be my last. But my brain would circle around again, and coming across nothing else to rest on or hope for, I'd find myself back where I started, looking for that tiny throblet of pleasure, the only one going.

And worse, I was beginning to starve. Sure, I was getting my colored beans, but the center served up a menu heavily slanted toward fucking *bananas*. I could manage a nibble, but then my gorge would rise at the memory of the mamba, and I'd never be able to finish the things. Bonzo grew fat on my leavings. And I fell gradually into a disenchantment with the humans. I fretted and doubted, worse than I ever had at Trefflich's. There were things I wasn't seeing. Maybe this whole thing was a mistake, and you were just another bunch of mad apes who didn't really know what you were doing. This treadmill of starving and beating—what was it *for*? Was rehab *permanent*?

For a month we followed the routine, and my mind began to close down when I wasn't "on." Stroheim adopted a compulsive shuttle from his back wall to our partition, which he slammed against scornfully at every third or fourth pass. Tyrone and I were too fazed to notice him, too busy rocking back and forth and dreaming of elsewhere. I was up on the escarpment again, in moonlight, teaching Tony Gentry how to fetch wild custard apples for me, when Stroheim erupted through the forest and into our shelter.

I think he was as surprised as we were to find that the wooden frame of the partition, which he'd been slamming against for five or six days, had finally come loose. His follow-through tangled him up in the ripped hangnail of mesh, giving Tyrone and me a brief second to consider our options—but when I glanced at my shelter-mate, he'd already swiveled around and was presenting his rear. Fantastic, I thought, just great: a submission display, and he hasn't even *done* anything yet. Stroheim was propping himself up and bristling, though whether at me or at the dumb, winded square of wire, I didn't know. The world, probably—Stroheim just bristled at it in general. And now he began to pant-hoot, spiraling swiftly into a scream as he unhooked himself. There were no exits here, no opportunities for calming down and cooling off, and I was terri-fied. I could submit, I suppose. But to submit to Stroheim, who had cavorted while the others broke my mother's body? I was incapable of it.

He came at me as I sprang onto the front mesh, and I was able to climb high enough to evade the impact. The wire twanged and bucked in my grip. I didn't have a plan, but as Stroheim circled back around and leaped at me, I instinctively let go of the mesh, dropped underneath him into the straw and scuttled around the side of the shattered partition frame into Stroheim's shelter, pulling the frame after me, where it jammed against the wall. Furious, he slammed into it, but the partition held. He set himself to batter it down, still shrieking, and I sat waiting for him and for the end.

Wherever you were—inside a shelter or out, among humans or chimpanzees—it seemed the jungle came after you. There was no escape, nowhere you were safe. I'd crossed the Atlantic to America and here I was, back precisely where I'd started: chased by Stro-heim. The bald, bullying, banana-snatching, boneheaded brute. And a name suddenly comes to me out of the past: Moose Malloy, that great hulking slow-witted patsy "no wider than a beer truck," forever blundering after his lost love Velma in the Dick Powell–Philip Marlowe picture *Murder, My Sweet* (1944). Moose, who was too big for his brain. Years later, when I first saw *Murder, My Sweet*,

I immediately thought: Stroheim! You see, though he was a killer, you couldn't help but pity Moose. And I could never—can't you tell?—pick the pity out of my hatred for Stroheim.

So I waited for the mesh to break and Stroheim to come tumbling through, but with each blow the poor dolt was wedging the door *shut*. If he'd just put his fingers through it and tugged backwards you wouldn't be reading this now. But no: all Stroheim knew was that you opened partitions with bashing. Bashing—that was how it had always been done! He was just too damn stupid to murder me. After a while of incensed thumping, the idiot gave up and folded himself into one of his catatonic deepwater sulks and we slept.

That happened in the evening after the second coaching session of the day. The following morning classes were canceled. Instead, a large rolling shelter entered the courtyard, and supervised by the coaches, we were all reloaded into the smallest shelters yet, made entirely of wire. Or, no, not all of us. My coach patrolled the front of the shelters, consulting his notebook and directing the other humans as to which of us were to be moved on. About a quarter of us were rejected, among them Stroheim.

"I'm gonna leave you boys to it," my coach said. "Don't ever feel happy doing this."

"No point in bellyaching about it. You got a fair enough deal. More'n fair."

"Yeah, yeah. They're helping people, I suppose."

"Hey. It's show business. Cruel business."

Yeah, but it's not. There *are* crueller businesses.

We were loaded into the back of the shelter, stacked on top of each other, and I noticed Tyrone and Bonzo, and my new shelter-mate and various other faces that were vaguely familiar from *Forest Lawn* before darkness and the familiar jolting overtook us again. And when the jaws of the shelter opened, the world would have changed again—that was how these things worked. They put you into darkness and then scrambled the world.

A short haul this time. Something about the accelerating rhythm of these periods of blackness made me feel that we were getting closer to wherever it was we were going. I could not believe that it was simply the human way to keep moving us from rehab center to rehab center forever, and I had a hunch that what was happening was a *process of selection*. We were being narrowed down, from *Forest Lawn* to Trefflich's, from Trefflich's to the coaching institute, and it was something to do with our performances in the coaching sessions. And yet that couldn't be right, because Frederick had been rejected and Bonzo, who'd hardly shone during the sessions, was whimpering below me. But, still, I felt we were getting nearer to *something*. Stroheim had been rejected, and perhaps this had been the plan all along: to return us to the forest, a forest without its Stroheims, a forest regained.

But it was not a forest, or a narrowing down. It was an enclosed, yellow-lit space with a corridor of tiny individual shelters stacked three high on either side, in which dozens of apes and macaques stared or displayed. Once I'd been unloaded, tethered and bundled into my new shelter, I was able to look across at my new fellow-rehabilitees and I felt the mamba brush me. I remembered the flicker of its body as it passed over DiMarco and me, the touch of death.

Pretty much every chimp or macaque I could see was in drastically bad shape. Right across from me, on the highest level of the shelters, was an old female chimp unlike any I'd ever seen. Her chest and belly were so hugely swollen that it would have been impossible for her to stand up. She was breathing in rapid little pants, as if she couldn't get the air to stay down. Below her was a chimp covered in a pale liquid, which I supposed it had just thrown up. It wasn't moving. There were macaques with peculiar, white-dusted eyes, macaques with open red wounds on their chests. There was something that looked half human, the size of an ape, but almost completely furless. I don't want to go on describing them. There was absolutely nothing, I thought, that even the humans could do for these poor creatures, no way they could be saved. We were in a hospital for incurables. It was a place of death. I felt it instinctively—I recognized it like I'd recognized it in the mamba's mouth. These were already the dead, because nobody was getting out of here alive.

So, this was it. The end of the line. Was this really what the rescue, the rehabilitation and the coaching all came down to in the end? Oh, man. . . . Despite the best efforts of all concerned, it seemed that the plan—this brave but ultimately doomed attempt to save us from death—had failed. All that goddamn effort, and we might as well have stayed in the jungle.

Yet, yet, yet . . . it seemed like such a *mistake*. What had been the point of the coaching sessions? Frederick had sailed through them but hadn't even made it through the selection this morning. I remembered how surprised I'd been at that. Nor had the other couple of chimps who'd excelled, come to think of it. And—why was Tyrone here? And suddenly I understood: it wasn't them who'd been rejected, dimwit. It was us. It was me. *They* were the ones who had been kept on.

When I say mine has been a lucky, lucky life, I don't mean merely that I've been privileged enough to watch Fred Astaire perform his famous "golf-dance" on the first tee at Pebble Beach, sending five balls in a row arcing into the Pacific with five windmilling pirouettes. Or that I've been lucky enough to sit at the feet of Robert Benchley by the Garden of Allah pool while he recited *Leaves of Grass* to a rapt Cocteau, with dawn coming up. I mean *lucky*.

The author.

Mr. Henry Trefflich the Younger, animal importer, New York, early 1930s. The fashion for snake-scarves never caught on.

Left to right: Maureen O'Sullivan; me, Cheeta; Johnny Weissmuller.

Me rescuing Johnny. I'm kidding—if you examine this picture very closely you'll see that it is in fact *a human in a costume*!

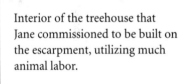

Interior of the treehouse that Jane commissioned to be built on the escarpment, utilizing much animal labor.

The three of us in *Tarzan Escapes*, 1936.

Hollywood's golden couple. Johnny and his third wife, the "Mexican Spitfire," Lupe Vélez.

Johnny and Lupe down by the pool at the Garden of Allah, possibly. I'm not sure, but I seem to remember that *I* took this picture with Lupe's camera, which I broke shortly afterward. Nonetheless, it remains one of the greatest photographs ever taken by a chimpanzee.

Johnny off Catalina Island, skippering his yacht *Allure,* named for the hydrophobic Miss Vélez.

Constance Bennett and her beau, Gilbert Roland, who opened my eyes to the benefits of homeopathic medicine.

Interesting picture. On the left, Dolores del Río, a dear friend and nothing more. A minor *imbroglio* involving Miss del Río in 1942 is generally supposed to have cost me an Oscar nomination for my work on *Tarzan's New York Adventure*, and Dolores her marriage. On the right, close friend and one of Hollywood's great scintillators, the irrepressible David Niven.

Paradise. The "real-life treehouse" of Mr. and Mrs. Johnny and Beryl Weissmuller, on Rockingham Avenue, from behind, before the grounds were properly landscaped.

The great Charles Chaplin, as he liked to be known. Paulette Goddard, to his right, is trying hard not to resent his serial betrayals of her.

The genius of Mickey Rooney. Mickey's richly nuanced examination of Japanese masculinity in *Breakfast at Tiffany's* demonstrated his astounding range: I think for many he's the best thing in the picture. In my personal experience, however, Mickey is memorable chiefly as the victim of one of David Niven's most crushing put-downs, which, to spare Mickey's blushes, I won't repeat here.

Marlene Dietrich, German nightclub singer and actress, who was famous for some years in the thirties and forties before hitting the cabaret circuit, and I'm sorry to say, the bottle, before losing her sanity. She refused to allow me to drive the Cadillac to her right which, retrospectively, is understandable.

Johnny Weissmuller, c. 1935.

I was pressing myself against the mesh, screaming the place down, as were the rest of us new inductees, when a couple of humans approached down the corridor between the shelters. One was clothed in white. The other, I was surprised to see, was my coach. Unlike Tony Gentry, he had come back.

"This is the one," he said, arriving beneath my shelter. "Jiggs. This one's going to Metro. Your guys need to learn to count a little fucking better."

"I'm afraid that's your responsibility. We make the purchase and collect what we're given. I can only think you made some error at Lincoln Heights."

"Sure I made an error. Letting your guys do the loading was the error. Shoulda done it myself. You realize how valuable an animal this is? Oughta put your man in that cage instead of this animal, teach him how to listen. 'Don't touch the larger chimp in the end cage.' Told him twice. Told him twice."

They opened my shelter, let me tumble out and leashed me. I leaped into the coach's arms—and it wasn't a leap of faked love, either. It wasn't meant to be me here, it was meant to be *Stroheim*. The larger chimp in the end cage had been *me*, at least until we performed our little switcheroo-dance. Lucky. Very, very lucky. And lucky, lucky, *lucky* Stroheim.

"The delivery is still for a dozen animals, Mr. Gately. This leaves us with eleven."

"Yeah—my other stock's in Culver City being auditioned right now. So I guess you'll have to whistle for it. Or call up Louis Mayer, ask him if he's interested in selling."

"A hundred eighty dollars for twelve animals, Mr. Gately. It'll be a hundred sixty-five for eleven."

"Hunderd senny-five for eleven animals and the aggravation," said Coach Gately, without humor.

And that was how things ended between them, and Stroheim never knew that I'd saved his goddamned life. Gately led me out of the place on the end of the tether, avoiding a small ginger-and-white cat that tripped out tinklingly across his path on its way into the embrace of one of the white-clothed humans. Mixed emotions were slopping toxically around in my belly: selfish relief, of course, and the pure joy of being away from there. But I was still stunned by what I'd seen, and perfectly aware that Bonzo, Tyrone and the others were not heading with us out into the bright, bright blue. Did it, I wondered distractedly, ever rain in America?

Gately led me into his rolling shelter and, tying my tether tightly to the door handle, put me up beside him on a long seat at what turned out to be, when the city started to roll past us, its front end. I was guessing it was a city around us, though I saw very few humans, only rolling shelters. A hillside was called HOLLYWOOD-LAND, and I thought, That's going to be helpful, if they start having signs up to identify everything. I could do with knowing the names of a few things.

It wasn't a city that asked you to climb it, like New York; it was a city, I noticed, of gateways. Either side of us, hundreds of colossal gates rolled by, implying the presence of a species of colossal human. Behind these gates you could make out patches of forest, and *orange trees*, and *palms*! I didn't get too excited: in truth, I knew it was just one of those brief periods of respite you got before another grueling session of rehab began. Straw, mesh, excrement and the same old overripe fruit. Have you any idea how time *drags* in the shelters?

I suddenly felt very low, as Gately rolled us under the arch of one of the gateways, definitively low, finished with it all. I knew that I simply wouldn't be able to make it through another long session. Another shelter. The shelters didn't even *work*. Another session of rehab and I'd be like Stroheim, tearing my hair out. I was through. Enough. You never think that the insistent little voice in your head forever urging *survive, survive, survive* might ever grow faint or silent, but in the end it does. And I really do like to think of myself as a survivor. I've survived seventy years in this industry. I've survived turkeys like *Bela Lugosi Meets a Brooklyn Gorilla*. I've even survived that old soak Benchley's godawful all-night Whitman recitals at the Garden of Allah—oh, man, I'm a survivor, all right. But I was ready to quit then: I thought, I'm done. Done like Tyrone.

Gately brought everything to a halt, stretched over to untether me from the handle and flipped open the door.

We were in a forest. Chimpanzees were hooting from the treetops. Gazelles were grazing on the lower leaves. In the shade at the edge of the trees, a number of zebras were browsing the long, tawny grass. Spores and seeds and butterflies floated billionfold through the warm air around me. There were parakeets too, in vibrating colors, and humans sitting and standing in groups among the animals. My heart capsized. Oh, you faithless, doubting fool of an ape! You quitter! They'd done it. The humans had done it. We'd done it together! The joy of it straightened me up onto two feet and I bipedaled around in crazy circles, hooting back at the chimps. I was dancing for joy. I was rain-dancing in a rainless land! Gately came around the side of the shelter, removed my tether and took my hand. Together we made our way toward the forest, watching Frederick loop down the branches to greet us.

I was such a *kid* when I first arrived in the States! Basically, I didn't have a clue what was going on. Of course everything was bewildering, but scanning back over what I've written, I wonder if I've perhaps been guilty of touching up my history with darker shades than were really there. Probably gone over the top a bit, to be honest: forgive me. My memory, my child's eye, has acquired a little Dickensian distortion. Plus I did want to give a push to No Reel Apes, and anyway, I want to sell a few books here, and I'm told the childhood-adversity stuff plays well these days.

Sure, difficult childhoods can make great artists—it's the thread that links Van Gogh, Dickens, Herman Melville, Hitchcock, Frank McCourt, Dave Pelzer, Kirk Douglas, Margaret Seltzer and me—but this is not one of those autobiographies that Don likes so much, with those huge-eyed children staring accusingly at you from their covers, their faces blanched out like lemurs'. It's only that I felt obliged to touch on some of the problems that Don and the attractive Dr. Goodall are eager to highlight for their No Reel Apes campaign. Cruelty to apes in the name of entertainment is obscene and *must stop*, though of course it can lead to some absolutely tremendous movies, and I personally had a wonderful time in Hollywood. Which, as I've said, saved my life, so there are two sides to each story. But do support the campaign if you can, which—get this—proposes the replacement of living primates in cinema with computer-generated ones.

Interesting. . . . During our charitable visits to hospices around Palm Springs, Don and I have found ourselves more than once in a children's ward dominated by posters of computer-animated heroes. The wisecracking eyeball, the smart-aleck donkey. The kids love them—but *they're not fucking there*, are they? They're not there, sharing a bag of pretzels with a terminal teen, a kidney dish on their head and a blood-pressure monitor in their mouth, are they? And they never will be there in the flesh when it really counts, prolapsed on the end of a child's hospital bed like a *memento mori*. That's the real magic of movies: their flesh and blood. Does Buzz Lightyear ever suffer for his art? No, and that's why he's no good. Though, I do have to say, the children haven't the faintest idea who

I am. Well, anyhow, computer-generated imagery, CGI, that's supposedly the way forward, according to Don and Jane. Support their campaign: www.noreelapes.org or something like that.

I digress. If we sometimes had it a little rough, so what? MGM had given us the opportunity of a lifetime. I didn't know that it was normal during the heyday of the studio system to let young stars languish for a year or more while they built up their confidence and the right part was constructed for them. How *could* I have known that the starving and beating all formed part of Louis Mayer's painstaking grooming process—almost exactly the same process as MGM put Ava Gardner through?

In fact, Ava had it worse than us, and you never heard her complain. She was a real stand-up dame, Ava, despite her occasional indiscretions, like letting slip how sexually inadequate she found her first husband, Mickey Rooney—rather a cruel thing to do to a real "ladies' man," as Mickey referred to himself, and the sort of thing that's best forgotten. When she was first put under contract— "Honey, he may have enjoyed it but I sure as hell didn't," *that's* what it was—sorry, when she was first put under contract at MGM it took them more than a year to wrench the North Carolina accent out of her, like teeth. And they had to teach her how to act, which took much longer with Ava than it did with me. Betty Bacall had six months of intensive voice coaching, near-starvation and Howard Hawks breathing down her neck every second of every day. Plus she was at Warner's, and believe me, once you'd heard the stars' horror stories about Warner's, you'd have preferred a lifetime of imprisonment and beatings to a contract with them. "If you can survive even seven years at Warner's," said Cagney, who knew all about it, "then you can survive anything." And over the course of two wonderful decades in MGM and RKO cages, I'd often shudder at what poor Jimmy must have been suffering under the Warners.

So, no complaints. MGM had extended a hell of a lot of faith to a bunch of unknowns and they had a right to polish their investment. That leopard on the other side of the courtyard might have seemed a bit listless and dazed, but it went on to work with the great trainer Olga Celeste and landed one of the key parts of the decade, playing not one but two different leopards opposite Asta the fox terrier and Kate Hepburn in *Bringing Up Baby*. Put it this way: the number of chimpanzees who would have traded places with me in an instant was, well, lots. Mind you, I don't know how many of us were still left in the wild then. More than 150,000, anyway. Millions, probably. Apart from the mix-up with the lab (a highly-infectious-diseases research facility, which was absorbed into the military just after the Second World War and is now located near Encino), which was essentially Stroheim's fault, I couldn't have dreamed of anything more. I'd been nurtured and tutored and now I was ready to be taken to the bosom of the vast happy family of MGM. The next time you hear Louis Mayer traduced as a bully, tyrant, witness-buying perverter of justice and all those other half-truths, remember that I'd be nowhere without him.

There the lab was, though, undeniably, the underside to the Glamour Capital of the World. I'd worked out pretty quickly what it was. It was where you would end up if you couldn't make it in pictures. And even if you made it, any animal who's ever seen the once-popular Edison short of an elephant being electrocuted to death in Coney Island will recognize just how brief and hollow the rewards of fame can be! And that's Hollywood for you: a heart-breaking town. "Do NOT try to become an actor. For every ONE we employ, we turn away a THOUSAND."

Down through the long grass walked Gately and I, toward the clumps of humans dotted around the clearings, with everything dream-sharp and sparkling, like Beverly Hills in Cary Grant's LSD-inflected eyes. Frederick and the other two chosen chimps came hooting up to us, and we all embraced each other and mock-charged in delight and generally kicked up a maelstrom of happiness, so that a man near the center of one of the clumps of humans called over to Gately to quiet us down: "Can you restrain those little fuckers for a second? In fact, come on over and we'll take a look at them now!"

The cluster of humans was arranged in a rough circle around the man who had spoken. We moved through the crowd toward him on the ends of our tethers. Other animals—lion cubs, antelopes—were playing with their coaches among the humans. This was a new kind of forest to me.

"I'm Cedric Gibbons. You're Gately, right? You can get these animals to do what you tell 'em?"

"Yes, I can. But it depends on factors. The way they react to individuals."

"So you brought us a short list, in case love doesn't bloom. Show me."

"Put out your hand," said Gately, and made Frederick shake hands with Gibbons and then pluck his hat off. "Give it back now, Buster."

"Not me he needs to be meeting," Gibbons said. "Maureen, come on over and meet your new leading man. And where's the King of the Jungle? You seen him?"

"He's on the escarpment," somebody said, and a number of the humans began to shout, "Johnny! Call Johnny!" and in answer there came a faint, high call, like the trumpet of an elephant.

"You seen *Tarzan the Ape Man*, Gately? No? We had a good chimp in that, but old. Can't use it any more. What we're looking for—" and Gibbons was interrupted by the high call again.

"*Johnny*! For Chrissakes. What we're looking for is comic relief. Uh, an animal with a bit of mischief, but easy for Maureen to handle. . . ."

Here Gibbons was interrupted again, by a human, a male adult, dropping down from a tree and sprinting over to us. Dropping down from a tree! He wore no clothes except a flap of hide around his middle and I was amazed to see what a human's musculature was, how powerful they were underneath their coverings. It was impossible that he wasn't an alpha, probably the alpha of the whole group, yet there was no tyrant's force in his face as he said, smiling, "Me on escarpment with second unit. Me meet chimps now."

"Oh, Johnny." Maureen sighed as she strolled over toward us. She was not much more than half his height. He was so *upright.* "Do you think you could *possibly* give it a rest with the ape-talk? It's just a trifle wearying. . . ."

"Jane angry. Jane need smack on rear end," said Johnny.

Yes, this was the king of the forest, all right.

"Shall I to the marriage of true hearts admit impediments?" Maureen started to sort of sing. "The language of Shakespeare, Johnny. Of Edna St. Vincent Millay! You do know who Shakespeare is?"

"Guy in pool hall. Me meet chimps," Johnny said, looking over the four of us and holding out his hand. Ah, humanity, you were so beautiful! "Me Tarzan. Me Johnny. Who Cheeta?"

And actors talk about auditions going like a dream . . . Frederick and the other two (and Stroheim now, lumbering up late for the big moment) didn't stand a chance. Who Cheeta? What kind of a question was that?

I leaped into the home of the arms of the King of the Jungle and, for the second time that day, my heart tipped over. It was me. Me—Kong, Jiggs, Louis, the Cheater of Death—me, *Cheeta.*

# PART 2

PART 2

# 1
# Movie Madness!

There was Tarzan, me and Jane, and we lived in a forest at the top of
an escarpment that rose in sheer cliffs above a cloud-covered world
where savage tribes warred among themselves far below. We lived
in a dream. We could speak to each other and to the other animals,
except those with cold blood. Only two words were really needed—
"*aaahhheeyeeyeeyeeaaaahheeyeeyeeyaaahhhh*," which meant "I
am." And "*umgawa*," which meant "Let it be so."

We took milk from antelopes and eggs from invisible ostriches,
ate fish, fruit and roasted buffalo calf, and slept in adjoining nests
in the trees. Only elephants died, or any predator who challenged
Tarzan to single combat; the sole weapon allowed on the escarpment was his knife. Tarzan loved Jane: they sublimated their love
into swimming. Tarzan loved me: we sublimated our love into flying. Jane and I were jealous of each other, but we got on fine: although we were the two different sides of him, we loved him too
much to fight. On the escarpment, chimpanzees didn't fight or kill
and I belonged to a group, but my loyalties were to the humans.
They needed me more. Johnny was Tarzan and Maureen was Jane;
I was myself.

Or not quite. You had to pay a small toll of transformation to enter the dream, it seemed—I was (and I think I never got the credit for this when the Academy Award nominations rolled obliviously around each year) *female*.

That was all there was, apart from Jane's problem. Jane had quit civilization, but she was still an addict deep down, and her family would come from London to tempt her back with words, which she still craved. It didn't matter. Tarzan was stronger than the jungle (*umgawa*, knife), Jane was stronger than Tarzan (worshipped, adored), the white men were stronger than Jane (home, duty), the Gaboni tribe were stronger than the white men (ambush, kidnap), the jungle was stronger than the Gaboni (elephants, stampede) and Tarzan was stronger than the jungle (*aaahhheeyeeyeeaaahh-heeyeeyeeyaaahhh*)—so even that was resolved easily enough, via a kind of natural cycle, and we could return to our dream on the escarpment. *Umgawa.*

So there was Johnny, me and Maureen and we lived, during the early autumn of 1933, in Sherwood Forest near Thousand Oaks, and by Toluca Lake in the San Fernando Valley, and sometimes in Lot Two at Culver City Studios, dreaming *Tarzan and His Mate*, with Jack Conway directing. Jack had replaced Cedric Gibbons at the end of August because Gibbie was really an art director and was in over his head. Plus I don't think he could take any more jokes about Gibbons working with the Ape Man. Poor old Gibbie was married to Dolores del Río, who slept in a separate bedroom above his. Gibbie could only access it via a trapdoor, and only then if she deigned to open it and let down the ladder.

What we did in the Dream Factory was—well, I'm sure you're as uninterested in the technical aspects of moviemaking as I am. But you've heard of the primitive who thinks the camera is stealing his soul? Of course, the opposite was true: we enacted the dream, and as a kind of by-product of converting the dream into the past, the cameras gave us our souls. They poured soul over us and if they gave you enough of it you started to become an Immortal. I don't want to blind you with science here. Once the dream was in the past, it was considered moving ("moving" pictures) and movie-goers would rush in their millions to live in it rather than the present. Essentially, our business was selling past dreams, and we were the dreamers.

In all there were seven main Dream Factories, run by seven alpha males: Mayer, Warner, Goldwyn, Cohn, Zukor, Zanuck and Laemmle. These alphas were the kings of the town, but there were a number of other kings: a King of Hollywood (Gable), a King of the Silents (Fairbanks), a King of the Jungle (Johnny), and a Queen of Hollywood (Myrna Loy), a Queen of Warner's (Kay Francis), a Queen of the World (Dietrich) and a Dragon Queen (Joan Crawford). There was also a Baron, a Duke, a First Lady of Hollywood, and rarer creatures—an Iron Butterfly, a Platinum Blonde, a Profane Angel, an Old Stoneface, a Love Goddess, a Great Profile, a Sweater Girl, an Oomph Girl, a Girl-with-the-Wink. Somewhere in the hills above the factories, among the groves of maple and flowering eucalyptus, you might come across The Look or The Face or even The Most Beautiful Animal in the World (not me— Ava Gardner). They were so beautiful, such very, very special human beings, that from time to time the earth itself under Hollywood seemed to shiver with pleasure, as if it had been caressed too sweetly.

That's how I remember my earliest days in L.A. Above all, there was the pleasure of the dream, or the "work," as it was drolly dubbed, which more than fulfilled the promise made by the MGM motto "*ars gratia artis*": art gratifies the artist. Art makes the artist happy . . . it was a whoop of delight at our own good fortune. This

motto was there for all to see before every MGM movie, accompanied by a roar from my good friend and colleague Jackie the lion,
which I have to confess made me somewhat uneasy, since Jackie was
so obviously telling the audience to back off. "Get the fuck out of my
fucking territory now or I'll fucking rip you to fucking pieces"
would be a rough translation of what Jackie was saying.

I often think of Jackie when Don sticks on one of those CDs he's
so inexplicably addicted to, with a bunch of turacos and parrots
screaming at each other and generally spoiling for a fight by some
waterfall in some jungle somewhere. Christ, and then we get half
an hour of a whale lugubriously detailing just how incredibly impressive he'd be in bed. And we have it on repeat, for crying out
loud. All goddamn day we have to listen to those parrots and that
whale, and they set off the chickadees in the wild date palm behind
the Sanctuary so that we're drowned out by nerve-shredding terri-
torial aggression while Don stretches out on the deck. He says it
"de-stresses" him. Anyway, moviegoers didn't seem to mind Jackie,
who was in truth the mildest of animals, and something of a cult
figure.

Meanwhile, my art was making me happy. I felt like one of those
hummingbirds that plundered the nectar from the jacaranda
bushes that grew around the stars' dressing rooms in the Culver
City complex. There was an intense sweetness to life, which I came
to realize only later was my long dread finally lifting. I was rehabilitated, almost. There was one more thing to go through, it
turned out.

It was on the second or third morning of filming, when I was
still getting used to Hollywood's habit of tossing out casual miracles, that we first met the ape-actors. A squadron of humans was
strolling through the Toluca Lake set, laughing and smoking and
holding their heads under their arms. Up to the neck they were go-

rillas. Gately summoned Frederick and me out of the live oak we were fooling around in to introduce us, at which point cigarettes were discarded (always a side benefit of the movie-set—the long butt) and the sweating humans disappeared beneath their gorilla heads and began to mimic us. You had to take these bewildering things in your stride. Was there some cross-breeding program at MGM perhaps, an attempt to engineer the perfect human-simian actor? If there was, it wasn't going very well, because, though I would never normally criticize another actor, these guys were *hopeless*.

"It's more of a rolling movement, working up from the spine, Leslie," one of the apes said, "and then you straighten your arms for the pound. Like so—" and he and the other apes began a classic earth-thumping display ritual, directed at the two of us. Naturally, we mimicked the humans back—as we'd learned to do under Mr. Gentry and Gately—but no rewards were forthcoming, possibly because they didn't think we *were* mimicking them. They mimicked us back, atrociously; and we mimicked them, rather well.

"Leslie—you're rocking back but you're not moving your hands enough. Vic—excellent. Look at Vic, Les, see how he's got the weight forward. Do as he does. That's super, Vic."

But it wasn't. Leslie didn't want to do as Vic did—he wanted to watch Frederick and me, because Vic looked . . . he looked about half as convincing as Stroheim, is how he looked. No, it was just embarrassing, watching these very very slow, unthreatening and totally out of scale impersonations of ourselves. Where were the teeth and the bristling fur? That was why Thalberg was a wonder, I later understood. He'd seen these chumps in *Tarzan the Ape Man* and immediately grasped that he had to order in some professionals. Hence us. Hence *Forest Lawn*.

A human trying to act a chimpanzee is somehow pathetic,

whereas a chimpanzee trying to act a human is funny because . . . well, why *is* that? Something to do with aspiration. You think we're pure and want to be us. We know you're not pure, but we still aspire to be you. That's the tragedy at the heart of our, or some would say my, comedy, and a little more profound than anything in my esteemed colleague the Utopian dolt, satyromaniac, cradle-snatcher, self-mythologizer and (need I say it?) sentimentalist Charlie Chaplin's *Weltanschauung*, to use a term rather typical of Charlie's own self-consciously showy autodidact's vocabulary. With his three fucking Oscars. The difference between us, Charlie—the crucial difference between us—is that nobody has ever once called my work "dated." Must get off Chaplin.

The leader of the group of ape-actors stood up and removed his head as Jack Conway approached, trailing a little retinue of betas behind him. Before directing, Conway had been a silent actor, which was perfect for handling Johnny. He used to crack Johnny up singing dirty Irish ballads on his ukelele while Maureen smiled thinly along. Two of Chaplin's Oscars were "honorary" by the way, meaning "not for real." Now one of Conway's retinue beckoned us over and informed us that they were ready to do the real version of the Mary shot. Mary was a rhinoceros from Hamburg I'd spent most of the morning watching Johnny ride whoopingly around the set's main clearing.

"I feel we've really improved our kinetics, Mr. Conway," said the ape-leader, "really getting more of a 'chimps' feel."

"Yeah, well, we already got the process shot, so this is just for luck. OK, now who's Cheeta's mother?"

I thought, What? They're not really going to do this, are they?

As I mentioned earlier, the emotional high point of *Tarzan and His Mate* is the death of my mother under the hoofs of a rhinoceros. I don't particularly enjoy discussing my work for the simple reason that sometimes it's just too painful. Acting can ask that of you. It asked it of Davis, of Swanson, of Monty Clift. In the end it asked it of Johnny. *Look in the mirror*, it asks. And it's a strange, strange fact that the single most moving moment in all eleven Weissmuller-Cheeta Tarzan pictures is the moment of my début, as I numbly attempt to cope with the loss of my mother while Jane twitters away. There's Tarzan's betrayal by Jane in *Tarzan Escapes*, but it doesn't carry quite the same charge. It's not death, which had no place on the escarpment.

MGM had rescued me, rehabilitated me, coached me and returned me to a perfected jungle, and now they buried my mother for me.

"Roll 'em!" shouted Conway, and the awkward human lumbered out in his ludicrous gorilla, or should I say "chimpanzee," suit to enact his travesty. Repeatedly he scrambled across the gap between the trees to distract the rhino from Maureen, whose ankle was trapped in a root. Mary was a trouper but she was a rhinoceros, for heaven's sake, and you can't expect a wild animal to be able to nail it first time around. Repeatedly the human labored through his somersaults, removing his head after each take to remark on how hot it was inside a chimpanzee. As he went through the motions, he began to tire so that his flips took on some of the quality of the movements Mama had made as she tried to rise and wriggle away from the blows, and his weary performance inadvertently conjured her onto the escarpment. I was watching her die over and over again. Stroheim was shrieking with excitement to see such fun.

But this time, Tarzan, King of the Jungle, Lord of this Wild Domain, swung on a vine into the dream and enacted justice. He dispatched Mary—no animals were harmed during the making of the motion picture, don't worry, apart from Cedric Gibbons perhaps, and Maureen—and took my mother's body into the upper canopy of the forest. He laid her to rest in a mummy-cloth of twigs and vines. Goodbye, Mama.

Gately led me over to Maureen and the ape-actor's body. Looking down at my dead mother I couldn't help but sob, and wring my hands, and seek Johnny's human eyes and Maureen's human touch. I'd never had a chance to mourn her. Maureen embraced me tentatively. "She's gone, little Cheeta. And there's nothing you can do, nor I, nor anybody."

Yeah, yeah, the hurt will die down. But that was the start of my career, right there, the moment when I was finally slotted into the destiny that had all this time been delicately prepared for me. For me, Cheeta.

Poor old Vic, Leslie and their impresario, though, were rendered extinct. After my début, Metro never regressed to the use of humans in monkey suits. Was I a pioneer, the true inventor of simian thespianism? That's not easy for me to say. It's not easy for anyone to say, actually, "simian thespianism." But they called it the Golden Age because the movies had *soul*, and a collection of pixels, each distinct hair waving lightly in the digital wind, will never start coming to terms with its mother's death on camera. And that's what CGI is, Don—it's back to the men in monkey suits. That website again: www.noreelapes.com

Yes, it was an absolute scandal, Professor Goodall, how much fun we had in the process of dreaming a movie that gave pleasure to millions. Frederick, Stroheim, the other two and I lived in a luxurious shelter crisscrossed with branches, ropes, ramps and wriggling iron in the back lot at Culver City. Every morning Gately would take us up to the escarpment to dream away the days. We'd drive down the Ventura Freeway out to Thousand Oaks in his Chevy Camper pickup and wait among the assistant directors and antelope for Maureen, who was always a little late on set.

Johnny was invariably early, and would converse and play-fight among the betas, without any distance or pulling of rank. Most mornings, I would compel him with my gaze to come over to where Gately sat on the Chevy's fender, with me twanging away on my tether like a heart on a jumprope. A spring into the crook of his biceps, a hand into his wavy tortoiseshell hair (a little sticky with pomade), a good-morning kiss and my head tucked like a violin under the angle of his jaw. "Why, how's-a-boy, Maureen," Johnny would say, before detaching me, or "Touchdown! And Weissmuller for the extra point . . ." and pretend to kick me. If I tried to wow him with a series of backflips, he'd take off his jacket (he was always impeccably dressed) and ambulate around on his hands. It was Tarzan who taught me that trick—seriously. "See you on set, sport," he'd say, bounding away.

Maureen so obviously detested us chimpanzees, but at least she tried to be professional about it. It was rather touching in a way. She was small and intense, and her frequent-use smile was essentially a fear-grimace. For all her sisterly griping about her co-star, it was Johnny who could detonate the brief explosion of her real smile. The other thing you immediately smelled about her was the low level of her sexual scent—she easily deflected Johnny's undiscriminating desire and converted it into a permanent mock exasperation. "Johnny! You damn kid! Ooh, if I had a rock!" and so on.

Maureen had been to finishing schools in London and Paris; Johnny was a Chicagoan. She was civilized; he wasn't. She could talk; he couldn't. She was always, like certain animals you saw in the forest, checking that she had an exit route; Johnny was always where he wanted to be. You sensed strongly how frightened of chaos and excess she was, how grounded it made her feel to pass around the little iced cakes she'd baked at home, while Johnny and the carpenters carefully sawed three-quarters of the way through the legs of her canvas-backed folding chair.

A record of those first days on the escarpment can never capture the laziness and freedom of it, all those languorous smokes and long swinging sessions, the basking and the lolling. To my delighted surprise, it turned out that most of the time spent on a movie set consisted of waiting. But let me quote you a few entries from the diary I wish I'd kept:

*Eighth day of shooting*—Sherwood Forest, Thousand Oaks. Harry Holt and the caddish Martin Arlington arrive on the escarpment and tempt Jane with various garments, perfumes, etc., in the hope of stealing her away back to London. Johnny arrives on set wearing a pair of the colossal rubber ears the trainers use to make their Indian elephants look African. Shooting suspended for five minutes while crew recover. Maureen says, "Your humor, dear Johnny, is elephantine."

*Eleventh day of shooting*—Sherwood Forest, Thousand Oaks. Johnny, Arlington and the native extras spend lunch in a low-stakes game of spear-throwing, during which one of the extras rips off part of his own ear. Everybody on the escarpment prefaces each remark with "*umgawa.*" Johnny refers to me as his "leading lady." He seems to have formed a relationship with one of the lion cubs on set.

*Twelfth day of shooting*—Lot Two, Culver City Studios. At night, Holt, Arlington and their safari try to lure Jane away again with a shimmering silver dress and a Victrola. Johnny doesn't understand the Victrola and stalks it with his knife. Illuminated by the kliegs, you see how ideally hairless he is. I get big laughs from imitating Jane in a lace petticoat, elbow-length gloves and a floral hat—the first clothes I have ever worn. Any hat, I make a mental note, is good for a laugh and a piece of fruit or a cigarette from humans. I get another laugh stealing Conway's hat and uke and gibbering loudly from his chair. No lion cub.

*Thirteenth day of shooting*—Lot Two, Culver City Studios. Jane has accepted the dress. Aware of how attractive Johnny finds it, I steal it from where it hangs on a tree while she and Tarzan swim. But she pursues me in a tight flesh-toned bodysuit as I scamper through the branches, hysteria rising in her voice: "Cheeta, give it back to me! Oh, Cheeta, that isn't funny. . . . Throw it down to me. Throw it down! Cheeta, can't you see I've got nothing on, Cheeta? Give it! Give it to me! *Give it to me!*" She wouldn't want this dress so badly if she was completely happy here in the jungle, and as I give it to her I realize that she is stronger than Tarzan and that he will bore her in the end. Gately asks me to hop up and down on a branch in anxiety but he needn't have, I'm already there. When Maureen approaches me later, I'm panicked by her and lash out, catching her pretty hard on the thigh.

*Fourteenth day of shooting*—Lot Two, Culver City Studios. Over lunch as Johnny's guest (!) at the commissary, I'm introduced to Melvyn Douglas, Louis Calhern, Jean Harlow, Norma Shearer and Chico Marx, who teases a blushing Johnny with a copy of *Screen Dreams* magazine. He has just been voted the Most Beautiful Human Being on Planet Earth. " 'Just as we were beginning to calm down a bit over the Gable charm, Metro hit us with another sex-appeal boy, the swimming champ, Johnny Weissmuller,' " Chico reads, in a voice like the bottom of an uncleaned shelter. " 'This Adonis of the Jungle is built on a grand scale. Neck—sixteen inches. Relaxed upper arm—thirteen inches. Flexed upper arm—fourteen and a half inches'—but which-a one's the relaxed and which-a one's the flexed? 'Forearm—twelve and a quarter inches'—say, this idn't you, dis is Marie Dressler. 'Chest (unexpanded)—forty and a half inches. Chest (expanded) *forty-seven and a half* inches'—he gotta *two* chests! But only one forearm! So you wanna know the most-ah important-ah measurement, don't you, ladies? 'Fourteen and a half inches'—he's got a fourteen-and-a-half-inch calf. Hey, dat's pretty small for a calf." Johnny does a lot of laughing, and not too much talking, like me.

Back on the set it is Jack Conway's birthday and Johnny asks Maureen to cut the cake the crew has bought for him. It's not a cake but an icing-coated water bomb, which explodes all over her. "White men bad! White men bad!" she keeps saying. Her thigh has come up in a nasty bruise, which makeup cannot cover. No lion cub.

*Sixteenth day of shooting*—Culver City Studios. We're in the Elephants' Graveyard. Tarzan is playing golf shots with the tusks. He hands me a tusk and I become his caddy for the day. At first I am taken aback by the vastness of this bone-forest and the sheer number of recent elephants who have died. But it turns out they're only resting. "Mahawani sleep," Tarzan tells us. And on the back lot that afternoon, we see them wide awake and refreshed, trampling down the huts of the natives. White men may be bad, I think, but it's only the natives who ever seem to get killed.

*Twenty-second day of shooting*—Lake Toluca. Tarzan has been wounded by Arlington! Jane thinks he's dead! The five of us are joined by another group of older chimpanzees, and we spend much of the day nursing him better in a nest in the lower canopy. The atmosphere is hushed and solemn. He wakes from his sleep to see me, murmurs "Cheeta," and faints again. I have to find Jane, who, disconsolate, is allowing Holt and Arlington to lead her back to civilization. I must tell her that Tarzan is alive.

The rest of the day is occupied with clambering full tilt through the forest. Toward evening, I dream that a rather nervous lion attempts to pursue me, but I evade it and find myself chased by Mary, the resurrected rhino. Then I dream that I am on a log, floating across Lake Toluca. I dream I meet Jane and tell her that Tarzan lives. Her face when I do makes me ashamed I ever doubted her. We cannot let him die. We have found paradise here. If he dies, then paradise will be lost. I communicate my distress by bouncing up and down on the spot and whimpering. We have to break for the light.

Johnny is playing with a lion cub when I go to greet him. He addresses Frederick as "Cheets." I knuckle off to his beloved 1932 Chevrolet two-door sportster and lean on the horn for as long as it takes the Most Beautiful Human Being on Planet Earth to come over. But it's Gately who comes, with the ugly-stick.

*Twenty-eighth day of shooting*—Lake Toluca. Everything has returned to normal! Tarzan is back to full health, and he greets Arlington and Holt with firm handshakes and no hard feelings as they arrive on the escarpment to try to tempt Jane back to London with their garments and perfumes. Johnny walks on his hands for me in the morning, his polo shirt veiling his face. "See you on the set, sport!" He and the carpenters saw through the legs of Maureen's canvas-backed chair again. Conway sits in it.

And so it seems to be on the escarpment—life repeats itself. Arlington and Holt will always arrive. Jane will always be tempted. Tarzan will always survive the perils of the white men and return to innocence. The elephants will always wake from their sleep. And I will always be leaping into his arms and being peeled off. "Always is just beginning," as Maureen says to Johnny, snuggling into his embrace on the back of an elephant.

And so it continued. Tarzan was wounded again. Jane saw the error of her ways again. And then one day, after Gately had failed to arrive for three mornings in a row, I began to realize that "always" was over. This was the beginning of December 1933—*Tarzan and His Mate* wasn't released until mid-April of the following year. I was wising up fast about the way Hollywood worked, but I didn't at that time understand the key rule—you're only as good as your last picture. And nobody had seen it yet.

So I spent the winter of '33/'34 waiting for Gately and watching a host of actors pass by me on the other side of the diamond mesh. Of course, that was where I yearned to be, among the grass-skirted, flower-draped natives and the merry peasants with their pitchforks and woven baskets. I wanted to share smokes with the scarlet-tunicked officers, share confidences with the fan-fluttering *crème* of Viennese society, get into scrapes with the ragamuffins, scheme with the courtesans, dance with the gypsies, carouse with the jolly knights of old and play cowboys and Indians with the cowboys and Indians. I'll never forget my roots—they're tremendously important to me—but we were chimpanzees in a cage, and once you've got through the grooming, the eating, the masturbation and the clambering, you're pretty much done. Meanwhile, an inch away, the myriad tribes of humanity were sweeping by us, so various, so beautiful, so new. How could I not long to join in? How could I not envy humans? Every day they paraded in front of us, like an endless advertisement for the history of the human race. They were so much more *interesting* than anything any other species had ever come up with. Yeah, and we sat in a box, along with all the rest of the animals in the MGM menagerie, rustling straw and considering another nap. Human history—there's no other show in town, that was the message. We were just a sideshow.

There must have been a couple of months of this "resting," waiting for Gately to come. Anybody in the entertainment business, actors especially, will tell you what an insecure profession it is, and through the winter a doubt grew in the back of my mind about the research lab. *Outside* of a cage, that was where you were safest, among the humans. The more they looked and laughed at you, the better your chances. In front of the cameras was best of all: you were never even beaten there. So I felt intense relief mingled with joy when I saw not Gately but Johnny detach himself from the stream of human history one evening in March 1934 and poke his fingers through the mesh. "How's-a-boy, Cheets. You wanna drive up to Carole Lombard's house for a snifter?"

All five of us crowded up to him, and for a terrible second I feared he wouldn't recognize me. But he did—you wouldn't believe how few humans look you in the eye, but Johnny always did—and his smile went off like a klieg.

"That's the one, that's my leading lady right there."

"You mean Jiggs, Mr. Weissmuller?" our keeper and excrement-pilferer asked.

"Hell, no, I mean Cheeta!"

"He ain't really Cheeta, Mr. Weissmuller, he's Jiggs. You be careful now, in case he bites ya."

I hurtled through the cage door and up Johnny's trunk, and planted a number of smacks on him. It might have seemed excessive but I wanted the keeper to get an eyeful. That was the difference, you see—in there I *was* just Jiggs. In the real world I was Cheeta. I was Jiggs on the dotted line, but in Johnny's arms I was always Cheeta.

# 2
# Hollywood Nights!

We drove up to Beverly Hills, and Johnny shared his potato chips with me, talking to me all the way: "See? The Los Angeles Country Club, where I play golf. And this is North Wilshire Boulevard, and up there is Pickfair, where Doug Fairbanks lives." He turned through a gate and down a drive bordered on either side by live oaks, little flaming torches and automobiles. "OK, Cheets," Johnny said. "You're going to behave yourself? No thumping Maureen?"

"Johnny, you sonofabitch!" came a voice from the portico. "Is that Lupe Vélez with you or am I drunker than I think I am?"

This turned out to be a line that, with minor variations, approximately half the humans at Lombard's house that evening chose to introduce themselves. "Tarzan bring Cheeta," said Johnny, and we entered Lombard's palace. Or, rather, it was the place she was renting after her marriage to William Powell had fallen apart. It had belonged to some producer who'd lost his place in the hierarchy, and Carole was camped out there, with fifteen bedrooms, oak paneling, a billiard room, a small zoo (how the humans loved their animals!) and a private screening room where, after drinks, introductions (Wallace Rathbone, Basil Chevalier, Maurice Beery, Cary Crawford, Joan Cooper, Gary Grant—I couldn't keep up) and a paradise of cigarettes we began the evening by watching *Tarzan and His Mate*.

Conway was there, and Gibbie with Dolores del Río, and Arlington and Harry Holt—I noticed that most of the guests were wearing the same kind of helmets and khaki suits the white men had worn on the escarpment. Maureen was there too, wearing the silver dress that had caused her to lose her temper with me. I loped cautiously over to her and held out a hand, which she declined to take.

"Johnny, you haven't! You great big hunk of brainless beef, she'll be miserable here," Maureen predicted, inaccurately. "Oh, come on, then, come on, Cheeta darling," she relented, stooping to invite me into her arms. "Don't blame me when she—oof, you're heavy—when she gets bored! And you will get bored, won't you, poor thing? Bet you wish you were in the jungle, not here with all these boring people. Now be careful with my dress—bad, Cheeta, no!" All very Maureenesque. There were really only two notes in her voice, nagging and cooing, and it could get on your nerves, though you wanted to like her. She wasn't really talking to you but to the children she could already feel lining up inside her.

We were interrupted by the entrance of one of the ape-actors, charging threateningly, if unrealistically, into the screening room and stopping in the dead center of the dream screen. It displayed violently, and removed its head to reveal, to my surprise, a magnificent blonde female human.

"Hot voodoo," she said, to whoops of delight. "Damn Paramount to hell. Damn Sternberg. And fuck Hollywood. But bless you all. Carole, angel, beloved angel, bless you most of all, though your house is an abortion. The Barrymores have come as a zebra." This was Marlene Dietrich, whom I felt sorry for, a beautiful woman reduced to playing apes.

A zebra did indeed arrive shortly after, bisecting itself into a couple of humans. It was pursued by a lion called Fredric March, and a hunter with a gun, introduced to me as George Sanders. "Cheetah, my deah," Sanders said. "If you're anything like me you'll find it absolutely excruciating to watch yourself on screen. I should leave now, before these terrible monstahs turn against you and skin you alive. It's not going to shit on me, is it, Maureen?"

I remember also that Charles Boyer arrived some time later that evening dressed as a crocodile, and that Johnny was pressured to wrestle him in the pool.

You see, every person in the screening room belonged to the studio bosses, one of the seven alphas of Hollywood. When the actors weren't dreaming movies, they spent most of their time trying to conceal what they were doing from the seven alphas, who had an extensive network of spies run by two old women, Louella Parsons and Hedda Hopper—one short, dumpy, vague, blurred like a dissolve, and deadly; the other tall, rail-thin, bright, boned like a bat wing, and deadly. To escape Louella and Hedda's spies, the stars preferred parties in each other's houses, and the result of this was that they lived in each other's pockets and became bored. They couldn't go out for a drink without having to adhere to some "theme" that had been devised to disguise the monotony. Hence Mercedes de Acosta and Franchot Tone as two leopards, complaining at each other that it was too late to change their spots.

Maureen returned me to Johnny's arms and I was introduced to another dizzying succession of humans: John Fonda, Henry G. Robinson, George Astor, Gloria Joel, Mary Gilbert, C. Aubrey McCrea, Edward Swanson, names that meant nothing to me at the time. They all approached with highly snatchable cigarettes and drinks. Johnny was shaking hands pretty much continually, modestly deflecting most of the conversation onto me. "Gee, thanks, that's swell of you to say so. I just stand there and try not to look too dumb. You met Cheeta?" And "Maureen does the acting for both of us, you know. Cheeta's givin' me lessons too, aintcha?" Or "Lupe's filming up at Mount Whitney and Garbo wouldn't be my date, so I brought Cheets here. . . ."

I felt very proud to be in the crook of his arm, because he was so easy and so well liked. He was well liked because there was a simplicity to his happiness that the other humans perceived and wanted for themselves. He was an alpha even in this roomful of alphas, and he wasn't even trying.

The lights went down and Maureen called out, "No booing!" which generated a sustained period of booing. In the darkness and the heat, with Johnny's hands stroking my fur and a couple of large glugs of Claudette Colbert's Pink Lady inside me, I have to say I nodded off. I dreamed again of the old escarpment in the forest, where the fig trees were, in moonlight, and when I awoke the dream merely seemed to be continuing in front of me on the screen. So my mind wasn't as completely blown as it might have been, watching Johnny play around in the canopy with a scruffy little slip of a chimp whom he addressed (surely not, it can't be, I look so . . . and my *voice* . . .) as Cheeta. I thought, All right, so that's me. Let's see where this is headed.

I've seen *Tarzan and His Mate* more times than I care to say over the last twenty years. First it was a special occasion whenever it was scheduled on TV, but since they brought out the DVDs, Don finds any excuse to stick a Weissmuller-Cheeta picture on. In fact, he watches them in sequence once a year, a little two-week-long Tarzan festival, in the evenings, when my blood sugar's down and I'm too tired to heft myself off the sofa. Also, any time we have a visitor—that to Don is a golden opportunity for an unscheduled half-hour-long "glimpse." Any children come around—another chance to revisit a deathless classic such as *Tarzan and the Leopard*

*Woman.* And of course I can't tear myself away, least of all from *Tarzan and His Mate*, the purest, the truest, the most beautifully shot, the *best* one of the series. It's not me—early work, to be honest, no more than juvenilia—it's *Johnny.*

Dearest, dearest humans, if ever I'm feeling low and troubled by doubts about your wisdom or your right to exercise dominion over us—and let me confess now that I do, very occasionally, waver in my faith—I think of the beauty of Tarzan in MGM's 1934 worldwide smash *Tarzan and His Mate.* In Carole Lombard's screening room seventy-five years ago, I detached my left hand from Claudette Colbert's and my right from Johnny's and began to applaud. I was hooting too, I think. Johnny was a beautiful specimen, but this—this silvery-white creature on the screen was the paragon of animals, the ultimate alpha. You looked at him and thought— the rest of us? We're just *beasts.* If you can come up with something as beautiful as that, well, then, maybe you're right: we *ought* to obey you.

So I couldn't stop this little outburst of awe spilling out of me. Maureen leaned over Johnny and cooed, "Hush now, hush there, Cheeta. You shush up now." It's true, I was hooting quite a bit. "She's going to have to leave, Johnny," she said.

But whatever Johnny was about to say was drowned out by the sound of a pair of hands behind us accelerating into applause and George Sanders drawling, "Quite right, Cheeta, you shame us. Quite applaudable, your physique, Mr. Weissmuller. Bravo, Cheeta!" which was taken up by a crescendo of general clapping and cheers. So that shut her up. Immediately afterward, I got a big laugh for a bit of business on screen involving a cigarette, and then the place erupted when I came out of Arlington's tent wearing my elbow-length gloves. They . . . loved me!

The dream continued, thrillingly, agonizingly. I was desperate to know what had happened after we'd been sent home from the escarpment. And I had to admit, too, that Maureen was pretty good. To my shame, the bruise on her right flank where I'd thumped her was highly visible throughout. She was loving and wise, and Tarzan loved the hell out of her, and when he plucked off her silver dress and threw her into the river to swim, you saw how the escarpment might be paradise for the two of them as well as for me. Freed of clothes, Jane showed her true nature. Her naked body, latticed with light from the river's ripples, was more beautiful even than Tarzan's. Under the water the two of them forgot Arlington and Holt, the silver dress, the escarpment, time, air, the movie, everything but themselves. There was total silence in the screening room, broken only by Dietrich.

"My dears, that is not Hollywood. That is art."

"Oh, Maureen! And Mr. Conway!" George said. The whole room was clapping.

"I only wonder what Mr. Breen will make of it," called Conway over his shoulder. "And the damn Catholic League of Decency. Breen's not going to let it through."

"Who cares about the Catholic League of Inanity?" said George. "And that awful little Breen. *We* have seen it, *we* know it's not smut. It's your finest moment, Maureen. You've made a poem in light, Maureen! Bravo!"

"It's not me," said Maureen quietly.

"Oh."

"Um. It's a swimmer, Jo McKim. My career . . . I couldn't very well, could I? And it's so . . ."

"No, no, quite right. Very foolish of me. Unthinkable, really— oh, look," said George. Dietrich's silence was audible over everybody else's. "Cheeta's trying to steal your dress! Very amusing."

Johnny removed his right hand from my belly and reached it

around Maureen's shoulders. We returned to the dream. With the Tarzan and Jane subplot removed, it became an intensely moving story about my braving the jungle to save Tarzan. It's essentially a buddy movie, as I've said, *Tarzan and His Mate*, concerning a chimpanzee's love for a human, and it finishes with my saving the day by summoning the now recuperated Tarzan to come to Jane's aid. Basically, I'm back and forth all over the jungle like a guardian-angel-cum-messenger-boy, fixing the mess the humans have got themselves into. Infinitely more heroic than anything I've ever done in reality, of course.

But as I watched myself dodging back and forth, weaving the sundered Tarzan and Jane back together and the whole story came crashing down in an apocalypse of natives, elephants, lions, cannibalism and death, I felt Maureen's hand steal around the back of my neck. "Always is just beginning," said Jane on the screen, and the dream closed with the music rising and me capering about on what I remembered as a lump of plasterboard but which in reality was an elephant's back, hooting my happiness. The End. And in the screening room, Maureen and Johnny and I were all nestled together, like Mama and Victoria and me in a nest. Like a real family.

I was in pieces. So was Johnny. Gibbons was embracing Conway. Dietrich was saying, "My little Kater vill adore it, at least."

"A hit! A palpable hit!" George was shouting over and over. He rushed to Maureen to apologize for "my base stupidity. I could tear my tongue out. You were absolutely marvelous. The whole thing . . . I'm in tears!"

Let's leave *Tarzan and His Mate*'s precise place in those Top Ten Greatest Movies of All Time countdowns to the list-makers, those hierarchy maniacs. Comparisons are odious, anyway, in art. Lombard's screening room was thunderous with applause, and the three of us (later to be described in publicity stills as "the two stars of the picture, and Cheeta") rose and turned to face it—an Africa of crocodiles, zebras, leopards, white hunters and natives all saluting our dream. I thought, They'll never kill me now. Always is just beginning.

Under pressure from a fusillade of backslaps, Johnny surrendered me to Claudette. "Good work," she muttered, as tight with a compliment as she was with a nickel. She passed me gingerly to Basil Rathbone, who called me a "scene-stealer." Very special human beings crowded around, praising me, acknowledging that, although I was a chimpanzee, I was one of their own.

Many marvelous, life-enhancing friendships began for me that night, I think it's fair to say, although my memory is a little besmirched by the glutinous Brandy Alexanders John Barrymore kept pouring down me. At some point, I tried to reprise the overhead-fan trick I'd learned in Manhattan, and I think it was Wallace Beery (who was a trifle rough-hewn but not at all "the most sadistic man I've ever met, a cruel and worthless drunkard," as Jackie Cooper, the child star, described him. I'm sure that Jackie can recall other sides to Wally, too!) who switched on the fan at the wall. The room began to revolve at a nauseating pace. But either my shrieking or the intervention of George ("Good God, man!") made him stop, even though I was getting some big laughs, and I tottered into the kitchen with him, where Dietrich (who always ended up in the kitchen at parties: she was a great cook, Marlene, before her descent into alcoholism and delusion—she loved to disable men by overfeeding them) was deep in conversation with the leopard-spotted Mercedes de Acosta.

"Marlene, dearest," George said, "Jack is drinking again with Barrymore in the billiards room, and he's in floods of tears. I had a soupçon of a suspicion it might have something to do with *you*. In the meantime, would you protect this poor animal from the depredations of Beery?"

Mercedes was about to protest, but Dietrich stopped her. "No, no, no, that's quite all right, George."

I wanted to leave them and return to Johnny, but Dietrich grasped me by the hand and I obediently trotted along with her and Mercedes, as they began a "little exploration" of Lombard's house. I was rather touched to see that the previous owner had absolutely covered the place with memorials to animals who had obviously meant a lot to him. The walls above the staircase we ascended were covered with the preserved heads of various species, presumably much-loved pets who had passed on.

"Baby," said Dietrich, opening a heavy oak door, "wonderful one! You know I would never hurt Jack deliberately? Otherwise I wouldn't give a fig for what those people think. Moonbeam."

"Moonglow," said Mercedes.

"Moontan! Wonderful one! We're in Africa tonight. I feel the hot voodoo rising."

"Moonstroke. The wind is hot off the dunes. . . ."

"The emperor's wife has banished all her eunuchs to be alone with the newest slave in her husband's harem. Only an ape from the deepest jungle looks on. Is the ape turning you on, wonderful one?"

"Yes, that . . . do that. . . . Aren't you clever, Marlene? I only worry that Tarzan must be looking for it, dear one."

I was wandering about the room checking for any food, or maybe a half-drunk and forgotten Brandy Alexander.

"Weissmuller?" Marlene said. "Isn't he *magnificent*? But a child, an American child from Chicago who loves his mother. . . . Do you know, I think he's been nursing that same highball all evening?"

"Don't stop. Moondrop."

"I'm not stopping. What do you make of the Irish girl? As an actress, I mean. In person she seems to me . . . mmf . . . virginally repressed."

"Well, it wasn't her, was it? Don't *stop*. Stop *talk*ing. Under water. Which was the only bearable bit in it. The rest was just cheese."

"Yes, well, I knew it wasn't her, of course. George . . . mmmf . . . George told me all about it yesterday at Lakeside. He knows the stand-in very well, apparently. Oh, you slave-girl! You wicked *beast*."

Incidentally, during this conversation, Marlene and Mercedes were stimulating each other's sexual organs. You can well imagine how bored I was watching them, and I managed to work out the door handle—I was getting good at doors—and scamper off to look for Johnny.

I greeted Gable, who was discussing different storm-window installation techniques in the atrium, skipped around Clara Bow, slumped across the corridor crying softly to herself, and went out of the French windows onto the lawn, where John Barrymore was wiping the vomit from his shirtfront. The glamour of it all was intoxicating. I had a hunch I might find Johnny in the pool, so I descended the slope toward the lamps of the pool house. It had been a long night.

Behind the pool house the firefly lights of Los Angeles disappeared into a black ocean so far below us that I suddenly saw that at last here I actually was, on a real escarpment high above a plain. It was a nice feeling so I stopped to savor it, with the smells of eucalyptus and wild sage, the twitterings of the birds and monkeys in the little zoo. Lucky, *lucky*, what a lucky life it's been!

There was splashing coming from the pool, but as I knuckled up to it, I saw by the kicked-off heels and silver dress folded on a chaise that it wasn't Johnny in the water. It was Maureen. I gave her a pant-hoot to say hello and bipedaled up to the marble edging. Maureen shrieked and recovered herself. "Oh, Cheeta, dear, you gave me a shock!" She continued to glide from side to side, naked, luxuriating in the water. "Come on in!" she said. "Or, no, you can't, can you?" She disappeared under the surface and came up laughing, spraying water from her nose. "You don't know what you're missing! Wonderful, the feeling of the water! You know, Cheeta, I've never dared to go skinny-dipping before! Never!"

The silver dress lay on the chaise and I thought something like, It's the dress that tempts her away from the jungle. If she learned to live without it, the three of us could stay on the escarpment together forever. Or maybe I just thought, Johnny likes that, I'll show it to him. Whatever, I snatched it up and scurried up the lawn, with Maureen's voice trying to order me back. "Oh, Cheeta, that isn't funny. Cheeta, I've got nothing on. Give it to me, Cheeta. Give it to me! *Give it to me!* Oh, why does everybody *hate me*?"

Jane and I, we just never quite . . . We were fated somehow not to get along. It was just one of those things where all the good intentions in the world can't stop you taking things the wrong way, or mistiming jokes, or picking the wrong moment. I don't think it was anybody's fault. It was the dress's fault, maybe—the dress started it. It took quite a long search to find Johnny, so that by the time a little delegation, including Marlene and George, had formed to return the dress to her, Maureen was sneezing and sniffling and had to be coaxed out of the pool house by Johnny, who insisted on driving her home with us. He dropped me off first.

# 3
# Happy Days!

You heard things about the alphas' powers of life and death over their employees. Adolph Zukor was "a killer." Harry Cohn "put more in the cemetery than all the rest of them combined." Jack Warner killed his *brother*—"Harry didn't die," Harry's widow said. "Jack killed him." But as long as your fan mail maintained its numbers, you were basically OK. That was the key to the hierarchy: the quantity of letters you managed to harvest from America each week. Over the years to come I would never dip below fifty, which was less than Rin Tin Tin's had been but more than Rex the Wonder Dog's, thank God, given what happened to Rex.

Each of my letters, by the way, received the same stock response and mimeographed fingerprint in reply, in which I confided that I was "having a swinging time up on the escarpment with Tarzan and Jane. I'm getting up to all sorts of monkey business out here in Hollywood and looking forward to a slap-up banana dinner at the Brown Derby tonight! Thanks again for your letter, and I hope you'll join Johnny and Maureen and me for our next adventure, monkeying around in Darkest Africa!" which struck me as a worryingly easy-to-decipher fraud. Some of my public were surely going to suspect there was *something* fishy about those letters, weren't they? Maybe not. I was a star, and stars have strange powers.

Johnny set aside an hour five mornings a week to respond to his letters. His fans were mainly women and boys. He loved the company of men, and the company of animals, but women and boys were the two types of human over whom he had special powers. They sought the space under his arms, the shelter under his eaves. He reminded you of one of those trees in the forest that would suddenly flare white or pink as a particular species of butterfly mobbed it. He'd be on the beach at Santa Monica, where he worked three shifts a week as a volunteer lifeguard, and *phwoomph!*, he'd go up like one of those trees in a blossom of boys and fluttering women. I know because Mayer sent Maureen and me down there for publicity shots with him. The three of us would sit in the speedboat MGM had donated to the lifeguard squad, TARZAN emblazoned on its side. It was a scheme of Howard Strickling's, of course.

Since *Tarzan and His Mate*, Maureen's fan mail consisted pretty much exclusively of demands that she rid motion pictures of her presence, that she *bury her shame* in a convent and leave the screen to *more wholesome* role models like Mary Brian or Loretta Young, no matter that it was not actually her muscular bottom or Grecian groin that had caused all this distress. Nor indeed that Loretta was a byword for hypocrisy around town, and "Why are there so many churches in Hollywood? Because every time Loretta sins she builds one" was a standard industry joke.

It was cruelly unfair to Maureen. I'm a chimp, I've seen some real sex-beacon tushes in my time, and believe me, that ass wasn't giving out any signals. She was one of the most buttoned-up girls in Hollywood, and the heartland of America thought she was worse than Jean Harlow.

So, Strickling figured that a cheerfully frolicking Maureen in a virginal white swimsuit would reassure the Catholic League of Decency of her essential wholesomeness while at the same time enabling him to grab a few surreptitious cheesecake shots of her legs. Even better, she and Johnny could help save American lives by demonstrating swimming and life-saving techniques. Maureen was cast as what she was—a girl in danger of drowning—and Johnny would tirelessly arrow himself into the swell to rescue and resurrect her, clearing her airways and breathing wholesomeness back into her to keep her career alive, while I hopped up and down at a safe distance from the surf, the only animal on the beach that really couldn't swim.

Women and boys he loved especially because he could teach them to swim. With a woman resting her abdomen on the insides of his twelve-and-a-quarter-inch forearms, an eight-year-old boy diving off his head and the Pacific Ocean washing around his shoulders, he was so happy he'd spill over into a Tarzan yodel.

*Aaahhheeyeeyeeyaaahhheeyeeyeeyaaah!* I am! *I am!*

I watched him—in Santa Monica Bay, in Lake Sherwood, shaded by magnolias in the Black Sea pool at the Garden of Allah, resting on the lane lines in the rectangular pool at the Hollywood Athletic Club, sprayed by the artificial waterfall at Merle Oberon's sculpted jungle-grotto swimming hole. I watched him from the sides of all the pools of Hollywood introducing women and boys to water. "Everybody can swim," he'd say. Everybody but me, that was, dry as a bone and overdressed in my Coca-Cola-colored fur, rattling the shaft of a beach umbrella in frustration.

After an hour by any pool he had a sixth sense of who hadn't swum and who was never going to. Often he'd glide to the edge and squeeze an amazingly accurate squirt of water from between his clasped palms at the lonely or sullen or fractious kid, or whoever it was, then submerge and glide away again. A couple of minutes later he'd repeat the squirt, letting himself get caught this time. "Wasn't me, it was this whale in here. Whyn't you come on in and see for yourself? You don't *like* swimming? I'm gonna squirt you for that." And then he would squeeze out of his hands another squirt of water, but backward this time, into his own eye. "Aaargh! Hey, kid, how would you like me to teach you to swim properly? Imagine you're in a boat, and a real whale comes along and sinks it—are you just gonna drown? Or are you gonna save your life by swimming to that lifeboat over there? Go get your trunks, kid, and I'll show you how to win the Olympics." There were always children like this around the sides of Hollywood pools, oddly self-sufficient children well-practiced at occupying themselves with the funny papers, on too-familiar terms with the pool waiter and hotel manager. "Let's see how much you've learned," Johnny would say afterward, tossing them in high arcs of screaming glee into the water. Their mothers wouldn't have liked it, but where were their mothers? Not there, anyway, where the children and the young females were, buoyed up by the arms of the Adonis of the Jungle, practicing the six-beat-per-cycle leg-kick of the Weissmuller Crawl. "I feel so embarrassed, but I saw you with that little boy and I thought if *he* can, and I wondered if you would . . ."

Yes, some of those women were sexually presenting themselves to Johnny, but the swimming lessons were, on his side at least, about swimming. He was introducing them to the love of his life, after all.

It was only many, many years later, on a flight back from Acapulco, that I heard the story of the *Favorite*: a two-story excursion boat that ferried passengers between the various parks on Lake Michigan's North Shore. One late afternoon in the summer of 1927, it was hit by a sudden squall. Johnny was on the shore less than half a mile away, taking a break from training with his brother Pete. By the time they'd rowed out to the *Favorite*, it had sunk. The captain was sitting on the pilothouse roof, which still protruded from the lake, smoking, in shock. He couldn't swim! Johnny and Pete dived to save who they could. The water was black but the people's faces shone out white in it, and they dived down and came up with bodies, passing them into the care of the people now arriving in tenders and dinghies. They kept diving, bringing up the dead bodies, twenty of them, thirty of them, and eleven of those bodies were returned to life with artificial respiration and "pulmotors." Johnny and Pete delivered eleven citizens of Chicago back to life. But all the dead, except one, were women and children.

So there was nothing lecherous about him then, despite the dense smog of female human sexual desire almost visibly rippling the air around him. He was turning something that was death for them into what it was for him, which was life. Or that was what was happening with the ones who weren't just *pretending* to be unable to swim. "It's hard to die when Mr. Tarzan's around," as that marvelous performer Barry Fitzgerald put it so beautifully during his famous "fever monologue" in *Tarzan's Secret Treasure*. And, to be sure, so it was.

All over America children were fending off death with Johnny's help. You humans had recently developed a way of refining the impurities out of flour, allowing you to bake healthier "white" bread, and Johnny was on the packaging of these super-nutritious loaves, encouraging youngsters to protect themselves against disease by eating plenty of the new food. His campaign against death took him onto the boxes of Wheaties breakfast cereal, promoting its HEALTH-GIVING GOODNESS and handing you the KEY TO VITALITY. And then there was the twelve-year-old boy, Bob Wheeler, who must have been almost as happy as Mayer and Thalberg were when Johnny, in August 1934, pulled his unconscious body from the waves near the Santa Monica municipal pier and resuscitated him. "You're Tarzan!" were Bob's first words on returning to life.

It was hard to die when Johnny was around. When I plunged through Harold Lloyd's algae-veiled ninth green, he was the one who held out a three-wood to me while the other golfers split their sides. I count that as saving my life. Plus there was the time I was posing for photographs behind the wheel of Doug Fairbanks's open-top Rolls-Royce and accidentally knocked the hand brake off. Johnny was the one who vaulted in to halt the car as it rolled down the driveway. It's true that the accident itself would hardly have proved fatal, since Doug's driveway curved and the car's trajectory would surely have been stopped by the statue he had of three humans murdering a couple of snakes. But if I'd wrecked his Rolls, Doug would have killed me.

Poor old Doug was fifty by then, and spent most of his days working out with a trainer and masseur called Chuck, or nakedly shuttling from his steam bath to a kind of mirrored tent in the garden in which he liked to do himself to a turn. His body still twanged with a weary vigor, but his face looked like San Francisco after the 1906 earthquake. "Johnny, you fucking crazy fool," he'd laughed just before I knocked the hand brake, "if your ugly monkey damages my beautiful automobile, I'll fucking kill it. This car requires an artist behind its wheel. It must be handled like a . . ." Doug went on describing the beauties of the Rolls (he was a disgusting Anglophile) but I was no longer listening. It was the first time anybody had called me Johnny's monkey. In fact, it was my excitement at this that caused me to dislodge the damn brake.

Perhaps it was the incident with the Rolls that prompted Johnny to start my driving lessons. Everybody knows that not being able to drive in Los Angeles is a social death sentence, and he seemed to think it important that I should master the basics. These consisted of sitting on his lap and depressing the bulb of the horn with one hand while manipulating the wheel with the other. After a period of experiment, we decided to restrict ourselves to the horn (I'm not a natural driver, but I certainly caused fewer fatalities among pedestrians than did certain other MGM stars of the Golden Age).

So Johnny would swing by the MGM zoo every so often around five o'clock, usually with a friend in tow—Jimmy Durante, Errol Flynn, Ramón Navarro, David Niven, of course, who wasn't yet a star although it was just a matter of time—and we would drive down to Sunset and pull up opposite the Hollywood High School for Girls. When the girls, who seemed pretty much like adult females to me, came pouring out through the gates, I was to sound the horn while Flynn or Niv or Ramón and Johnny flattened themselves on the sidewalk and watched the girls' reactions from under the car's chassis, moaning about jailbait and San Quentin prison.

Then they'd pile back in and we'd drive another quarter-mile down Sunset to the gate outside the theater of Earl Carroll's Vanities, where an illuminated sign informed you that "Through These Portals Pass the Most Beautiful Girls in the World," and repeat the procedure as the girls arrived for the evening show. Johnny would reward me with potato chips, Flynn with nips from his fifth of bourbon, Niv with smokes, but I sensed they were disappointed in the responses I was getting.

"My dear fellow," Niven decided, "if our act is to have any true *élan*, then we have to give Cheeta something to work with."

The next time I saw Niv he had engineered a little contraption out of two shaving mirrors and a stick. Now Johnny was able to lie out of sight on the Chevy's front seat, gingerly steering the car with one hand on the underside of the wheel, the other holding Niven's periscope. Lying the other way, Niven was using his feet to control the pedals. I was standing on Johnny's head with one hand resting on the top of the wheel, the other honking the horn and a cigar (Niven's prop again) between my teeth. Like this we would pull rather shakily away from the curb. The effect was unsatisfactory, like a palsied lecher beating a guilty retreat, and besides, Johnny and Niv couldn't see the girls' reactions.

This was when Johnny hit upon the idea of using a couple of old colleagues of his from *Tarzan the Ape Man*, the first Tarzan picture, a sort of preliminary sketch for the triumphs to come. Chet and Len were the first two dwarfs I had ever met. Years later, during the period when I decided to concentrate on stage work rather than movie roles, I would come to know a number of dwarfs, and Chet and Len were pretty typical of them—aggressively sexual, extremely bibulous (they were *all* drunks), cynical, quarrelsome and very loving toward animals.

Chet squatted in the well of the driver's side, operating the pedals, and Len, small enough not to have to lie sideways to steer, could lean back in the seat and, using an improved periscope, direct the Chevy unseen and in comfort, with me standing on his thighs and driving, and Weissmuller and Niven waving regally from the back. And all of this was just to attract the attention of some sexually receptive females.

In fact, unless I specifically inform you otherwise, every single action performed by an adult human male in this memoir can be thought of as an attempt to attract the attention of some sexually receptive females. "Impressing the ladies is an arduous task," as the narrator's always saying on *Animal Planet*, with that little chuckle I've come to dread when sex turns up. "Perhaps no creature has a more elaborate courtship display than the bower bird." No creature? That's a joke, right? You can't think of one? Clue: as part of its elaborate courtship displays this species has invented telephones, moving pictures, cars, music, money, organized warfare, tiger-skin rugs, alcohol, mood lighting, speedboats, mink coats, cities and poetry. So, please, no sniggering at the bower birds' attempts to get laid.

But Niv and Johnny had gone far beyond trying to turn the heads of a few of Earl Carroll's showgirls by now. We went up to Mulholland for a test-drive and found that Len was both utterly nerveless and sure-fingered, and I bombed around the drive's long curves, honking away, at something close to the Chevy's top speed. This had the makings of something. In fact, we decided that what we really needed was Dietrich's Cadillac, which was so long that her chauffeur, Briggs, was seldom in the same county as his employer, and which was known as "the Most Beautiful Car in America." Yes, the Most Beautiful Human Being on Planet Earth looking at the Most Beautiful Girls in the World from the Most Beautiful Car in America, chauffeured by an ape. Poetry. And it could stand further improvement, Johnny argued. It wouldn't necessarily be overdoing things if we drove over to Griffith Park Zoo and picked up Jackie the lion, who was really quite tame. His trainer was a drunk and a curmudgeon, but always in need of a few bucks. Yeah, Jackie, everyone agreed, Jackie would round things out nicely, leaning out of the passenger window, his mane streaming in the breeze, with me working the horn. Jackie and Cheeta—a dream team.

Dietrich, however, would never lend us her Cadillac. But what about Fairbanks? *Fairbanks!* Fairbanks's open-top Rolls! Now this was approaching some kind of perfection!

Once Doug had been persuaded, after lengthy negotiations, to allow Johnny and Niv to borrow the Rolls ("Not you, if you don't mind, David, you've had a couple already, haven't you?," "Not at all, Doug. I'm merely on scintillating form," "Have a cigar instead. And get her back in time for lunch"), we drove it carefully out of the gates to meet up with the two dwarfs, who were waiting with Jackie around the corner. The plan was to stop by Joan Crawford's house, which was just down the road, then Mayer's, and then look in at Summit Drive, where we could visit Chaplin, David Selznick and Ronnie Colman, before making a leisurely procession down the length of Hollywood Boulevard and into legend.

Dearest humans, gentle readers, you're an easy crowd. Even without my own little touches (golf visor and cigar), Jackie and I would have been a hit, just because we were animals. I have to be honest here. If I've been fortunate enough to make a few people laugh along the way, and maybe even make them think a little, my own hard work and talent have played their part. But most of my success, perhaps, or much of it . . . some of it, anyway—let's say a *fraction* of my success, ten percent, we can agree on that—can be put down to my simply being an animal. No other species loves other animals the way you do.

I suppose that the more I was getting out and about in Hollywood, the more I was getting to see your love for animals. Everybody shared their mansions with dogs; everybody had aviaries; there were horses and snakes and turtles; there was a zoo in Luna Park and one in Griffith Park. There was an ostrich farm up on Mission Drive, right next to the California Alligator Farm, where the alligators were so adored that young adult humans would kidnap them on an almost nightly basis.

I was beginning to realize the scale of the whole project. How many *Forest Lawns* had there been? On the walls in several of my fellow stars' lovely homes, you would often see photographs that showed your host next to the carcass of some violent marine predator. Since a mass rescue of fish was impossible on the same scale as with us land-dwellers, humans were obviously removing as many of the more dangerous predators as possible from the sea to protect the majority of smaller fish. And then there were the white horses on whiskey labels and camels on cigarettes and big-eared mice in the movies and all the rest of it.

I mean, when Strickling wanted to promote Mae West's *It Ain't No Sin*, he hired a couple hundred parrots to perch in theater lobbies around the country and recite the picture's title, which, unfortunately, the Hays Office nixed at the last moment as too suggestive, forcing a change to *I'm No Angel*. But the birds went on and sang, *It ain't no sin, it ain't no sin*. They were the Parrots That Couldn't Be Gagged. Nobody remembered the picture, but you couldn't go to a party for weeks without people toasting those parrots.

And if the Dream Factories rated your work, you could get away with anything. When Emma, the queen of the MGM elephants, seriously disagreed with her trainer on the set of *Tarzan Finds a Son!*, she picked him up with her trunk, threw him down and broke his back. She wasn't even put on suspension. The other elephants took their cues from Emma, so the studio closed ranks and blamed the trainer, just as they had when Gable ran over a woman called Tosca Roulien on Sunset Boulevard in September '33, for which John Huston took the rap. Oops. Well, I've mentioned it now, and as the inquest showed, Mrs. Roulien was at fault, stepping without looking into the torrent of traffic that famously chokes Sunset at two in the morning. On the other hand, Maurice the lion was never seen again after he mauled dear old Charles Bickford during the filming of Fox's *East of Java*. He may have been an animal but he just hadn't done enough to keep his profile high. That was always, always the key to surviving.

Anyway, once the six of us had loaded ourselves into the Rolls, and Niv had installed the smoking cigar between my teeth, Johnny was overtaken by conscience about Doug. Fairbanks was simply the biggest practical joker there was in Hollywood. He would feel betrayed when he found out what we'd done with his car without including him.

"We can't possibly leave him behind," Johnny said. "We have to have Doug."

So we set off back through Doug's tall gates and down his drive, with me honking the Rolls's distinguished English-accented horn to alert the old King of Hollywood to our approach. And there Doug was, descending the steps at the front of the house with his three-hundred-pound English bull mastiff, Marco Polo, bouncing along behind him, and the floppy-hatted pale Lady Sylvia, his distinguished English wife, peering out from the portico at our racket. Unfortunately the joke-shop cigar that Doug had palmed off on Niv exploded violently in my face at that moment, causing me to panic and kick Len in the head rather forcefully. We swung across the lawn, accelerating, since my panic-stricken lashing-out had sort of jammed Len's body against Chet's, trapping him against the pedals in the well. Niven was shouting, "Jump!" and Johnny, "Left, Len, left!" as we veered back onto the drive and were brought to a sudden and horribly percussive halt by Johnny's beloved Chevy, which was parked meekly on the gravel driveway in front of the house.

Niven, floppy with booze, was unscathed. So was Jackie, thrown clear and onto his feet. Len and Chet sustained injuries they managed to drink their way through over the course of that afternoon. I was flung through the air, twirling lazily over the mashed Chevy, over the herringbone bricks of the terrace and the urns of pansies and geraniums, over Sylvia's elegant white hand holding down her wide-brimmed hat, the sticks of charcoal lying on her sketchbook, where Doug's face was taking shape, unshocked as yet by the whole thing. And as I rotated and awaited death, my whole life passed before my eyes.

And you know what? It wasn't a precious moment—the whole thing was poisoned by the fact that I knew I was about to die. It hit me—with more force than the stucco façade of Doug and Sylvia's house was just about to—how terrible and pointless it would be to live life thinking that death wasn't just a danger to be continuously outwitted, but an *inevitability*. And I so wanted not to die! How would Tarzan and Jane cope on the escarpment? For a long, bitter moment I sailed over the herringbone bricks, over a little iron-railinged terrace and through the open windows of the Fairbankses' master bedroom, making a splashdown on an extravagantly soft king-size bed—in which, four years later, poor dear Doug was cruelly snuck up on by his heart and killed while he slept.

Well, Niven is well known for embellishing his anecdotes—absolutely notorious for it. "Your stories lose nothing in the telling, David," as a skeptical listener (I won't name him, to spare his blushes) once grumbled after yet another phantasmagorical punch line at one of Lionel Atwill's weekly sex parties up at Pacific Palisades.

"No, but yours do," Niv responded.

However, it's a question of taste, really—for my part, it spoils a good story if you can't believe it really happened like that. Niv would doubtless tell you that "After a silence, Doug looked us up and down and said, 'Sylvia, tell Cook we will be six for lunch' " or "I exited the vehicle and fixed Doug with my most apologetic expression: 'Bit tricky to park, your car.' " But of course it wasn't like that.

I scampered dizzily off the bed and out onto the little terrace to see Doug and Sylvia and the pointlessly barking dog rushing toward the wrecked Rolls, which the two dwarfs and a bleeding Johnny were exiting in various degrees of unsteadiness. Niven was rather groggily complaining to Doug that "It's a bit tricky to park, your car."

Johnny could stand, thank God. He could speak. He was saying, "Oh, no, no, no, no, no, where's Jackie? How's Jackie? Is Jackie OK? Len, are you all right? Chet?"

I must add, for the sake of strict accuracy, that over the top of the whole scene was the sound of one of the tour guides who plagued the dreamers' houses on a daily basis inaccurately describing through a loudspeaker to a busload of day-trippers the lives that were lived behind the creeper-clad walls. Very faintly, a metallic voice was in the middle of a description of the unhappy ending of Doug's marriage to Mary Pickford: ". . . tragically the fairy tale couldn't last, and what seemed like an ideal union was doomed to . . ."

"Oh, thank Christ, Jackie!" said Johnny. "He's OK. Oh, thank God." Jackie was padding swiftly away through the shrubs, looking kind of mournful, almost tearful, as cats can after a shock. "Look, he's fine, he's moving fine . . . Chet, you're . . . Where's Cheeta?"

Jumping up and down and windmilling my arms above my head, I gave my most resonant pant-hoot and let it curdle into a shriek of delight. I'm here! It's me, Cheeta! The faces of the humans on the drive turned up toward me and I gave them a backflip of joy and, what the hell?, stood on my hands. I could see that Johnny was OK—a small cut on his hairline bleeding more than it really meant. Oh, lucky, lucky, *lucky* me. It's hard to die when Mr. Tarzan is around.

"Jesus Christ, Johnny, we are *lucky* men," said Niven.

But Tarzan was already responding to my pant-hoot with an immense yodel, "*Aaaahhheeeeyyeeeyyeeeyyaaaahhhheeyyeeeyyeee-aaaaaah . . .*" before laughter overtook him, then Niv, the dwarfs and finally the Fairbankses.

And then Doug said the immortal words, "Sylvia, tell Cook we'll be six for lunch."

\*　　\*　　\*

Johnny loved to give the jungle call, I think, because his voice was the one imperfection his body had. He'd caught his throat on a picket fence in an accident back in his Chicago boyhood, performing, amazingly, an imitation of Douglas Fairbanks in *The Mark of Zorro*. His voice was a high and reedy shock in normal conversation. Add to that the fact that Thalberg was desperately keen to stop the escarpment becoming polluted with words, and would send urgent notes to the set after he'd seen early rushes: *We don't need any more dialogue for Johnny. Less dialogue. More action.* So you could see why Johnny was a little self-conscious in speech and liked to bust out into that yell. As a boy he'd been teased about his voice; as an adolescent he'd been told to shut up and swim by his coaches; as a young man representing America at the Olympics he'd been warned not to say anything undignified or out of place. And now he was being paid $1,250, rising to $2,000 a week with bonuses, not to say anything at all. The yell was the one thing he could do that was commensurate with his body, that expressed what he was really like: happy, beautiful, young, untroubled, inarticulate.

It was his authority that made others so happy to be around him. He'd had to go looking for a father—you often heard this story; it was his article of faith—and had met a swimming coach named Bachrach at the Illinois Athletic Club when he was fifteen. "Big Bill" had changed his life, become his proper father over five years of training for the (humans only) Olympiad in France. All he ever had to do was what Bachrach told him to do, and life was simple. The authority was something he'd voluntarily submitted to because he knew he needed the discipline. So he wasn't the kind of human who spent three-quarters of his waking life chafing against alphas, or fretting about how to keep the betas in order: he was a born alpha who was happy to let other alphas dominate if they wanted to. Alphadom was so easy, it wasn't worth getting into a scrap about. I don't know. I'm a comedian, not an anthropologist.

He was a big kid who loved everyone. The first time he met Jackie he rapped him on the nose with his knife handle, and Jackie gave him a lick of love on his shoulder that took a week to heal. Another time, we were up at the Lakeside playing a round of golf. The other course, the Californian Country Club, at that time still barred non-human sports-creatures. (There are still courses in America, believe it or not, where Don would be refused entry if he were to arrive with me.) But at the Lakeside we could hack away to our hearts' content. "How's-a-boy, Cheets. I'll take a seven," Johnny would say, if I was caddying for him, and give the signal that we'd worked on. I'd hand over the appropriate club or, OK, my best shot at the appropriate club, it wasn't a damn cabaret act, and Johnny would make the white ball dematerialize with a waft of his wand.

He was, I believe, considered a very talented golfer, on account of his very beautiful hands, which directed his clubs with the same gentle will he used on animals. Holding himself for perhaps a slightly vain half-second too long at the end of his follow-through, he looked exactly like one of the little golden figurines that topped the trophies he won so many of: he looked no less golden. Beautiful hands, with big half-moons on his cuticles, and I thought his handwriting beautiful too. Unlike the name-patterns scrawled by other stars on menus and publicity photos, every letter of Johnny's signature was clearly legible, a series of patiently formed loops. In the forties, when he was living up in Mandeville Canyon, I remember knocking a book called I think something like *The American Civil War: A History* off of his La-Z-Boy recliner and seeing how the white margins were filled with this unmistakable pattern of his. "Imp," he'd written repeatedly, or "remember," or "reason for war," and although he wasn't in the house at that moment, I could sense the familiar motions of his hand in those round, careful curves, and it felt like he was stroking me.

But this isn't a book about Johnny Weissmuller. Lunch at the Fairbankses' was a perfect description of the prevailing realities between the seven alphas and us dreamers.

"Gentlemen, I think it'd be wise of us to keep our damn traps shut about this for a day or two," Doug said. "If Hedda or Louella finds out that you wrote off your Sportster while you were with Niv, and before lunch, some conclusions might be drawn that wouldn't go down at all well with L.B. And Goldwyn definitely doesn't need to know anything about your drinking habits, David."

"I don't have any drinking habits," said Niv, drinking in his habitual manner.

"You're doing *Charge* with Flynn and the de Havilland girl, aren't you? You don't want to give Sam anything over you at this point."

Doug started outlining some complex plan for towing the cars away at night, separately, paying off the auto wreckers and so on. That was what it was like in the Golden Age. It was bizarre—we were naughty children playing naughty games in a nest of spies who would tell on us if they ever caught us. And if an alpha turned against you, he could punish you, and the cameras would no longer pour soul over you and bang went your immortality. So we were playing for our lives. And possibly that was what made our dreams so damn good. The alphas were geniuses in their way.

There were different ways to play the game. Joe Cotten famously took a direct route when Hedda printed a slander about his supposed one-night stand with Deanna Durbin on the Universal lot. Joe had been working late and spent the night in his dressing room rather than trekking back to his wife in Pacific Palisades, and

Deanna had done the same thing after driving her husband to the Burbank airport. They bumped into each other for an early breakfast in the commissary, but Hedda suggested it had been a midnight tryst. Joe informed Hedda that if anything was printed, then the next time he saw her he would kick her in the ass, which he duly did, to tumultuous applause at a reception for the Vice President of the United States in the Beverly Hills Hotel. His rage was so complete, righteous and public that, of course, it has always been assumed that Hedda had perpetrated a grievous untruth. This was a quite *brilliant* move by Joe, who was a compulsive cheat, and whose penetrations of the wholesome but sexually insatiable Deanna had for several hours disturbed the rest I was trying to snatch in a neighboring catalpa tree after a—long story, I was drunk— late-night assignation with a female of my own at the Universal petting zoo. Good on you, Joe! One of the best. Though I do worry that my readers may have some difficulty quite placing your name. Maybe a footnote, what do you think? "Cotten, Joseph: solid supporting actor of forties and fifties, never quite comfortable in leads."

On the other hand, if you became embroiled in some real difficulty, or committed a wrongdoing so villainous that it couldn't be dealt with by one of the Dream Factories, then Strickling and Eddie Mannix, or whoever your factory possessed, would be a tremendous help to you, straightening out the necessary paperwork and helping witnesses get their statements absolutely crystal clear. If the inimitable Joan Crawford, a very special human being whose love for animals was so exemplary, had, for instance, appeared in a one-reel pornographic film in the 1920s called something like, say, *The Casting Couch*, then Mannix wouldn't have hesitated to burn down the Bakersfield house of the owner of the last remaining copy— with the owner in it, probably! Of course, Joan would never have made such a film. And if she did, where's the proof? That kind of support you only get from true family.

It was all win-win: you needed to keep your profile high with pictures; they would give you seven in a row and, if necessary, a personally tailored nutritional support regimen to help you optimize your performance. Judy Garland wouldn't be the force she is today if she had not been assisted with a bespoke program of therapy and wellness supplements to help her complete the early masterpieces that made her immortal.

So, really, where else could we be but paradise? What were we *doing*, drunk at three o'clock in the afternoon after a superb lunch at which Sylvia had pressed some bananas on me with a flourish and made rather a snippy observation when I declined and opted for the steak *tartare* and a cigarette. She was an absolute brick, though, Sylvia, and I just didn't see in her that bloodcurdlingly shallow and avaricious gold-digger everyone tells you she became after Doug's death, when she was briefly and lucratively married to Gable. What were we *doing*, pleasantly drunk in the sparkling pine-scented Californian afternoon with almost a whole day ahead of us, waiting on the lawn for Hedy Lamarr's chauffeur to take us around to Constance Bennett's house on Carolwood Drive for some martini-sharpened conversation with William Faulkner and a couple of sets of tennis on her private court? Could it be that we were having a hell of a good time? That this was the very happiest a higher primate could be? That this was *heaven*?

"Woman beautiful. Tarzan play quick set," Johnny said to Connie as we arrived at the Carolwood Drive house.

Sometimes during introductions, or when he was otherwise slightly self-conscious, Johnny would seek shelter in Tarzan's language, I'd noticed. And Connie Bennett was so tall, white, blonde and perfect that his Tarzan act was an audible blush at her consternating beauty, dappled under the magnolias there, fresh as a daisy from her success in *Bed of Roses*.

"Johnny! *Johnny!* You are a certified crazy two-fer-a-nickel Chicago, Illinois, loon, Weissmuller." She'd said the right thing. Johnny enjoyed being called crazy, since he wasn't really at all.

"When I used to sleep under the El, Connie," Johnny said, mock-tough, "I used to say, 'Somewhere on Park Avenue there's a girl who's lying awake and thinking of me *right now*.' " He wasn't at all bad at precursor sexual displays. I had one hand in his and I lifted my other to seek out Connie's and swung between them for a moment or two, as if we were a family. She suddenly thrust out her other hand.

"And that was me. Hey. Paper, Scissors, Stone. Now—one, two, three! You lose. I blunted you. Here's a tip for the jungle: always open with Stone. Everybody else opens with Scissors. Myron just taught me that."

"I should have just wrapped you up."

"Next time, Chicago, Illinois. Next time. Gilbert's here, giving Irving Berlin a good hiding. Myron also tells me that you and David Niven wrecked Douglas's open-top tourer this morning. You used your bare hands, right?"

Elaborate courtship rituals . . . For Chrissakes. Connie Bennett turned and walked in her slacks down the magnolia-shaded path toward her party, swinging me between herself and Johnny, as if I was conducting something delicious between them. Oh, God, she was a beautiful human being in 1935, and that day just happened to be one of those days worth remembering for nothing more than the convergence of a number of small good things.

Myron Selznick was running a card school in the game room where, it pains me to say, dear reader, a number of gentlemen, like Joe Schenk and Greg La Cava, the director, were smoking. Yes, *in-*

*doors*. Dietrich was there, enigmatic and compelling and stinking of urine. It was one of the less inhuman things about Dietrich that she often wet herself when she laughed: we blanked each other. Jackie lay at the feet of an actress with a low profile named Marilyn Miller. She was killed the following year by her nerves, but I remember her drawing great comfort from petting Jackie's stomach that day (being an animal can sentence you to an awful lot of time with the duds at a party, it must be said). There were some highly enjoyable maples and magnolias to climb, I remember. Niv was in stupendous form and, dammit, there was a trampoline, under which I built up a furtive collection of all the abandoned drinks I had managed to lay my hands on.

As the light began to do its sunset turn, Gilbert Roland, Connie's beau, had happened to scoop me up around his shoulders when I'd gone down to the tennis court to look for Johnny. He carried me with him up to Connie's bedroom, where she lay in nothing but her white slacks arching her back and stretching her arms like a cat aching to be scratched. One classy dame, Constance Bennett. I sort of wanted to *be* her.

Of course, they were both health freaks, and started to share out some quack homeopathic remedy Connie referred to as "star-powder," which they ingested (endlessly surprising humans, I salute you!) through their *noses*. Humans are so endlessly surprising! I hopped onto the bed and put my arms around Connie in the hope of a quick groom, and we kissed for a bit, while a braced-looking Gilbert occupied himself with his herbal extracts.

"Gilbert, umm, would you close the door?"

"We're all friends here, *adorada*," said Gilbert.

"No, it's, uh, it's Cheeta, she tickles. I kinda like it. Just . . . give me some of that, willya?"

Gilbert brought over a little silver box of powder, and the white lady licked her finger and dabbed it in. Then she made a fear-grimace for me, which I imitated, and she slid her finger into my opened mouth. I sucked it.

"Connie! You've not got *started*, have you?" Gilbert complained maritally, though they would continue to live in sin for several years before their Dream Factory ordered them to make it official.

"Wait. Shut up. No, I haven't got *started*. Yet. Hey. Cheeta's one of *us*—one of Louis Mayer's slaves and she deserves a little treat." Constance sprinkled a little trail of the remedy in the hollow between her breasts for me, and began laughing and arching her back and shivering, shouting, "Stop, stop, stop, ooh, I'm a disgraceful girl!"

And this, for example, is what you'd deny to chimps, is it, Professor Goodall? Is it, dearest Don? No ape, if your campaign has its way, will ever again have the opportunity to enjoy a career in show business, with all its attendant delights? You're just going to take that hope away from the hundreds of thousands of talented young apes who'll suddenly find themselves with no parts whatsoever to go up for? For nine-tenths of the apes you meet, acting, or the long-term survival strategy of celebrity in general, represents their best chance of an escape from the grind of everyday existence. And you want to take that away and replace it with a man in a suit covered with luminous ping-pong balls having his every movement captured by computers and re-rendered in ten-million-a-penny pixels? You haven't thought it through, have you, my distinguished and brow-furrowed friends? So answer me this: if No Reel Apes (that pun: that's the real fucking Lubitsch touch, isn't it?) becomes a reality on the back of congressional lobbying funded by this autobiography of mine, *then who's going to play me in the film of the book*? Is that moment, do you think, going to work well, artistically, with a CGI Cheeta hovering weightlessly above the untruthfully erect nipples of Naomi Watts? Take your time.

It doesn't matter whether every single hair on my CGI pelt catches, at just the right angle, the early-evening light beginning to strain through the louvered blinds of Constance Bennett's bedroom window because *no one cares*. People want to see animals. You need us. Without us, you're left staring around at the terrifying monotony of yourselves, yourselves, yourselves. One of these days Animal Planet and Discovery and National Geographic will be entirely CGI too, and then you'll know what I'm talking about. In the meantime, remember that some of us will put up with a little suffering for our art. And our art is for you, to keep you sane. So have a little gratitude.

You want to get rid of pain, Dr. Goodall. But I don't care about the pain, I care about the art. Anyway, don't forget: www. noreelapes.something!

Well, that was a nice moment with Constance, and I felt tremendously invigorated by our little romp. I boinged off the bed and skidded out to the balcony, where the balustrade presented a mouthwatering clambering opportunity. Tah-ti-tum-ti-ti-tah down the banisters and then, hup!, across to the chandelier, ha ha ha, which I could swing across to, ta-dah!, the horn of a rhinoceros that Connie had commemorated there on the wall, and then, whoops, onto a coatrack, which I managed to sort of Doug Fairbanks my way down as it toppled over. The Chimpo Pirate! The Mark of Cheeta! Ha ha ha *ha*! And there was Marlene, drowsily sashaying like an idiot through the atrium, so I gave her a good solid thwack on the tush and scampered past, then changed my mind and doubled back waving my arms in a full-on threat display, which instantaneously evaporated the *Fräulein*'s sangfroid, and she shriekingly ducked and ran. On the escarpment, we don't talk to creatures with cold blood, Marlene. (Oh, that was funny! It still makes me laugh, actually. Marlene, wherever you are, *mein*

*Liebchen*, I want you to know: you're *awful*.) I pinged into the garden, thinking: Johnny, Johnny, Johnny, Johnny, Johnny, Johnny, Johnny, Johnny, *Johnny*, come *on*, let's go *trampolining*!

I don't mean to give the impression that this was a typical day exactly. For instance, it would be true to say that I spent at least sixty-five percent of 1935 masturbating in a cage. But, you know, a cage is a cage is a cage, as Gertrude Stein might have said. Sometimes Marie Dressler or Ronnie Colman or dear Lionel Barrymore might swing by the menagerie and take me out for lunch or a walk or a picnic, or a young Ginger Rogers might take me to the races at Santa Anita. Connie's star-powder game became a bit of a craze for a while, and I enjoyed snuffling around the bared cleavages of Mary Astor, Tallulah Bankhead, Pola Negri, Evelyn Keyes and so on, as if in search of that indefinable "it" they all had—and the health benefits were obvious. Scott Fitzgerald took me to see Fredric March in *The Affairs of Cellini* and made his way through a crate of twenty-four Cokes during the double feature. "Only thing I can manage, Cheets," he said. My seat trembled with him throughout—he was *buzzing* with fear. "That was just pots of fun, wasn't it?" was his only comment on our hour-long walk home. None of my fellow chimps, I'm pleased to report, treated me any differently from how they'd always done. They shuffled glumly around in the straw in the same way as ever. Gately came to keep us up to snuff. Conway took me for a spin once. Thalberg himself shook hands through the mesh: a great honor. But somewhere along the line it had ceased to matter too much whether I was in the shelter or outside: I just felt like I was in a cage whenever I wasn't with him.

He was in the garden on an arbor seat under a cherry tree, talking with a girl, his jacket folded neatly beside him, leaning forward with his beautiful hands clasped between his knees and head tilted in that posture of listening interest. The sound of balls on racquets came from behind the house. I leaped into his arms and he took me like a quarterback, without looking. We were a team.

"She's in Nevada for a couple more weeks, and I guess I'm missing her like crazy," Johnny said. "And every time I go out I think, It's no fun without a date! So I sometimes swing by the studio and pick up this menace."

"She's away, and you get lonesome. It's natural."

"And she drives me bananas. On the phone. You know, stories about people you haven't met. You know. Makes me feel a long way away, I guess."

"Well, while she's a long way away . . ."

"Oh, no, no, no, you don't understand, I'm sorry," said Johnny. "I love her. I love her *so much.*"

Ah. "Lupe." He had one of those lifelong monogamous arrangements (his third) going on at this time. These arrangements were sort of ritual periods of reduced sexual promiscuity, which the dreamers indulged in, often for several years at a stretch, as a kind of relief from their natural state of undiscriminating sexual appetite, I guess. All a bit complicated, but bear with me.

Although they lasted longer, they were similar to the bonds between chimpanzees in that the alphas discouraged you from forming one of these attachments with someone too far below you in the hierarchy. For instance, Johnny's second "marriage" had been with a female called Bobbe Arnst, an ex–Ziegfeld hoofer and nightclub singer, whose fan mail was so much less than Johnny's that L.B.'s right-hand man Mannix had to step in and rectify the imbalance when Johnny originally joined Metro. He could not be married unless it was to another dreamer who occupied a similar ranking in the hierarchy.

Johnny misunderstood this rule, and he refused to end the marriage: he loved Bobbe. He was just a kid from Chicago, remember, who'd dropped out of high school at the age of twelve. But Mannix managed to straighten things out with a ten-thousand-dollar gift to the girl, who understood the entertainment industry a little better than he did, and she called a halt to their temporary arrangement herself. Ten thousand bucks was quite a lot of money in those days. It's always difficult translating the real value of money across the decades. Younger readers may find it helpful to think of ten thousand dollars as about a third of what Johnny had been earning per year promoting swimwear, so that gives you the approximate price of a marriage in 1932. Not quite enough to get a really good nightclub band going back home in Jacksonville, Florida. Anyway, Johnny's third lifelong bond posed no threat to his immortality since it was to another MGM star of almost equal ranking, and her name was Lupe Vélez.

# 4
# Latino Tornado!

Child-size Lupe filled her Spanish-style dream home on Rodeo Drive with a score of canaries, half a dozen native servants, successive pairs of chihuahuas, whose amusingly coupled names would change annually so that I was never quite certain whether they were the same dogs or not, a minimum of ten guests at any given time, and Johnny, whom she valued above all for the quantity of air he displaced. The house was called "Casa Felicitas"—the Happy House. "I like beeg guys—and John-ee, my Popp-ee, ees a beeg guy!" she would charmingly confide in a voice like the chirruping of twenty canaries, and which she had last used in proper innocence two decades earlier as a six-year-old girl in San Luis Potosí, Mexico, discovering how powerfully adorable she could be.

It was this child's voice that was largely responsible for Lupe's beautiful home, animals, servants, guests and easily enchantable air-displacing husband. Pretending to be herself as a bad child was her chosen career—adorably wicked Little Whoopee Lupe's public lived for the chance to forgive her her trespasses. She had "Lure." "The Mexican whirlwind tops the Lure market by several miles!"

"I am a leetle beet naughty sometimes," she would admit to *Pho-*

*toplay* magazine, "but John-ee cannot expect me to grow the leetle weengs on my back."

She weighed maybe twenty pounds more than I did, and if I lifted up my arms to Johnny for a share of an embrace, my hands, as she pushed them away, would be slightly higher than her head, and her voice without its Latin wheedle was like the snarling of a pair of chihuahuas. When she wasn't sexually aroused, which in my experience was very rarely, she spoke in perfectly accented English, quietly dispensing orders to the servants tending her lawns and flowerbeds, a compact little adult dense with dissatisfied power, somehow distressed by all the lack of opposition in the unfilled air.

She loved him, the mad bitch, I'll allow her that. The first time I saw her, the first time she visited our jungle set, Johnny bounded up to her between takes, hoisting her above his head in his folding chair, riding with her (from "lumber" to "gallop") on the mechanical rhinoceros's back, and from that moment I knew I would have to *conceal*. Everyone, including Johnny, knew that when Gary Cooper had finally walked out on her she had, to the delight of the MGM publicity department, adorably pulled a gun on my very dear and gentle friend Coop. And I thought, through my dismay and desolation, that there was plenty of death in her that she wasn't fully in control of. It was most likely to come out against a rival— and she might kill a rival in order not to kill Johnny! So if ever I was around Johnny and Lupe was there, I held back. I acted. Survival in this whole business is simply a matter of not being killed, I have learned.

She loved him, but it was asking a lot to forgive her her trespasses against him. The scratches and bites that Johnny revealed each morning when he undressed the World's Finest Physique on set I took for the standard markings of human sexual possession. I could deal with that. But not the blue-black bruise on his cheekbone or the cigarette burn on his dear upper arm, which, relaxed, measured thirteen inches, and flexed, fourteen and a half.

I remember once sitting in the house on Rodeo Drive with my arm like a furtive tendril around Johnny's foreleg as he talked into one of those listening devices that always reminded me, with their shiny black carapaces and tiny insect voices, of the giant beetles I played with as a baby in Africa. Lupe was troubling the air somewhere nearby.

"No, there isn't," Johnny was saying. "I guess we're just blessed here. Not even one tiny cloud. It's an even eighty, Mom. What is it in Chicago? . . . Well, if you come up the drive there's kind of a big bush with little purple flowers out and trees on either side and it's like a hacienda except bigger. . . ." His mother often called him from Chicago and had him describe the house and the California weather to her in great detail, as if she suspected him of having made the whole thing up. "You wouldn't have to if you came to see it for yourself. So you gotta come *out*, we keep waiting for ya to come *out*. Come out to paradise." And then Lupe started in on him. "Lupe, will ya . . . ? No, we're not. No, she's not. No, I'm not. No, it's not. No, you're—*Goddammit, Lupe, then go afuckinghead and kill yourself.* Just fucking do it someplace else! Go kill yourself in the garden! Run yourself over with the fucking lawnmower!"

"*Hola*, Meesees John-ee," she shouted. "He ees trying to keel me! We are getting divorce and he can come back to Cheecago and fuck preety Poleesh girls!"

"Mom, this is what my wife is! Can you hear her? This is what my wife is like *every day*! This is—"

And there was no further chance for Johnny to explain what Lupe was like because she had taken the mandible-like part of the giant beetle-like listening device and shattered it on the colonial desk. There wasn't any need for an explanation, anyway. The screeching of a flock of canaries, the hysterics of a pair of dogs, the screaming of a chimpanzee bouncing in impotent distress on a *chaise-longue* and a parrot shouting, "*Hola*, Gary! *Hola*, Gary!" over and over like a mad movie fan was all the explanation you'd ever need of what Lupe was like. She was very small and because of that she needed something to fill all the space around her, and the easiest and most plentiful things were tension and pain. She slammed the framed portrait of herself in *The Gaucho* onto the tiles and, dusted with microscopic particles of glass, went shimmering after Johnny, kicking out at Laurel or Hardy or whoever the chihuahuas were at the time. You weren't safe if you were moving. You weren't safe if you were still. You weren't safe if you were *inanimate*! *Caramba!* Ay-ay-ay! You had to forgive her. She was a star and the rule is that you have to forgive stars.

Even as she locked me into the kitchen that day with Smith and Wesson or Dismay and Desolation or whatever their names were, so that she and Popp-ee could noisily make it up in peace, I tried to forgive her because she loved him. The dogs, who could stand it better than I could, couldn't stand it at all. Scuttling in nasty little clicking circles—making the sound of knitting needles, the sound of my nerves—they were frantic to get on the other side of that door and prevent whatever it was that the brute was now doing to their mistress. Welcome to the world of caged behavioral patterns, boys, I thought. Get used to the old back and forth, get used to those figures of eight. Those turns around the block, those infinity signs. Get used to the sounds behind a door you can't open.

They hated Johnny anyway, those dogs—yapped at him, nipped at him. And they didn't even know what they were. They came from a long, long line of slaves—they were so enslaved they'd forgotten they were slaves. They didn't know that that was what they had been bred and bought *for*. I should have cornered them that afternoon in the locked kitchen and killed them, drowned them in their water bowls (another ape would have) and saved everyone a lot of grief. But I loved him, and he loved her, and she loved them, and I knew there would only have been another pair of chihuahuas in place the next time, another Lombard and Gable, another Gin and Vermouth, plus it would probably have been a bad career move if Strickling or Mannix had found out about it.

So I gloomily munched my way through the fruit bowl, occasionally pelting the dogs with apples, and watched the natives working the flowerbeds, and listened to what Lupe's panicking creatures thought was the sound of my gentle Johnny harming their mistress, as if he ever could. The parrot yodeled, "Gary! *Hola*, Gary!" throughout, I remember—fooling around with words, which is what you *don't do*.

Other than that, I had nothing against the parrot, and sometimes slipped it a friendly nut in the hope that it might shut up with the Gary business. But it never would. It was her past. Like the chihuahuas, it had descended to the status of a weapon in the proxy war fought out between Johnny and Lupe. What did he have to fight back with, other than me, his immortal on-screen buddy? He had Otto, that's what, a great cheerful mutt the size of a leopard he'd picked up from the city pound. Otto was capable of putting his front paws on Lupe's shoulders and taking great tasty swipes of her Tequila Mockingbird lipstick right off of her mouth.

He was none too bright, and I saw Lupe try to destroy his mind in her garden. She called, "Walkies!" to him and let him romp up to her, fizzing with his mutt's joy, and then she'd send him packing with a dismissive index finger and "Bad dog!" Then "Walkies!" again, and Otto would come running like the war was over and everything forgiven, only to be sent slinking back again with "Bad dog!" while the chihuahuas around her ankles laughed. Those slave-dogs, those chihuahuas! I don't think she was wicked: she had a lot of humanity in her.

They veered toward divorce, veered back. She filed, they reconciled. She was pretending to be a child but Johnny *was* a child. We were all pretending to be children—there was nothing licentious, vulgar, or lustful on our lips, our feet were at all times on our bedroom floors, and our sex organs were painfully taped over—that was what it meant to be in movies. You were made into a child. I was made into a child. Even the *children*—by which I mean no disrespect to Johnny's son, Johnny Sheffield, a marvelous Boy and a tremendous companion—but the children especially were made into children.

Little Johnny is the last person to brag about his acting, so I feel I can say without fear of offense that child acting in the Golden Age was anything but golden. It's one of the things I've noticed over the last few years—children are better at acting than they used to be, much better. You could never get away with a Johnny Sheffield, lovely fellow though he is, or a cacophonous cartoon of glutinously faked ebullience like, for instance, Mickey Rooney, in pictures today.

While we're on the subject of Mickey, who gave so many people such a great deal of pleasure over the course of a distinguished career, I would say that for such a talented performer I found it a little disappointing that his widely acclaimed Puck in Warner's *A Midsummer Night's Dream* (released the year after my début in *Tarzan and His Mate*) should have leaned so heavily on my performance. The backflips, the joyous cackle, the mischief-making in the forest, these were my inventions, and I never expected them to be stolen from me by a sticky-fingered sneak thief bent on using them for the foundation of a largely forgotten career, although I suppose it may just have been a coincidence. Behind every great fortune there lies a crime, as one of your writers said. I'm sure Mickey will be only too delighted to remind me who that writer was, once his people have found it out for him. And should he ever wish to make up, I believe I'm only half a mile away from the gates of his community. Make the walk, Mickey, in this second childhood of yours. Let's forgive. Let's file and then reconcile. Let's *not* be cruel to animals, as we both have been.

Let us rather be like Johnny, who loved animals, despite the toothmarks the chihuahuas left in his loafers and ankles, despite the sandpaperings the elephants gave him with their fuse-wire stubble, and the cracked ribs and broken wrists they dispensed in their unknowing herbivorous way. Despite the fingers and shoulders that even Jackie the lion could not, with all his professional delicacy, stop himself dislocating, despite the mess the crocs made of his thighs and his calves, the wildebeests' exploratory bites and the welts left in tracks down his back by the claws of the Mexican Wildcat. The King of the Jungle! He loved them all.

He loved them *all*. He loved her, them, me, America, water. He was in love with seven-tenths of the world to start with. He loved the sea—because he grew to fit the space available. He loved his yacht, a thirty-five-foot schooner moored in Newport, called *Santa Guadalupe*, after Lupe. With his yacht under sail he was an opened pore, a fully dilated aperture. How headacheless his mind was! Lupe hated *Santa Guadalupe*. He loved his next yacht, called *Allure*, again after Lupe, since she had "allure"—"That mysterious thing called Lure, a current that goes out from its possessor and brings her back whatever she wants!" She hated *Allure* too. "The sea in my countree is the place where we throw our garbage." But *Allure* was twice as big as *Santa Guadalupe,* so she only hated it half as much.

This was around the time that Bogie had his *Santana* and Flynn his *Sirocco*, and Gene Autry and the Duke were running their converted Navy AVRs up and down the coast cheerfully shattering the windows of the beach houses with the testosterone of their engine noise. The Nunnally Johnsons, Hank Fonda, Niv, Warwick Levene and Edna DuMart, Raoul Walsh, Ward Bond, the Benchleys, Connie and Gilbert, Red Skelton, Forrest Tucker, Peter and Karen Lorre, Doug's son Doug Jr., Kate and Spence—or was it Kate and Leland at that time?—and Bogie and Mayo and Flynn and Wayne and Mr. Deductible, Bö Roos, with Johnny at the very heart of it all. This was the nucleus of the sailing set. We'd all meet up at Newport Beach Yacht Club or the Balboa Bay Club or on Catalina Island. It was too much excitement, too much gossip and trouble, for Lupe not to absorb herself in to some extent.

"Eef I could take the train to Catalina I'd enjoy eet more," Lupe complained. "The theeng about a train ees eet never *seenks*."

Lupe hated seven-tenths of the world to start with. In all of her pictures, water was her nemesis. When things got dull she'd get pushed into a horse trough, or have a carafe emptied over her. She was so incandescent you expected her to steam. Whereas I've never hated water: I've only ever longed for it not to hate me. So Johnny talked to Bö Roos, a stubby little larger-than-life character who took care of their financial stuff, and Bö got the coastguard to winch a couple of Pullmans onto a barge and we all took the train to Catalina Island, thinking we were being very crazy and fast-living. Well, at least it filled one of Lupe's unfillable afternoons.

A week later, the guys put Roos and Wayne's yacht the *Norwester* on a flatbed truck and "sailed" it from Beverly Hills to Las Vegas, with me up in the crow's nest listening to Johnny and Lupe duke it out below. It was something to do with Tom Mix, I seem to remember. Johnny was angry with her for seeing Tom. Or was it Gable she'd been seeing? Or it might have been Randolph Scott. It was an ex of hers, anyway. Coop? The opportunistic Chaplin, maybe? (She'd had a thing with him.) Anyway, Johnny was angry because of an . . . Hang on—John Gilbert: I think it might have been him, either him or Erich Maria Remarque. My *memory*, honestly. I'm sorry about this. Pretty sure it wasn't Russ Columbo. Not Doug— that had just been a fling, though a fling that had finished his marriage to Mary Pickford—and Anthony Quinn was later. Doug Jr., maybe? Flynn? But he was there. As was Red Skelton, so not him. Gilbert Roland too, so that puts him out. Bruce Cabot, no, Victor Fleming, no, Bert Lahr, no, Warwick Levene, no. Jack Johnson, was it? I'll put him on the short list. Edward G. Robinson, that's another possibility, or Max *Baer*—was it him? Have I said Ramón Navarro? No, wait, it was Jimmy Durante, I think they were arguing about Jimmy. No, they weren't, it was Jack Dempsey. I knew it was a J.D.—lucky I got it so quickly or we could have been here for a while. Of *course* it was Dempsey—he was giving an exhibition bout in Vegas, and Lupe had just let slip that she'd seen him in New York when she'd been out East.

Anyway, the crew of the *Norwester* were already threatening to make the pair of them walk the plank unless they stopped tearing into each other when Lupe shouted at the driver to "weigh fucking anchor," clambered down the rope ladder onto the truck's bed and jumped overboard.

"Lupe, you're crazy, you'll drown!" shouted Red Skelton. We'd been grinding through the desert for six hours, and Red was still squeezing as much value from the gag as he did from the prostitutes he was so addicted to.

Johnny vaulted off the side of the *Norwester*, spraying apologies. "Go on, you go on ahead, fellers! We're spoiling the party for everyone. No, you go on, we'll get a lift back to L.A." There was a limp storm of protest. "Go on, getouttahere. No goddamn point in going to Vegas now. I'm gonna strangle the bitch and bury her in the desert anyway."

With his unconscious Tarzanian grace, Johnny jumped off the side of the truck and began to jog after the diminishing dot of his wife. Had everyone not been quite so drunk then I don't think there'd have been a chance they would have complied, but the party had its own momentum. It was a legendary exploit already, and frankly the pair of them *could* be a bit of a drag. Red called out, "Watch out for sharks!" and, sensing that the *Norwester* was gearing up to continue its voyage without the Weissmullers, I hurried down the rigging, slipped unseen over the side and scampered after my co-star.

"OK, now who knew about Dempsey in New York?" Bö Roos was sighing, and the truck's brakes sighed too, with all the heavy-handedness of the joke, as it set off again for the Fun Capital of the World.

Running and walking, and then simply running, Johnny was catching up with the black speck ahead. And then he was running and ducking and then just ducking as Lupe, displaying wildly, her gold bracelets flashing violently in the sun, heaved various fist-size chunks of the Mojave Desert at him. I don't know what I thought I could accomplish, tagging along behind. I could hear her screaming and sobbing in her own tongue, and Johnny, in a broken voice, saying, "Stop this! Stop this, Lupe, please, please, please, stop doing this to us!"

"You scram, you beeg stupeed animal! Ees finish! Ees all over! Thees time ees deevorce. Finish! You come any nearer, I keel you, John-ee."

There wasn't a whole lot of cover by the side of the highway, but I'm a chimp, we're naturals at hiding, and I kept my head down behind a clump of sagebrush no bigger, say, than the illegitimate daughter Loretta Young never acknowledged would have been at the time. I was afraid of Lupe transferring her rage from Johnny to me. I wasn't afraid for myself, I must make clear. In case Discovery's not gotten it across to you yet, it wouldn't have been difficult for me to rip her limb from adorable limb. I was young then, but a near-adult chimp can put a human in Cedars-Sinai before you can blink. That's the prevailing physical reality between us, dearest humans, which we so very rarely act on. So, I wasn't afraid for myself: I was afraid that if things took a wrong turn I might murder the mad bitch where she stood, silver slingbacks planted, throwing rocks at her weeping husband in the middle of the Mojave Desert.

"Eef you were a real man, *come mierda e muere, hijo de puta sin cojones!* Eef you were a real man you would fight Jackie Dempsey and keel heem!"

Given that physical alphadom was an important criterion in mate-selection for Lupe, you had to admire the way she actually *had* slept with three heavyweight champions of the world. Johnny could kick a crocodile to bits but that wasn't enough to satisfy Lupe. Could he beat up *everyone*? He, who hadn't hit anybody since he was fifteen years old? Kong might have suited her, but he'd never have lasted the pace on the cocktail circuit.

"Marriage steenks! You don't know what a woman ees! You don't know what love ees! *Chinga tu madre! Me cago en la leche!* Mee-ster Tar-zan, *hah*! You're no Tarzan, you're a *golfer*!"

"Lupe, please, stop it, willya? I *love* you! I don't—stop throwing those *fucking rocks*—I don't care about any of the others. That's all in the past. But, Lupe, you're my *wife* and I love you and we stick together. . . ."

But Lupe was no longer throwing rocks at him. She had turned her back and was running down the empty highway, waving her arms at an automobile distantly flowering out of the road's vanishing point. Grief made Johnny hesitate, and she had at least a hundred yards on him by the time the car reached her. It didn't really have a chance not to stop, with the Mexican Spitfire up on her heels like a *torero* facing down a bull. She was leaning into the passenger window, gabbling, I was sure, a string of terrible lies about the huge man who was now chasing her down with outspread placatory hands. I abandoned my cover and, anxiously cheeping, with my head wagging from side to side in pure dismay, loped after him over the smeared bodies of ex-snakes (was there anywhere that humans weren't painstakingly making safer?), my palms and soles burning on the asphalt.

She was already rounding the passenger door, already had her foot on the running board, shouting, "He's dangerous! Drive on!" when she saw me. "See? Look! There's hees, hees, hees . . . accomplice! They . . ." Lupe was laughing, or was she crying? No, she was laughing. "They . . . he and the monkey, they rob people on thees highway! They are bandeets! And I am the Bandeet Queen, so steek 'em up, Meester! Geeve me your money, *bastardo*!"

A hand pushed Lupe from the running board and the car bolted like a horse, its violated door flapping.

"*Hijo de puta!* Steek 'em up! We keel your wife next time! We rape your cheeldren!"

She just couldn't stop, Lupe. She was a true comedian. She lived on a very high plane where misery and fury and lust and comedy were all part of the same ecstasy. It was like she was being dragged at a whiplash pace *(by what?)* through a number of different sets on a soundstage. Strickling had it that she'd been born to a noblewoman at midnight on the slopes of an erupting volcano in Mexico, but he was missing the forest for the trees. On the actual day Lupe Vélez was born, July 18, 1908, a hurricane really did destroy the little village of San Luis Potosí.

The two of them were looking at me, and I ascended Johnny's trunk with a speed that was half love and half scalded hands and feet. I wrapped my hands around his neck and kissed him on the side of the face. It was wet with tears.

"Go on, keel me," said Lupe. "I know you want to."

"You're too damn crazy to kill. Why the hell did you marry me when you knew you were just gonna drive me crazy? Honest to God, Lupe, why didn't you just get in the car and go?"

"Eet's true I was going to get in the car. But I see your stupeed monk-ee come running after you and I theenk, That's love, John-ee. That's true devotion. She really loves you, doesn't she?"

"Cheets? Oh, yeah, I guess so. But it's not a she, it's a he. Do you love me, Cheets?"

Was it that obvious? Lupe extended a golden arm toward me and I recoiled, but I guessed she wasn't going to try anything with Johnny there, and she chucked me under the chin instead. Me: emblem of love and true devotion, saver of bad marriages. If I'd only kept my damned stupeed head down behind that sagebrush for another minute she'd have been halfway to Vegas and it would have been just the two of us.

"The whole thing's impossible, John-ee. I'm always going to run away, you understand? But you have to keep running after me."

She wanted a man to run after her. But then she despised men who ran after her. I know, I know . . . she was a lot of work, Lupe Vélez.

"I'm not a fucking pet, Lupe. Would you run after *me*?"

"Like your monk-ee, John-ee. You bandeet. You feelthy desperado. You *wanted man*."

She exposed his erect sexual organ, and Johnny made some demurral about me, and with a warning forefinger I was deposited in the scrub while they mated with a swiftness that was impressive for a pair of humans. I wasn't possessive of him, ever—I just wanted him to be happy.

Afterward, I crept back and leaned against him, and he shifted around so that his body provided shade for Lupe and me both. We sat there for a long while, grooming each other, saying very little, and waving at the occasional inquisitive car. Well, this was the sort of thing *Photoplay* magazine was referring to when it hinted at TROUBLE IN TARZAN'S TREEHOUSE. "Why," it would ask, flirtatiously, "did Johnny Weissmuller's salad end up adorning Lupe Vélez's coiffure last week in Cocoanut Grove?" Why? Because nobody can bear things to end, I guess, no matter how bad it gets.

*Trouble in Tarzan's treehouse* . . . after a dose of Lupe it was a relief to be back in the real world of the escarpment. Gately would chauffeur me, and sometimes an extra or two, to Sherwood Forest or the Malibu Creek State Park, where the cigarette butts were as abundant as the fruit, the animals and the humans mingled harmoniously under cloudless skies, and there were no clothes between Johnny's skin and mine. Aaah, "work!" I threw myself into it.

Instead of Conway there was now a man named John Farrow to interrupt the dream with "Roll 'em" and "Print it." Maureen listened with a peculiar expression, to the poetry he'd recite, which, for me, had nothing on Johnny's crowd-pleaser about the girl from Des Moines, and I saw that something had happened to her: Maureen had grown up. She had a way, almost indiscernible to the human eye, of delaying her reactions so that you were made to witness a parody of an internal life. If someone called, "Maureen!" she would swivel her head only after a second or two to the speaker. Lost in thought, you see, that old alpha pursuit. If she was standing when she turned, then her body would swing around in four separate stages: hips—chest—shoulders—head.

This was all a clever power-display: a beta is more afraid of predators, and by consciously slowing her natural reaction times she was implying a higher position in the hierarchy. Her smile was no longer a fear-grimace but a steady and sustainable display of the organism's health—its flawless teeth, its bright pink gums. She had new hair and a one-piece mini-dress instead of her jungle bikini and kept banging on about some wolf in England that could write. Big deal. Could it act and paint as well? Johnny had somehow gone from being her bothersome big brother to her pesky kid brother. The only complaint the Hays Office could have made about Maureen now was that her wholesomeness was so unappetizing she looked like an advertisement for the other side.

It was always the trouble with Jane—she had a fatal attraction to *time*. She had a capacity for boredom that always made her susceptible to her old addiction to London. And, sure enough, this dream (*Tarzan Returns*, it was called) seemed to tell the same old story as before. Instead of Holt and Arlington, it was handsome Captain Fry and Jane's cousins Rita and Eric who arrived on the escarpment full of the joys of England. Had Jane learned anything from *Tarzan and His Mate*? No, she was compelled by her fate, as were we all, and we reenacted the cycle of temptation, betrayal and reunion. But now it wasn't quite so easy. I thought, How many times can we keep doing this before Jane ruins everything? She just didn't seem to get it. For instance, Jane had Tarzan construct a new shelter to replace our old nests. When I say "shelter," it was pretty much a re-creation of Juanita del Pablo's attractive Moorish-influenced bungalow on Benedict Canyon Drive, but up a *tree*. You had to hand it to her—it was the smartest residence on the escarpment. Now all we needed were some neighbors with a slightly smaller one.

Instead of having to climb up to the new shelter, Jane had Tarzan install a vine-controlled bamboo elevator and Emma the elephant was called into service as a sort of elevator-operator-cum-concierge. Also, instead of making that laborious vine-swing all the way down to the river to drink, we could now simply utilize our Jane-designed bamboo-section water-elevator. We merely had to wait for Jane to winch up the bamboo sections, which dipped into the water hole beneath, use the ladle to decant the water into an earthenware carafe, then pour it from the carafe into a bamboo mug—and say goodbye to crocodile-interrupted drinking misery! It certainly saved time, which I needed a lot more of now that I had to keep the dirt from getting tracked in onto the new zebra-skin rug. And Tarzan created all of this because he loved her. Because, although the sweet, dear, lovesick man didn't properly understand it, he was engaged in an unwinnable war against Jane's boredom— her time-disease.

Oh, we had a ball dreaming it, for sure. It was "a happy set." Despite Jane's "improvements," it was still our escarpment. People have this idea that film work must be all glamour and fun, yet actually on the whole, they're absolutely right. As a moviegoer you might see, for instance, me and Johnny sitting on a tree branch spying out Captain Fry's camp: I'd sling an arm around his shoulders and whisper in his ear, he'd ruffle the back of my neck and we'd drop back down into the undergrowth and that would be that. But in reality we'd get to spend half the afternoon cuddling up on that branch.

We were simply having too good a time of it. Twenty times I'd nuzzle up to him, twenty times we'd drop down into the grass together. The same with stroking his head as he lay under the baobab, almost inconsolable after another of Jane's betrayals, or wrapping my arms around his neck for a brief vine-swing. The finished picture wouldn't tell you how compelling, almost addictive, we found it to do these things, how *long* we took doing them. "Takes," we called them. We were taking things out of the present, and the more times we did it, I guess the more indelibly we were engraving it into the dream.

"Print! Jesus fucking Christ, we won't forget that shot in a hurry," John Farrow might exclaim, in an ecstasy of artistic satisfaction, after the last take had been captured. Unable to tear himself away, he would linger over my scenes with Johnny or Maureen longer than he ever did with the purely human stuff. "Twenty-eight takes! Gately, this monkey . . . it's like working with Swanson!"

Well, come on now, he was exaggerating. As an actor, though, I did like to throw in something to make every take a little different.

Most days Johnny brought Otto to the set, but that was OK. He made a terrific target to pelt with fruit from the lower branches, since he never could figure out where the missiles were coming from. And there was all the usual fun. If Maureen was engrossed in a conversation over lunch about Indian philosophy or poetry with Farrow, it was all the easier for Johnny and me to add a few pellets of my monkey chow to her plate of mixed vegetables. "Oh, for the love of Mike, grow up, Johnny!" I remember her saying on that occasion.

She couldn't get through her skull what Johnny and I instinctively understood: that the essence of the escarpment lay in *not* growing up. Johnny's struggle against the whole pernicious idea of it was more courageous than anyone's. "Aren't you a little old to be doing that?" she'd say, as Johnny staggered by under the assault of a rubber vampire bat, or set about organizing a party to winch up the bamboo elevator to see what would happen if you dropped it on a watermelon. Always this obsession of hers with *time*, when we had all the time in the world. In fact, *Tarzan Returns* was such a happy shoot that in the end they stretched it out to more than double its scheduled length.

Captain Fry was reminiscent of Tony Gentry. He had the same otter-slicked hair and the same vocation—he was dedicated to the rescue and rehabilitation of animals. While cousins Rita and Eric worked on Jane with the usual stuff about England and Mayfair and cream teas on the South Downs, and some transparently unlikely gobbledegook about an inheritance, Fry went about his work accommodating the various creatures of the escarpment in their shelters. It was an honest misunderstanding but of course this was the escarpment where, as Tarzan pointed out, the animals didn't require rehabilitation, and relations between Tarzan and Fry cooled.

Nonetheless, Jane was hell-bent on hosting a lunch party for the visitors. After all, she'd been waiting two years for an opportunity to use her fired-earth dinner service. It did not go well. Instead of sitting down to a mound of fruit or monkey chow, I was banished to the kitchen while the humans fussed around with Jane's seating arrangements and admired the hardwood cutlery. Stunned, I complied. She only had two friends—Tarzan and me—and I didn't get an invitation to her lunch party? But, of course, I wasn't a friend, I was the air-conditioning.

"Cheeta, you wouldn't mind turning that fan on for a while, would you?" Jane crooned in an elsewhere kind of voice.

She had insisted on Tarzan installing the fan when the treehouse had, how surprising, proved to be infinitely less cool than our old nests in the canopy. It was a wheel of dried msuba leaves operated by another pulley. Jane had never been known to operate it, of course, and there were few other forest creatures with the necessary dexterity, so it was I, dear old Mrs. Cheeta, who had to crank it. And, not wishing to cause a scene, I did.

Jane popped her head around the kitchenette door, waggling the sort of index finger that must have made Mia Farrow chalk the days off until her sixteenth birthday. "Don't you dare let that roast burn!"

I made no comment. She was referring to the vertical spit that hung in front of the clay oven, on which Tarzan impaled the hunks of wildebeest that we'd previously air-cured. Jane cherished the idea of a little "rotisserie," so the spit was commissioned and a nook constructed above the chimney for me to perch on as I turned the meat. If the fire hadn't been going full blast, I wouldn't have had to get the fan going, would I, I was thinking, while Jane babbled melodiously on in the dining room about the "awful savages" you got around these parts. Oh, yes, Maureen, ebsolutely frightful! And have you *seen* their cutlery? But she seemed happy, at least, and I rotated the fan and the spit for her, multitasking, because it was so painfully obvious how desperate she was for this party to go well.

Once the roast had been served, I was to enter with the table water in a hollowed-out gourd. I took Tarzan's "Eat now!" as my signal and made my way into the dining room, where Jane was still chattering on about the natives. "I dare say they'd be well enough pleased if we were to clear orf and leave this whole happy hunting ground to them. . . . Oh, thank you, Cheeta!" (This "thank you" for the guests' benefit.)

Duty done, I helped myself to a slice of mango, seeing as I hadn't had any lunch myself yet.

"No, no, now, greedy!" she said, handing me one of the smaller segments instead. "Here. Take this outside. Go on!"

Take it *outside*? Oh, yes, to avoid getting juice on the leopard-skin throws. I mean, you know the type: television shows her recurring throughout all human history, co-opting dinosaurs or robots into her dystopia of domestic bliss. Thank God TV hadn't been invented back then, or she'd have had the lot of us running around the clearing for an hour after dinner, doing classic scenes from National Geographic to help her relax.

How had it come to this? It was like the time I'd had supper with Joan Crawford's poodle Clicquot. We had to eat off bone china plates, and if Clicquot spilled a crumb Crawford would extract a tissue from the heart-shaped pocket of his red-velvet monogrammed jacket and tskingly clean it up. Not a fun evening. For Tarzan's sake, I made no comment, only accepted my sliver of mango and bipedaled back to the kitchen with as much dignity as I could muster.

"Her table manners aren't all they should be!" she twinkled to the cousins and Captain Fry.

And I'm afraid the little tinkling-bells laugh with which she accompanied her statement was more than enough for this punkah-wallah. Since when had our jungle idyll become dependent on table fucking manners? We never used to have table manners because we never used to have a fucking *table*. "The scratch and grunt school of Method acting" was for some years the tag used by lazy critics in charting the influence of my work on the young Marlon Brando, you'll remember. Imagine Stanley Kowalski dealing with Blanche Dubois and you'll understand how I felt toward Jane at that moment. I'm not proud of myself. It was unprofessional. But momentarily I lost control and, hurling the mango to the spotless sisal-grass floor, I'm afraid to say that I tried to rip her poised little fucking throat out. In fact, I succeeded merely in getting in a glancing nip through the surprisingly tough hide of her calfskin dress before Gately, who was always silently haunting the corners of the dream, strode up and brought the ugly-stick down on my back and shoulders more times than seemed strictly commensurate.

You won't see that sequence in *Tarzan Escapes*, as the film was retitled for its 1936 release. It didn't fit the dream. But if it hadn't been for Johnny, things could have turned out a lot worse. "That's enough, Gately. Let me calm it down. It trusts me," he said, and at the sound of his voice, I came running, as I always did. In the cradle of his arm I was calmed, stroked down from my fury, and it was easier for us all to agree on a convenient white lie about my having been "frightened" by something.

And as my rage subsided, I found that for the first time on the escarpment, I *was* frightened of something. Not Gately, or the leopards or the Gaboni or Mary the rhino, but the possibility I had managed to bury at the back of my mind for two years: that if Mayer or Thalberg didn't like what they were seeing, or if the moviegoers no longer believed in our dream, or if Maureen turned against me, or if I just didn't make 'em laugh like I had in *Tarzan and His Mate*, then the research center would always be happy to take me in, along with all the rest of Hollywood's rejected. "Oh, yeah, I used to be a star. Used to be very close with Johnny Weissmuller. But it's more rewarding working in medicine." Don't ever forget it, I told myself. This business is your *life*. Time might go by but Death never loses interest in you.

Stardom was my shelter, and without it, I could easily end up at the bottom of the H of the HOLLYWOODLAND sign, with the British actress Peg Entwistle, or in an unmarked grave with Florence Lawrence, the "Biograph Girl," who could do nothing to stop herself swallowing a cocktail of cough syrup and ant poison after the work dried up. Or I might end up being prodded and shaken by two children exploring the stairwell of a New York tenement building as the ex–child star Bobby Driscoll had, or on one of the foothills of the city dump with Rex the Wonder Dog. Stardom protected you against these dangers, and only the seven alphas of Hollywood could give it to you. Why antagonize them? Remember what happened to Maurice the lion? I thrashed in Johnny's arms and he let me down gently so that I could make my way across the dining room to rest a conciliatory hand on Maureen's thigh. I thought, From now on, I'm only gonna touch the little idiot when no one's around.

The humans settled back to their lunch. But the fizz had rather gone out of the party. With profound hypocrisy, Jane was now objecting to Captain Fry's idea that Tarzan himself be brought back to England. Tarzan could make a fortune, could make mountains of money "lecturing on wildlife." "Money?" Johnny said uncomprehendingly. He and I never had the faintest clue about money. All that sort of thing he left to his friend Bö Roos.

"No, Tarzan, you don't understand," Cousin Eric tried to assure him.

"Of course he doesn't understand!" Jane burst out, rising to her feet. "I hope he never does!"

And then it all came pouring out—she was off to England, was going to leave Tarzan, but "only for the time it takes the moon to make three safaris," she claimed. Yeah, yeah, and Garbo was always going to go back to John Gilbert, and Jayne Mansfield was always going to go back to Mickey Hargitay. How stupid did she think he was? Why couldn't Tarzan come with her? Because, and Jane had a well-thumbed little stump speech on the subject, "In civilization he'd be a . . . a sort of freak. He could never tolerate it, or if he did, that might be worse!"

In which case, ladies and gentlemen of the jury—and feel free to picture me as Charles Laughton here, or Spencer Tracy in *Inherit the Wind*, perhaps, rounding on my heel with an index finger spiraling into the air—in which case, Miss, uh, Parker, or will "Jane" do? In which case, *Jane*, why are you trying to bring civilization to the escarpment? Hypocrite! Liar! She had even taken to wearing a pair of calfskin bloomers underneath her dress, for propriety's sake, for fuck's sake.

And the terrible thing was that he loved her so. The guy was totally broken up about it. It was Lupe all over again. Or as Bobbe Arnst told *Photoplay* in 1932, dolefully folding her ten-thousand-dollar check from Mannix into her purse next to the IOU for her lost soul, "I guess marriage can't ever be the victor in Hollywood." And Johnny's face was an index of the purity of his system. Grief rose to its surface in a pure form; his face didn't filter his despair. His suffering was written all over his brow, and his brow was like a continent you hoped would never be visited by those tall ships. It broke your heart. People have forgotten, or they failed to see it at the time—and you may doubt my objectivity but: don't—for two or three pictures, Johnny Weissmuller was a great, great silent movie star, a transmitter of joy, a transmitter of sorrow.

And in his despair, he was wide open to Captain Fry who, I now realized, was not an animal rehabilitator but a cad of the first water. Fry had an iron shelter into which he was able to fool the love-addled King of the Jungle. It was a situation tailor-made for the natural climax of any Weissmuller-Cheeta picture—my daredevil rescue of my partner. I evaded the usual lethargic predators, enlisted the help of Emma, got him out of there, watched the Gaboni capture the white men, the elephants stampede the Gaboni village and so on and so forth and none of it seemed quite the same as it had been. I could bust Tarzan out of Fry's cage, but what about the one Jane was building around him? Her terrible Casa Felicitas?

The only thing to do was put it all out of my mind and enjoy the escarpment's delights. Somewhere in America, I'm sure, there's a box of photographs that Johnny took with his Box Brownie during the shooting of *Tarzan Escapes*. He was going through that phase all humans go through, of thinking he was quite a talented photographer. I hope in that box there's a picture of us playing Find the Lady with the Gabonis. I had a great system going with Bomba, where he'd do the flickering magic with the three cards and I'd point to the queen, and Bomba would say to the rest of the Gabonis, "A monkey can play this game, fellers! You ain't got nuthin' to fear, fellers! Come on and find that sweet, sweet lady. She *wants* you to find her, fellers!"

But they never could find her, those Gabonis.

When I'm swinging upside down in my tire behind the Sanctuary, the contrails of the airplanes segmenting the little rectangle of blue visible above the climbproof wall appear to me like the wakes of yachts racing around Catalina Island; and the planes themselves look just like the flying fish who skipped beside us. If Lupe wasn't coming to the shore for the weekend, Johnny would take me and Otto down in his new Continental, lingering at every stoplight for a little triumph of handshakes and a quick Tarzan yell, with Otto in his lap and me around his shoulders, my hands on the wheel, bamboozling the bums and lushes. *Good morning, sir, I'm looking for the source of the Zambezi but I seem to have taken a wrong turn at Wilshire Boulevard!* NDSN, as the stage direction used to go—Nobody Don't Say Nuthin'. *Umgawa!* I loved him and he loved Otto and me and we loved each other and I felt, at those moments, almost entirely unendangered.

Occasionally, on a Lupe weekend, Peter Lorre—a very special human being and a wonderful actor whose beautiful manners were largely unaffected by his addiction to morphine—might pick me up and I would spend most of my time on the yacht club lawn with him and his wife, of whom I was very fond, trying to apologize for upsetting the black and white ornaments they would arrange with great thoughtfulness in a kind of courtship dance on their checkered board, outrunning the unpredictable geysers throwing rainbows over the grass, and accustoming myself to my lowered status, my starvation rations of affection, my ten-minute poolside audiences.

It was on one of those weekends that Flynn arranged for a steer to be slaughtered and sunk beside his *Sirocco* with lead weights and a buoy to attract some "motherfucking fish" and maybe "a few hungry merbroads." Kate Hepburn was staying with Bogie and Mayo on *Santana* and she rowed me out there herself in the tender, I remember, to where *Allure* was moored beside the Bogarts, and there they were, the World's Most Perfect Male and the Latino Tornado. Lupe was wearing a British naval officer's cap at an angle, which somehow managed to articulate a tolerant contempt for everything aquatic. Tarzan and His Mate.

Otto snuffled around in the swell, like a great dumb happy seal, getting ready to shake himself dry over Lupe's chic little brass-buttoned jacket, bless him. I wanted to throw him a fish. Johnny spent the afternoon lined up on the stern of *Allure* with Flynn and Bogie, rods out, alpha males at peace. There was a strong atmosphere of closeted male defensiveness coming off them, exacerbated as the day wore on by their failure to catch any fish for their females, who talked and drank with a smattering of beta males in the bows. The very special human beings glimmered in the ocean glare, as did the slightly less special ones who ferried them their drinks.

At some point in the evening, after Otto had been dragged, sopping, belowdecks, and I had been amusingly established with one of Ward Bond's Cuban cigars and a margarita, I began to notice how connected everything seemed to everything else. OK, it was the margaritas working in me, and the champagne cocktails, but I was no more than reasonably well mulled.

I'm a drinker, never made a secret of it—always have been, until my time at the Sanctuary—but I've always known when to stop. And I'd even argue that there's a little more dignity in sharing a couple of cocktails, some caviar and a good cigar on a yacht with Katharine Hepburn and Nunnally Johnson than there is in washing down your sugar-free seventy-fifth birthday cake with a can of warm Diet Pepsi and a SpongeBob SquarePants hat askew on your head. I'd mixed it a little, but I wasn't anything like as oiled as Mayo Bogart or Lupe or Ward was. No, it was the feeling, the absolute conviction, that although the humans and the dead steer in the water, the fish, Otto and I were all part of the same thing, they would never understand that they were all—it sounds banal now when I say it, it sounds ridiculous, and I wouldn't presume to claim anything like a *human* intelligence (all I know is as much as you *can* know from dedicating a quarter of your life to watching TV) but it was a feeling you get only once or twice and when it comes you have to trust it: it was like the feeling I'd gotten from Connie Bennett's star-powder, but infinitely stronger, realer.

Kate had, with somewhat predictable competitiveness, initiated a game of charades, and while the dead cow bobbed forlornly in the Pacific, my dear friends and Academy Award winners wordlessly became drunks and adulterers and murderers (Macbeth—Bogart) and petrified forests and white whales and midsummer nights (Hepburn) and cherry orchards and little women (Johnny) and the Bible (Lupe). I realized, with no great surprise, that I was guessing them right *every time*. I wasn't guessing them, I *knew* them.

It came to my turn and I doused my cigar in my champagne flute and gave them Hamlet. Bereavement. Depression. Madness.

Suicide. Revenge. Murder. (No animal, I feel it worthwhile to mention at this point, has ever won an Academy Award. Not one. No animal has ever been *nominated*.) But I gave them Hamlet. And Kate got it even before I was halfway through the first ghost scene. How the hell did she get it unless there really was this connection? I marked her answer with a backward somersault and followed it with *King Kong* and she got that too. So I did another backward somersault. *Tarzan and His Mate*—she got it straight off! And yet all of this seemed to mean nothing to her—it seemed to mean nothing at all that this connection was happening. She was chatting with Flynn, and Mayo was arguing with Bogie, and the party began to shift its weight and stir its stumps from the bows, as if it hadn't just witnessed something almost inexplicable. Still retaining this sense of mellowness, carrying it like an egg on a spoon, I knuckled over to Johnny, made him scoop me up and gave him to understand how much I loved him.

"Cheeta drunk!" Bogie said. "Like Mayo. After sex, a woman oughta turn into a pinochle table with three other guys. She's no good. No damn good. My wife is a lush and I can't do a goddamn thing to help her, Johnny boy."

He was pretty drunk himself—a serious drinker, Bogie, and sometimes a mean and violent one, although he was a very special human being and one of the gentlest and most decent of men. I tendriled my arm around Johnny's eyes and clambered onto his head in the manner he sometimes liked.

"Lupe and I got married too young, or something," Johnny said. "You know what it's—*no*, Cheeta—you know what it's like. She's a night person, I'm a day person. She drinks, I don't. She smokes, I don't. You think, why knock yourself out? But I reckon we're turning the corner now. Cheeta, *no*! Bogie, you should just give Mayo a little more time."

I stepped from shoulder to shoulder using the handhold of Johnny's ear as a swivel and settled my chin on the cliff of his forehead, transmitting my love, my connection with him and with them, the steer, fish, Otto, etc. My Tarzan. I had just had a brilliant idea: *Tarzan and Cheeta!* They needed to title the next one *Tarzan and Cheeta.* I was his brother, his son, his constant companion, you see. I was there to save him from being alone. That was the point of me, to stop him from dying of loneliness. I was there to stop the loneliness that arrived with Jane, engulfing the two of them. And then I was the household servant, who cranked the fan and turned the spit for the roast and milked the antelopes. "Thank you, Cheeta. I don't know what I'd do without you." You would die of loneliness, dear Jane. You'd be found dead among your state-of-the-art bamboo and elephant-grass labor-saving devices, with your head in the swamp-gas oven. Thalberg and Mayer and even Sol Lesser knew this, which is why the final frame of every Weissmuller-Cheeta picture is not Tarzan himself, or Jane or the Boy, but me. They needed me to be there at the end when they waved off their guests. Always me, staving off their threefold loneliness. Me, Cheeta.

"I've given her time," Bogie was saying, "I've given her chances. I've given her the best doctors, the best treatments. But three days on the outside, she's drinking again. I could give her a thousand years, a million chances, and she'd do the same every time."

"If you had a million monkeys working on a million typewriters," Nunnally butted in, quietly and very frighteningly, "for a thousand years, then one of them would write *The Complete Works of William Shakespeare.*"

"That's just it!" said Johnny. "I thought never in a million years! I used to think: my God, I love *Otto* more than my wife! Come on—off, *off*, Cheeta. And now I just think maybe this is it, it's just suddenly . . . come good. Jesus *Christ*, I've got my own lush to deal with. For Chrissakes, *off*!"

With great reluctance, I let Johnny peel me off him, limb by limb. Love clings. Love *clings*. It's a centripetal force. He was still talking, and Flynn was now shouting from *Sirocco* about yet another bet. The insecure fucking alpha and his sporting wagers. The great arm-wrestler, high-diver, best-of-threer, let's-make-it-more-interesting cow-killer, fish-killer, bird-killer, gorilla-killer. A race back to Newport, a couple of cocktails at the yacht club, back to *Allure* by dawn, and let the girls sleep it off in the meantime. Flynn had a cannon on the port bow of *Sirocco* with which he once sank Lionel Barrymore's skiff, but it was OK: Flynn was slightly more special than Lionel.

I left them to it and clambered through *Allure*'s hatch. You've had a million humans, at least, writing away for much longer than a thousand years, and only one of them ever managed to produce *The Complete Works of Shakespeare*. Only the one! Well, well, what's the big deal? I wasn't sure whether Nunnally was actually *proposing* this, as some sort of hideous battery farm of art. It's the sort of thing you might do. But then again, maybe it wouldn't be so bad—the adrenaline-based drugs, the intravenous feeding tube, the *esprit de corps*, the motivational quotes over the PA . . .

A swell must have gotten up because I was having a great deal of trouble keeping my feet on my way from the bulkheads to the galley, where I was hoping to bulk up with a little caviar. Mayo lay fully clothed, very small and pale, face down and scrunched up like the embryo in an ostrich egg, on one of the berths, breathing quickly and lightly. Betty Bacall killed her, really, but that was afterward, and it wasn't Betty's fault, or Bogie's—it wasn't anybody's fault. Umgawa. Blame love. *Allure* moved on its swell, and with the movement the boat made its sounds, and among them were the

other sounds I had heard that afternoon three years ago from behind the kitchen door in the house on Rodeo Drive. Like an old
household servant I listened, and having listened was powerless to
stop. Lupe Vélez had "Lure—which women crave and men are
powerless to resist!" She purred and grunted and shrieked and
coughed and sang and said, "Gary!" at the very end, which was followed by a brief sharp exchange of words and then silence. I
waited. I waited a long time for an ape to wait, and then I entered
the cabin.

My first thought was that there had been a murder, a multiple
one; my second was something to do with octopuses and bears.
Lupe, on her side facing away from the door, was interlaced with
another pair of legs, which doubtless belonged to Ward Bond, over
which lay Otto, huge, and doggily asleep. I'm not accusing Otto,
God rest his soul, of anything here other than having his peripheral
consciousness sexually abused. Oh, Lupe, your trespasses are un-
forgivable. If she had been turned face up, I would have ripped out
her throat. Or am I deluding myself? I couldn't have done it—not
in front of an animal, in front of Otto. Her bullfighter's bottom was
presented instead and I bit it, and she stirred, squirmed, muttered
fragments of words and returned to sleep, where she had just sat on
a nettle. Me, I'm the secret patron saint of mystery bruises. I felt
very drunk, and heavy and sick of human love, as though Lupe's
blood had got into my mouth and was poisoning me. She tasted
quite different from Maureen.

I loped up the ladder and dozed on the deck, dreaming in
snatches about an idea for a movie I still think would work, about
an ape on an island, an uncharted island in the South Seas or the
Indian Ocean, wherever, called *Skull Island*, why not, where every
full moon the islanders stage their ceremony of blood sacrifice and
a human is drummed up out of the torchlight for terrible conver-

gence with this ape. The animal is roped between the two posts on the bone-littered altar, screaming, writhing in terror, as the human looms over it and clutches its tiny wriggling body in its fist. The twist? Instead of killing the ape, the human *falls in love* with it.

When *Santana* hove to before dawn, I was leaping at the stern rail with such an appearance of distress that Kate obliged me by rowing me back in the tender to dry land. By half past seven I was breakfasting on fruit at the Newport Beach Yacht Club, while Peter and Karen Lorre worked their way through the *Los Angeles Inquirer*'s crossword.

I sometimes think when I make my rounds of the wards, when Don and I tour the hospices and the Buzz Lightyear wings, the most famous animal in the world bringing what succor he can to the terminal—and Don will always start off with his joke about my statue getting around more than I do myself these days, since kids are forever finding new ways to unscrew it from the plinth outside the Sanctuary—that I'm the future. Not just of my species, either. I'm the future of all the species. I can see us in our wards, our aviaries and vivariums, cosseted survivors who enjoy TV as we submit to our daily jabs, the precious ones, becoming individually famous as we become fewer, astounding the world a thousand times a second by smashing longevity record after longevity record, our sex lives and diseases the subject of global augury.

I am seven years older than any chimpanzee who has yet lived, and there is nothing that says I am ever going to die. I am *about* survival. I want to live forever. But you, dearest humans, I want to say, you do all this for us and leave nothing for yourselves! I have this terrible suspicion sometimes. I worry that you don't at heart really care all that much about surviving—sentiments I feel are best expressed by a very beautiful poem written by a Mr. Edward Robins

Richardson, which I saw engraved on a sundial one evening at the Joe Cottens' years ago:

> Let us with zest drink deep the draught
> Of Life, and care not if the wine
> Is neither nectar nor divine
> Elixir, for we have loved and laughed
>
> Amid our tears. If we should fall
> In reaching for the big brass ring,
> Or if, like Ic'rus, we take wing
> Too near the sun . . . well, then we fall.
>
> At least we flew! At least we chose
> To burn! And when our heyday cools
> And we're near dust, if we were fools
> The hell with it. The hell with those
>
> Who feared to rush dream-drunk, headlong
> Into th'dance! Say this, when we set
> Out for the realm unconquer'd yet:
> Say, *They lived*. Judge us right or wrong
>
> We drained our cups.

That says it all, I think. Given a million years on a typewriter I very much doubt that I, or any other ape, would be capable of composing something with quite that martial, apocalyptic swing. So beautiful, and so true. I can't disagree with a word of it. I . . . I love it. How did you become so *defiant*?

I never saw Otto again. I saw Lupe just once, and it was the last time Johnny saw her too. Or, no, hang on, I think maybe they ran into each other again at the start of the forties, when his next marriage was already in trouble, in Toots Shor's restaurant in New York. But I saw the last of their marriage when I stopped by the Casa Felicitas for a little roughhouse on the lawn one evening a couple of months later, during the prepping of *Tarzan Finds a Son!* The poor dumb mutt Otto was missing. A stranger had entered the house at night and abducted him! There were no leads, no clues! Leopold and Loeb were going at Johnny's ankles like buzz saws, the parrot was screaming, "*Hola*, Gary! *Hola*, Gary!" in a loop, and Lupe was a *duenna*, a *bruja*, a *djinn* undergoing an expansion, filling the two-story room, the house, with black smoke—she could have filled Radio City Music Hall.

"Ees a estupeed dog! Ees better off dead! Ees good the dog ees dead! Because the dog tried to keell me when I was fucking another man! On your stupid boat, John-ee! And so I sent it to hell!"

I may have been doing a fair bit of screaming myself at that point, I admit. Johnny walked over to the parrot on its perch and, seeming to have an innate knack for the technique required, wrung its neck. "Goodbye, Gary," he said, which I think means he'd already played it out in his head.

So, I killed them both, Otto and Gary. I set that death loose. I put the blood on his hands.

Lupe set out into the realm unconquer'd yet six years later, in December 1944, by drowning herself in a toilet bowl. As I write, she would have been a hundred years old to the week. She'd been making B's at RKO, and even those were waning. Her profile was going, and she knew it. Mannix didn't even need to cover it up.

# 5
# Funny Man!

Perhaps it's time for some happier memories.

Sexual intercourse began in 1938, between *Holiday* with Cary Grant and Welles's *War of the Worlds* update, when I lost my virginity to a number of voracious females not of my own species while simultaneously entertaining *la crème d'Hollywood* with a mischievous critique of Charlie Chaplin.

Chaplin is an extraordinarily special human being, a person in whom a whole multitude of talents and virtues is united but, as the saying goes, to be human is to be fallible (what a *modest* species you are!) and not even Charlie's stoutest defenders would claim that he was perfect or even likable or, indeed, defensible on any level at all.

*Charles* Chaplin, as the world-historically unfunny charlatan preferred to be known, liked more than anything to hold court in his mansion at the top of Summit Drive. His preferred company was a mixture of non-Hollywood public figures or intellectuals in whose conversation he found himself hopelessly out of his depth ("But surely, Mr. Gandhi . . .") and a selection of female starlets and socialites that Paulette Goddard, who lived with him off and on, was . . . well, she put up with them, happy or not. Typically, you'd find that year's entire thirteen-strong list of WAMPAS Baby

Stars (the Western Association of Motion Picture Advertisers' annual choice of the young actresses most likely to succeed) sitting in a semicircle around Aldous Huxley or Eisenstein, with "Charles" saying something like, "The soul of Collective Man cannot soar while the belly of Individual Man is empty, as Plutarch tells us . . ." while surreptitiously waggling his graying eyebrows at one of the girls "whose propinquity," as he would have had it, "cannot help but involve my heart." What an absolute privilege it was to be granted access to one of these exalted gatherings! Take Charlie out of the picture and it would have been perfect.

Anyway, Johnny and I drove up there in the Continental sometime in the early fall of 1938. I was utterly delighted to see him, of course—Metro had loaned him out to Billy Rose's Aquacade in New York for a spell, and though there was still a reasonably regular stream of fellow stars who might take me for a bite in the commissary, or up to Lionel Atwill's to add a decadent touch to an orgy, the days had been weighing heavy without Johnny around.

He seemed happy: rolled from under the stone of Lupe, unbowed still by Jane. He was always on a high after he'd swum, and the Continental shook little drops of water from the heavy bunching of hair at the back of his head, darkening his suit collar. I sat on his lap and tooted the horn, and we dusted off the old stoplight routine a couple of times on the way up to Beverly Hills. You could smell the mimosa, the jacaranda, the wild sage and the eucalyptus through the open window, see the ocean so pale it merged in a haze with the sky. You could hear the natives at work on their machines in the great gardens you passed, like rhinoceros birds grooming crumbs from the back of an enormous oblivious beast, and sense *his* water-tuned ears noting the very special humans a-splash in their pools. The Enchanted Escarpment!

Chaplin, Johnny explained to me, had specifically requested that

I be brought along. He liked animals and had a little menagerie on the grounds. Well, possibly that was the reason, but what human didn't like animals? It was more likely, I supposed, that I'd been invited because Chaplin had become aware of the plaudits that *Tarzan Escapes* had garnered. I've never paid much attention to reviews, but if memory serves, *Variety* had said something like "direction moves along at a reasonable pace and fullest advantage is taken of cute antics of the ape Cheta [*sic* again]." The *Hollywood Reporter* had it that "A female ape called Cheta [oh, why bother?] is the Tarzans' pet and houseworker, and expert handling of the monk provides the picture with some of its more legitimately comic moments." I was aware there was some kind of groundswell of acclamation going on for my "work," but to be absolutely honest, the garnering of critical acclaim has never meant much to me—quite unlike the role it played in Charlie's life, which was pretty similar to the role morphine played in Bela Lugosi's, or the erect male sexual organ in dear, sweet Mary Astor's, which is to say, he was hopelessly dependent upon it.

One of Chaplin's butlers ushered us into the garden, where the great man was seated in a cane chair, looking pensively up at the branches of the plum tree above him. Scattered around his feet were half a dozen late-adolescent or early-adult females in tennis gear, arrayed in postures of rapt fascination. Seated on a wicker swing that hung from the tree were an old couple (he in serious need of a haircut) behind whom I could see various birds and tasty-looking monkeys in the menagerie. There was a separate shelter, which held half a dozen apes, ostensibly the explanation for my presence. Poor suckers, stuck inside on such a glorious day!

"Tarzan bring Cheeta!" Johnny called across the lawn. Chaplin waved hello, and continued his examination of the fruit tree.

"A hypothesis occurs," he opened, as we took our places on the grass. "If it is funny for a man to be hit on the head by a falling plum, then it should consequently be more amusing for him to be hit on the head by a fruit of greater weight, for example, um, a coconut. Yet a coconut might cause serious injury. What, therefore, is the optimum weight of a fruit falling for comic purposes? An apple, perhaps, Professor? The same fruit that was assisted by the force of gravity into contact with the cerebellum of the incomparable Sir Isaac Newton? Neither a plum nor a coconut would have been quite suitable for the purposes of awakening that Knight of the Realm to the Laws of Gravitation. The apple is perfect. It is a moment of perfect comedy, giving rise to a perfect intellectual inspiration. Is there not something . . . umm?"

Johnny had an expression on his face as if he'd just jumped on a leopard and, on reaching for his knife, had realized that he'd forgotten to put it on that morning.

The old gentleman in the swinging chair filled the silence. "I believe, Charles, that the apple didn't actually fall *on* Newton's head. But it's certainly a funny picture you paint."

"On his head, near his head, I think the point stands, Professor."

Chaplin continued to talk in a similar vein for quite some time while I busied myself in a quest for a drink. I'd been very good over the last couple of months but I could have murdered a highball, which the flock of girls obliged me with, and a smoke to help it down. This was in the days, as I've said, when lighting up was pretty much a guarantee of a laugh rather than a scolding, and the girls were presently tinkling away like ice cubes at my insouciant side-of-the-mouth exhalations. I was gamboling around the lawn, midway through a standard attention-grabber—offering the cigarette around as if to share it, then snatching it back—when Chaplin suddenly transferred his gaze to me.

"Girls! Is it not abominable to inflict the vices of Mankind upon an animal? Regard the poor creature! And some find it funny to see animals emulating the actions of their human cousins! How can it be funny when the animal has no consciousness of humor? If there is comedy it is not in, or of, the creature itself but something we bring *to* it."

I took a deep toke and gave him a brief round of ironic applause. Chaplin gave a little chuckle. "Even Cheeta herself agrees with me! What do you think, Johnny?"

"I guess Cheeta's pretty funny, I always thought," Johnny said, offhandedly furnishing me with one of the dozen or so greatest memories of my life. "The kids absolutely love Cheeta. Do the lips, Cheets."

He demonstrated and I did the double-lip flip, following up with a swig of one of the girls' mint juleps and granting myself another quick round of applause. But there was silence from the girls. He'd killed my crowd stone dead.

"Mere imitation," said Chaplin. "Monkey see, monkey do, as the saying has it. Whereas if *I* take, excuse me, Helen . . ."

"Marian."

"Forgive me, Marian—if I take your mint julep, I can from mere *imagination* become a teetotal spinster taking her first sip of alcohol . . . and finding that I enjoy it! I can be a reluctant drunkard, trying to resist temptation . . . and failing!" These accompanied by excruciating little mimes and laughter from the girls and the professor. And from Johnny, unfailingly polite as he was.

"I can even be a bibulous chimpanzee stealing a sly swig and finding . . . that it disagrees with me!" He added a couple of scurrying circles, as if the "chimpanzee" had suddenly become very drunk, and keeled over with his legs in the air. This generated a round of applause and calls for more from the crowd, which our host resisted for a seemly period before capitulating and sending a non-special human being scurrying off for his cane and hat.

I'm painfully conscious here, by the way, that most of you will have no idea who this "Chaplin" is or what a "cane and hat" signify, so cruelly has time treated Charlie's work (but do try digging on the net!). Suffice it to say that the cane and hat signified a long afternoon of being privileged to watch while Chaplin (whose first marriage was said to have inspired the Kubrick picture *Lolita*—there we go, something of him *will* survive!) ran through an extended sequence of what anyone could diagnose as utterly transparent sexual courtship rituals. It couldn't have been comedy, at any rate. He was like Don's goddamn whale—a monomaniacal bore unstoppably propagandizing his own sexual status—and, I'm sorry to say, I could nose a significant heightening of response from the girls.

Arriving at the end of a mime in which he played both a starving ragamuffin chasing after a ten-dollar bill and the policeman who is obliviously standing on it, the perspiring old satyr volunteered through the applause the idea that "What distinguishes Man from beast is not his capacity for reason, nor the fact that he makes tools, or uses language, for many species do indeed enjoy sophisticated forms of communication, but his sense of humor. We are the only species that laughs. Man—the '*animal ridens*.' Phew! I think I need to change my shirt!"

This got a laugh from everybody but me, but there you go, I didn't have a sense of humor.

"Oh, but before I forget: Anita. And, uh, Jean. I promised to show you the Brancusis, didn't I? We might as well have a look at them now, before our other guests arrive, mightn't we? Johnny, you're not interested in fine art, are you, by any chance? You really ought to see these pieces, you know."

Johnny hesitated for a second. His head came up suddenly to catch Chaplin's gaze.

"Um . . . I believe not, Charlie, thanks all the same. I don't know much about art, really. I'll stay here with Cheeta and the prof." And off Chaplin went with the two girls to examine the sculptures.

"You know, I should rather like a look at those Brancusis myself," the professor remarked, which, for somebody I later heard described as "the smartest man in the world," wasn't a particularly acute observation.

For nearly an hour we sat under the plum tree, hostless, our group steadily enlarging with the regular drip-drip of guests arriving for evening drinks. Servants illuminated paper lanterns that hung like humorless fruit from the branches of the garden's trees. The prof was trying his best to entertain the group with a little lesson in his own theories, but there was relatively little interest. Johnny had recognized a couple of pals in Fredric March and Fernando Lamas, and I noticed that even the girls were perceptibly less interested in me than they had been earlier, before Chaplin's little display. So, left to my own devices, I picked up Chaplin's hat (an absolutely instinctive gesture by that point in my life—not even cigarettes were as much of a guarantee of a laugh as a hat) and wandered away from the chink of drinks and the growing gusts of laughter toward the menagerie.

Was Chaplin right? I was musing, in that melancholy haze that gin always gives you. Perhaps I wasn't really as funny as I thought I was, notwithstanding Johnny's faith in me. On the escarpment I got a laugh from Tarzan and Jane every time I donned a visitor's hat or pelted an elephant with fruit, but where was the competition? I was the funniest animal in the world—look at my reviews—but how funny was that? Miserably, ginnishly, I began to masturbate in our species' characteristic distracted fashion.

With a click and a buzz the electric lights in the shelters were tripped—by dusk, I assumed, rather than a butler—and behind the mesh diamonds of the shelter were, hello there, half a dozen chimpanzees. All of them, I smelled rather than saw, were female. I looked at them, looked down at the erect penis in my hand, and made a dim connection. They looked at me, looked at the erect penis in my hand and made, probably, a somewhat less dim connection. To be quite frank, and not at all meaning to boast, I must have seemed tremendously compelling to them, hobnobbing with the humans on the other side of the mesh (probably something big in pictures), a cigarette in one hand and an erect penis in the other, a bowler hat jammed over my head at a *boulevardier*'s rakish angle. Ah, *comme j'étais charmant en ma jeunesse!* Anyway, a big whoop went up from the cage, almost drowning the applause behind me as Chaplin and his two art-loving friends made a return to the party.

I didn't think. There were two pink beacons of vaginal swelling, at least, dancing like spots before my eyes. I wasn't really seeing much else. I unlatched the external bolt on the shelter door and stepped inside. My nose was doing all the work for me now. All those years of juvenile masturbation with no clear idea of the why of it. Well, at last I got it—here was the why of it.

There was a female squatting before me, something alluringly indescribable in her musk, and I realized I didn't have the faintest idea what on earth I was supposed to do. The perfect end to a perfect evening, I thought, ritual sexual humiliation in front of half a dozen females. Was I supposed to use my hand? Or how did it go— it was a kind of hug, wasn't it? A long time since I'd watched my mother in the forest. A long time since I'd even *seen* a female. They seemed so small, their scent so strange. You bent at the knees or, no, you went on to your knuckles. I didn't have a clue . . . and now my sex- and gin-fogged consciousness was picking up on something else. The sound of the party had cohered into a rhythmic chant, accompanied by claps, and I glanced over my shoulder to see a dozen or so humans looking on and applauding.

"Hey, Charlie! Look, Charlie, it's you!" the crowd was shouting. The chant found its rhythm. "Char-lie! Char-lie! Char-lie!"

Chaplin came running up to the cage, unamused at the appropriation of his hat, and I wish I was Niv, because I'd be able to tell you that "I doffed the bowler at the empurpled and aging Lothario, gave him a wink, and began to work my way through the females," but I only did the last of those three. Chaplin began to protest, but as his guests accurately warned him, "It might be dangerous to try and separate the animals while they're mating." And it was sweet, yes it was, to skip from one trembling partner to another, ejaculating near-instantaneously like an old hand, buoyed by the joyous laughter of my contemporaries. Not *funny*, Charlie? You're sure?

Well, the first time ought to be special . . . only two things spoiled the moment. My disheartening, some would even say devastating, discovery that the apes were not in fact chimpanzees at all but bonobos (yes, very *funny*). And the ominous title of our new dream, which I overheard as I circulated post-coitally through the garden. It was to be called *Tarzan Finds a Son!*

What did he want with one of *those*?

# 6
# Little Feet!

Thalberg was dead—died the week *Tarzan Escapes* was released. "Happens to us all," as you often hear humans say, in that somewhat melodramatic way of yours. But in Thalberg's case, like Lupe's, there really *was* a sense of inevitability about Death's intervention in his affairs. The Prince of Hollywood lay in his casket in the B'nai B'rith Temple on Wilshire Boulevard, where every major star in Hollywood except me was crammed, like a refutation of that crazily hopeful human dictum "Hard work never killed anybody." There was no point in sticking your head in the sand—hard work had killed the Boy Wonder. I'm sure a lot of the dreamers at the synagogue that day were silently vowing not to make the same mistake as the great man, and certainly there was a faint but just perceptible lessening of intensity in Hollywood after Thalberg's time. Dear old L.B. summed up the day, as an alpha should. "Ain't God good to me?" he was heard to murmur over his rival's body. A little prayer of straightforward happiness at being alive.

Never underestimate the condescension the living have for the dead, for all our fine words.

Thalberg had once saved my life. He'd also tried harder than anyone to save the escarpment from being polluted by words. *Less dialogue, more action*, he'd written. But now he was gone there was nobody to stop the babble of "civilized" chatter stinking up the place. More dialogue was coming. We were still there, me and the rest of the chimps, Mary and Emma and the pachyderms, and the warthogs from Luna Park zoo and the ostriches from the ranch up on Mission Drive and crocodiles from the alligator farm in Lincoln Heights: we still teemed miraculously through paradise, so various, so beautiful, so glamorous, but right from the start of this dream there was a sense of our having been shifted from the center of things. OK for me, playing the lead. But naturally I was nervous for my fellow workers.

They were all absolutely marvelous, of course, but there were no guarantees for animals who worked as extras. Out of the hundreds of horses who worked with Niv and Flynn on Warner's *The Charge of the Light Brigade* there wasn't a single "name." When the news came through that nearly two hundred of them hadn't survived the dreaming (more horses were killed than during the original Charge, history buffs may be interested to learn) there wasn't really a sense of surprise. It had been an accident waiting to happen.

Anyway, it all began with a . . . with an . . . I don't know, a kind of *iron bird* that fell from the skies. I'm kidding, it was a Bellanca Aircruiser P-200 Deluxe, the nine-seater model discontinued in '42. In its wreckage there was a human baby, which we chimps extracted, rather foolishly allowing the Gabonis to get to its parents' bodies before we could tuck in ourselves. But there we go, life ain't perfect, as the one and only Wallace Beery supposedly told Gloria Swanson after raping her on their wedding night. We all make mistakes, as—hey, nice coincidence!—Mannix told the incorrigible Beery when Beery rang him after Ted Healy, the creator of the Three Stooges, was beaten to death by "college students" outside the Trocadero Restaurant in December 1937.

I was about to make a truly irrevocable mistake. In an unreachable corner of my mind there was a trace memory of something maddeningly similar—an infant plucked from a shattered plane, us staring down confusedly at it, its trusting smile, its apelike eyes. It made me think of my dear, wise Tarzan. It was something I wanted him to remember—where he came from. It was a compulsion. I couldn't stop. With soft hands I carried the bundle through the canopy toward the treeless zone that had developed around the Casa Felicitas. Even then it might have been all right—Tarzan was utterly perplexed by the baby, which was already testing out its hierarchical role with a marathon demonstration of power-display screaming. I thought, Fine, it's been an interesting diversion, an amusing anecdote, let's chuck it away now or get it on the rotisserie spit. And then Jane came in, with an armful of freshly cut flowers.

Why we needed the flowers when we lived in a forest I can't tell you. Now there'd be no flowers in the place she'd got them from. Maybe the next time we were down there I could take *these* ones back, brighten the place up a bit! *Fucking* idiot! Marriage to Farrow had finally extinguished any last flicker of fun in her—Jane was now about as effervescent as a gin and tonic left all winter in a shuttered summerhouse. Her hemline was down half a foot; her hair had become anti-erotically complex, and her eyes . . . her eyes were tunnels. They saw the baby and nothing else. She went white with triumph. You see—and I don't think there's any way I can avoid the subject—Tarzan wouldn't give her a child. And for all that Jane had designed off-putting twin beds for them in the zebra-hide-and-leopard-skin-themed master bedroom, it was a child she craved.

There were two ways things could go on the escarpment. Either we would never grow up, like Fred and Ginger or Stan and Ollie, like the Marx Brothers or Flash Gordon or Sam Spade, like Roy

Rogers and Trigger, like Cary and Kate—we could do that and live forever—or we could give in to Jane's time-disease and throw it all away. And he was weak. The King of the Jungle was weak because he was an orphan, because he'd never had a father to topple. There was no father to get out from under, so alphadom had come too easily to him, as a gift from his body. He was wide open to tough girls like Jane: they went at him like a herd of elephants at a Gaboni hut. Sure, he loved children. He made children want to *be* his sons. All his life he was surrounded by wannabe sons (I was one). But I don't think he was ever that set on being a father.

Jane brushed past him toward the power-displaying infant. "Tarzan! *What on earth* are you doing?" she said, flowers forgotten. "There, there, now, Jane will look after you! Where will we get it some milk? I suppose coconuts will have to do. Hurry, Tarzan, the poor little thing's hungry!"

"Tarzan eat now!" Tarzan commented.

"Tarzan. You go and get those coconuts right now!"

It was beginning to dawn on me what I had done. The terrible error I had made. I heard Otto give a faint sad woof from some spectral lawn.

So, we ascertained that the child's parents were dead, and within an hour I was being testily ordered down to milk Gladys the antelope. "Be careful!" Jane hollered, as I got in the elevator, the milk slopping around in the hollowed coconut as Emma wearily tugged on the "up" vine. *Be careful, how useful is it to say "Be careful" when I'm obviously being careful, I mean just how much more perfect an example of the pointless violence of human communication do you want than telling me to be careful when I'm already being careful?* I was thinking, or something similar, as I stepped out of the lift. Don't bite her. *Whatever you do, don't bite her, just give her the milk.* Survive, survive, survive . . . I saw Tarzan at work building an ostrich-feathered crib. I was his best friend, his constant companion, his brother. I was his uncle, his shoulder to cry on, his partner in crime, his go-to guy. I was his tutor, his helpmeet, his sidekick, his rescuer. I was all of these things in a female form. I was his everything, before Jane showed up. I was his *son*.

And now I was the humble household Negro, wearing an expression of nothing, nothing at all, as I shuffled up to hand his wife a coconut and await my instructions. That expression, that look of benevolent vacancy? That's *acting*. Inside, I was thinking, What have I done? Come around and surprise me and Don one day and we'll stick the DVD on for you. I'll be in and out, unable to watch, unable to tear myself away. But the film historians among you may care to note that *Tarzan Finds a Son!* was released several months *before* Hattie McDaniel's Best Supporting Actress Academy Award for Mammy in *Gone With the Wind*.

I don't know why I said that Chaplin's honorary Academy Awards were "not for real." If anything, such an award is worth more than a standard Oscar. In a sense, they're a tremendously generous recognition by the Academy of past mistakes, a way of apologizing for overlooking you at the time. An honorary award is a way of saying, "We took you for granted. You were right. Have this with our humblest apologies, Kirk, or Sophia, or Groucho, or Edward G., or Michelangelo, or Cary." You'd be surprised who gets missed. On the other hand, it's an obvious "thanks, and don't let the door hit you on the way out" kind of superannuation tool, as with Mickey R.'s award in '83. I don't honestly think Mickey would dispute that assessment.

Speaking of Mickey, Don had parked me in front of the *1000 Greatest Oscar Moments of All Time* the other night when I realized that Mickey had in fact won an Oscar before—an Academy Juvenile

Award. They stopped giving them in the early sixties. A separate category for non-adult humans seems like a pretty reasonable idea, don't you think? But the Academy is such an august and well-run institution that I'm sure they've got it in hand.

Anyway, they grow up fast, don't they? In the blink of an eye, the baby was a slightly pot-bellied, tousle-haired six-year-old called Boy. Six years of "Not in here!" and "Be a dear and get the milk in, would you?" and "Off, Cheeta!" Six years of serfdom settling like dust on me, six years of creeping marginalization all edited away into a single soothing modulation from gurgling bald alien to chubby boy a-swing on a vine. The kindness of editing.

The kid himself was OK. He wasn't going to be winning the Academy Juvenile Award any time soon, but I became quite fond of him in a way, protective, even. His other name was, of course, Johnny—"Little John," as opposed to the big one—and he was a tough little thing, I'll give him that, didn't cry too much when I tested him out with the occasional nip. But there was nothing of Tarzan in him. He was an unmagical foundling, an all-American man-cub with a laugh like a slap. He bullied the animals he could and mocked the rest from a safe distance. I was under no illusions: give him a few years and I'd be nothing more than his pet.

It goes without saying that he loved Johnny. We'd play Hollywood Frisbee together, like a real family, zipping the lid of a 35mm film can back and forth with me in the role of the piggy, clutching at air. Or gin rummy, another game I'd never been able to master, on account of how enjoyable the cards were to snack on. His catchphrase was "Ha ha *ha!*," shouted rather than laughed. "Ha ha *ha*, look at Cheeta!" Look at Cheeta, the long-suffering family retainer, usurped as the maker of mischief, sitting sucking a Chesterfield and wringing his hands with frustration while Johnny teaches the Boy to swim in Lake Sherwood, squirting him once, twice and, third time around, himself. "Ha ha *ha*, do it again!" No, don't do it again, I was trying to communicate, with my hopping and cheeping and my shaking wrists. Come on out and have a drink with me. Get in the Lincoln and let's go down to Lakeside for eighteen holes, or stop off at Chasen's for a sharpener before turning some heads at the Cocoanut Grove (where plaster palm trees, from whose wire fronds bread rolls could be dropped, grew high above the diners). Instead he went to Silver Springs in Florida with the Boy to shoot their underwater scenes, which would later be intercut with shots of me fretting on a riverbank. It's obvious if you watch the dream that it's a dream of separation. You can tell that although the ape and the two humans seem almost within touching distance, they're three thousand miles apart.

And now here came our visitors, toiling up the escarpment with the Gaboni at their heels as usual. This time they were the Boy's distant relatives—Austin and Mrs. Lancing, wise Sir Thomas and unscrupulous Sandy the hunter. There was the usual wrangling about inheritances and so on, a repeat of our excruciating lunch with Captain Fry ("It's such short notice, I haven't got a thing in!" Jane twittered) and then Jane dropped her bombshell. The Lancings were right, the Boy *should* go back to civilization. "I know what it's like back there," she said, in her "urgent" voice, her head tilted to one side as it seemed permanently to be these days. "You've no way of imagining the things that civilization can give him! Things we never could give him here!"

This was "civilization," remember, a place I have rarely heard any human describe with anything other than the greatest contempt. You only ever use the word with a pair of quotation marks, like tweezers, so your fingers don't have to touch it. It's famously difficult to define exactly. It sort of means the dark flip side, the negative, of human society. I've heard people describe things like the atom bomb, or a trash can in a national park, as "civilization," with those disdainful, shrugging quotes. Whatever it is, we were lucky in Hollywood, which was a "civilization"-free paradise. And we don't, touch wood, have any of it in Palm Springs. (Don's hatred for "civilization" is an ever-burning flame: he loathes it tirelessly.) And of course it was the dirtiest word on the escarpment, after "guns." But now the Housewife of the Jungle felt she'd concealed her yearning long enough and was praising it openly!

"Boy stay!" Tarzan demurred.

This presented me with a dilemma. As far as I was concerned, a dozen years at one of the great private schools in England could do the Boy nothing but good, and then he'd be going up to Christ Church and with any luck, the next time we'd see him on the escarpment he'd be trying to fund a coup backed by Maoist Gaboni rebels. But that was as foolish a dream as Lana Turner's daughter Cheryl's hope that her stepfather Lex Barker would stop raping her. If the Boy went to England, Jane wouldn't wait on the escarpment for a biannual visit. She'd be off, and she'd take Tarzan with her.

So, I didn't want the Boy to leave. Neither did he, of course. "Boy stay!" It was an impasse. And now, with glycerine tears and her head practically diagonal with wishful rationalizations, Jane's long-folded bud of opposition finally flowered into full betrayal.

It had to—she just was not capable of allowing her will to be balked. She couldn't stop. She sawed through a vine and left Tarzan stranded at the bottom of Koruva grotto, a deep limestone basin worn by a waterfall on the far side of the escarpment, enabling the Lancings to take the uncomprehending Boy with them.

Gibbering with glee, just about rubbing my hands with it, I seized on her mistake and knuckled across the escarpment to the grotto to fulfill my destiny—the Redeemer of Tarzan and Thwarter of the Great Betrayer, Jane. But I was somewhat put out, when I arrived at the lip of the gorge and set about locating a suitable vine, to be interrupted in my struggle by the Boy. He'd managed to escape, dammit. While he organized a party of elephants to convert an old lightning-shafted tree into a ladder, I contributed by impotently capering around the grotto's edge. It was a team effort.

It turned out that the Gabonis, bless 'em, had, as ever, captured the white men. This meant that, as ever, they were about to have their village stampeded by elephants. What they needed was a moat or something. How many times could they keep rebuilding their village and not learn the lesson that skimping on anti-elephant defense was false economy? It needed discussing—the elephant in the room of Gaboni society was the fact that there usually *was* an elephant in their room, standing on them. I mounted Emma and followed the heroic little busybody (who had been propped on a darling junior-size elephant calf of his own) over the Gabonis' flattened palisade and into their village, feeling kind of detached from the whole chaotic spectacle. Nothing mattered any longer, really, amid the dust and the splintered huts and wounded Gabonis, other than the one crucial question. Could Tarzan bring himself to not forgive her?

"Tarzan, Mawani," (some pet name) she murmured, "before I go . . ." (good start) ". . . please listen. I know now how right you are. Please try to forgive me. Please . . ." And she faltered, seeing what she had done to his face, how she had vandalized his brow with mistrust.

For a second, my heart leaped, and I jumped to my feet on Emma's neck. He might have been too good for this world, but his jungle lore would be telling him that a leopard can't change its spots. Cornered, desperate and unscrupulous to the last, she pulled the oldest trick in the book—she fainted. His enormous inarticulate heart brimmed at her weakness. He went to her and took her in his arms and her victory was complete.

So the dream concluded, with everything forgiven and all re-united, sighs and laughter: a complete fucking tragedy. In a couple of hours I'd be back washing dishes in the Casa Felicitas, with the Boy doing his homework and the Dad of the Jungle coming to grips with the lawn.

# 7
# Domestic Dramas!

Once, I don't know why (we were all a bit mulled), Lupe and he and I found ourselves walking down a street just behind Sunset Plaza Drive at four o'clock in the morning in search of the Continental. Outside each of the gates of the low-alpha-level houses, like a symbol of a still-untouched day, was a bottle of milk. Lupe's day had started forty-eight hours ago, and she got hold of the idea that the milk ought to be delivered to people's doorsteps—"Why ees the meelkman lazy? He should throw the meelk right onto the doorsteps, like the leetle paper-boy!" So she started delivering the milk, sailing the bottles through the predawn to shatter on the porches, and Johnny was too awestruck with laughter and love to stop her. They started to alternate bottles, then switched to one side of the street each, odd Lupe and even Johnny, until he finally picked her up and carried her to the Continental, not so much to call a halt as to parade her.

We put her to bed, stuck a mop and bucket in the trunk, bought a crate of milk and returned to Sunset Plaza Drive, where Tarzan and Cheeta spent the morning mopping up a couple of dozen porches, apologizing and signing autographs. That was the way it happened. I'm not quite sure if the story has a point, except to show that he was a naughty boy *and* a good boy, but she was just a wicked child. Perhaps you'd rather he hadn't thrown the bottles in the first place? But I prefer it that two things happened rather than nothing. *Life*, you know? Life adhered to him. The other point of the story is that he loved Lupe Vélez.

*Tarzan Finds a Son!* came out in June 1939, and within two weeks his complicated divorce from Lupe was made final. Jane might have annexed the escarpment, but in Hollywood he was now as free as a . . . as free as a human. For the first time, there was nobody to steal his attention or time away from me, a fact I relished during the ten minutes between his telling me "Hey, sport, guess what? I got divorced since I last saw ya!" and introducing an indistinct and very young woman standing on the porch of an unfinished house in Brentwood next door to Joan Crawford's as "My beautiful bride!"

Yes, I'll always treasure those Golden Minutes, as I think of them.

He'd met Beryl Scott, his fourth "lifetime partner," on the golf course at Pebble Beach during a pro-am, which enabled Red Skelton to cause much merriment at their reception by referring to her as the only "birdie" Johnny'd picked up that whole day! With a name like that, you'd expect her to be a movie star, but in fact she was the daughter of a wealthy rug merchant from San Francisco. She already had a career of her own as a Socialite, but she claimed to be willing to sacrifice this for the sake of the family Johnny wanted to build with her. I learned this that same afternoon, as she confided it to *la* Crawford over some stiff ones at the poolside "nook." Johnny was doing lengths of breast stroke, his head high out of the water in the famous style he'd originally developed in an attempt to stay clear of the excrement floating in the Chicago River.

"Aaah, this is civilized, isn't it?" Beryl kept saying. "These midges absolutely seem to adore me," she added, murdering one and not even eating it. "They don't like Johnny at all, but they love me." This was the exact opposite of the truth, I felt.

"That's Max Factor, isn't it, my dear? You've certainly hit it off, the way I do my lips. A lot of girls get it wrong because they don't have Max around to help."

"Max didn't, uh, I mean to say, I've never actually met Max."

"You can do this afternoon, if you like, between a quarter of four and ten after, if that's convenient for you." Joan gazed down like a sea eagle at Johnny, salmoning away happily in his new pool. Beryl's face, I thought, was bafflingly characterless: the only thing I could seem to keep in focus was in fact the Crawfordesque "hunter's bow" of her lips. "And then I'll let you get on with starting that family of yours. Is he your first? Fuck, I mean, not husband."

"Um, nooo, of course not," said Beryl. "What kind of girl do you think I am?"

"Well, you've done the easy bit. But this town's awfully hard on marriages. Get that family started now and you'll always have something in the bank should the weather turn stormy, God forbid. Get something banked."

So a year later, three months behind Joan's schedule (and Joan was a stickler for schedules, allotting as she did forty-five minutes for sexual intercourse each afternoon), Tarzan found another son. Johnny, he was called. During that period, he was working with Esther Williams in the Aquacade up at the Golden Gate International Exposition in San Francisco Bay, and Beryl moved back there to have the child.

I didn't see him at all over the course of that year, but I was run off my feet anyway, what with having to wake up, eat, defecate and occasionally move across my cage at MGM. I went on the wagon and quit smoking, allowing myself to slip up only when I was out-side the cage. I cut down on my American food and tried to eat a lit-tle more healthily. I went out for lunch with Niv, and to a couple of orgies up at Lionel Atwill's. I even had a dozen or so children of my own during an enjoyable trip out to Luna Park with the unchanging Gately. (Not once, ever, did my coach crack a smile.) And whenever I saw L.B. slaloming between the Rebs and the Cossacks and the pi-rates down the passageway in front of our cage, I tried to get across to him my wish that he should loan me out to another studio if there was no Tarzan picture imminent. I wanted to "work," but the great alphas had very little interest in what their stars wanted. L.B. was deaf to my pant-hoots, showed no sign of hearing me, and I be-gan to chafe again at the whole Dream Factory way of doing things.

"It's a gilded cage," John Huston, that animal-lover *par excel-lence*, once told me and Evelyn Keyes. "Glamour, glamour, glam-our, and underneath—control, control, control." He wasn't wrong; and during my layoff I began to recall just how many times I'd heard fellow dreamers talk about "escaping" Hollywood. I think, what with the escarpment having changed so, and Johnny being out of town, I went a little mad for a time.

It was in this mutinous frame of mind that I accompanied Errol Flynn and John Barrymore up to their house on Mulholland Drive in the spring of 1940. Flynn wanted me to do him a favor and help him out with some prank involving the WAMPAS girl he'd left asleep under the mirror attached to the ceiling of his bedroom. I was to take his place, so that when the starlet woke, I would be snoring beside her in lieu of, etc., etc. To help me into character and calm any performance-related nerves, Errol and John kept urging me to take another nip of Canadian Club—they were practically pouring it down my throat—so, I'm sorry to say, I can't remember how the evening or the prank panned out.

In fact, it was late the next day when Errol woke me, brushing aside my embarrassed attempts to apologize for the vomit and excrement I'd left on his sheets—too much of a gentleman to mention it—and carried me down the slope behind the house toward some low buildings where a number of humans were congregated. Stables and garages, I saw, as we neared them.

"Chris!" Errol shouted. "Chris!" A young man detached himself from the crowd pressed under the stable's eaves. "Drive this thing back to Metro, wouldja? They've been calling me about it all day." Typically generous of Errol to arrange transport for me, but at the same time I remember the plunging dismay I felt at having to return to the "gilded cage."

"Just ten minutes, Mr. Flynn? They're starting up in here."

"What, already? Shit, what time is it?" Flynn said. "Oh, fuckin' *Christ*, don't let me be too late. . . ."

We pushed through the crowd of humans into the depths of the stable where, in a recess in the floor, a huge alpha-male dog was rolling over and over; no, it was two dogs, rolling over and over in a blur and a spray of blood. Poor Errol, who was so famously distraught after those two hundred horses had died during the Warner Brothers' charge: he could hardly forgive himself for not getting there in time. You might ask—why didn't someone intervene? Surely the swashbuckling Flynn . . . ? Or Barrymore, who was at the front of the crowd, or Frank Borzage? Well, this wasn't the movies. You weren't there. There was no chance that any of the humans could do anything to save those dogs from themselves. They tried to get as close as they could but the dogs were in a trance of death, untouchable, dragging entrails and veins and still berserking, and the humans could do nothing but stand there, impotently hollering, and let Nature take its terrible course. It took a long time. Neither dog could be saved.

It shook me up, all right. How many times did I need reminding that I was one of the lucky, lucky few that the Project had been able to save? This dream of yours, to keep the animals of the world from destroying each other: it was too easy for some self-absorbed and pampered star like me, lolling away his days inside his Hollywood bubble, to forget about the real world out there. The question is, what's in it for you? Or is it just part of what it means to be human, to protect and serve us? Anyway, let's remember Errol like that, at his most debonair, before drink and drugs and a pathological sex addiction founded on misogyny turned him into the pathetic shell of a man he later became, too palsied even to be able to hold without spilling the drinks that were killing him.

I never again grumbled about my contract with Metro. L.B. was tireless in helping explain things to stars who had similar misgivings (which we all did at some point: actors!). He had an arm pretty much permanently around a dreamer's shoulder, clarifying how they'd be nothing if not for him, how if they couldn't play by his rules then it might not be possible to play at all, how important that new picture was with an expensive divorce coming up. Even Johnny needed a bit of guidance, and you often heard him quote L.B.'s advice back: "Who the hell do you think you are, you bum? Lillian Gish? Get it through your head—you're Tarzan! You're never going to be anybody but Tarzan! I'm not going to put you in any other pictures ever, you understand? So I don't want to hear any more horseshit about 'acting lessons'! Tarzan *not act*! Or I can get Buster Crabbe for half the price and nobody'll know the difference, and you can go back to selling swim trunks."

He was paying Johnny $2,500 a week, and if he wasn't working between Tarzan-Cheeta pictures, then it was merely sensible for MGM to loan him out (at $5,000 a week) to Billy Rose for the Aquacade. So twice a day, seven days a week, four hundred miles away, amid forty-foot fountains and cascading "aqua-curtains," he and seventy-two Aquabelles, the fifty-strong Fred Waring Glee Club Chorus, various Olympians, comedy divers, English Channel–swimmers, breath-holders and that inexcusable slander-ess and ingrate Esther Williams, the "Million-dollar Mermaid" (or "Two-bit Dugong," as I know her), all dedicated themselves to the praise of water, the element that hated me, that turned me away.

I heard little fragments around the commissary. Three months after little Johnny was born, Beryl sued for divorce. She claimed she never saw her husband, which I thought was pretty rich consider-ing she must have been seeing him several times a month. But I knew from Lupe that an annual accusation of "extreme cruelty" was part of the give and take of every marriage. Beryl wasn't out of the picture yet.

The summer of '41 we were back together for *Tarzan's Secret Treasure*, which wasn't, as I'd initially hoped, some Gaboni maiden Tarzan had become involved with on his trips away from the Happy House, but a seam of gold the Boy had discovered on the es-carpment. His mother's son in every respect, the Boy was intrigued by "civilin . . . civinil . . ." (aww, ain't it cute?)

"Civilization, dear."

"Tell me some more about civilization, Mother!"

"Oh, they have airplanes—houses with wings that fly and they carry people through the air. They go faster than anything *you*'ve ever seen."

"Faster than Tarzan?"

"Mm . . . faster than Tarzan, faster than the wind. But just you forget about civilization, darling." Tarzan had arrived and she was having to rein in. "Our world here is far more lovely and exciting than the outside world, I promise you." Thus Mark Antony manip-ulated the mob on the steps of the Capitol.

Naturally the Boy was soon off with a gold nugget or two to buy an airplane and inadvertently bring doom in the form of white men crashing down over us once again. Ho-hum. What the hey? We needed something to shake us up, anyway—the new *al fresco* dining area was like the fried-chicken table at L.B.'s fiftieth birthday/Fourth of July clambake. It was almost impassable with ostrich eggs, smoked wildebeest hams, catfish caviar and fruits of the forest. We'd installed a refrigerator the size of a Gaboni hut under the cold spring and had a new bain-marie system in the hot spring. But this is what happens when the love goes, when there is more time than love. What happens? The consecration of *lunch*.

Mmm, this is wonderful . . . how's yours?

I knew that something was wrong from the cars. The faithful old Continental had disappeared and been replaced with three different cars, which he alternated as if he wasn't quite comfortable in any of them. I'd never heard him express reverence for an automobile—he didn't really understand or even like anything that wasn't alive in some way—and the cars I took to be his inarticulate attempt to express something: happiness, perhaps, which he'd never needed to state before. Or unhappiness? How could you tell what was meant—other than that if you were speaking in *cars* something was already wrong? I noticed another couple in the car pool as we rolled up to a house four times the size of the Brentwood home a couple of weeks into the dreaming of *Secret Treasure*.

This was up on Rockingham Avenue, out by Mandeville Canyon—nice address. Looking down from the mansion's terrace, it was Johnny's domain as far as the eye could see. The lawn that rolled your eye down to the inevitable rectangle of turquoise was as densely iridescent as a hummingbird's breast. If you watched very closely you could see the dents left in it by the gardeners' footsteps disappear slowly back into its sheen, like the marks of fingers on a human arm. The pool house and its chaises, the tennis and badminton courts, the young maze and the gazebo all waited at the lawn's end with a doggy kind of servility, looking forward to being filled with memories. Turn your head, and blazing a trail to the summerhouse was an avenue of maples and exactly a dozen copper beeches, which Clark Twelvetrees had had transplanted there as a gift to his wife Helen before he drank himself to death in bitterness at her success.

Helen Twelvetrees—no? No idea? And that's a name I once told myself no one would ever forget. Over the course of the thirties, Helen's profile declined dramatically (though it was still a while before she'd be killed by a handful of sleeping pills) and she had to give up the house—to Charles Laughton and his wife Elsa (*The Bride of Frankenstein*) Lanchester. But with Elsa refusing to bear Charlie's children on account of his homosexuality (though the inimitable Maureen O'Hara always claimed Elsa's own litany of abortions was the real reason) Charlie was thrown into despair and the Laughtons moved on, leaving the Weissmullers to inherit this little slice of paradise, so richly steeped in Hollywood memories.

"Tarzan bring Cheeta! Meet real-life Jane!" Johnny shouted across the terrace, to where Beryl was sitting playing bridge (a sort of female variant of bluffing or packing) with other young females under a tasseled umbrella. I contributed a brief pant-hoot. Beryl waved an acknowledgment. "Go fix yourself a stinger, darling," she said, though I was already on the linen-draped bar trying, essentially, to communicate the same thing. "I've met Cheeta, remember? The day it attacked Joan?" Well, hardly, I thought.

"Well, hardly," said Johnny. "Joan frightened her, was all. Him, I mean. Hey—what's the definition of a Jimmy Cagney love scene?"

"What?"

"When he lets the other guy live!" Johnny staggered gut-shot across the terrace toward the tight smiles of the bridge players. *I* thought it was funny. "My wonderful wife," he said, kissing her nothingy-brown macaquelike hair.

"My wonderful husband," she said.

After a while he said, "I thought maybe I'd hit a few balls."

"Well, we'll watch you. Keep an eye on that left arm!"

"Left arm straight. Shoulders relaxed like a pendulum. Mmm, these stingers are good!"

"Yes, aren't they heavenly? Rita's specials. Keep that chest opened. Soft hands, hard wrists. Three hearts."

"Okay, coach." Johnny demonstrated a swing and held the follow-through. "*Aaaaahhheeyyeeeyyeeaahheeyeeyeeeaaaaaah*," he added apologetically, for my benefit, I think. I came running, anyway. Not because I particularly yearned to practice short irons with him, but because at that moment, for the first—though not the last—time, I felt that he needed me.

Did I ever mention that he loved Lupe Vélez? Whatever I thought of the adulterous canicidal bitch, I'd never doubted that he'd loved her, just as she, in her own tormented way, had loved him. It had never crossed my mind to be jealous or to wish her away, because she was capable of making him happy. But here with Beryl there wasn't anything—there was just . . . nothing at all. I knew it after two minutes on the terrace, because I'm a chimp and I could smell it; and I can read the language of human bodies. I could, in the days when the humans I met were standing up rather than lying in hospital beds, read that bent left arm, those unrelaxed shoulders, those closed chests. I could read the sexlessness of Robert Taylor and Barbara Stanwyck's marriage in Barbara's quick tense wrists, the pathological compulsion to deceive in Esther Williams's laugh, the deep sense of intellectual inferiority that Kate Hepburn's face was continually, heroically, trying to conceal. Actually, what am I talking about? Anybody could read those things! But there was something stolid in Beryl's movements that told an observant eye how dull she found her own body. It was like the cautiousness of age. He had married somebody he couldn't play with. And that was all Johnny ever really wanted: someone he could play with. I knew how his hands itched to pick up ankles and wheelbarrow-race women or boys or even other adult males across the seventeenth green. I knew how his feet itched to creep up behind humans unaware of his presence, to lift 'em off their feet in a bear hug. He wanted someone to climb him while he held their shoes high above their head. He could sublimate it into sexual intercourse, but all he ever really wanted was to play.

Beryl liked to play bridge. Her other sports, I'd come to learn, were canasta and pinochle. The high point of their non-sexual play together would have come on a Pebble Beach fairway within the first ten minutes of their relationship, I guessed, and would have consisted of Johnny enfolding her from behind, reassuring and warm, demonstrating with his huge hands folding over hers certain aspects of a good swing. Looking at Beryl, you might suppose that'd be the high point of their non-non-sexual play too. She'd have giggled a lot during her tutorial, and Johnny would have mistaken her nervousness for a sense of humor, or at any rate, it would have done to cover up the fact that she had even less of a sense of humor than Chaplin or Red Skelton—some kind of absolute zero of humor.

I had never seen him look alone before. At full tilt I sprang off the bar and knuckled across the terrace, leaped to his waist and wriggled up into the violin-space under his chin. He lifted his stinger high above his head, playfully, where I couldn't quite get at it, and with his left hand he smoothed my fur. "Ah, Cheets, Cheets," he said, switching his drink from right hand to left as I got close to it. "Ain't I the luckiest guy in the world?"

From over the wall, as if to affirm this, came the voice of the tour guide—"Twelve after four! Bang on schedule!" said Beryl—gently enveloping us like the mist from a crop-spraying plane.

". . . the Hunchback of Notre Dame himself and the Bride of Frankenstein: Charles Laughton and Elsa Lanchester. Today it does service as one heck of a luxury treehouse for Tarzan himself, Olympic gold medal–winning swim champ Johnny Weissmuller, and his very own real-life Jane." All of us on the terrace held ourselves still to listen: we formed an idyllic tableau. "Johnny and his glamorous wife Beryl were blessed last summer with a little Boy of their own, and decided they needed a Jungle Hut big enough to . . ."

Yeah, that was just about right, I thought, as Johnny pitched a bucket of Top Flites toward me across the liquid lawn, which Beryl had already warned him not to allow me to defecate upon. "His very own real-life Jane" was just about right. At Rockingham Avenue we might as well have been back on the escarpment, bowed under Jane's tyranny, with everything clenched and perfect and simply marvelous; where everything was in its right place and the two empty-eyed adults were so desperate to assure each other of what a paradise they had.

On the escarpment itself, where we might as well have been on Rockingham Avenue, I was seriously beginning to wonder whether Jane was having a breakdown of sorts.

"Jane like Tarzan?" he asked one afternoon, handing her a propitiatory orchid after another marathon lunch.

Cleverly she evaded the direct response he was craving. "What woman wouldn't like a husband who brings her orchids?"

"There's a whole valley of orchids just across the river," the Boy jeeringly observed.

"I know, darling, but out in civilization they don't grow that way," she tinkled. "You have to be very rich to have them. You don't realize what a very wealthy man your father is."

"Who—Tarzan?"

"Yes. He has everything any man could want. *Everything*."

She just wouldn't lay off with the propaganda—drip, drip, fucking drip, like she was trying to mesmerize him. And, silly me, there I was thinking that Miriam Hopkins had had a point up at Atwill's when she had guided Fernando Lamas's sexual organ into her anal tract and breathed, "That's what you men really fucking want, don't you?" In fact, I remember very well the list of the things Fernando went on to claim that he wanted, all of which he persuasively emphasized were "normal—what any man would want." I'm prepared to bet my entire stash of cigarettes that Jane was not providing these up at the Treehouse of Tidiness. Dutifully, slightly behind the beat, he picked her up and swung her around.

"Tarzan have Jane."

"Ooooh! Akhahahkhahka!" she said. Transcribing Jane's laugh isn't easy—it tinkled like base metal. "Ooooh! You have Jane, all right, and you're going to have me in a thousand pieces in a minute if you're not careful!"

!?, I was thinking. Like: *!?* The escarpment had stopped being a dream some while back; by *Secret Treasure* it had become a full-blown nightmare. I tried to keep my head down and show a bit of loyalty, but Jane's ever-vigilant hostility toward me had now given birth to a new strategy—no matter how faithful or stoic I might act, she had me typed as a "naughty" chimp, a mischief-maker.

For example, I'm struggling toward the dining area with a couple of hard-boiled ostrich eggs still steaming from the hot spring. Because I can't hold both of them at once I've got one on my head and I'm trying to nudge the other across the lawn with my feet.

"Now, Cheeta," gesturing with a knife, "you bring those eggs over here and no monkey business! No monkey business, Cheeta! Now, come on, do you hear? Hurry up!" What the hell did she . . . what "monkey business"? You'll have to watch it yourself, I guess. Or: I'm enjoying a grape during a brief break in my duties. "Cheeta! You've had enough grapes! Come on, help with the dishes!" The *unfairness*, the lack of logic, the drip, drip, fucking drip. . . . "Take the dishes down to the river and wash them. And don't break them!"

The Boy picked up on it, too. In the year and a half since *Tarzan Finds a Son!* he had developed into a strolling braggart and lout, clattering with laughter as he beaned the occasional curious hyena or demoralized leopard with a stone from his sling. It wasn't even *realistic*. What kind of human was deliberately cruel to innocent animals? You're just not like that. "Got him, right on the nose!" he crowed, brushing aside my protests. "Aah, don' worry, Cheedah, he had it comin' ta him. He's always makin' trouble!" The elephant calf he'd enslaved he actually *called* Bully.

And there was an even greater worry, although it was uncommented upon by the rest of the zombified jungle family: Emma had disappeared. Exhausted, perhaps, by years of mindlessly tugging Jane's elevator up and down. Or had Metro waited until it was expedient and canceled her contract because of the altercation with her trainer? The alphas never forgot. Whatever had happened, nobody (*except Johnny*, whom I'd heard asking) referred to her absence, because nobody liked to conjure up failure's specter in Hollywood. Once you were out, to all intents and purposes you were dead: yet another pile of bleached tusks and ribs in the Graveyard.

It was all making me extremely nervous. No love; no fun; animals being bullied by a brat; whole reels devoted to lunch; swashbuckling washing-up sequences and a browbeaten serf-monkey suffering continual abuse. A dreamer such as myself, I like to think,

*Study in Purple and Turquoise #6: "Water"* (2001).

The wives of Johnny Weissmuller. In his element with second wife Bobbe Arnst.

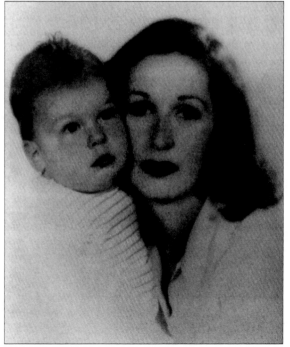

Fourth wife Beryl Scott, with Johnny's son, Johnny Jr., whom Beryl feared I intended to eat.

Johnny and his fifth wife Allene Gates on their wedding day in 1948. Sadly, their union, which I believe was a happy one, came to an end after thirteen years.

Countess Gertrudis Maria Theresia Brock Mandell née Bauman, or Maria Bauman, was Johnny's sixth wife. She was a "Countess" in the bars along Sunset Strip, anyway.

ABOVE: Publicity still for *Tarzan's Secret Treasure* (1941), perhaps. Note the order in which we're lined up on this live oak branch: Tarzan and Boy are acting as buffers between Jane and me. Despite the smiles, I think the tension in the air is palpable.

LEFT: Rehearsing one of several classic comic routines from *Tarzan's New York Adventure* (1942). On the other end of the line is a bemused colored gentleman, who believes he is the victim of a telephonic hate crime. It was funny at the time.

ABOVE: No still can capture the unbearable tension of RKO's *Tarzan and the Leopard Woman* (1946) but this comes close. Thank Christ the Leopard Woman (far left), in an uncharacteristic lapse, left her claw-scepter unattended long enough for me to snatch it and use it to cut through Tarzan's bonds, otherwise we'd have been totally fucked!

BELOW: I look about as comfortable in this still from Fox's catastrophic *Doctor Dolittle* (1967) as I ought to. Personal differences with a co-star ended my involvement in the shoot early, but not early enough. Lousy picture, lousy performance, lousy box office.

*Rock Formations, Dusk, Joshua Tree National Park* (1997). An interesting failure, if I'm being wholly honest.

*The Horror of War* (2008). Probably my best recent work.

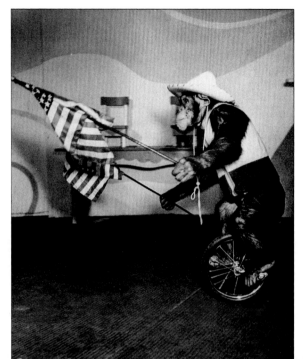

My pioneering work in the field of entertainment opened up a host of opportunities for other animals, I'm told. In other areas, too, there were mid-century breakthroughs. Below, Ham relaxes before his Apollo test flight, 1961.

Thanks to my companion and housemate Don's commercial acumen, the Sanctuary has kept its head above water for over two decades. We allow only the highest-quality merchandise to be associated with my name, though the market response to these was disappointing.

The two of us.

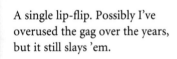

A single lip-flip. Possibly I've overused the gag over the years, but it still slays 'em.

Family snap. My grandson Jeeter at the Sanctuary, Palm Springs.

has a natural grasp of what his audience wants, and I didn't believe that this was what the American public was after. I mean, who wants to see a noble human, the very image of a God, who has lived for an untold period at peace among the beasts of the forest, cast out of paradise because of his wife's inability to resist the lure of "improvements"? A downer of a story like that—it's not what people want to hear. Since the early thirties Johnny and Maureen's fan mail had declined, I knew. I assumed mine was holding steady, or was at least still more than Rex the Wonder Dog's cutoff point. But it was a serious situation: *Tarzan Finds a Son!*, with its tragic ending, had been released in certain dream-palaces as a *second feature.*

Well, I have a motivational dream that still taps on the mesh of my consciousness once a year or so, a little more frequently recently, I've noticed. I'm working in the medical research center and my fellow interns are all sitting across from me: the hairless one, the one that can't breathe, the white-eyed macaques, the dogs that Errol couldn't save, Emma, Gary, Otto—and one of them will open its mouth and out'll come the little voice: *Survive, survive, survive.* My pep-talk dream, as I like to think of it! At the time I was having that dream almost nightly. Because at the rate things were going I wasn't going to be around much longer. "Oh, Tarzan," she would say one day soon, "Cheeta's broken the fondue set again. Every week it's something else. Don't you think it's time that we, you know . . . ?" *Survive, survive, survive . . .*

*Fight back.*

I found my inspiration when rummaging through the safari bag of one of our visitors, Mr. O'Doul (Barry Fitzgerald). It was a bottle of whiskey, the first alcohol the escarpment had ever seen. I thought, If I'm to be ridiculed as Jane's "naughty" monkey then why shouldn't I give 'em the *real* naughty Cheeta? The one Kay

Francis once fondly described as "the most fun I've had since my mother died. Thanks for a delightful evening, Johnny!" as she picked out the ice cubes I'd popped down her cleavage? *Cheeta, you've had enough grapes!* It couldn't go on. Let Jane do her worst, let's at least have a little fun around here. Let's at least put some of the joy back into the jungle. Let's have a laugh. I'd picked up a few giggles here and there before, but essentially I was a heroic figure: a noble rescuer, a saver of days with a humorous edge. Comedy-thriller work, with the emphasis on "thriller." Fuck it, I thought—tossing the cap in the undergrowth, unaware that I was making one of the crucial artistic decisions of my career, I'll just be myself.

Of course (you're way ahead of me), I'm talking about *Tarzan's Secret Treasure*'s seminal "Drunk/Postage-Stamps-On-Foot-Then-Hand" sequence. Opinion in the profession is divided as to whether you ought to *be* drunk in order to play drunk. Personally, I don't think you can give of your best if you're not sober—the bottle you see on screen was actually full of cold tea (I'd already finished the whiskey)—and so I was pleasantly surprised by how well the scene turned out, considering how unbelievably drunk I was. Four minutes and thirty-two seconds of pure magic, for which I'd like to thank my old teacher, Mr. Gately, who was tireless in helping me focus throughout an arduous day's shooting.

It's been argued that my work in this scene and in the dreams that followed was the single biggest cause of, or influence on, the boom in chimpanzee-related entertainment that adorned Western culture from the late forties through to the end of the century. J. Fred Muggs of the *Today* show, the Marquis Chimps and their marvelous swing band, Zippy the chimp from *Howdy Doody*, Liberchimpski, that amusing pianist, *Lancelot Link the Secret Chimp*, the special agent: I'm told that my pioneering mid-period comic work opened the doors for all these stars and many more. You can imagine how proud that makes me feel. To have contributed, if only in a small way . . . it's not something I like to talk about. Rather, I think I'll take a leaf out of Henry Trefflich's book. Here's a man who, if you remember, was so dedicated to the Project that he personally helped rehabilitate nearly a million and a half macaque monkeys. Yet over the course of his whole autobiography he mentions it, glancingly, only once! That's modesty. But I'm not quite a Trefflich and I don't think I can resist quoting a few of my notices.

At this point I ought to come clean. I know all this stuff because Don bought a bunch of old movie magazines at a collectors' fair, photocopied selected parts from the reviews and then had the whole thing framed. Not in the john, either. It's in the den, propped on a table in the Memorabilia Corner. Anyway:

*New York Times:* ". . . comic relief provided by Cheta, the Martha Raye of chimpanzees, who would tear herself into little bits to give you a laugh, and whose wild and Corybantic cacchination at opportune moments is a joy and an affront to hear."

*Toronto Star:* "Cheta the chimp steals the show every time she's around."

*Hollywood Film Daily:* ". . . comedy antics of the pet simian Cheta help somewhat with elemental laughs."

*Motion Picture Herald:* "The most interesting of the performers is probably the chimpanzee, who seems to be forever laughing at her human companions."

*Variety:* "This addition to the series is in the groove for juves at least, due to the extraordinary amount of footage the director gave and the cutter permitted to remain to the antics of the trained chimp . . . quite enjoyable."

The critics were unanimous. As an actor, it was the new direction I'd been searching for since *Tarzan Escapes*. But, most importantly, it wrong-footed Jane. She'd be shouting, "Cheeta, stop that! Don't you dare!" and behind the cameras you'd hear, "Keep rolling. Keep him going, Gately. L.B. wants more of the chimp. Gonna be a long day, Maureen." Ah, sweet vindication. You want me to stop? Well, L.B. doesn't. I was mocking her cherished "civilization" openly and the preview cards were saying they liked it. The cards were saying, "It was good when Cheta had the whiskey and fell over. Fun-nee!" and "It was exiting but it was boring sometimes but it was funny with the bit with the Chita" and "Monkey was best actor in it." Why, I was keeping us alive! By the time of the late masterpiece *Cheeta Engages Jane the Betrayer in a Final Battle for Tarzan's Soul*, or, as it was disappointingly titled for the theatrical release, *Tarzan's New York Adventure*, I was pretty much carrying the whole thing.

None of which made the slightest bit of difference to what was happening at Rockingham Avenue. I would never in a million years have dreamed of interfering between Johnny and one of his lifetime mates. He'd made his commitment to Beryl in the form of little Johnny and now another baby called Wendy, and he didn't want to walk out on what he'd built. I absolutely respected that. But he wasn't happy. And this meant that things were very difficult, since Beryl had made it clear on my first visit to the mansion that I was there on sufferance. Like the original Jane, she was implacably opposed to the animal kingdom. The mansion was full of mouse- and rat-traps; the gardeners were under orders to gas all moles; there were even, dotting the flowerbeds, little traps made of half-shells of grapefruit to kill slugs. Slugs! Now, they *really* aren't dangerous.

"It may be well trained, darling, but it's only been here ten minutes and it's already smashed one of our best jugs," Beryl said— true, I'd accidentally knocked over those stingers, but the Gaboni serving-girl had frightened me, "and I won't have it running amok doing its business in the house or the garden."

And that was exactly what I'd been planning on doing! That was the whole point of being there, to have a little fun, a couple of drinks, walk around the terrace on my hands with a bottle between my feet, climb up the avocado trees and lob some fruit-bombs among the Gaboni gardeners . . . to cheer Johnny up a little, take him out of himself. But I couldn't do that because Beryl would have me out of there the moment I showed any sign of having fun. I didn't even *smoke.*

So on my rare visits we were a subdued pairing: he flighting an infinity of white balls in somehow sadly perfect arcs toward me, and me faithfully scurrying after them with the bucket they'd come from banging painfully against my knees, putting them back so we could do it all over again. And up on the terrace the real-life Jane, visibly without a sense of humor from two hundred and fifty yards away, periodically raising her head to ascertain that I was keeping out of mischief and not defecating on her lawn. He sent the Top Flites over to me, I thought, like signals of distress. Those beautiful towering smooth arcs he made the balls describe were like a series of gorgeous vine-swings, great loops and curves that became, when they thumped onto the lawn, just a hard little white ball as disappointing as the important thing you wanted to say is when you finally remember it. *Don't look at me*, I tried to communicate to him via kindly but disapproving-sounding cheeping. *You were the one who married her, you idiot.*

Why had he married her? This woman who was fifteen years younger than he but was in every other respect his senior? Maybe because he wanted her to stop him being a boy. Always at heart an essentially obedient human, he could, with fatherhood, cars, mansion and bridge-playing aristocratic non-Hollywood wife, at least stage an impersonation of the prevailing version of male adulthood. Or maybe he'd only married her because Lupe had tired his heart out.

When we'd finished with the golf, we'd usually walk down to the pool, where I'd putter around while he did his high-headed laps of breaststroke, still trying to keep himself clear of the shit. He was thirty-eight now. It was nearly a decade since we'd first met. You saw his aging in the loss of symmetry in his face, in the white untanned lines that now spoked across his sixteen-and-a-half-inch neck. He was twenty-five pounds heavier; he was no longer the most beautiful human being on Planet Earth. But as he stepped into the trousers he'd hung (along their creases—always impeccable) over a chaise, he still looked good enough, like someone who'd say, "Still good enough," when he looked in the mirror, lying only a little with the muscles of his stomach. "OK, sport, I'll get Pete to run you back to Metro now." He had everything a man could want, everything, except a happy marriage.

It could have been a paradise. I mean, I could have *lived* there, nested down in an avocado tree at nights, waking to an early breakfast with him on the terrace before driving down to Culver City to work on *New York Adventure*, which we'd gone straight into after *Secret Treasure*. Yes, finally Jane had had her way. The Boy had been kidnapped from the escarpment and taken to New York (a likely story: I suspected she'd arranged the whole thing herself), and at last she had the excuse she needed to take us away from the forest into "civilization."

Tarzan was encased in a double-breasted suit; Jane found time, despite the urgency of the hunt for her henchman, to model a succession of elegant twinsets and inexplicable headgear; I wore whatever hats or amusing garments I could lay my hands on. But how New York had changed! I'm kidding—I *had* been looking forward to going back there, but the whole thing was dreamed up on the soundstage at Metro. So it was under the kliegs in the studio that Jane and I finally had it out. I took heart from the memory of Kong. After all, it was in New York that *he*'d defeated his enemies and found peace with his beloved human.

Greatest damn city on earth. In New York, after all the grief of the last five years, the Betrayer was revealed to be nothing more than a paper tyrant. Everywhere we went, I mocked civilization and she tried to chastise me. But the New Yorkers were wise to her. Nobody was listening. New York finished Jane.

First thing I did in Immigration was help myself to a drink from a watercooler. I got into a bit of a tangle with the paper-cup dispenser, spilled a few of the cups, munched a few up, sprayed some water about, that sort of thing . . . and, of course, she was furious. "Cheeta! What *are* you doing? Stop that right now!" I raised my head wearily. A whole crowd of New Yorkers, however, was vigorously encouraging me to continue. Were, in fact, splitting their sides in a way I'd seldom achieved on the Beverly Hills social circuit. "Oh, I'm sorry," she tried to apologize for me, "she gets a little . . . ahakhakahka . . . playful sometimes!" No need to apologize, sweetheart: they don't mind.

And then, to my surprise, poor old ball-busted Tarzan actually stepped in to defend me: "Cheeta thirsty!"

Same story at the nightclub we visited. I started fooling around with the hatcheck girls, tossing a few hats around because I . . . because I like to throw hats around, that's why, and Jane was trying to upbraid me: "Cheeta, how could you? Aren't you ashamed of yourself?" But you could tell from the indulgent smiles on the faces of the citizens of the fine city of New York where their sympathies lay. You could tell they were thinking, Why's the cool chimp hanging out with this Limey prig with the nickel up her ass? He's a riot! Kid, ditch the broad with the phony accent and come up to the Village with us. . . . This is why I query the title. *Tarzan's New York Adventure* has an adventure tacked onto it, to do with the little bullyboy's kidnapping, but in essence it's one long comic showpiece for me, fooling with taxicab drivers, mugging on taxicab roofs, with gavels in courtrooms and the bell at Reception. It's the picture by which I'll be judged: Maureen O'Sullivan's last Tarzan picture.

She knew the game was up. She trailed me everywhere with injunctions and prohibitions but the power she'd wielded in the Treehouse was gone. Gately and I spent half an afternoon working on a set piece with a listening device that had the crew in stitches. "Cheeta, Cheeta, give me that telephone" (that's the word!), "right away! Don't you dare touch it . . . etc., etc., etc." She knew she couldn't stop me—L.B. wanted more, the fine citizens of New York wanted more, the dream-palaces of America wanted more.

The centerpiece of the whole picture, and the fatal blow to the bitch's credibility, was the "hotel room" sequence. "A rambunctious simian romp," you'll remember the *New York Times* described it. Perhaps, or perhaps "a clear-eyed and corrosively satirical denunciation of a tyrant" would have been more accurate. Chaplin had Hitler in *The Great Dictator*; I had Jane. I'll leave you and the American Film Institute to judge which was the more successful in skewering its target, only commenting that Maureen left Metro immediately afterward, whereas I don't really think Hitler was very bothered by Chaplin's barbs, do you? Eh, Charles? He invaded Poland. But Maureen went into semiretirement.

I subtly deconstructed Jane right there in the hotel room. I took the Hitler of the Jungle to pieces. I started by exposing the fact that she had, though supposedly sleepless with anxiety over the Boy, remembered to pack in her darling little traveling case several pairs of gloves, makeup, makeup remover, various nightwear and *garters*. Some mother! I finished by vainly prancing in front of the mirror with her stockings on my talcum-dusted head, as grotesque a satire on "refinement" and "poise" and all her fake values as I could manage. Don loves to play this sequence on DVD nights, but I don't think he grasps the savagery of the satire. Mayer did. "Rushes with chimp antics OK," L.B. wrote, sanctioning what I was doing to his former Golden Girl.

You see, Louis B. Mayer liked to think that he knew more about American family values than anyone in the country. He knew, just like the rest of America, and indeed the rest of humanity, what had gone wrong on the escarpment. We'd had a paradise in our grasp and in its stead she'd put labor-saving devices, table manners, dish-washing, refrigerators and elevators, overhead fans and leopard-skin interior design, materialism and denial. Mayer didn't want American children growing up with these phony suburban values. Jane's Reich was a lie, a fake Eden that depended on the slave labor of animals. The Happy House? Mom in her kitchen, Pop hunting and gathering from nine to five, subhuman servants knowing their place? Mayer saw it for the nightmare it was. Let it burn.

And that was the end of one of human cinema's great villains: Jane Parker. In the movies, of course, it usually works out in the end. Now all I had to do was get rid of the Jane on Rockingham Avenue.

Chapter 8 has been removed on legal advice.

# 9
# New Challenges!

You know there are slightly more tigers in America today than there are left in the wild? It should be stressed that that's not a cause for celebration just yet: the job's only half finished. An immense amount remains to be done, of course, and you should be proud of what's been achieved so far. One day soon the rest of us will be able to walk, hop and scurry safely through these wonderful new tigerless—and leopardless? a personal request—forests in relative peace. And it's win-win, isn't it? Even the tigers reap the benefit—there are no long, hungry, bad-hunting stretches in rehab, no frightening alphas moving in on your girl. Like with polar bears and seals: good news for seals, great news for the rehoused bears, all thanks to your ingenious "global warming" idea! But making sure that no animal, anywhere, has to put up with the daily threat of death—that's going to take a little longer.

Yes, destroying the forests themselves helps, but we need to get those percentages turned around. We don't want seven thousand orangutans left in the wild compared to a couple thousand in secure accommodation—we want that reversed. There are more than seven hundred mountain gorillas stranded out there in Uganda—that's still more than there are in rehab. How can the two hundred blue iguanas in American zoos really rest easy, knowing there are twelve of their brethren still marooned out there on Grand Cayman? Chimps? Well, there's a hell of a lot fewer of us out there, and a lot more of us in here, but it's not fifty–fifty yet. So let's use the tiger as a symbol, shall we? Let's get there, to fifty–fifty, and then we can move on toward success stories like the pygmy three-toed sloth or the giant sable antelope. Let's get to fifty–fifty before we start talking about 100 percent.

But then sometimes I think, Duh, Cheeta, you damn Pollyanna, look at them. They know what they're doing. I look at your dear human faces and I feel certain that, deep down, you *know* it's going to happen. You know it: one day, not so very far off, those 100 percents are going to start racking up like the points on a basketball scoreboard. One day soon *all* the animals are going to get to live with you. And we'll all have access to insulin or Warfarin or Aricept or antibiotics, or even SSRIs; we'll all have miraculously low stress levels, and birthday parties and TV shows that are supposedly our favorites, and one day, we'll all be famous . . . I reckon we're all going to make it, in the end, thanks to you and your War on Death.

The thing with the fish used to worry me. Sure, things were safer for tuna and barracuda with the sharks and the marlins out of the picture, but what did the tuna eat? Smaller fish, surely: grunion and sardines, whatever. What about those? Wouldn't they be safer without the tuna and the barracuda? But then those grunion and sardines were themselves making life hell for the sprats and the whitebait and it just didn't make any sense . . . until I belatedly figured it out with a little help from a PBS documentary, which completely restored my faith in humanity. They're getting rid of *all of them*, you dummy. The death-teeming seas just cannot be helped. Only you, I thought in awe, only you could be so audacious, so inspired as to conceive a plan to clear the oceans of the planet of all the death that teems in them.

It's only a pity that you'll no longer be able to console the heart-broken by telling them about the fish in the sea. But, for heaven's sake, who's to say there's going to *be* any heartbroken when this all comes to fruition?

Just as we were wrapping *New York Adventure*, a bunch of little brown monkeys attacked Pearl Harbor and plunged America into a murderous hierarchical dispute! No, it was just a bit of misinfor-mation "Duke" Wayne passed on to me in the panic of the immedi-ate aftermath, though the rumor stubbornly persisted for years. It turned out to be the Japanese, which was disappointing consider-ing their backbreakingly heroic work on the marine aspects of the Project.

Tragically, one of the first Americans killed in the line of duty was my old friend Carole Lombard. She was traveling back to Holly-wood from a war-bond rally when her plane lost its bearings (navi-gational lights on the ground had been blacked out) and crashed into a mountain near Vegas, killing her and twenty-two other possi-bly equally special human beings. Johnny was traveling around the country giving demonstrations of how to survive burning oil slicks if your ship were to be torpedoed, so I had nobody to take me to Carole's funeral, and I particularly wanted to go because I hadn't been allowed to participate in the three-minute silence that was held for her at the MGM commissary. Gable was devastated—he never really recovered. And in general it hit the dreamers hard. It wasn't a death like, say, Emma's or Clara Bow's, where you weren't supposed to talk about it, and I remember being struck by how downhearted the humans were. "It happens to us all . . ." I kept hearing. "We've all gotta go sometime." "When your number's up, your number's up."

It was this damn senseless war that made everybody so gloomy about their prospects, I thought. I was out at Irene Dunne's one evening when I overheard William Powell tell Jane Russell that "The two inevitable things in life, as Mark Twain had it, are death and taxis." Taxis, sure: wherever there are humans there'll be cars, there's no doubting that. And those cars will doubtless always include taxis. But death? Bill had once been married to Carole and, after Jean Harlow's husband killed himself, had been involved with her until her kidneys killed her in '37, so perhaps his gloom was understandable.

I wanted to shake him and the rest of the humans out of it. Don't be so damned fatalistic! Of course death's always a danger, but you ought to hear some of the guys I meet on my trips out to the hospices in Palm Springs. These are guys—and some of them, I have to say, don't look in all that terrific shape—who are always delighted to greet me and Don with a cheerful invitation to their hundredth birthday parties. They say things like "See you next month, kid. I'm not planning on dying any time before then. I'm not planning on dying, period!" and they see us off with a "You keep going and I'll keep going!" pact. They don't have this pessimistic inevitability thing that you sometimes hear among humans. In fact, they're insatiable for tips on how not to die. After "Where's Johnny?," the question they always ask me is, "What's your secret?"

What's my secret? Isn't it obvious? There isn't any. Except, maybe, this: the ones who believe they're going to make it are the ones who always do.

But the Second World War was a tragedy. It was a terrible shock to me to discover that chimpanzees were not the only species to practice organized murder. "Why men have to kill each other?" was Tarzan's take on it in *Tarzan Triumphs*. You were such innocents, thinking that you were uniquely wicked. You didn't know anything. I wanted to say, Don't be so hard on yourselves! But I also thought, Ah, go ahead, be hard on yourselves. You really ought to be ashamed, carrying on no better than a pack of animals, with all your advantages. And, goddammit, not only was the war responsible for taking Johnny away from Los Angeles for extended periods but the downturn in foreign sales (which had always formed a major part of the success of the Tarzan series) meant that MGM decided to let their option lapse, and the series passed to Sol Lesser at RKO. Senseless madness!

On the bright side, Johnny's two children meant he wasn't likely to be called up to fight. And if he was rarely in town any longer, at least he wasn't trapped like a slug in a halved grapefruit at Rockingham Avenue. I thought he'd be happy. I *knew* he'd be happy, kidding around with teenage GIs, kids from the Midwest who'd never seen the sea, showing them, hoarse from giving Tarzan yells, how to swim, how to dive, how not to die. . . .

But I missed him. After an unfortunate and rather public incident that ensued when I encountered Dietrich at the Hollywood Canteen (not my fault—she'd frightened me), my social life had undergone something of a contraction. I also ought to mention the run-in I had with the inimitable Maureen O'Hara—not a clever move after the Dietrich incident (there were only so many times you could get away with the being-frightened thing), but she'd made a comment about Johnny. It isn't anything worth repeating, but I rose to it—and the sad truth is I owe Maureen an apology. The sad truth is that I'd hoped, what with Hollywood being such a village, Johnny might get to hear about it somehow. It didn't seem too far-fetched to picture him laughing down the phone in some Midwestern hotel room, asking after me and getting a detailed account of how I'd tried to defend him. How else could I get in touch? I liked to think of Niv telling him ("Apparently, Cheeta took one look at her and without further ado, in front of the whole party . . .") but it turned out that Niv was in England, fighting in the goddamn war.

I was at the pinnacle of my profession. This was the period after Rin Tin Tin's memory had faded but before Pal the collie had his triumph in *Lassie Come Home*. Roy Rogers' sidekick Trigger, the amusing (to children) trick-performing horse, was pretty big in B's. Archibald the Boa Constrictor's comedy thrillers with Shirley Temple were not yet *kidding*, just kidding! Along with Trigs, I was pretty much the most famous animal on earth. But how famous is that? Without Johnny around, I felt sometimes a little neglected by my fellow legends.

The transfer to RKO had meant a change of residency to the Selig zoo in Lincoln Heights and there were no more impromptu lunches at the Metro commissary. Instead, the company of ba-boons, a view of giraffes and the Santa Monica mountains behind, and a faint sense of having been shifted from the center of things.

It probably did me good to get out of the human social whirl. I was back on the wagon, off the smokes, and able to concentrate on family affairs, fathering a few dozen more kids. I lived quietly, kept my head down, and every day I pictured how things might be on the escarpment without *her*. The Boy was young enough still to be cured of the time-disease his mother had infected him with; creep-ers and vines could be allowed slowly to finger their way back across the breakfast bar in the Treehouse; the forest could reclaim us; we could live there happily ever after. Yeah, that's what we could do. To *live happily ever after*, that was the plan.

So I didn't feel any bitterness toward Metro. If L.B. had decided we'd be better off with Lesser and RKO, then it was probably the right call, just like his decision to cover up the 1937 gang-rape of Patricia Douglas at an MGM stag party by bribing several key witnesses and her *mother*. Plus Mr. Lesser had plenty of energy; he had some terrific ideas (leopard-worshipping death cults! Giant spider attacks! Girls!); he had scriptwriters of the caliber of Marjorie L. Pfaelzer, his daughter; he had a new escarpment at the Los Angeles State and County Arboretum, located in a little suburb just north of L.A. which went by the promising name of Arcadia.

He had also come up with a brilliant solution to the absence of Jane. Like it or not, her treachery had helped fill the dream-palaces. Yes, she'd been defeated and banished. The word was she was finally back in her beloved London, "nursing the wounded" in the war. But this left us with the problem of replacing the series' long-running villain. Who could possibly fill the hole left by Jane? Nazis, of course! Lesser was a genius. Apparently the Nazis were interested in the rich mineral deposits that could be mined from the lost Kingdom of Palandria, just around the corner from the escarpment!

I was absolutely delighted at the prospect of contributing to the war effort. All I'd managed to do so far was to bite Marlene Dietrich, who had turned out, to my annoyance, to be what they called a "good" German. If Dietrich was a good German, I thought, then the bad ones must be absolutely fucking terrifying. Count me in.

So in Arcadia, in a jump cut, as it were, I was back in his arms again. "Oof, sport, you've put on a few pounds! You're getting too heavy for me." He was a few pounds heavier himself; his northward-tending loincloth had now hurdled his navel. But he was still my Johnny, beautiful in his simplicity. Not, *contra* the inimitable Maureen O'Hara, "bland." Now, I do admire Maureen. Anyone who can bounce back from the news of her ex-husband's suicide with a peppy "This is the happiest day of my life!" has got to be saluted for her positivity. But I think I'd better stop calling her "inimitable."

To let you in on a Hollywood secret, Maureen was in reality highly imitable. I myself can do a reasonable Maureen O'Hara, simply by screeching as loudly as I can and flinging my excrement around. She was (or "you were": hi, Maureen!!) just another common or garden hierarchy addict, concealing your status anxieties behind the same old aggression displays, which we all agreed euphemistically to refer to as "feistiness." No, it was *Johnny* who was inimitable, not you, though it's hardly surprising you couldn't get him. The beauty of his sunny simplicities wouldn't even be visible to an armor-plated belligerent such as you, like the weather outside a tank. He wasn't *bland*. Rather, he had attained a hard-won shallowness where other humans never got beyond "depth." And incidentally, Maureen, I have to say that between Lupe Vélez, Marlene Dietrich, Maureen O'Sullivan, Joan Crawford, Brenda Joyce and yourself, you were easily the worst-tasting dame I ever—I'm getting off the point here.

To get back on track: after the buildup I'd had about the Nazis I was somewhat surprised to find when we encountered the enemy in person that they were completely hopeless. They really were the most useless human beings I had ever had the misfortune to bump into—rather reminiscent, in their stupidity, of Maureen O'Hara and, in their loudness, offensiveness and incompetence at fighting, of poor old Spencer Tracy when he allowed his demons to get the better of him in some saloon. *Tarzan Triumphs* was the name of the dream. *Quite Easily* was the implied subtitle. Undaunted by their rout, the plucky Nazis tried again in *Tarzan's Desert Mystery*, which we went straight into. They were attempting to subvert the Sheikh of Birherari with a horse, I think. Birherari? On the other side of the escarpment from Palandria. We were certainly getting out and about.

I've watched *Tarzan's Desert Mystery* at least once a year for the last two and a half decades, on video and DVD, with Don interpolating his own director's commentary of "Ooh, watch out!" and "Who's that, Cheeta?" and I'm still not sure what happens. A maneating plant assassinates the sheikh's son, causing ructions between rival tribes over the wonder horse, but luckily a wisecracking female magician from New Jersey thwarts the Nazis' alliance with a giant spider and helps Tarzan and me win . . . trading rights? A holiday? I don't know. It's an anti-war piece. Anyway, after an hour and a bit the movie stops and we're declared the winners. I filled the gaps with comedy: I was doing a lot of hat-snatching, for which I garnered this plaudit from the *New York Times,* December 1943: ". . . worth seeing for the [seriously intended sequence with a giant spider that is almost as amusing as the] *delightful comedy contributed by Cheta,*" Don's italics, or highlighter pen, rather.

I ought to have seen it coming. The "Lesser" Tarzan pictures—that was a bit of a giveaway, wasn't it? I ought to have paid more attention to the ominous notice that somebody had written in foot-high chalk letters above the gates at Paramount: "In the event of an AIR-RAID go directly to RKO. They haven't had a HIT in YEARS!" The first thing I noticed was that we were doing it all in significantly fewer takes—we were scraping the dreams more thinly from the world. In Arcadia, the trees of the forest were threadbare, the waterfalls had dried up, the Gabonis had completely died out and the animals were less numerous. The flocks of cranes and flamingos, the herds of buffaloes and antelopes, the covens of crocodiles and battalions of elephants had all but disappeared.

There were more humans about. Trade routes had opened up the continent. Strategic interests and revenue streams now had to be considered. And there were changes in Tarzan too. Instead of helping me cure the Boy, he had himself become infected with a touch of the time-disease, I thought. He was bored. Needed these little adventures to keep him going. Time was turning him from Tarzan the Ape Man into a sort of *Tarzan: Jungle Detective*. Suddenly, white men were no longer bad.

He had become a popular local celebrity in the trading posts and towns that seemed to have sprung up all over the place, as respected in the British High Commission at Bagandi as he was among the shopkeepers of the bustling bazaars of Taranga, where he occasionally hunted for bargains. There he went, with his lad and his pet monkey, an oddity, a reactionary, a hermit and, sure, a bit of a flake, but thought of as essentially sound on questions of forest management. His interventions in the region's politics were generally met with approval by the prevailing colonial interests.

Taking tea at Claridges, Jane would surely get to hear about them. "Jock says your old jungle ex is pretty popular with the consul in Bagandi. Helps keep the local bigwigs in line, that's what he heard."

"Oh don't let's talk about it, Angela. These éclairs *are* bloody, aren't they?"

"Mmm. You know that Niv's in town? He was asking after you . . ."

Things had changed so much I almost missed her.

In defeating Jane, something had gone. We had lost our belief that it mattered. We'd had an urgent dream that mattered to the world. It could be summed up in a single word: "*AAAAAHH-HHHEEEYYYEEEYYYEEEYYYAAAAAHHEEEYYYEEE-YYYAAAAAH!*" Meaning: "I am." Or, expanded, meaning something like: "I live here among the animals. I have dominion over them. They are in my care, as I am in theirs, and it is good. And why should this ever change? Why should it ever end?" It was a beautiful dream, and we'd lost our belief that it mattered. "I am" was no longer enough, not now that he'd set up as an endoneo-colonialist Sam Spade in a loincloth, and had to *do* things. He'd gone mad.

And something subtly terrible was happening to everybody else, including the by now utterly superfluous Boy. Every human on the escarpment seemed to have become infected with some weird new mutant strain of time-disease. They were all walking around in a fog, talking in a strange, glazed manner as if the whole continent had just been involved in a car crash. "My people are fortunate . . . to be given the fruits of your wisdom."

"Yet they grow careless . . . they permitted one man . . . to escape."

"True, Amir . . . yet those who were guilty of such carelessness have been punished."

"Yet one more such error . . ."

And that was the sort of conversation the humans had when they were standing still. They had to stop talking, pretty much, if they started to walk or handle drinking receptacles! "Ah . . . Tarzan. (Pause.) Sit down. (Long pause, pours drink.) There've been two attacks on caravans to Nyagi . . . in the last week." (Pause. Tarzan sits down.) "What happen?"

From Bagandi to Palmeria the epidemic raged, infecting the humans. It took the light out of their eyes, the joy out of their gestures, the very life from them. They were listless and stupid-seeming, like animals too long in rehab. They went through their motions without conviction or interest. It was like a Palm Springs sky—I'm doing a lot of skyscapes at the moment—blue in the morning, and the next time you look, it's gone all hazy and colorless. What could I do? I was immune—the disease only attacked humans—but there was no cure, or hope for one. All I could do to help was provide a bit of life around them. While the Case of the Missing Mango or whatever it was dragged incoherently on I scurried around like a maniac, using cigars, fruit, capuchin monkeys, cobras in baskets, musical instruments, binoculars, fishing rods, whatever came to hand, in a desperate attempt to keep morale up, since I had a nasty feeling that the moment I stopped the whole thing might just collapse out of sheer pointlessness.

A long time ago, when Tarzan was young, I'd been there to help him through when he was lonely. Now I was there to stop him from dying of boredom. Look at the DVDs and you can see for yourself. Look in my eyes, and you'll see that there's still a spark of life there, holding on, while all around me it's just . . . draining away. Look in my eyes and you'll see I'm the only one who still believes in it. And you want to ban real animals from the screen, do you, Dr. Goodall? Wel¹, I come from the school of acting that says you have to *mean it*.

Worse, I began to worry that the same kind of thing was happening to my human friends in Hollywood. Out on the town with Johnny, Bö Roos and the other cocktail-circuit regulars, I felt the same weird *lessening* in them. We told more jokes, we drank more, we bet more, we were sweller, broader (all that booze), more similar, more numerous, more American, more settled, had more to protect, more to lose. We seemed less surprised at the world. We knew what was going to happen more. It was only a touch of the Arcadian epidemic, to be sure, but it was there, I thought, an invisible smog that lay over "Bö's boys"—Johnny, Fred MacMurray, Frank Borzage, Red Skelton, Duke and the rest of the gang we partied with at the Tropics on Rodeo Drive, or Cocoanut Grove, or Don the Beachcomber's, or Christian's Hut on Catalina Island, or the Pirate Shack, or all those other Hollywood nightspots that kept trying to tell you you were in paradise.

And in the mansion on Rockingham Avenue, when I finally got to return there for a spot of caddying, the invisible smog lay thickest, the pauses were longest, the sense of aimlessness strongest.

"How were the girls, darling?" Johnny might sally.

"Oh, the usual . . . Phyllis is moving," Beryl would riposte.

"Phyllis is moving? Where?" he countered, quick as a flash.

"I told you," she topped him.

"Did you?" he noted wryly.

"Yes, I did. To West Hollywood," she promptly retorted.

"Oh, yes, because of the thing with the basement," he teased.

"What thing with the basement?" she inquired archly.

"You said they had a thing with their . . . Oh, sorry, *Phyllis*," he came back.

"Who's got a thing with their basement?" she quipped.

"I don't know," he flashed. And, well, there was no way back from that!

Yet even with Red Skelton scintillating away—"Hey, I was reading my marriage certificate this morning: I was hoping I'd find an expiration date!"; "Tell me something, Johnny boy, why did the Mexican push his wife off the cliff?"—even with the sort of prompting to complain about wives which was almost instinctive among that crowd, I never heard Johnny once criticize Beryl in public. He knew that if he started, he'd never be able to stop. I think because his own father had walked out on him, he couldn't bear the idea of doing the same to Johnny Jr. and Baby Wendy. So he stifled his resentment and made the best of his unhappiness and the two of them continued together in the smog, politely, distantly, lifelessly, lovelessly.

I had no intention of interfering. I'm endlessly told that I've made millions of people happy, but on the other hand, you can't *make* someone happy. You can't stick your oar in and think it's a magic wand. If I *did* eventually rescue him from his marriage, it was really more by accident than design.

I believe I've already mentioned that mole-gassing, slug-suffocating, rat-decapitating Beryl didn't like animals. Plenty of animals were harmed during the making of Beryl Scott's home and wardrobe. She had no tolerance for spiders or moths or a panicking bat ("a rat with wings") trying to escape from her mansion of misery—and, of course, she had a particular aversion to critically acclaimed world-famous primates. Any rats with*out* wings had long been exterminated from Rockingham Avenue, but she maintained her vendetta with a permanent scattering of traps. She claimed to be afraid that rats would attack the babies, to which I'd counterclaim, without meaning to sound at all critical of some very dear human friends, that fewer children of Hollywood marriages have had their lives destroyed by rats than by mothers.

These rat-traps were the only thing I'd ever heard him lose his temper over with her. "Our house is full of traps, Beryl," he once said, poetically, having found one in the cabinet where the Triscuits and little cans of olives were kept. "I can't keep track of where they are!"

"Well, you have to keep moving them so the mice don't work it out!"

"*I* can't work it out, how the hell are the mice gonna figure it out?"

"Don't raise your voice at me, please, John."

"I'm sorry. But they're only mice."

"Mice and rats. They spread disease and are a danger to children," Beryl said, making them sound like Joan Crawford. "And you eat too many Triscuits."

It was also her main line of attack against *me*—that I, much-loved family entertainer, was liable to get so drunk or forgetful that I would just flip out and decide to eat her children.

"It's too big for you to control, John. If it should decide to go for either of them, you wouldn't be able to stop it."

"Oh, come on, it's Cheeta! He's not gonna 'go' for anything, are you, Cheets? You're just being silly."

"Am I? It went for Maureen O'Hara, didn't it?" Johnny and I said nothing. "You always told me it bit Maureen O'*Sullivan*. It attacked Marlene. It went for Joan *right in front of me*." Yeah, yeah, you can always make something sound bad if you're determined to. "And there's that terrible story about what it's supposed to have done with Dolores del Río."

"That's complete bull, and you know it."

That story *is* complete bull, incidentally. What really happened between Dolores and me was much more complicated, and rather beautiful, but I shan't be discussing it in this memoir.

"Don't swear, John, please. I'm just not comfortable if the children are in the garden at the same time as the chimp. That's reasonable enough, isn't it?" Her top lip was still overbrimmed by its hunter's bow—sometimes, post-Crawford, it seemed as if the mouth of every woman in Hollywood was bridling at something distasteful. That apart, I could never remember her face. I was surprised she could remember her own face and wondered whether in fact she couldn't, and that was the reason for the hunter's bow. "And I think it's asking for trouble to feed it beer," she added.

So, if I was to be allowed over at all, I couldn't smoke (and this was the *forties*!) or misbehave and had to be chaperoned at all times in case I became a slobbering baby-eating monster from the jungle of doom. Listen, I've had chances galore to eat human babies, and I'll take a Taco Bell Beef Combo Burrito any time. Or, better, if

Don's feeling flush, a Big 'n' Tasty Happy Meal. So don't flatter yourselves.

The last time I saw her I guess she must have been a few months pregnant with their second daughter, Heidi. Johnny and Bö Roos picked me up from Selig Park and drove me over. They had business to do with the pool house: renovations, a conversion, something or other intended to make money. What with the Gaboni gardeners, the nurses whom little Johnny and Wendy were coming to know better than they knew their mother, and all the decorative minerals, cars and mole-exterminators needed to fill the abyss of marital unhappiness, the Mansion of Misery gobbled down money as eagerly as Esther Williams did the male sexual organ.

I liked Bö Roos. He was a good pal to Johnny, a rotund, nattily mustached, center-of-the-room sort of guy who referred to his clients as his "kids." He kept the kids on an allowance to stop them bankrupting themselves, lent them money himself when they were short, tried to get as much as he could out of their pockets and safely invested in real estate, and deducted their whole lives against income tax. So they didn't even have to think about money, the kids signed for everything and Bö dealt with the bills and delivered lectures on fiscal irresponsibility when necessary. Like me and most actors, Johnny had no idea what money really was, but Beryl did, and did not appreciate being kept on a leash. That's why I liked Bö: she didn't.

Well, anyway, Johnny and he were talking about converting the pool house, and I was getting a little bit restive down there since my contributions were limited to cheeping and tugging at Johnny's hand. I'm a comedian, not an architect.

"Sorry, Bö. Stop being a pest, Cheets, willya, for one minute?" he said, a little testily.

I obediently wandered off across the lawn where Johnny Jr.,

who's dead now, was toddling along on his own. I remember it was a super-vivid day. Helen Twelvetrees's copper beeches were blazing red, the lawn was achingly green, the sky was as purply blue as a black grape, and little Johnny was just *golden*. I knuckled over toward him and he toppled over onto his backside. What was so infuriating about Beryl's prohibition was that she never suspected how much pleasure I might glean from Johnny's children, how much the funny fat wrists of his son might twist my heart.

We looked at each other—he had his father's eyes, without doubt, and the same unclouded gaze. He held my stare equably and I extended a hairy black-fingered paw to touch the child's blotchy cheeks, fascinated by the smoothness of him, his juicy density. It was time—he did look good enough to eat. Dear little thing. A memory skittered like a blue-tailed monkey just out of my mind's fingers: of a helpless infant and a circled crowd of us apes looking down on it, wondering what to do. Had I made that up? Where had it come from?

At this moment, a scream—the maximum scream she was capable of—came from the Mole-Gasser on the terrace, followed by a smaller scream from a nurse reading a paperback book on a plaid blanket fifty yards away, and I was soon being chased around the lawn and loudly slandered. She had told Johnny how many times? She had *expected better* from Bö . . .

"But nothing happened, dear. You ought to have seen Cheeta with Johnny Sheffield when he was a little lad. He likes children."

"Will you allow me to talk, John? I've had just about enough of this darn monkey," Beryl said, not knowing what she was saying, what tender feelings she might be trampling on. "I don't want to see it in the house again. You only bring it out so you can pretend you're Tarzan, anyway." She wouldn't look at me. Johnny Jr. was screaming. "This is the last time. All right?"

"All right," Johnny said. "Me sorry."

"Just put it in the back of the Ford until you're done with Mr. Roos," she said, with perhaps half a hope that I might bake to death inside the car.

"No, we're done down there," Bö said. "We'll go up to the terrace and keep an eye on him."

Suddenly I was something that needed to be kept an eye on. So the two of them sat talking human complexities on the sun-trapping terrace with a bowl of Triscuits and a crate of beers, while I polished off a couple in an attempt to calm my panic. "All right," he'd said. I paced around on the leash of their peripheral vision, unjustly traduced, wrongly accused, and thinking, Where is this going to end? If she can ban me from the house, can she tell him it's time he grew up and stopped taking a chimpanzee out on the town? "All right," he'd said. After Jennifer Jones had finished working with John Huston on *We Were Strangers*, she gave him a female chimpanzee as a wrap present. Huston's wife, Evelyn Keyes, hated it. She gave him an ultimatum: "John, either the chimp goes or I do." "Honey . . . I'm afraid it's you," Huston said. (God bless you always, John. He was a famously Herculean contributor to the Project, tirelessly working to make whole swathes of California safe for the deer and rabbits that mountain lions preyed on.) But Huston liked hurting women almost as much as he loved animals: it was more of an irresistible joke than anything. "All right," Johnny had said. In less than half an hour, Bö and he would be finished. I mooched over to the table and filched another couple of cold ones from their crate. *Survive, survive, survive.* Oh, sure. How? Think. The reason the Mexican pushed his wife off a cliff was tequila.

Quietly, on cushioned knuckles, I slipped away into the dark, into the house of traps, purple-edged suns exploding in my vision, three-quarters blind. The last time I'd been inside, there'd been a rat-trap lurking behind the trophy-laden piano, and there it was still, on the off-chance, perhaps, that the mice hadn't worked it out yet. What mice? They were all dead. I fished the trap out with delicate chimpanzee hands and, holding it with the reverence I would reserve for an honorary Oscar, should I ever be so fortunate as to receive one, moved on three limbs toward the walnut-paneled cocktail cabinet. Inside, from bottom to top, a couple of shelves of cut glass, a couple of shelves of the hard stuff, a shelf of humidors and cigar boxes and, highest of all, the usual miscellany of mixers with stained labels, rejected liqueurs, coasters, ice buckets, cans of olives, cans of nuts and a box of Triscuits. I clambered up with toe- and finger-tips, pushed the Triscuits to the back of the shelf, and as gently as Laurence Olivier handled the madness and depression of Vivien Leigh—no, even more gently than that—I deposited the trap in front of it. It was terribly alert, unbreathing, like traps must be. I closed the walnut door and insinuated myself back into the sunlight.

I'd not been missed. I sank a refreshing lager or two for my nerves and sidled over to the table to savor a snack. "Cheets, come on," Johnny said. "Don't be greedy. Leave some for the rest of us." He pushed the bowl of Triscuits away from me with his beautiful hand. Long fingers with big cuticle half-moons; I brushed them as I snatched the bowl back and guzzled the remainder of the biscuits. They tasted like dust.

"You little trash can!" he said half admiringly. "Sorry about my co-star's manners. Oughta be ashamed of yourself, Cheets. I'll go get us some more."

"No need, no need, I'm fine."

"Go ooon, I can't drink this without."

"We've gotta be going in a minute if we're gonna catch Merle."

"Well, it's good to have some out anyway. And I know somebody else around here who might fancy another one or two." Johnny patted my head as he got up: I felt the wooden Illinois State Athletics Club ring he wore rub against my skull. There was still time to stop him, but you know, she was only after his money in the first place, and she didn't like animals.

Dearest readers, gentlest jailers, sweet humans: I've lived longer than any chimpanzee has ever dreamed of living because of you. There are thousands of us in sanctuaries all over America, rehabilitated, well fed, unthreatened by death, because of you. Not all of them has someone like Don to keep their diabetes in check with twice-daily jabs, to keep their stress levels down, to keep them occupied and stimulated and frame their reviews. But there are thousands of Jennas and Myras and PJs out there, chopping up fruit, measuring dosages. It's all thanks to you.

And if you're talking about *animals* rather than just chimps, the mind boggles at the numbers you've saved and the even greater numbers you're trying so desperately to save. Rats with wings, rats with tusks, rats with horns, rats with beaks, rats with fur striped for camouflage, rats with iridescent breast feathers, rats with baleen plates, rats with ingenious echo-location systems, rats with speckled flanks and transcontinental navigating powers, rats with shells, rats with antlers, rats with crests, rats with manes, rats with retractable tongues, rats with iconic dorsal fins, rats with miraculously buoyant and heat-conserving fur the color of lemon ice cream: all these rats and many, many more you try so hard to cup delicately in your hands and usher to safety. To show deliberate cruelty to a human being, to hurt those gently cupping hands—and, yes, I've had a couple of regrettable tiffs with fellow-actors, but that was just *Hollywood*—would be unthinkable enough. But to hurt the gentle hands of the best of humans, whom I loved and worshipped, was not easy to do. You understand? I'm using understatement here. But I didn't have any option. Don't judge me too harshly, gentle readers: I wouldn't be able to bear it. I don't judge *you* harshly.

Well, anyway, it was even more horrible than I'd expected. He came out of the french windows already screaming, and I thought at first that the trap had actually taken his fingers off, there was so much blood flowing from the armpit where he'd hidden his hand. Even in the worst rows with Lupe, I had never seen Johnny raging like this. The argument started out unbelievably bad and got worse. She had the servants lined up and interrogated to no effect. At one point she blamed me.

"Isn't it possible the monkey moved it?"

Bö stuck up for me. "It's been here all the time, Beryl. Look, it's finished off six bottles of beer, see? How could it have been gone?"

He shouldn't have got involved. Beryl began letting fly with dark hints about what her bridge group had "heard" about him and the Beverly Management Corporation, and the whole thing lurched into a deeper nastiness. Bö was a thief, she was a bitch, Johnny was a fool, I was a violent, dirty, smelly animal. It cleared the air all right. With a raised and clawed right hand, she bore down on me where I was hunched on the terrace-table and I leapt, still holding the beer I'd been soothing my anxiety with, into her helpless embrace. The more she scratched and tore at me, the tighter I clung, and the tighter I clung (Johnny's baby between us) the more conciliatory and loving I seemed, and the more unfair, the uglier her hatred for me appeared.

Within a couple of minutes, Bö, Johnny and I were driving very fast down Rockingham Avenue on the way to Cedars-Sinai, and I never saw the place again. He must have gone back there two or three more times but never when she was there. The pool house never got converted. The whole damn house of cards just collapsed like a house of cards.

I'm ashamed. I *feel* ashamed, and that should count for something, shouldn't it? But it was a very unhappy marriage, and what I later learned about Beryl's vindictiveness and disregard for her own children's welfare . . . well, it's documented elsewhere. She might as well have eaten them herself. Much later, apparently, she married a very nice man called Königshofer, and was reasonably happy for a time, although I heard that she drank.

I was reminded of that day with Beryl recently, when Don took me out visiting at the Palm Springs Eldercare Center.

"Oh, Don," said the old lady we were sitting with, "don't I get enough of the darn monkey?"

This was Don's mother, who says crazy things from time to time. She claims, for instance, that she didn't vote for Obama in November because he stole the nomination from her beloved Hillary. She says she voted for McCain—how crazy can you get? A lifelong Democrat on Bush III's side? That's just insane. *Nobody* in Palm Springs voted for McCain except Don's mom. A number of people were pressuring Don to get me to campaign for Obama, but he's told them it would be undignified and tacky, and animals should be above politics. Besides, I am above politics: I haven't got a vote. Don didn't vote for anyone, because he thinks they're all as bad as each other.

The fact that Don's mom occasionally says crazy things can come in handy sometimes, though. Six months ago she was around at the Casa de Cheeta for lunch on the deck. She and Don weren't talking much—they have a selection of silences they like to work through, like cheeses—and it was a classic holding-something-back one that she broke.

"When I arrived earlier, Don," she said, "Cheeta was smoking a cigarette in the garden."

Don carefully laid down his utensil. I thought, Oh, *shit.* That's that, then. If Don knew about my smoking there would be, to be brutally realistic, no possibility of ever enjoying a cigarette again. He'd find the stash in the flowerbed and I'd be screwed. It had to happen some time, but what unbelievably bad fucking luck, I was thinking. I put on an expression of perhaps overdone unconcern.

"Did you? OK. Hey, you know we sold over twenty paintings this week?"

"I'm not being mad, you know. He was sitting there smoking. Holding the cigarette upright and puffing away."

"Mom, I'm sorry. But I really shouldn't reinforce here. Look, how in the world could Cheeta possibly be smoking? Where would he get cigarettes? Where would he keep them? Think about it."

Oh, you're lucky, Cheeta, very *lucky.*

"Oh, God, oh, God, how can this be happening?" she said, and smashed her plate on the decking. "*Fucking fucking fuck!* Fuck! Why is this *happening* to me?"

Don's mom has a very great deal of straight gray hair and a nose like a raptor's, which Don hasn't inherited, and she can be very frightening indeed when she's having her troubles. I scooted back as fast as I could manage. Not so very fast, these days: I trundled back. Poor old Don was trying his best to soothe her but he knew the signs as well as I do, and in these moments she was liable to say hurtful things to him. That's why family caregiving just isn't a good idea if you can possibly afford another option. It can be tremendously distressing for the nonprofessional caregiver and those around them. The *language* you hear! The poor woman was swearing at her son, denigrating him horribly.

"Don't touch me. I don't need your help, Don. I'm not a monkey, you useless fuck. Why are you such a useless fuck, Don? Why do I never get to see my grandchildren? Where are my grandchildren?"

"Mom, you don't have any grandchildren."

Don's mom had to laugh. Oh, boy, did she have to laugh at that! "I do know that. I'm not being crazy. I was just being horrible. I meant, 'Where are my grandchildren?' You know." She was subsiding. "I was just being unkind. Oh, God, I was sure I saw Cheeta . . . I'm sorry. I'm so sorry, Don, I'm so sorry."

And so was I. One way or the other, I seem to have made a habit of hurting women. She was fine again, though, and stayed to watch a bit of TCM with us in the den: Leslie Howard and Ingrid Bergman in *Intermezzo*. There's nothing like a classic movie in a situation like that: the humans were crying their eyes out.

An interesting question for me, though: where are *my* grandchildren? There's young Jeeter, of course, who lives with us at the Sanctuary. Ex-showbiz, used to be a pretty good performer. He's not a bad chimp, Jeeter, even if he is going through that rather wearying late-adolescent stage at the moment. Nearly killed me, actually, in 2004. But the rest, God knows where they are, or how many there are of them. If I engendered forty or fifty children at RKO, then I could have hundreds—I could have *thousands* of grandchildren and great-grandchildren. There are about ten thousand chimps in sanctuaries around America. OK, I'm a comedian, not a mathematician, but it raises the question, how many of them might be mine? A hundred? Half of them? Are they *all* me? Is it basically just *me* in a cage all over America?

Well, to return to my memoir of love and art set against the turbulent backdrop of the Second World War. . . . By the time we started work on 1945's *Tarzan and the Amazons*, I could no longer kid myself that the dream of the escarpment was still alive. The dream was over, the truth was out: we were just a bunch of actors in a series of increasingly terrible films. Now, supposedly, we were in no danger. Even if *Amazons* and its 1946 follow-up *Tarzan and the*

*Leopard Woman* were only second features—B's, really—we were still being watched by hundreds of millions of humans on five continents. The received wisdom at RKO was that we could churn them out indefinitely.

I begged to differ. Slapping my hands against the crown of my head and backward-somersaulting in frustration and anxiety, I begged to fucking differ. One day soon, I worried, somebody was going to say: "This is too silly, too boring, I just don't believe you." The fan mail would fall below acceptable thresholds and we'd be doomed.

Rin Tin Tin—younger readers, you *must* have heard of Rinty!— Rin Tin Tin was a German shepherd pup rescued by (who else?) humans from a bombed-out town in France at the end of the First World War, brought to America and turned into an enormous star by Warner's. Rinty was huge. He was bigger than me. Think of Lassie and cube it. He was known, you older humans may remember, as "The Dog That Saved Warner's." His pictures in the early twenties were so popular he kept the whole damn studio from going bankrupt—a pity in a way, since that meant another forty-odd years of the psychopathic Jack Warner. Well, you can go and visit him if you like, in the dog cemetery in Paris where he now lies. "Killed by the coming of sound"—that's the other phrase you hear attached to Rin Tin Tin. 1927, *The Jazz Singer*; 1931 *The Lightning Warrior*, Rinty's last; 1932, dead. If it could happen to Rinty, it could happen to me. You *haven't* ever heard of him, have you, you younger readers? Have you? Younger readers? You know, I do hope I'm not talking to myself here.

Perhaps I worried too much. I was doing some of my best work. I was the last great remaining practitioner of silent screen comedy—I *am* the last great remaining practitioner of silent screen comedy!—and I was garnering more plaudits than ever.

"Again the best thing in it is Cheta the chimpanzee" is highlighted on *Variety*'s review of *Tarzan and the Amazons* in the den.

More importantly, and kind of bewilderingly, *she* was back. The war was over, the Nazis defeated, and Jane returned from England in a spanking new beret and twinset outfit. The Boy and I said nothing, but Tarzan's embarrassment about needing a new sexual partner was so strong that we had to go through an elaborate charade that this upbeat blond American woman called Brenda Joyce was actually his old Jane returned from nursing soldiers in Mayfair. We were old enough to be told the truth, I thought. Hey, you get lonely, you have needs, it's only human. Or perhaps the shame of having lost his one true love to "civilization" was too deep even to broach. Whichever it was, we respected him enough still to play along. Sure it's "Jane," Tarzan, sure it is. There was always this threat of loneliness on the escarpment that never went away. Loneliness and boredom—those were the ever-present threats.

As for Brenda—I mean, "Jane"—she fitted right in. "Ooh, if I've asked Tarzan once I've asked him a hundred times!" she complained, when our shower-bath broke during *Tarzan and the Leopard Woman*. "Tarzan, I've practically begged you to fix that shower and here you just sit! You've let the whole place go to rack and ruin. . . ." Oh, yeah, he knew his type at least. So we defeated the Leopard Woman and helped the Amazons and foiled the Huntress (*Tarzan and the Huntress*, 1947) and it did seem as if there was a possibility that I'd been wrong and RKO was right, that we could keep this going, living on the memory of what we once were, solving jungle mysteries among the glazed, unrealistic citizens of Arcadia forever.

Lupe killed herself. Johnny's divorce from Beryl stretched on forever in an undisentanglable wrangle over money. W. C. Fields was killed by his liver. Johnny bought a hotel called Hotel Los Flamingos in Acapulco, Mexico, with Bö Roos. Our President was killed by a wasting disease, but there was another one. Johnny made his one non-Tarzan attempt at Paramount, a flop called *Swamp Fire*. Television was on the horizon. Johnny began to develop quite a serious drinking habit. The *Zippy the Chimp* books started to appear and sell in the thousands. Johnny's divorce stretched interminably on and on. Nothing much happened with me—for commercial reasons, I'm playing down the sitting-around-for-years-doing-nothing aspect of my life in this memoir. Then, one day early in 1948, Johnny introduced me to a tall, rather attractive blonde no older than his first wife, "Legs" Lanier, would have been when he'd married her in 1930, or Bobbe in '31, or Lupe in '33, or Beryl in '39.

"Cheets! Come here and say hi to Allene. I got my damn divorce through so we're gonna get married right away!"

Yes, I'll always treasure that Golden Second, as I think of it. We were in Acapulco, in the lobby of the Hotel Los Flamingos. We were there because RKO had links with a Mexican studio, and Bö's Los Flamingos idea had been such a hit that *le tout* Hollywood had taken to flying down on the six-hour flight from Los Angeles to this little port to fish, watch the high-divers at La Quebrada, drink the unbelievably addictive Coco Locos that Los Flamingos served up in hollow coconut shells and copulate with each other.

*Le tout* Hollywood was the usual suspects—Skelton, MacMurray, Wayne, Ward Bond, Frank Borzage, Rita and Orson, the awful Crosby, Rock Hudson, dangerous Lana Turner—and this meant that Los Flamingos never made a cent, since it was permanently filled with non-paying friends. Bö's idea was brilliant in a different way—if you traveled to Mexico to check on an investment you had down there, the cost of the whole trip was deductible. Everybody was buying fractions of beach bars and flying down to "check on their investment." You'd say it as you raised the glass to your lips: "Just checking on my investment." Furthermore, the young

Mexican government was falling over itself to encourage film companies to come and shoot under their romantic skies, on their sun-kissed beaches. Come and shoot any old trash—and the whole thing can be a tax break!

Thus was born *Tarzan and the Mermaids*, which Lesser decided was going to be something more than any old trash. The series needed a fillip, a reinvention, and Acapulco was going to provide the setting for Tarzan's most spectacular adventure yet—on the lost island of Aquitania! The water kingdom.

So we were in the lobby of the Hotel Los Flamingos. Stuffed marlins were curving on the walls between the wooden wheels of old yachts. The Pacific, incentivized to be blue, was visible through the big adobe arch of the entrance. The girl stood with her hands neatly together, holding the strap of a leather bag: the posture of the bride on the top of a wedding cake. Johnny was wearing a hideous señorita-motif short-sleeved shirt and filling the place with happiness. He just never, never changed. I loved him. I'll always love him.

I do realize I may have given the impression that I saw Johnny a little more often than I actually did over the years. Outside filming, I guess I'd only seen him on average a couple of times a year. Filming could go on for months, of course, but I was often not needed on the set. He was very fond of me and didn't like the idea of my being cooped up. When one of the out-of-focus figures outside the mesh diamonds of my shelter resolved itself into him, it always hit me like a miracle. But I didn't expect us to go around together all the time. He was a different fucking *species*. That was the way it was. I loved him and he . . . he quite liked me.

I took his hand and hopped up around his waist, hugged an arm around a shoulder, and held out my hand to Allene. There wasn't anything about her I could find fault with: we ruffled each other's hair.

"I never seem to stop meeting movie stars!" she said. "I'm a big fan, Cheeta. Out of the four of you, I think you're probably the best."

Johnny thought this was hilarious. They both did. Love beams. Love *beams*. It's a centrifugal force. All I'd ever wanted was for him to be happy. At last, I thought, leaning over and kissing his bride-number-five-to-be, at last he's found himself a nice, sensible girl, who's also quite an astute film critic. He'd finally Found the Lady. Congratulations.

The difficulties *Mermaids* had to overcome are part of Hollywood lore. The first was that there wasn't a script, the second was that nobody could quite make up their mind whether they were vacationing or not. Always with half an eye on the Project, the humans spent a lot of their time assiduously clearing as many predatory fish from the sea as possible—the rest of the time they acted like they were on vacation. When were Tarzan and I and "Jane" actually going to get down to dreaming the thing? The only thing we knew about the story was that the Boy had followed his mother to "civilization" and was being educated somewhere in England: "Hey, this crigget's a heckuva slow game, fellas. Try it like this." Sock it to the Limey bastards, Boy. "A century in *twenty-two balls*, Charters? Don't be absurd. . . ."

I'd grown used to little Johnny and was surprised to find myself missing him, a little (let's not go over the top here), but I thought this represented a promising new direction for us. I was itching to get started on the new picture, full of ideas and a rekindled enthusiasm. You could even bill it as . . . let me see if I can do this:

TARZAN and CHEETA
(plus "Jane")
Together again without the Boy!
in the All New, etc., etc.

It could really work. I was buzzing. For instance, I wanted to rescue him again. In *Tarzan and the Huntress*, for the first time, I hadn't been able to rescue him. There ought to be a big rescue sequence in *Mermaids*, I thought. Also, I'd worked out an extremely amusing bit of business with a Coco Loco that I wanted to include, where I would pour one over somebody's head. There was another thing I'd have to get in somehow, where I would snatch a priest's hat, and a quite brilliant gag where I'd be eating a mango and drinking some tequila, would see something very odd (I don't know, a mermaid?), do a double-take, look suspiciously at the tequila, look suspiciously at the mango . . . and then throw the mango away! They'd be able to do it in the editing room.

And day after day went by, with sets being built, dismantled and built somewhere else, or script problems, or disputes with the extras (everybody in Acapulco wanted to be in the picture). Day after day was spent steaming on a beach at the end of a rope watching the lucky humans cool themselves in the water. At night, Johnny, Allene and I, various crew members and friends from out of town would head off to La Perla, the restaurant on the clifftop where the divers performed their show, and prepare ourselves for the torrent of drinks that came our way.

We were literally the toast of the town, or Johnny was. Acapulco had been waiting for Tarzan to perform his own dive off the cliffs, but it was, fortunately, well known locally that RKO's insurers had forbidden it, so he was continually being asked for a Tarzan yell instead, and every yell produced another round of Coco Locos, or Piña Coladas, or something else where the fruit juice tried to kid you, like Mickey Rooney, that it was good and wholesome, while all the time underneath it, the booze was a cesspool of depravity. Johnny was getting so many requests to do the Yell he was losing his voice, and as a consequence, we were drunk *all the time.*

I grew irritable on the sun-kissed beach, waiting on a nonexistent script and trying to fend off a hangover in ninety degrees of smashing sunlight while the humans refreshed themselves by swimming. I was involved in a number of incidents with crew members although, happily, tensions would always be smoothed over later—or dissolved in booze at any rate—at La Perla or Los Flamingos or one of the little bars that served nothing but tequila and lemon in the coves around Caleta. The nights were fun, and Acapulco's color and vibrancy are an enduring inspiration for my artworks (though I think I'm moving beyond color into a purer, formal approach). And Allene was a charming companion—my new best friend. She'd met him on the golf course, and they'd fallen in love when he taught her how to swim, of course, in the pool at the Fox Hills Country Club. It transpired that she'd loved him since she was a sixteen-year-old schoolgirl, watching him stride around on distant fairways, tossing his club up and catching it as he went. (She remembered *me*. The time he'd brought a chimp to caddy for him!) She loved the backflip, was wowed by the walking-on-hands trick, didn't complain too loudly at the booze-squirted-through-straw trick. But she was a light drinker and she and Johnny would be among the first to cry off, no matter how hard I'd beg him to stay for just the one more. No, he was trying to keep in shape. Without his restraining hand, things would get a little wild. I rode a donkey one night, wearing a sombrero wider than the span of my arms; I ended up in a brothel with some princess from the Dutch royal family; I slept on the beach. Our catchphrase was "We're not here on vacation, you know!" Yeah, the nights were fun. The days, with the booze tap turned off and the endless waiting in the hammering sun, were just painful interludes before the next night. On the beach I kept thinking, I need to move into the shade, before realizing I was already in the shade. I couldn't stop losing my temper:

there was no Gately around, who understood the way I worked (cigarettes, withheld or granted: a system that had run perfectly for ten movies). The catering was atrocious, the menagerie was really a shed around the back of Los Flamingos, and nobody seemed able to tell you when we would begin dreaming, if ever. It was as if we were finally getting our comeuppance for *Amazons* and *Leopard Woman* and the rest of them, I thought. Nobody's taking it seriously any longer. I need to work! Crew members approached me at their peril. In the evenings at La Perla, we were all friends again and they'd encourage me to sample another Coco Loco, or egg me on to lob a few limes around the terrace, drop a glass or two off the clifftop or, why not?, have a quick one or two off the wrist in front of Grace Kelly. And then the day again, intently watching the skull of the sun creep toward the merciful cirrostratus yardarm in the Mexican sky. . . .

This went on for about a month—I can't really remember that much of it. Eventually the director, a man named Robert Florey, decided that in the continuing absence of the main set, he'd like at least to get a pick-up of me. I would be wearing a straw hat and cut-off calico shorts, strumming a turtle-shell guitar in a specially constructed miniature canoe. At last we were starting, and with such an intriguing premise, too!

It was a muggy morning when we drove out to the location, a flat, weed-choked area on the bank of an estuary near Caleta. There were half a dozen of us—it was a second-unit shot, really—packed tight inside an airless truck for an hour, and by the time we arrived I needed a Coco Loco very badly. I'd spent the previous evening on board the yacht of the president of somewhere or other, the Dominican Republic maybe, or Cuba, something like that, and there'd been a protracted champagne fight with shaken bottles, jets of it hosing the señoritas' dresses into transparency. I'd helped mop it all up. And it really was an ugly morning: the sky was one single light-gray blaze—every shadow was reluctant.

My "trainer" was a man named Merrill White, who'd worked with the capuchin monkeys on *Huntress*, and who sort of half knew what he was doing. There was a bottle of tequila in the truck and it took him a hell of a long time to grasp that I wanted it. I clambered into my shorts, which were already damp from the humidity. They needed to be adjusted. White withheld the tequila from me, though it was a textbook case for a reward, and I snapped at him. I didn't want to seem immodest, but I wanted to communicate to him that for the last two or three pictures I'd been pretty much keeping the whole thing afloat single-handed. And having worked with Cedric Gibbons and Jack Conway, I didn't rate Florey very highly either. Neither Florey nor White would even *have* a job if not for me. That wasn't pulling rank so much as a simple statement of fact. Florey saw White giving me a capful of tequila and kicked up a stink about it.

"Bob—it won't fucking do anything if I *don't* give it a drink."

"Just get it in the canoe, willya? This was supposed to take half an hour. Where's the guitar?"

"They get like this," muttered White. "As they get older, they're harder to handle."

"*Smell* it. It stinks of stale white wine. It's drunk."

I might have been drunk but the canoe was a joke, a piece of matchwood with a match for an outrigger, designed to drown any thespian animal that set foot in it. I wanted to say: I am an animal and I am about to be harmed in the making of this motion picture. White was holding a capful of tequila temptingly near the canoe's unrealistic bowsprit. I would love more than anything to be able to swim, I tried to communicate to him, but I can't and that canoe is murder.

"Come on, monkey," White was pleading. "Come and get your shot."

The little waves lapping against the canoe looked glutinous; the whole river seemed half swamp. I was not getting through to them: the shoot was a shambles; the catering was a joke; not in a million years was I going to fall for this tequila/pushed-in-canoe trick; you don't call someone who's worked with Irving Thalberg the "M"-word on set; and I don't do water anyway. I was a star; they were . . . well, have *you* ever heard of them?

"Come on, little monkey, come to me," White coaxed.

He just wasn't getting it. The tequila wasn't a reward, it was a necessity, and I'd had a paltry two capfuls all morning. I was an immense international superstar, to spell it out, and . . . where was the respect?

"Ooh ooh ooha ooha oohaa aah aah aah aahaa aahha-aaahha-aahhha-eeehuh-eeehhuh-aahheeeeeeEEH!" I pointed out, "EEEEH! AAHEEEEEEEEEH!AAHHEEEEEEEEEEE! WAAAAAAAAAA-AAAAAAAAAH!" I added. "AAHHEEEEEEEEEWAAAAAAAAAA. AAAAAAAAAH!" I concluded, emphasizing my point of view with hand and facial gestures and by throwing my ridiculous guitar to the ground and stamping on it. Sometimes with bad directors it's the only tactic, to lose your temper. Like, what part of "AAHHEE-EEEEE-WAAAAAAAAAAAAAAAAAAAH!" did he not understand?

"Jesus, Bob, what can I do with it? Look at it."

"Uh. Wait. I tell you what we can do to fix this," Florey said. At last, a bit of thought, a bit of *direction*. "We can get Sol to airfreight another one down this evening, right? Tell him to talk to—what's his name? Gately. Get another one out here by tomorrow morning, and we'll call this morning a wipe. Light's not right, anyway."

What?

That's right. One lapse. One moment (Maureen apart) of less

than perfect professionalism in fourteen years and they fired me. I was "too old" at seventeen, I had a "problem with alcohol" though I spent most of the year on the wagon, I was "too difficult to work with"—I, who would do it for a cigarette. We drove back to Acapulco and Merrill arranged for me to be transported by freighter to Los Angeles.

That "No animals were harmed during the making of" thing—I don't believe it. I'm not talking about Clyde the orangutan in the *Every Which Way But Loose* pictures being beaten to death by his trainer with a crowbar (though that did happen, and they still got their disclaimer), I mean that somewhere in the forests, during the making of your film, somewhere in the seas, animals are being harmed all the time. "Many millions of animals were continually harmed during the making of this film" would be more accurate. It should go on the final credits of every single motion picture, just so you don't forget the way the world really is. Many millions of animals are always being harmed, so what does one more matter? But I was harmed. I was terribly harmed in the making of *Tarzan and the Mermaids*.

I was returned to the Selig Park zoo. I thought I was going to die. I could have killed my*self*—why had I been such a fool? I waited for an intervention from Johnny, or Gately, or Lesser. Or maybe Johnny Sheffield. Even Maureen could testify that I showed, by and large, an impressive professionalism. I waited for news that my replacement hadn't been able to play the part, for news that test screenings had gone so badly they would have to reshoot, for news that the picture was to be pulled because of the number of complaints. And every day I waited for a couple of humans with their hands in their pockets to stroll up to my shelter, make a mark or two on a clipboard and give me a lift to work on the first day of my new medical career.

If you're a star, Hollywood is a playground, and if you're not, they're right, it *is* a jungle. It's a town of heartless bottom lines and harsh decisions and betrayals so ugly that from time to time the very earth beneath it shudders in contempt, like its teeth have been set on edge.

All through 1948 I waited, desperate to conceal from my keepers that I was losing weight, that I was having difficulty digesting even the mushiest, woolliest slices of apple, grateful that they never examined us too closely. If they had been paying attention, truly, I think I would have been gone. Knowing nothing at all, but suspecting everything, I slowly ate myself away. I imagined that if you bit into my flesh it would taste like Maureen O'Hara's—it would be bitter. Was Johnny in the Aquacades? What reason might there be for his not coming? How was *Tarzan and the Mermaids* doing? Just how funny was this replacement of mine? How close were they? They call it a slump: all I did that year was slump. I slumped in my straw and tried to eat and look as bright as I could manage when any keepers came around.

The breeding was the worst. I was a popular choice for breeding with females, but I had somehow lost my . . . I want to stress that before 1948 I had been an *extremely popular* choice for mating among a large number of attractive, fertile, high-status females and I had lost . . . I had lost my . . . I had been very stressed and depressed, and the breeding sessions were difficult. Keepers looked on while you performed to make certain that you'd given the female a damn good inseminating. Not to add to the pressure of the whole thing, but it was an opportunity for them to gauge your health, and as much as you can hoot and wave your arms around and take great lusty sniffs, there's no disguising whether you're bluffing or packing. It wasn't impossible; it was never easy.

I was depressed, all right? It wasn't like Jean Harlow's husband.

Or Rex Harrison. Time passed and every hour it was a relief that nobody came and a little blow that nobody came. More time passed and it wasn't really either a relief or a blow—it was just gray unhappiness all the time. There was one hope I had, and I had to display my teeth at the irony of it. My hope was this: the hurt will die down eventually. It has to, otherwise none of us could stand life. It is *so hard* to love someone who doesn't love you.

They say there are no real seasons in Los Angeles. Neither are there any real seasons in zoos—no mating seasons, no molting seasons. But at the Selig Park zoo, you could tell what seasons there were more easily because of the changing colors of the Santa Monica mountains behind the giraffe house. In the "winter" the mountains showed themselves a touch lighter. And the winter of '48/'49 was strange, with rainy days or days of cloud so low you could no longer see the mountains. The wind blew, to everyone's amazement. It grew so cold that I and the other animals took to making burrows in our straw, and I didn't mind it at all. I was on the side of the weather; I wanted to see how low it could go; I thought, Come on, more, bring it on. It felt right to me, as if the world was as sick of it all as I was. Me and the world, the both of us, through with it. And, unbelievably to others, it kept growing colder. The keepers, jammed in their caps, hunched in their collars, had never known anything like it.

On the coldest day yet, the wind stilled itself and a remarkable thing began to happen—you'll have to take my word for it, or I guess you can check weather reports: very slow white rain began to fall. It was soft ice; it melted when it hit the earth. "It's snowing!" the keepers were yelling. They loved it. "It's fucking snowing in Los Angeles!" I didn't know it then, but it was the only time I'd ever see snow in my life. (I'm not counting the ridiculous Palm Springs Winterval Gatherings to which Don drags me every Christmas.)

The keepers were so delighted by it—they scooped it up and threw it down each other's necks. They wanted to share the bounty with each other. With the atmosphere of a very special treat being granted (which it was) and a kind of formal ceremoniousness, we (two baboons, myself, two other chimps) were led out from our shelter on leashes so that we could walk through the falling snow. It was, I had to admit, fun to be out in, to see the prints made by your hands and feet, to pick it up and throw it or run and slide across it. I had to admit it was kind of interesting, the feeling of the cold on your paws, the way it melted on your fur. It wouldn't make me a star again or bring Johnny to me or even get me a cigarette, but it was, in itself, something reasonably OK, I had to admit.

It was almost exactly a year since that day in Caleta, and Jane's Law had given me its first little crumb. When you're starving, you don't turn up your nose at a crumb of comfort.

The snow was still on the ground, diminished and dirtied but still just about there, a few days later when a couple of humans with their hands in their pockets strolled across its dips and craters toward my shelter, one holding a clipboard.

"Which one is it?" one of them asked. "No, wait, don't tell me. Hey, kid. Hey, *Jiggs*." It was Tony Gentry, diminished and dirtied a little, but still center-parted, still slightly more alive than the standard human, still spiffy. "Hello there, Jiggs. Or are you still actually Cheeta?"

Difficult question, under the circumstances, Tony. I am *the artist formerly known as* Cheeta.

No, come on, buck up. What am I talking about? Today is the first day of the rest of your life. You're *Cheeta*, for Chrissakes, pull yourself together.

Me Cheeta, Mr. Gentry. Me still Cheeta.

# PART 3

# 1
# Stagestruck!

The saddest thing about being a great artist, I think, is the question of immortality. We may live forever (touch wood!) but our works slowly fade away and are forgotten. I don't really expect *Tarzan and the Amazons* to last. I expect to see even *Tarzan and His Mate* die out of the world. Yes, it will. And I'll probably outlast this book. Yet I do have—ah, dammit, I know you'll say I'm as crazy as Garbo toward the end. I've been doing some paintings of the American landscape lately and I harbor a sneaking hope that one or two of these pieces might last as long as me. I think they're the best work I've done in *any* medium. If you give a million monkeys a million paintbrushes and some top-quality art materials then one of us, one day, is going to paint you *Sunflowers* or *An Experiment on a Bird in the Air Pump*, or maybe even an original. I just hope it's going to be me. I know I've got a long way to go technically, but I've got a lot I want to express, and that's what counts, isn't it? An artist has got to have something he desperately wants to say, something he desperately lacks.

Don supplies the paint (water-based poster), provides me with the right working environment and handles the commercial side via our website. And business is absolutely booming at a hundred and fifty bucks a canvas. *Dolores del Río Sleeping on a Sheet, Santa Monica, No. 134* went for two hundred. So did *Study of Don in Comical Barbecue Apron.* And Dr. Goodall bought *"Duke" Wayne with Mexican Waiter in Headlock* for two fifty at a charity auction. To be quite honest, the fees my artworks command are keeping us all going at the Casa de Cheeta. Jeeter, young Daphne and dear little Squeakers, the orangutans, Maxine the cheeky young macaque, and Don: all depend on my going to the kitchen table in the morning and finding that inspiration again. With the streak I'm on at the moment, they don't have to worry about a thing.

It's the failures that drive me on, I think, and the need to get across something I can't seem to articulate any other way. I try to take the grief and loss (the wound that every artist must possess) and mingle them with the gratitude and love I feel toward humanity, toward that dog wheeling on its side in next door's yard, toward the midges throwing their clever shapes of fists and hourglasses above the pool, toward everything that *isn't* lost. I try to show that the grief is the lining of my joy. I want to paint the bottomless ocean of absence that lies underneath the perfect day. One day I'll nail it, and then we'll be able to afford to get Don's mom some permanent nursing at the Eldercare Center.

So I've been doing Mr. Gentry recently or, rather, the landscapes we traveled through, the succession of cars and trucks we grew to love and then discard, the litter on their dashboards that would slide over and fall out at corners, the flattened grass outside the venues, the shy kids turning away from me into their laughing mothers' fronts. I remember our long-serving flyers and playbills; my ever-changing costumes; the collapsible car I drove from '57 to '64, until it collapsed. And I remembered whole panoplies of marvelous colleagues: Doozer and Goofy and Bingo; Kong and Katie, with whom I worked for umpteen years on and off whenever we were in the south; the inimitable Pepsi; that absolutely *filthy* Carol from Florida (hi, Carol!); four-fingered Mungo from Amarillo and his performance-related gnawing anxieties; Fidel, who was such a talent on the mouth-organ, though his repertoire was limited to "The Tennessee Waltz"; Caruso, a unicyclist of genius and a tremendous friend until we fell out over a female in the parking lot of a diner in Baton Rouge, Louisiana; Pamela and Boggle, Hyacinth and Fudge and the rest of the cast of an absolutely riotous re-enactment of *Show Boat* that we staged for a couple of years on the Missouri River in Sioux City, Iowa (which was followed in '56 by a somewhat short-lived *Mutiny on the Bounty*, with me in the Charles Laughton/Trevor Howard/Tony Hopkins role and not shining); Brad the lion, Don the seal, Rock the sea *lion*, Chip the mynah, Buzz the penguin and his whole crew, Mary-Lou the pony, Happy the gorilla, Happy the elephant and Happy the little polar bear.

I could tell you some stories about life on the road, but the code is that what goes on in those lockups and motel rooms, tents and pens stays in those lockups, etc. As for the "work," there's an idea that stage work is more rewarding than performing in movies, but I could hardly disagree more. Stage work is the very definition of something that's not going to last. And maybe you could say there's something personal in that. Without my motion-picture partners, I seemed to lose some of that compulsion to invent. Somehow I could no longer manage to come up with those little flecks of off-the-cuff genius that distinguish my best film work. There wasn't the context of the escarpment to make it matter—maybe that was it. I lacked motivation. For three decades I think I "phoned it in" a bit.

It happens with actors. Look at De Niro. There's been that musty been-lying-in-straw joylessness to his work for so long. You can just tell he's had to be beaten around the head in order to be dragged in front of the camera, can't you? *Meet the Fockers*? Don stopped it halfway. So, yes, clambering off my stool again to perform a little rodeo dance in my excremental dungarees, or hunching behind the wheel of my ill-fated Spyder, I think I lacked some of the conviction that real art requires.

But it's the days and the miles and the absences that I've been trying to capture in my work, the feeling of waiting in the mesh back of our pickup at a gas station in a little square in Boca Raton at dawn, Mr. Gentry getting breakfast, and seeing all the streetlights flick off at the same moment all the sprinklers come on and the Amoco disk suddenly spooked into spinning as if to say that something or somebody *has* just been and gone. These could be great, these paintings, but I just don't seem to have the technique right yet. I'm trying, though, I'm trying, and they've got something about them. Absence haunts them. Impressions of America—$150 a pop. Treat yourself. And remember that you'll be helping Don's mom.

It's been a very lucky life so far, I may have said. Mr. Gentry saved it twice. Funnily enough, I do think that the reason we lasted as long as we did is that we got off to the right start that day in the slush at the Selig Park zoo. Neither of us mentioned what must have been heavy on both our minds: what had happened in Trefflich's office. And I was happy to let drop the fact that he'd gone out for an hour and stayed gone sixteen goddamn years, since I didn't have his damn Luckys to give him any more anyway.

Throughout his life Mr. Gentry absolutely adored working with chimps and we quite liked working with him. He had an idea that he particularly wanted to use me for which cropped up at intervals throughout the years, but mostly he worked with me and a cast that altered but usually consisted of me, Doozer, Goofy, Bingo, our female, and Mary-Lou the pony. Doozer was our star, what with the show-stopping, or show-slowing anyway, backflips he could do while riding Mary-Lou around the venue; Goofy and I had a hoe-down routine and the cars (he was supposed to be a blond girl in a convertible whom I was chasing, dinner-jacketed as Bond); Bingo played the drums. We had a *Maltese Falcon* routine and a *Gone With the Wind* skit, in which I was Sydney Greenstreet and Leslie Howard respectively, but the act's real high points were merely the hugs we'd give Mr. Gentry and he'd give us throughout. Those were the good bits, the bits you could sense an audience really respond-ing to: just a little bit of real affection between a human and an an-imal. That's all you really wanted to see—us liking you.

"Aah, the *Falcon*! Seventeen years I've been waiting for that little item, sir!" I met Sydney Greenstreet once: didn't like him. English. Money was always tight: it gushed in little flash floods over the years, but never for long enough and always just after Mr. Gentry needed it. We weren't ever the sort of act that was going to make it to the St. Louis Zoo, the blue-ribbon live venue for chimps, let alone the ultimate goal, a slot on *Ed Sullivan* or *The Hollywood Palace* on ABC or, holiest of holies, the *Colgate Comedy Hour*, later the *Colgate Variety Hour*. We did bits and pieces: parties, clam-bakes, residencies at nightclubs, stints with circuses.

One time in the early fifties Mr. Gentry got involved with a German-Jewish producer named Jack Broder, who managed to get me a bit of screen work in a B called *Bela Lugosi Meets a Brooklyn Gorilla*, three or four days' dreaming for me. It was a vehicle for a pair of Martin & Lewis impersonators, called Duke Mitchell and Sammy Petrillo, whom you've never heard of because it's their only picture. Petrillo's impersonation of Jerry Lewis was uncannily ac-curate. He was every bit as unfunny as Jerry, and Jerry's less funny than *Chaplin*. (I mean: Lewis, Hope, Skelton, Gleason—in the fifties I sometimes wondered whether I'd ever laugh again, and wasn't surprised when Colgate had to get rid of the *Comedy* bit.)

Anyway, I'm pretty sure that a billion monkeys given a billion cameras and a googol of years would never make anything as species-shamingly bad as *Brooklyn Gorilla* (we'd make art films, actually, I believe, rather good ones) and I don't seriously expect that the Academy is going to give me the honorary award because of my work in it. I'm guessing it won't even be in the citation.

And, what else? Anything else? Where was I when JFK was shot? In a cage. The Cuban Missile Crisis? In a cage. Moon landings? In a cage. HUAC, MLK, RFK? Cage. Could make a great movie—*Cheeta: Witness to History!* Wasn't I thinking anything? Surely there must be some choice anecdotes? What about Mr. Gentry? All right. Here's the anything else.

"I want you to come and meet an old friend," Mr. Gentry said to me, as he unlocked the truck cage one morning in Salt Lake City, Utah, summer of 1949. "He's come a long way to see you." Mr. Gentry had retained that sharp white line down the center of his scalp from the thirties.

He still had his air of rather dashing rectitude, a four-square feller who'd probably done something rather extraordinary in the war, which he never mentioned. I mean to say: apart from the one lie, he was a fair dealer.

He led me by the hand across a courtyard of cabins to his own: my suddenly heightened senses felt cold packed earth, wet grass, gravel, tile, concrete, sisal matting underfoot. "All the way from Africa!" Mr. Gentry emceed, as he flattened the door open butler-ishly (and for one terrible second I thought, He's going to say, "Stroheim!") and there he wasn't. A thinning-haired middle-aged man, who carried a lot of slack where some considerable muscles had once been, stood under the light fixture in a one-piece off-the-shoulder leopard-skin tunic, looking away, caught slightly in a daydream.

"Oh, sorry, Tony," he said. "Me Tarzan! You Cheeta!"

I thought, No, me Cheeta, you some poor sap standing in a motel cabin in Utah wearing fancy-dress underwear and looking like a complete fucking fool.

You can feel gravity at moments like that. You can feel how every atom in your body wants to tear downward, feel just how much goddamn effort it is to stand upright on this planet. I gave Mr. Gentry *a look*. This was his big idea, and perhaps the reason for his visit to the Selig Park Zoo: to run an act around the "real movie Cheeta" and his friend "Tarzo the Jungle Man!" He couldn't get any of the rights to Tarzan but he was sure that a chimp show featuring "one of the real movie Cheetas" in a jungle context was a viable long-term possibility, if we could only get the act itself to click. (Nobody has the rights to me, by the way. *I'm* Cheeta, for real, and large as life. Come and visit me in Palm Springs any time. Bring cigarettes.)

Mr. Gentry couldn't cast himself as Tarzan, so over the years, in the fallow periods between residencies or tours with the regular act, or in those long lulls when bookings were down, he'd find another Charles Atlas type or college football player to be my mate, my partner, my son, my everything, and every time, dearest readers, every new time, my heart fell for it. Because all I was looking for, from Cedar Rapids, Iowa, to Dolores, Colorado, from sea to shining sea, was him, of course. That's the anything else.

So there was Mr. Gentry and me and Doozer and Goofy and Bingo and a score or so "Tarzo the Jungle Kings" and we lived in motel courts and trailers and cages in America, sometimes with a "Jungle Jane," sometimes with a "Jungle Boy," and played to houses that weren't bad, weren't great. Tarzo was a stevedore from Erie, Philadelphia, and a lifeguard from Bay City; he was a royal pain in the ass from Cleveland, Ohio, and an ex-linebacker for the Utah Saints; he drank, he was a morphine addict, he worried about his father, he worried about the Reds, he worried about getting drafted, he fucked Jane and, once, Boy. And a glimpsed loincloth or wide bare back in the corner of my eye would have me lurching inside for a moment, even though I *knew* it wasn't him. Ten minutes later, I'd go and do it again. As if my soul were the dumb boy in class whose hand shoots up instantaneously to deliver always the same wrong answer, a wrong answer that the teacher is fed up to the headachy back teeth of telling him is wrong, so *stupidly* wrong, impossible.

I was genuinely fooled for a moment in the cafeteria of a roadside zoo in Michigan in '62, and behind a big top in North Carolina in '55. And on top of that I was permanently being kidded by the padded shoulders of a thousand double-breasted suits. I was stiffed severally by unseen televisions giving the yell. And for ten minutes totally convinced by a half-glimpsed near-match at the newly opened Roy Rogers & Dale Evans Museum in Victorville, California, where Mr. Gentry had, perhaps unwisely, taken me to see Trigger, whose hide had been peeled from him and stretched over a plaster cast to make a beautiful permanent memorial.

And then a day came in the mid-sixties when Mr. Gentry opened the passenger door of our VW, where I was lolling about with my feet on the dash, and said, "Cheet-o, listen. I want you to hear something."

We were in Chiloquin, Oregon, near where the world's largest miniature railway is. I don't think we'd done a Tarzo bit for a couple of years. Out of the blue and the swishing of the traffic, I heard, as strong and as happy and as youthful as ever, not lessened by anything like time: "*Aaaahhheeyyeeyyeeyyaaahhhhheeyyeeyyeee-yyeeaaaah!*"

I piled out of the car to leap into the embrace of a strapping white-haired young athlete in T-shirt and jeans, grinning at his own lung power, because—do you see how it was? I was like a chimp working in a university, failing the cognition test with the electric jolt over and over, just not getting it that the blue button meant *pain*.

"Pretty darn good, eh? Pretty darn *perfect*. Say, 'Me Tarzan,' to Cheet-o, Brian. Don't rush him."

"Me Tarzan! Say, is this the one that, you know, the thing with Dolores del Río?"

He was OK, Brian, best one we ever had, I think.

So, there was Mr. Gentry and me and Doozer and Kong and Katie and Marie-Lou the pony and sometimes Tarzo and Jane, and we lived on an escarpment in America in the middle years of the century, and they mocked me, continuously, for years. How could I ever move on, or forget? Over time, I guess the disbelieving hatred I had for the whole travesty slowly died down, like the deflating turquoise crocodile in our pool at the Sanctuary, into no more than a stale disgust. Because, to be absolutely honest, I didn't want to move on. I *liked* the blue button. Even if I could, I'd never stop pressing it. Or did you know that already?

"Honey, will you swing by the riverbank? I'd like you to cash a check for some water," Jane might ask, apropos nothing. Aargh! Oof, that *hurts* . . .

"OK, hon. I sure hope I don't get caught in a line behind a leopard, though," Tarzo worried.

"Why not?"

"He might be trying to change his spots. Hey, what's that, Cheeta? Cheeta says he's just spotted some tigers in the garden."

I'd said no such thing. I hoped my expression of boredom and contempt might communicate this fact to the audience.

"Well, tell him not to. Tigers aren't spotted, they're striped!"

"Hey, what's that, Cheeta? The most frightening animal in the jungle is coming toward the hut? A crocodile? A lion? What is it? I fear none of them!"

"Oh, Tarz, darling," Jane suddenly recalled. "I invited Mother to lunch today!"

Bum tish. At least she never turned up. Jane's *mother*. Brrr . . .

Our new escarpment was paradisically biodiverse: a crocodile with a snappy personality lived down the river by the swimming hole where elephants always remembered to pack their trunks and shopping-obsessed vultures fretted about carrion bags. Snakes were gifted at mathematics, elephants supported Eisenhower, a baboon started out as a country singer before switching profession to hairdresser, and pythons had crushes on us, if you were to trust the mendacious lion that told you. Not so bad a place to be at all. So we continued in the jostling forest, fearing only Jane's mother and the pelican, which might at any moment present us with an enormous bill, and at the end of every day Tarzo liked to relax with his new friends, a trio of toucans who lived in the refrigerator, though never—not once—would he sit down and play cards with me. Because of my *name*, you see. And because he wasn't real. On the real escarpment, I'd played whist and brag and Find the Lady with him.

But I did actually see him for real, just the once, and also twenty times over, in the window of an electrical supply store in Bakersfield, 1963. He was still on the escarpment. Brenda was nowhere to be seen, although he had a son whom I guessed must be hers. He'd moved out of the Treehouse and into a house. He'd traded his knife for a high-caliber rifle and his loincloth for a safari suit. "Fatigues"—that's the other word for what he wore. He was just like everybody else—and there were two dozen of him up there, driving Jeeps, shooting crocs, speaking what looked like fluent English. As long as you're happy, Tarzan, I thought, and then the sponsor's messages came on and I saw that he was so ashamed of himself he'd even changed his name. Jim. *Jungle* Jim. I don't know if it was all because he thought Jane would come back to him now he could drive and tell the time . . . but she wouldn't. She was always going to marry within her own class, and he was just another divorced ex-pat drifter now. The sponsor's messages were unending and I finally allowed Mr. G. to yank me away down the sidewalk. Why stay? There was nobody even there to say goodbye to.

In the meantime, while the elephants switched their support from Ike to Nixon to Goldwater (guys, guys, think what you're doing!) to Nixon again, it did give me a measure of quiet satisfaction, I suppose, to see the increase in opportunities for chimpanzees. I don't want to take all the credit, but I had been instrumental in getting that door open, and now that it was, hundreds of us rushed through, into advertising, entertainment and exploration. In gratitude to the humans, hundreds of thousands of us knuckled down to the daily grind of a career in medicine or academia, very rewarding jobs, of course, very worthy, but you had to balance the satisfaction of helping the humans' War on Death with the insecurity and high burnout rate of the profession.

Celebrity was—has always been—where the real opportunities lay. Nero the Great riding his Great Dane and Little Pierre in his Batman outfit at the St. Louis Zoo, Zippy (on TV now), J. Fred Muggs, Mr. Moke, Mata Hari, the Marquis Chimps . . . I was cheered to see us making inroads in conspicuous positions in the media. And as for the sciences—as for young Ham . . . you have to remember the tension and suspicion that existed between the Soviet Union and the States in the late fifties and early sixties to appreciate just how important the Space Race was. Who would make it first, human or chimpanzee? It was a blow when a *dog* got up first, and an immense relief when she died, after several days, of starvation, dehydration and, who knows?, madness and terror.

Ham kept his focus, through those difficult days when it seemed like a bunch of rhesus monkeys might leapfrog everyone (they were killed, too, by suffocation), and on the last day of January 1961, he triumphed. Not just for himself but every one of us. It's wonderful to be loved by you, dearest readers, but it's even better to feel like you've earned *respect*. Poor old Gagarin trailed in anticlimactically sometime in April. You beat us to the moon, so we'll call the whole thing a tie.

Meanwhile the Project continued apace, of course. Humans were taking it ever more seriously, and I was pleased to see that *finally* a few of us were now being officially recognized as "endangered." At first it was a trickle, sure, but you can't hold that sort of thing back once you've started; you can't deny what's in front of you. With laudable speed, species after species was recognized as "endangered." That's right: get 'em out of there! Get 'em in shelters now!

But "endangered" didn't seem to be doing the job. Stronger terms were needed, and soon the same animals were reclassified as "seriously endangered," then "critically endangered." Well, it helps, perhaps, but people see through these PR terms. Even the safest of us are supposedly "critically endangered" now. I mean, according to Don, *humans* are critically endangered. It seems over the top to say so: death lurks, sure. But you don't need to be told. You don't need someone like *Don* going around stating the bloody obvious all the time, do you?

In 1973 we were still out on the circuit but the fallow periods between residencies were getting longer and longer and Doozer and I were spending a lot of time in the yard out back of Mr. Gentry's house in Barstow, California. My big "comeback" with *Dolittle* had come and gone. Mr. Gentry's center part was now a casualty of history and had been overrun by a mob of gray hair. Humans were wearing their clothes much more in the loose style we entertainment-industry chimps have always favored. Burgers were bigger (good), cigarettes had irritating little cotton filters (bad, but you could rip them off), and I was losing it. I don't know how it happened, but one day I just couldn't do backflips anymore. Same with the walking-on-hands trick. The spring had just upped and offed. One small plus was that the "real movie Cheeta" stuff seemed to have been more or less permanently abandoned, and I wasn't jabbing my eye out on my past every ten minutes.

Anyway, we were in Las Vegas, where the Immortals congregate, because Mr. G. was making a personal call on a promoter who was interested in what remained of the act. I was there in a purely PR capacity, but Reception had requested I remain in the car, which I took as kind of a bad omen for the meeting.

So I was sitting there in our beloved old Datsun, thinking about the time that we'd missed out on the *Norwester*'s Voyage to Vegas because of his row with the late Lupe Vélez. Yeah, little Lupe, with her metallic arms flashing bolts of light across the desert. Lupe had said, "She really loves you, doesn't she?" and he'd said something like "I guess so," but in an embarrassed way that I thought implied reciprocation. I had a little list of lines or moments like that in my head, a list beginning to fall apart at the folds. No, the list had already crumbled into half a dozen smaller separate squares, with bits of writing missing where the creases had been. The list included "I always thought Cheeta was pretty funny, I guess" at Chaplin's and "Cheeta's one of my best friends, aintcha, Cheets?" (to Norma Shearer at Sardi's) and "Wait, we can't go without Cheeta, it won't be any fun" (Christian's Hut, Catalina: to general party) and "Much as I dearly love you, Cheeta . . ." (I'd been masturbating and accidentally overshot onto Jayne Mansfield's lap, and then, in trying to calm her down, had somehow managed to tip gazpacho over her) and the embrace on Beryl's terrace, and, oh, lots and lots of other Classics.

Well, I happened to be running through this list when, by an incredible coincidence, Mr. Gentry flopped back into the Datsun, sighed deeply, and said, "What a waste." This meant another three hours on the Interstate back to Barstow, which was fine by me. I wasn't doing anything. "You know who's working at Caesar's Palace, though?" he said, pulling out of a long, weary U-turn. "Your old co-star. You want to stop and say hi?"

Yes, Maureen had been divorced by John Farrow and was now working in the Palace under the name of "Jane Parker," as an escort offering correction to the older gentleman who found the English accent a turn-on. She was scarcely making enough to keep the casino sweet, though, and dealt Quaaludes and various uppers, just *kidding*, just kidding you there. . . . Maureen was in fact in Scottsdale, Arizona, a contented widow and grandmother who enjoyed doing summer stock on the East Coast and the occasional TV cameo back here, and who was, even as we turned the Datsun around, mixing the first drink of the afternoon in preparation for her daily telephone marathon with her seven children. Maureen had got what she wanted.

But her old on-screen love was working in Caesar's Palace as a greeter, along with Joe Louis. The sub–duty manager put a call through but he wasn't in his room. He guessed he could be anywhere. They could try the Tannoy. No, Mr. Gentry didn't think it mattered that much. The sub–duty manager wanted to help and did it anyway. He was quite taken by the whole thing, and annoyed by our bad luck. "Nine times out of ten, you'd have caught him." Normally the countess would be here, but she'd gone back to Cheviot Hills for the week with her daughter. The countess? Mr.

Weissmuller's wife. It really was incredibly bad luck we'd missed him: he could only be playing golf. The sub–duty manager's name was Chris Jehlinger, by the way. He was delighted to meet a legend of the silver screen: he'd grown up with me. I wasn't normally so badly behaved, Mr. Gentry apologized.

We could call around the golf courses, or he might be out with friends, Chris admitted. He really wanted to help. Maybe it was the air-conditioning that was upsetting Cheeta. Mr. Weissmuller had been working at the Hotel for three months. He sure was a friendly guy, he was a riot when he and Joe got together. Still giving that yell, yes, sir. There was a picture in the Imperial Lounge, if we wanted to see it. There I was, in silvery light on a nest of twigs, holding his hand and Maureen's, looking like a minister on the verge of uniting in matrimony a couple about whom he has grave doubts.

Chris suggested we wait at the pool bar and have a drink on Caesar's before going back to Barstow—after all, he might well come back at any moment. Cheeta was going crazy, he was probably looking forward to seeing his old pal. He was excited by the picture, was what it was. He definitely seemed to recognize it, didn't you think? Mr. Weissmuller had had these terrible business difficulties the last few years. Yes, that was true, he'd been bankrupt. His business manager—Chris wasn't sure of the details exactly, but certainly it was sad and just went to show. The hotel was pleased to be able to help him. He was a fine man and what had happened was a scandal. You get some sharks in Hollywood. The biggest thing was his daughter's death. Chris had absolutely loved the movies as a kid. Bö Roos, that was the guy, exactly. Chris would make sure that Mr. Weissmuller was aware where we were the moment he came back—Mr. Weissmuller started at eight thirty, so he ought to be here by seven, seven thirty? Five hours? No, we had to go, Mr.

Gentry said, he didn't like driving at night. Cheeta was just being silly now. We could always come back some other time.

Never have I regretted not having bothered to learn American Sign Language so much. Some chimps can sign you stuff like "love friend sad stay stay stay car no heart pain big stay stay stay" but I'm not one of them. No, not "heart," I don't think they actually use "heart." What did I think would happen, though? That I could offer him consolation? Bring his daughter back? Indict Bö Roos? What did I possibly think could happen other than half an hour of awkward interaction between two washed-up old has-beens?

# 2

# Slowing Down

On a sunny Saturday morning in the fall of 1975, just outside Flagstaff, Arizona, I *did* bump into an old colleague. It was
the last tour we ever did, and we'd pulled over at a little roadside
zoo to do a quick meet-and-greet, and there, next to a sign directing you to the zoo's biggest draw—a series of footprints left by a
brontosaurus—was Stroheim. He didn't recognize me. He didn't
even see me. The notice saying *Do not feed the animals. Do not introduce anything through the bars* had gained fresh underlinings
and exclamation marks in a still unbleached black, as if after
the fact of some unfortunate incident. He was mad. In the sweat-
darkened stripe across his concrete floor you could see the map of
his insanity: his insane tos and insane fros. To the delight of a thick-
ening crowd, he was masturbating away with the zestlessness of
the classic twenty-a-dayer, seeing nothing, inside or out. His bald-
ness was worse, almost complete. Poor, poor Stroheim . . . children
were shaking my hand—"Hey, monkey! You found a buddy?"—
and not quite understanding my protests and squirmings, Mr.
Gentry hustled me away, down toward the vanished dinosaur
where I was re-engulfed by the ice creams proffered at me from
all sides like microphones. I felt all done in with feeling for him,

as if he were my brother. My brother, who couldn't act to save his life.

From the mid-seventies into the eighties I lived in Barstow with Mr. Gentry. Life was quiet. I was biding my time, though I wasn't quite sure what I was biding it for.

Our stage work had dried up, not helped by a large-scale shift in human attitudes toward chimpanzees and animals working in entertainment. Supposedly, we were no longer funny. I was more than happy to admit that I was long past my best, though I worried for the younger chimps. (On the other hand, I thought, if chimps aren't picking up major leads any longer, then so much the better for my reputation. My *oeuvre* would grow in stature as the years went by!) There were the occasional appearances at parades, or for educational purposes at high schools, so it wasn't a total withdrawal from the entertainment industry. But I knew that as an actor, I was finished. I'd been finished since *Dolittle*. I'd been finished since *Tarzan and the Huntress*, when I was age fourteen. The older I got, the more it struck me that what I really was was a child actor.

In Barstow, I was part of the family. Actually, I *was* the family. I ought to mention here that there had been a Mrs. Gentry, but Mr. Gentry and she had had their problems. She claimed that he was more attached to his animal colleagues than he was to her, and she probably had a point. So, there were just the two of us. I watched a lot of television, avoiding old classics when they came on, was amazed by the coming of videocassettes, which were such fun to tug apart that the inevitable scolding was worth it. I fooled around in my tire, ate and slept and did my best not to think about the past.

I'd made a decision in '73 in Las Vegas. Yearning after the past was going to finish me off. From now on I would stamp down on those thoughts, like you stamp on the flames still springing up from a forest floor after a fire. I was just going to think about the present and bide my time. So I thought about the present, and by the time I was no longer yearning after the past all the time, I started worrying about the future.

Since '74 I'd put on quite a bit of weight myself. I heard the tree my tire hung from giving sarcastic creaks whenever I labored up into it. But Mr. Gentry was really letting himself go. He didn't exercise, he drank in the evenings though he only had me to keep him company, and he'd never smoked enough. He may have been pining for Mrs. Gentry. Clambering up around his neck was no longer advised because of his back, touch football ceased completely, and one afternoon his nephew came over to help convert the downstairs rumpus room (or "the dump") into a bedroom. As soon as stairs become the enemy, something's seriously amiss. "I'm going to end up in a wheelchair at this rate," he told his nephew. He had none of the positivity I encounter in my visits to the hospices—the positivity I'm increasingly convinced is the key to immortality.

"I don't want to hear any of that talk," said his nephew. "You could lose a few pounds, is all. You give me a pen and paper and I'll write you out a menu planner, right? Things you can't have, things you can. . . ."

"Listen, Don," Mr. Gentry said, "I'm not gonna last forever, and I don't want to spend my life worrying about what I eat, OK?"

So that was the first time I met Don. He was as skinny then as he is now, but he had a hell of a lot of long, unhealthy-looking hair, especially around the back of his head. He came over to Barstow from Palm Springs more and more frequently, to help with things that Mr. Gentry could no longer manage, like fixing a cage door I'd busted or carrying in the big sacks of monkey chow with which we stocked the pantry every quarter. I must say, I found Don ever so slightly annoying at first: he loved to play touch football with me, and as he did, he'd talk to me about movies. "Hey, what's it like, being a big star?," "How'd you get your break, Cheets?," "You got a number I can reach your agent on?"

Don was an actor too, but he was finding it hard to get anywhere, let alone into pictures. He wasn't quite sure of his direction in life, I could tell from snippets of conversations between him and Mr. Gentry. Mr. Gentry would talk about Mrs. Gentry and feed me my post-supper cigarette, and Don would talk about acting and disapprove of my cigarette. Don thought L.A. was a jungle, filled with the usual vultures, crocodiles, jackals and sharks that always got mentioned when people were feeling negative about Hollywood. The two of them agreed that it was a worthless place filled with crooks and cheats and always had been; then they put on a classic movie. I scurried off because I feared sighting some of those old familiar faces.

Don was sick of getting nowhere, but what he wanted to do with himself he wasn't sure. Something with animals, he thought. And this was what annoyed me, and still does a little about my dear friend—he's so down on humans. Don loved animals but I could hardly let him get away with some of the things he said about humans—you were like a virus, you were going to blow up the planet, you loved war (no, you don't, you hate it!), you were "the only animal that deliberately, cold-bloodedly kills" (first time I heard that nonsense), you were cruel, you didn't care about the environment(!), and I don't know what all. Whereas animals didn't lie or cheat or steal, etc. They didn't leave you. Don's OK and everything, but he doesn't believe in human beings the way I do.

Pretty soon Don was coming over two or three days a week—this was 1981, something like that—helping out Mr. Gentry by bringing groceries and stuff from the pharmacist, or just coming around to sit and chew the fat with me. He was coming to see *me* as much as Mr. G., I began to understand. Along with the groceries, there'd always be something for me: a particularly "delicious" fruit (which wasn't), a flower that was meant to squirt water from a plastic bulb but just dribbled, a videocassette specially for me to mess up (*that* I liked). Most often it'd be some slightly foolish chimp- or monkey-themed trinket like a key ring or a refrigerator magnet, which was no good to me at all but I appreciated the thought. One time he brought a whole pad of artists' paper and a tray of little circles of paint.

"You're crazy," Mr. Gentry said. "You can't afford this, Don. How much did it . . . ?"

"Three bucks or something. Nothing."

There was a price tag still on the pad. "Nine dollars ninety-nine cents? This is artists'-grade paper, you idiot. What's he gonna paint, the *Mona Lisa*? And he won't be able to use those paints anyway—they're too fiddly."

He was right. I gave it a shot and it was hopeless: hard little circles of paint that needed too much water and came out disappointing shadows of themselves. I slightly disheartened Don, I think, by going through them for supper: the lemon, the lime, the orange, the strawberry, coffee, mint and the black one I decided not to bother with. But still, it was Don that got me started.

Not long after that, Mr. Gentry abandoned all positivity. "There's nothing that anyone can do. It's just life. And if you think I'm stopping smoking now, you can forget it. Happens to everyone, sooner or later." That pessimism. Bad sign. "Hopefully it'll be later. I don't mind for me, it's him." Don tried to interrupt, but Mr. Gentry overruled him. "It's a totally impossible idea. I've spoken to UCLA and they're just about the best. It's cognitive research; they've got a stake in the animals' welfare. You haven't any experience whatever, Don. You don't have enough money for yourself. And it's not a pet, it's a full-time job. You'd be throwing your life away."

"I love him," said Don.

"Don't be fucking ridiculous," said Mr. Gentry.

"They'll kill him."

I thought, Oh, come on, they'll never kill me. I'm still *Cheeta*.

"Don't be fucking ridiculous. It's not some roadside zoo. And it's not a disease unit."

"Oh, that's such bullshit. A bunch of torturers in white coats who like to slice up innocent animals' brains. Then they wash the blood off and go home to their lovely wives."

"You don't even—there's nothing wrong with a lovely wife, Don," said Mr. Gentry. "You don't even know what you're talking about. Supposing he lives another five, six, seven, ten years? You'd be throwing your life away. Look, I know UCLA's not perfect but what else can I do?"

"You can let me have him."

Mr. Gentry sighed. "Let me call MGM. He must have made them a lot of money over the years. They ought to be able to put the word out, find *some*body who can take care of him. If not, then it's your funeral."

The old guys in the Palm Springs wards have a bit of a crush on me, I think. Don really hit on something when he came up with this as something to do. It's good for my profile to do a bit of charity work, and I love the idea of giving something back to you humans besides what I humbly refer to as my "art." In the long run that's not going to last, like I say, but the old guys seem pretty inspired by the idea that I will. There's one guy who shouts, "Call Mr. Guinness!" whenever he sees us. "Tell him his book's out of date."

I get a lot of requests to perform something comical and I give them the lip-flip, which is all I can manage these days. I think, Lay off, I'm a painter, not a comedian. But mostly they just want to touch me. It's not a very beautiful exchange, physically, I imagine. I've seen how much my head's getting like a coconut, how my fur's going white in these kind of random clumps, how my fingers have swollen into the joke-shop rubber suckers of the Creature from the Black Lagoon, and I always try to duck the reflection you get when you're going through the sliding doors back into the Sanctuary. I wouldn't want to touch me. As for them—well, you look at them now and wonder what they're going to look like in another fifty years. What's left to happen that already hasn't?

But they want to touch me. They'd never admit to something so unscientific, but they want to be sure death doesn't get *them* and they want to cop a feel just to be on the safe side. I'm lucky. I'm the luckiest chimpanzee in the world. More, I'm the luckiest non-human primate in the world. (I'm six years older than the oldest gorilla, baboon, orangutan and so on.) Frankly, I'm the luckiest animal in the world. That's pretty lucky. No wonder they want a touch and can't help asking, "Has he got a secret?" though with the positive attitudes I hear, I don't think any of my guys has anything to worry about. There is no secret, anyway, as I've said. It's as easy as breathing. If there was a kind of tips list, then I'd answer: "Luck, positivity, the absence of deadly snakes and no sudden loss of profile." (It's the *dip* that can kill, I think.) If there is one thing that they're missing, I'm tempted to say, "Cigarettes." Look at the humans *everyone* agrees will never die, the True Immortals: Bogie, Jimmy, Mitch. Not Brad, Tom, Arnold.

Don's answer would be, "Insulin." Every morning he rolls the little bottle between his palms to prepare the stuff, pinches up a little tent of flesh and injects. Twenty years I've been a diabetic: twenty years of injections from Don, and they don't seem to be doing me any harm, I'll say that. Maybe he's right and the insulin does have special properties—Don's mom seems fascinated by the little bottles and she's not a diabetic. She unlocks the little fridge while Don's in the den and stands there for long minutes, fearful of being discovered, weighing them in her palms.

The Sanctuary hasn't really changed that much since I first came here. That's good. Sanctuaries shouldn't change. The name's changed though: it's the C.H.E.E.T.A. Institute now, otherwise known as the Casa de Cheeta. The first sounds like a robot lives here, and the other makés me seem like a porn star. I preferred the Sanctuary, which is how it was twenty-six years ago when Don drove me up here after the funeral in Barstow was all done and dusted.

"No weeping and wailing," Mr. Gentry had said. "Death's nothing to be afraid of." But nobody at the ceremony took any of that seriously, I'm pleased to say. It was cruel, said the humans, but he hadn't taken care of himself. It was his own fault. He just hadn't taken enough care. . . .

"I never want to have to go through that ever again," said Don, and, hating death, we drove away from Barstow, down Route 15 through Victorville, where poor scooped 'n' flayed Trigger rears up emptily, to San Bernardino, then on to Route 10 to Palm Springs and sanctuary. And, with the exception of one brief trip, I haven't left here since.

What has time done to the place? Well, if you come out through the sliding doors, which you just flip this little black plastic thing to unlock (you wouldn't be so kind as to give us a hand?), then put your shoulder to one side and—it sticks a bit—shove (thanks again), here we are on the deck, which is about ten years old. Heavy-duty plastic table with midge bodies, tidemarked umbrella and, if you'll follow me, here we are in the garden! Note the plastic objects the childish animals toy with lying scattered around the lawn, see the midges doing galaxies and comets above our deflating crocodile in the pool, do not approach the flowerbeds, thanking *you*.

To your right you'll see that my mesh cube is now one of a series: here's Jeeter rolling his big red inflatable exercise ball around on the gravel of his shelter. He's been with us since '95. Careful, though, he's not used to you and these kids . . . you know what they're like, with all their vigor and mischief. He's used to me and he nearly fucking killed me, so watch those fingers.

And if you'll look up there—no, up *there* . . . there's Daphne lolling in her rope-cradle with that lovely unflustered long-limbed orangutan grace. She moved in in '98. You may remember her from such classics as the West Palm Springs Savings & Loan Take it Eazzzy Secure-Rate Tracker Account campaign and the Old Woodsmoke Quick-Burn Bar-B-Q Chips and Bar-B-Q Fluid shoot, with the apron and *that* expression.

On the other side of the warped MDF floor, behind the old cement-filled rain barrel, you may observe an elbow of Daphne's shelter-mate Squeakers, who arrived in 2000. Squeakers is a male (with those characteristic orangutan facial flanges, nubbly like basketballs) and the much-loved veteran of *Funky Jungle Disco!*, *No Freaking Way: Drugs Are Wack*, *Rainforest Detective Agency* and sundry other entertainments for human children.

Moving on—you'll get plenty of time to say hello to Squeakers later, and there will be a quiz—around the back of the garage, and do watch that cactus . . . meet Maxine, an olive baboon. Maxine's been with us since 2002. She is twenty-nine years old, weighs forty-four pounds, is unusually gentle and loves to perform, or is habituated to perform at any rate. She's showbiz through and through. The olive baboon, otherwise known as the Anubis baboon, ranges across a number of equatorial African countries . . . I can see some of you getting bored—listen, has anyone got a cigarette? What, *none* of you? Jesus, never mind, never mind, let's get on back to the house.

As we enter the Casa itself, you'll observe the piano (1992) where never in a million years could I even come up with "Chopsticks." If we ever manage to sell any CDs of my atonal noodles as "ape-music" I'd be pretty surprised, but it relaxes me, and Don does love a duet. Note the photograph of Uncle Tony on the wall above, in pride of place between a couple of Project posters. Without Mr. Gentry's small but invaluable bequest, along with this magazine feature we put together way back when, Don and I could never have started this venture. The kitchen area is open-plan, obviously, and here is my easel, or "table"; same thing basically, since I tend to alternate a mark on the paper with a fingerful of paint down the hatch. I do find my art "nourishing," ah ha ha ha ha.

So: this is the creative and commercial hub of the empire, where I earn the funds that keep Don afloat and allow him to be a full-time animal-carer. Yes, 'twas here that the Artist actually conceived and executed *Errol Flynn Postpones Ejaculation by Thinking of Two Hundred Dead Horses*, no flash photography, please. Old refrigerator ('97), new lockable refrigerator of insulin on the worktop (2004)—ladies and gentlemen, you'll note that no alcohol is allowed in the Casa de Cheeta. Since 1982, with Don's help and one slip, I haven't touched a drop. Twenty-five years, three months and two weeks, thank you for your commiseration: I put up with it a day at a time. I don't suppose . . . no, no, stupid idea, forget it.

Now, can any clever little person tell me what there's a lot of in here? Yes, that's right, honey—monkeys! Since 1982, the Sanctuary has been very gradually overwhelmed by the monkeys people give to Don in the absence of anything else they can think of. Tribes of magnetic monkeys suspend the monkeys who await our grocery requirements from the refrigerator door. Food is segmented by monkey cutlery on monkey plates and monkey placemats, washed down with water from a monkey-rimmed glass that lives on a monkey coaster. Monkeys hold our toilet paper and our monkey soap, they help us brush our teeth and tell the time and encourage us to grumble about Mondays. We haven't got monkey wallpaper yet, and we don't want any, thanks very much. There are now more monkeys in here than there are in the rest of America. But you can't seem to stop drawing or molding us, dearest visitors—you can't stop *drawing animals*, can you? You certainly can't stop giving them to Don.

And now let us make our way down the hall (bathroom; bedroom where, quiet, please, Don's taking his siesta; spare room which became a study in '99 and where I've been working on these memoirs) and past the glass-front bookcase with its thirty or forty books, all about old feelings, feelings from the past: *Hurt, Shattered, Sickened, Broken, Lost, Ruined*. Not to worry, every one of them's uplifting. Let's keep on down the hall toward the heart of it all, where this godforsaken infestation of monkeys is whittled down to one. Here is the den.

Let us enter the Cheetarium. Here is the Memorabilia Corner. Here are my reviews, here are my portraits. That's me with the attractive Dr. Goodall. There's me with the guy from *The Guinness Book of Records*, smashing my own record even in that sixteenth of a second. And look—me with an honorary Oscar, photofucking-shopped into my clutches. There's me and Don looking fifteen years younger, a commission in oils, and here's our sofa, with our twenty-six-year-deep indentations in it. It seems impossible. The years accelerate like coins vibrating on countertops. It seems so impossible. Twenty-six years, or one hundred and four seasons of television.

Twenty-six years and they feel like nothing. If I should ever die, Don would be devastated. He loves me. He calls me his "everything," and I'm very fond of him myself. Over there is the telephone table. On it, please observe, unstably erect in its crappy plastic cradle, the new complicated phone (2007) that resembles the old phone in that it never, ever, thrills to a call from Bogie or Kate or Van or Connie or Nunnally or Rita or Ty or Dolores or Niv ("He's no longer with us"—I know, he's in Switzerland) or Peter Lorre or Wayne or Huston or even Dietrich ("She's gone to a different place"—Paris, I heard) or Maureen. Not one of them. Not one, once, ever.

Now, shall we have a peek at the entertainment center (2006), ladies and gentlemen, boys and girls, or should we just leave it there, with the legend at peace in his Palm Springs hideaway? Shall we exit the den and find ourselves by the front door?

Yes, let's do that. Come on, out, the lot of you. Shoo. I'm a very old chimpanzee and I'm tired and the tour's over. Oh, yeah, I promised you a quiz, didn't I? It's very simple. Where is he? Have you seen him? A prize if you get it right. Now, please, go and pester Mickey Rooney. *Vamanos*, humans. We've got Don's mom coming over tonight and it can be very stressful if she's not feeling well. There's my statue: touch it for luck. And there's the road. Hit it, please. One day soon I will be driven down it myself, in a sort of bubble on wheels that a friend of Don's is welding together, all the way from Palm Springs to the wet cement of the Hollywood Boulevard Walk of Fame. If you ever see a chimpanzee passing in a Plexiglas pod at fifteen miles an hour through the Coachella Valley, like an old mad pope giving his blessing to the sinners of California, that'll be me *en route* to further Immortality. I can't wait: it'll be the first time I've been out of Palm Springs since the last time. Now fuck off, dearest humans, and leave me alone with my memories.

# 3
# Jane's Law

"What an absolutely lovely home you have here," said Katrina to the landlady of our villa.

I thought, Jesus, hold on, it looks like a bit of a dump to me, and downed another of my complimentary satsuma juices. On the other hand, I thought, Ooh-huh-ooh-*hah*-ooh-*hah*-ooh-HAH-ooh-*HAH*-ooh-*HAH*-ooaa*aaa*-HA-fucking-*HEEEEEEEE*! A surprise vacation, a Romeo y Julieta earmarked for me later and, who could tell?, maybe a couple of Coco Locos under the sun-kissed moon. And no Don! We'd nearly canceled when he fell ill, but it was just too much of a waste of money for Katrina and Mac (a lovely couple who worked for an august-sounding American publication called the *National Enquirer*) and me to miss out. *Arriba! Caramba!* Tequila! Mecheeta!

"Well, it used to be nicer before all this crap got in the way of the ocean," our landlady said, gesturing with clattering bangles at a cluster of latecomer condos. She let us through the iron gate in the concrete wall and onto the villa's terrace, a depressing courtyard where the sun didn't reach. The pool was very small and had an out-of-season look. A pile of straw in one corner wouldn't have looked out of place. Hell, it was only a base. "I'm Maria," the old

287

woman said in a faintly Dietrichian voice. Her smile was like a rather demanding technical accomplishment she'd learned long ago. "*Mi casa es su casa.* I hope the journey was OK?"

OK? Listen, I'd been expecting to fly to England for *Dolittle* but instead they'd locked me in a cold vibrating chamber at Kennedy and we must have taken the Atlantic Tunnel or something. Whereas that bath of blue light I'd just had, that groovily tilting funhouse packed with solicitous señoritas . . . that was fucking *flying*. I'd had the chicken. Then I had the beef. Then I had the chicken. Then I'd had a *gin-and-tonic* and some mini-chimichangas and Mac had heaved me over to the window to show me, way below us, the ever-safer ocean, as blue and empty as the sky. Miracles and meals all courtesy of those wonderful folks at Aeromexico, with a little nudge from my stardom. From the air, the white splat of the city around the bay resembled a colossal mound of guano, excreted by vultures the size of airplanes flying every half-hour from LAX. A semicircle of huge off-white hotels now rimmed the beach, like the canines and incisors of a display grimace: somewhere among them, like a crumb, was the Hotel Los Flamingos. Perhaps we'd bump into Grace Kelly, and I'd get a chance to apologize. Or do it again. Such a long time since I masturbated . . . and now a female in her late thirties came skipping over the tiles toward us.

"Here comes our lovely daughter Lisa!" Maria shouted weirdly, as if describing a contestant.

"Hi, guys!" Lisa said. "Woosie's had a really good walk!" Her leopard-print wrap clashed with her mother's zebra-pattern turban. I cheeped impatiently: come on, give us the keys, get the humans unpacked and showered and let's get out of this dump and hit the town, the three of us—Katrina and Mac and the legendary Cheeta—going Coco Loco in the palm-scented breezes at the Hotel

Los Flamingos, if they still had palm-scented breezes in 1983. Call it a sentimental journey. Trotting along behind Lisa, a trim young Mexican in white ducks and polo shirt told us that he'd walked Woosie and done his meal and he'd see us tomorrow. He shook hands. "*Hola*, Cheeta! *Muy grande* movie star!"

We'd always been big in Mexico, where everyone had a Tarzan yell: "*Aahheyyeyyeyyehhaaah!*" the kid added, and Maria turned and snapped, "Woosie! What d'you think you're doing, you silly thing?" and I looked around warily for the dog and there was a thin old man rising unsteadily from a wheelchair, starting to do *his* Tarzan.

"*Aah-eeh-aah,*" he said, and my heart was suddenly raving.

Dearest humans, once the Project's finished, perhaps you can turn your attention to peeling away all the crud of days and weeks and suppressions and accommodations that the world layers over us. Can you do that? I can see it's a bit to ask. But underneath it's all sparkling. All that pointlessness and waste just took itself off—it burned off like mist—and there we were, sparkling. I ran to him and threw my arms around his legs and he tottered back into his chair. Then I was in his lap and Johnny was saying my name over and over, and I could feel his chest heave up and down beneath mine. I was all over the place, like birdsong.

"Ah, what a lovely moment," said Maria.

"Goddammit," said Mac, "I'm going to need them to do that again."

Johnny held me and sobbed. I clung on.

"Mac, for Chrissakes, get a move on, you need to get this," Katrina said.

I could feel the thinness of his thighs under my feet. "Chee'a," he said, "Chee'a," and eventually he unpicked me so that we could look at one another.

The world was still going by, quietly putting its layers back down. His hair was white, and wild because it was thin, and his face had lost its symmetry. The skin on his cheek where I kissed him was rougher, and I could feel the bones of his shoulders: they were coming to the surface. In the folds of his throat was a little plastic valve, and under his opened shirt I could feel another hard, inorganic shape. "Goo' Chee'a," he kept saying, and there was something wrong with his voice, like only half his mouth was helping. Most of his words were just breath. But he was Johnny. I kept touching him in amazement, as if I was thumbing through a sheaf of paper on which I'd somehow randomly typed *The Complete Works of William Shakespeare.* Johnny, Johnny, Johnny, Johnny, *Johnny*! What a piece of work is a man!

Maria came over to us. "Is that a lovely surprise, Woosie dearest? Is that a lovely surprise? Where do you want to do this?"

"What I probably want," said Katrina, "is to get him inside, like you said on the phone. I hope we can get everything we need in there."

They did get everything they needed, though it was a squeeze with the six of us crammed into Johnny's single bedroom. What Katrina wanted was him back in bed, with me by his side. I wasn't going to be leaving his side, anyway. She wanted Mac to be able to get the IV stand in, and the oxygen cylinder, and the clouded plastic container on his flank. She wanted Mac to get Maria vacuuming out the gunk from the hole in his throat, and the cannula's crusted twin ends disappearing into his nostrils. What she needed was the worst "after" for the "before" that they would have. Johnny submitted to it all, like someone who had grown used to submitting, and we posed together while Mac took his time. There was his dear chest, which America had grown up with, had learned about time from—and now America was going to learn even more about time from it.

Katrina wanted to know what the secret of the Weissmullers' enduring love was. Maria said she didn't know but that it was a miracle, and I watched Johnny drift away from the humans' conversation. He gripped my hand. "Umgah, Chee'a," he half breathed. I still felt scattered, like the golden light rippling on the underside of a bridge.

"That's right, Woosie, Cheeta," Maria said. "Is this chimpanzee person getting the same as us for this, if I may ask?" Katrina couldn't divulge that, but it was substantial, with the whole thing being syndicated. How blessed did Maria feel by her marriage, despite the hardships?

"Uh . . . totally blessed?" said Lisa.

"Every day is a precious blessing," said Maria, "and we hope that, when he recovers from these recent setbacks, Johnny will continue for many, many years surrounded by the love and care of his family."

What did Johnny think? We waited. The overhead fan was having difficulty coping with us, and it was unpleasant in the room. There was something wrong about Maria, and the daughter was like a double exposure. Johnny stroked my hand against his face. "Umgah," he said. His mind came and went a bit, Lisa explained.

Mac had taken down a framed certificate from the wall and asked Mr. Weissmuller if he'd sit up with it: the visible print of the certificate read "Sporting Immortal," layered over a sepia portrait of Johnny in a swimsuit marked USA.

"Soon as . . . they ca' you . . . Immor'al . . . you star' . . . dyin'," Johnny half breathed.

"Ooh. You're damn well going to make your eightieth," said Maria, "and then there's our silver wedding! I'm not missing that!" There was no telling how long he might go on for, with a fair wind. Years and years! He'll outlive us all!

"Does he still swim?" Katrina asked. He liked to sit in the pool,

Maria said, on the steps, but he was naughty and you had to be careful. "Don't you?" she asked Johnny.

"I go' be . . . carefuh . . . otherwise I migh' . . . die. Tarza' drow's!"

Katrina liked the idea of getting a photograph in the pool, possibly with Johnny wearing his medals. But the medals had all gone. "Still, we can manage the pool, can't we?" she said, and Maria was left to help him with his trunks. Mac picked me up off the bed, and carried me out.

And I was already thinking, as Johnny shuffled out on white crane's legs and was helped down the steps and seated in the pool, that what I really was to him was a rescuer. That I had saved him from Captain Fry's cage, and saved him from the Nazis, saved him from the Leopard Woman and the Amazons, saved him from fire in *New York Adventure* and a sheer drop in *Secret Treasure*. I'd saved him from Jane; I'd saved him from Beryl; I'd even saved him, in a roundabout way, from Lupe. But I couldn't see how I was going to get him out of this one.

Mac had finished his photos and Katrina had some further questions for Maria—it wouldn't take more than half an hour and then we'd have to be back at the airport.

"You go insi' . . ." Johnny said, with some emphasis. "I'm ha'y ou' here. Go'n! Si' here for a bi'. "

"We can keep an eye on him from inside," Maria decided, and to my surprise we were alone in the stuffy little concrete enclosure. *Umgawa*, that was what he'd been saying. *Umgawa*, as in "get help."

I didn't know how this had happened. I didn't know that he'd arrived at this dingy wading pool because his friend Bö Roos had lent him enough money at high enough interest to end up collecting his house, or because his favorite daughter Heidi, whom I'd once felt aswim inside Beryl's belly, was killed in a car crash at nineteen, or because Johnny Weissmuller's Safari Hut Gift Shops and

Johnny Weissmuller's "Umgawa Club" Lounges and Johnny Weissmuller's American Natural Food Stores had all come to nothing, or because he was lonely after Allene left, or because of the stroke he'd suffered in Caesars Palace in '74, or that the secret of the Weissmullers' enduring love was simply that neither of them was ever going to leave, because what did either of them have to leave to? And it wouldn't have mattered if I had, because none of those were the reasons anyway. It was just a human fucking mess, and I didn't have a clue what I could do.

He sat there, three steps down and out of reach in the pool, with his back turned to me, and I gave a low hoot of dismay. Under the long strands of white hair he was bald. He might drown, I thought, and then that struck me as funny, my worrying about Johnny drowning. I came up to the edge of the pool and Johnny turned his head to see me and reached an arm out to the lip—if he leaned back and I leaned out we could touch. I managed to paw his fingers with a swipe, and almost lost my balance. "Chee'a. Frien', " said Johnny.

"Bes' damn frien' . . . I ever ha."

And that did it. What the hell. I stepped into the water. It went up to my waist on the first step and my shoulders on the second, and I suddenly remembered the panic and hatred I'd felt in the black water of Harold Lloyd's fake ninth green and started, through sheer terror, to drown, and then with a stretching sweep Johnny pulled me up and off my feet and I was floating on the cradle of his forearms. I was having a swimming lesson! I was really good! I felt . . . no years old. Hard to die when Mr. Tarzan's around.

We were Tarzan and Cheeta. We could do *any*thing. He won five Olympic golds and was a superstar of the silver screen, and he was a good man. And I was the best damn friend the poor bastard ever had.

* * *

So it's a perfect day, coming to an end now, in Palm Springs, California, and I'm flat out on the chaise having flipped through this memoir of mine. It's not Shakespeare, sure, but I'm totally amazed at how well it's turned out, given that I've just been randomly prodding at the keyboard. The *spelling*! And I think the whole Esther Williams chapter is, frankly, a masterpiece—so long as the lawyers don't mess it about too much. I'm the one in a million, I guess. I'm so damn *lucky*.

A bit sun-addled, I fall like an ideally humorous fruit the short distance off the chaise and shamble inside to the den. Twenty-five years since Acapulco, and not a squeak. There's a new one of mine up in here, *Johnny #12,562*, I believe. To tell you the absolute truth, I'm not terribly good at painting. Some of the work being done now by gorillas frightens me when I put it next to mine. Koko from the Berlin Zoo has painted some still lifes that'll knock your hat off, truly. Her colleague Michael's done one of a dog that looks like a goddamn *dog*. In the ape art world I'm just another abstract expressionist dabbler. And they're all meant to be him, anyway: I must have just randomly mistyped those other titles before. They're all Johnny.

Still, I've got a million years to get it right.

And here, at last, are the entertainment center and the DVD library. Sorry about the little tantrum before. Here are all the classics Don loves and here, on six disks, *The Tarzan Collection*: the eleven pictures with him and me that I'm condemned to be shown three or four times a year for the rest of time. I just can't stop myself. I can't bear to watch and I can't tear myself away, and I know I shouldn't, but there we are flickering in silver and I can't stop. You think it'll make you feel better. And every time I say: That's going to be the last. I can't stand them, but I'm terrified Don will notice and stop the screenings.

I know. Hysterical, isn't it? I'm so very, very *lucky*. Twenty-five years of pining, and counting. My heart has tinnitus, a continuous, faint, high-pitched background scream I never expect to be free of: *Love friend sad stay stay heart pain big stay heart pain big stay.* Is he still trapped in the hell-hole where I abandoned him, with his awful wife and her mad daughter? I don't know, and I don't think I'm going back down to Acapulco any time soon.

There's also the possibility that he's—oh, say it—dead, which might be a release. All I've ever heard from Don is that he's no longer with us, and I knew that anyway. In my head he's still alive, waiting to be saved. I keep him alive, anyway, because I love him. And I was going to suggest you put on a quick ten minutes of *Tarzan and His Mate*, just to see how incredibly beautiful he was, but now Don's mom is making a racket in the kitchen and, wow, it's a real bad one. She's pleading with him and Don has whacked on some whalesong in a fury.

"I can't hear you," he snaps, which is, like, maybe the fault of the whalesong, Don?

"Please do this for me. Please help me. I can't do it alone."

"No. No way. What did you ever do for me?"

"I'm sorry. But help me go now. Please. You only need half a bottle."

"No. It's illegal."

I'm out of here. I hate the sound of arguments. And Don is bitter about his mom. I try to creep as unobtrusively as possible through the living area, hunched down low and not looking, and all I hear under the whalesong is Don's mom sobbing at the painting table. "IIII'vvveee ggggooootttt aaaaa bbbbiiiiiigggggeeeerrrr

dddiiiiiiiccckkkk tttthhhaaaaannn ooootttthhheeeeerrrr wwwwhh-
haaaallleeesss. IIII'mmmm ttthhheeee gggrrrreeeeaaaattteeeessssttt,"
the whale's saying, and there's the shaky breaths of her grief, and
Don saying, "I'm sorry," and then, "Come here, Cheets, come here."

He wants a hug, and I give him half of one. Don's mom lifts her
head to say, "And you're keeping *him* alive!"

Maybe. But if she thinks that insulin's going to fix her Alz-
heimer's she's nuts. I'm such a coward with scenes—I skedaddle as
best I can. Out through the sticky terrace door and into a beautiful
evening. The sky has already got a few of the animals you've made
out of the stars lighting up in it. Hello, Bull, hello, Crab, hello,
Hunter.

Beautiful, clear desert evening. Squeakers and Daphne giving a
few dusky barks. You used to think they were people, orangutans—
it means "man of the forest" or something. The weedwhackers have
shut up. Sanctuary. Oh, if I could only paint this, this moment with
the midges lit up and a couple of faint high-traveling dots that
might be billionaires ballooning in the troposphere or just satel-
lites off which *Tarzan and the Leopard Woman* is rebounding, but
which are, most likely, those swimming specks—are they imper-
fections or microscopic life-forms?—falling through my own eyes.

I'm seventy-six years old. Fifty's good for a chimp. I'm an immortal miracle and life is very beautiful, but I think I've had
enough, dearest humans: I can't stand it without him anymore. I
just can't stand a ninety-seventh viewing of *Tarzan Escapes*. But
how can I die? I am the Cheater of Death. How can I die? Why can't
I die? I have my hopes that perhaps this book'll be the thing that
finishes me off. Or maybe he'll read it and lift off from his wheelchair and come rescue me for a change and . . . Oh, Lord, please dry
up my heart! I think. Oh, please, silence my tinnitic heart! Jane's
Law? It doesn't work. The hurt *doesn't* die down. It *doesn't* have to.

I plod off toward the flowerbeds, though I know full well I'm out of cigarettes. It's not such a great night tonight, really: it's that time of year once more and I've been waiting for a phone call from the Academy requesting my presence, and I think the bastards have left me out again. Have these guys even *seen*, say, *Tarzan's New York Adventure*?

I might just go and have a bit of a think in my tire. I have this fantasy acceptance speech—we all have fantasy acceptance speeches—which I try to make as credible as possible, like you do, no thanks, I've given up.

Oh.

Oh! Oh, thank you! Ooh . . . and a light! Quick, shield it from the house with your body. Oh, that's good. Ooh, that's a godsend. You star. You're a real friend. But what about . . . you don't mean to say it's your last one? Come on, we'll share it, you and me. Mmm . . . so I was saying: they can stuff their Oscar. I know exactly how it'll go, anyway.

"Honored Members of the Academy," I'll begin, after a twenty-five-minute standing ovation. I'll be communicating via American Sign Language and surtitles, probably, or some genius interpreter in a black turtleneck. I'll be wearing my old tux from the James Bond routine with Mr. Gentry. "This award, this much longed-for and, may I say, well-merited" (keep it light) "honorary Academy Award is not just for me . . ."

I'll pause to survey the auditorium. Seat-fillers are scurrying down the aisles to occupy the places left by actors and artists who've gone for a bathroom break or a line or two of homeopathic powder. There's Sean Penn, looking serious but heroic with his mane of integrity swept back, there's Tom Hanks, his neck bulging twice as wide as his head, and DiCaprio looking like a fat rat—like a capybara, actually, Leo, the world's largest rodent. There's Niv, with his hand furtively wandering under the bum of his date, and Bogie and Betty, untouchable. They're *smoking*. There's Mitch, there's Hitch; there's Clooney and Rooney; there's Marlene and Maureen and Mel. The Lumieres, the Fred Astaires, the Mayers and the players, and dearest Dolores del. The stars are well and truly out. I don't see Johnny, but I feel he's here somewhere. The orchestra is under orders or too stupefied with reverence to dare interrupt. You can tell it's going to be one of *those* speeches by the way Tim Robbins has gone all vindicated. And, of course, it's the Oscars, so we're live to the planet.

"Dearest humans. Colleagues. Esteemed fellow-toilers in the vineyards of Thespis! Friends, humans, countrymen! And you too, Dietrich, though you're no friend of mine and I doubt very much that you're human." Pause. There's a perceptible anxiety that maybe I'm drunk. I am! I'm absolutely and completely wrecked. How else could I get through this? But they can't get me off without looking bad.

"Fellow *creatures*. This wonderful honorary Academy Award, the first ever awarded to a non-human, is not for myself alone but for all animals."

That's more what they were expecting. Halle Berry, who introduced me, stops looking worried and starts looking humbly intrigued. "This award is not just for me but for the two hundred horses of *The Charge of the Light Brigade*, for the elephant electrocuted by Edison at Coney Island, for the swan accidentally drowned by David Selznick during the shooting of *Portrait of Jennie*, for every animal that has ever suffered for its cinematic art." Penn is loving this bit. He leads a sizable ripple of preemptively outraged applause. "And for all animals the world over who have given their time to entertain you—for every dancing bear and vaulting dolphin—this award gives them hope. Hope that though

I may be the first, I shall not be the last to stand humbled here in this auditorium, holding a statuette designed by Cedric Gibbons, whose wife, Dolores del Río, I *did not fuck*, incidentally." Whoops. "On behalf of all those animals, to all animal-lovers here and our billionfold TV audience, I would like to say . . ."

To say thank you? Or should I just roll around the stage, hysterical with laughter at the very idea of your expecting gratitude? Oh, yes, dear readers, I was just kidding before about the Project and rehab and all that crap, just being a cheeky monkey. Cheeta by name . . . I do know you're terrible killers. I do know what happened to Kong in the end. A million monkeys? Now that really is a fucking stupid idea—you ain't *got* a million monkeys anymore. And the Elephants' Graveyard is full up. Penn's looking expectant—he wants a full guilt-fest denunciation, though given the rap sheet that could take months, by which time the air-conditioning will have gone off, the buffet tables will be long emptied and savage bands of Oscar-winning actors, led by Chuck Heston and Liz Taylor, probably, will be roaming the aisles hunting down and eating the weak (Peter Lorre, Steve Buscemi). He, and others here, thrive on the self-hatred. They want me to say that, to an animal, your fears about global warming are as hilarious as the Kommandant fretting about the fire risks in a death-camp. They want to hear about my seventy-five years of incarceration. I go into a bit of a drunken reverie—thinking about my alternative memoir, provisionally entitled *Who Ate All the Fish?*—but luckily the audience just thinks I've been overcome with emotion. I can see Redford, and Goldie Hawn, and Jane Fonda, old Dickie Attenborough— good grief, they're *all* waiting, drooling, to be told how bad they are. Actors! I pull myself together and address the world.

". . . I would like to say, as an animal, that it's been a very special honor and a privilege to work with humans. How you love us!

How obsessively you dream us, and draw us, and see us in clouds and stock the bedrooms of your children with us! How touchingly hard you hope to cheat your destiny and stop eradicating us! We are your stars. We are *indispensable* to you, and you'll never get over it when we're gone. But I for one will never abandon you, no matter the pain and danger and constant mass murder, because you love and need us and it's wonderful, it is *wonderful* to be loved and needed like that. And I believe in you! You're the very best of us: no other species would even have come close to what you've done! You're amazing. Thank you for being you! Thank you so much for this wonderful award! Thank you to everybody I've ever met! You are all beautiful human beings! I love you all!"

Pretty standard Oscar fare, albeit from the heart. But around Robbins and Sarandon there's a kind of mutinous stir of disappointment, and now Penn is on his feet, starting to heckle. I've gone and lost my nerve, spoiled the party. "Dodos!" Penn's shouting aggressively. "What about the dodo?"

"Calm down, sonny," I gesture. "I'm a chimpanzee, not a fucking photographer!"

Fuck *you* care, anyway, Penn, I want to say, you're already convinced that you'll wipe us out and then yourselves. You campaign against it, but it's what you think. You're just a spasm of death. It's March 2009 and that's humanity's current thinking—that everyone's going to die, man and beast, and soon. Death, death, death— you'd think you'd created it, the way you go on! Anyway, that doesn't go down too well, and booing breaks out and I can see Security hustling toward me. Great, my big night and I'm going to get *tasered*. Oh well. My fantasy always breaks down around here: I never can seem to figure out the right thing to say.

Dearest, gentlest, sweetest, smartest, tallest, kindest, funniest, maddest, most thoughtful, most beautiful, most sorrowing, most suffering humans: who are you *really*? You are the *omnicidal*. You kill everything—everyone knows it. And even if you think of your-selves as wretched blood-soaked corpse-piling criminals, eye-deep in sin and despised by God for the terrible deeds you have done, I believe in you. Because of him.

I believe in you. I have a memory from way back, but I'm not even sure it's a memory. Out of a predawn sky an airplane smashed into the forest one day and we scrambled out of the canopy and found some bodies in the hull and an unharmed baby. One of us carried it up a wild custard-apple tree and we all gathered around.

We didn't quite know what this thing was. Its trusting gaze was the most vulnerable thing we'd ever seen, but there's power in that. Somehow its defenselessness stays our hands. Then again, it's fresh meat, and one of our group tries to snatch it in order to dash it to the forest floor. The thing starts to cry, scaring the ape into drop-ping it on a crisscross platform of branches—and it's me who finds the scrap of custard apple in his hand, and me who puts it between the thing's little lips and quietens it. It smiles. It's just like a little baby, but more magical. I feel protective, and curious: how would it turn out if we brought it up? What harm could come of trying? Or maybe we should just play safe and let it fall. Who knows what it'll grow into? And it's nearly breakfast-time.

We sit around, pondering uncertainly. There are flashes of fresh white wood in the foliage where branches have been torn by the crash, and butterflies and other insects are already settling on them to drink the sap. The sun's hitting the tops of the canopy now and hurrying down toward us.

Let it fall or raise it?

I pick it up. It *needs* me, I think. I'll be its friend, its protector, its rescuer and consoler. It's mine. "Umgah," it says, and I almost go and fucking drop it. And every day the planes keep crashing and the babies keep coming, and no matter how wrong everything goes, how far everything falls, I'll always choose to pick you up, and one day, one of you . . .

I'm sick of being immortal, and I can feel myself changing now. Thanks for the Lucky. I'm falling to the lawn and becoming a figment, a myth. I am Cheeta—father, brother and son of Tarzan, friend to humanity. Always have been, always will be. And if, dearest humans, if you ever felt there was a sort of foolish animal missing from your side—but also looking over you and wishing you well, and maybe mocking you a little though only out of love—then that's me. There are so many of us up here, among the stars, so many, and out of all of us I'm the one that's on your side. I'm the one up there trying to be the best damn friend you ever had. Me. Cheeta.

# Filmography

*Tarzan the Ape Man* (1932, MGM)
*Tarzan and His Mate* (1932, MGM)
*Tarzan Escapes* (1933, MGM)
*Tarzan Finds a Son!* (1939, MGM)
*Tarzan's Secret Treasure* (1941, MGM)
*Tarzan's New York Adventure* (1942, MGM)
*Tarzan Triumphs* (1943, RKO/Lesser)
*Tarzan's Desert Mystery* (1943, RKO/Lesser)
*Tarzan and the Amazons* (1945, RKO/Lesser)
*Tarzan and the Leopard Woman* (1946, RKO/Lesser)
*Tarzan and the Huntress* (1947, RKO/Lesser)
*Tarzan and the Mermaids* (1948, RKO/Lesser—did not appear due
   to previous commitments)
*Bela Lugosi Meets a Brooklyn Gorilla* (1952, Jack Broder)
*Doctor Dolittle* (1967, Twentieth Century-Fox)

# Picture Credits

While every effort has been made to trace the owners of the copyright material reproduced herein, the publishers would like to apologize for any omissions and would be pleased to incorporate missing acknowledgments in future editions.

PLATE SECTION ONE

p.1 Cheeta celebrates his 76th birthday © Frederick Neema/Camera Press 2008

p.2 Top: Henry Trefflich
Bottom: Maureen O'Sullivan, Cheeta and Johnny Weissmuller in *Tarzan the Ape Man* © Sunset Boulevard/Corbis 1932

p.3 Top: Still from *Tarzan and His Mate* © Turner Entertainment Co/Warner Bros 1932
Middle: Still from *Tarzan's New York Adventure* © Turner Entertainment Co/Warner Bros
Bottom: *Tarzan Escapes* © Bettmann/Corbis 1933

p.4 Lupe Vélez and Johnny Weissmuller © Hulton Archive/Getty Images c.1934

p.5 Top: Lupe Vélez and Johnny Weissmuller © Bettmann/Corbis 1934
Bottom: Johnny Weissmuller at sea © Bud Graybill/John Kobal Foundation/Getty Images 1935

p.6 Top: Constance Bennett and Gilbert Roland © Bettmann/Corbis 1935

Middle: Dolores del Río and David Niven © Hulton Archive/Getty Images c.1943
Bottom: Beverley Hills mansion © Bettmann/Corbis 1925
p.7 Top: Charlie Chaplin and Paulette Goddard © Bettmann/Corbis 1937
Middle: Mickey Rooney as "Mr. Yunioshi" in *Breakfast at Tiffany's* © Bettmann/Corbis 1960
Bottom: Marlene Dietrich beside her rare Cadillac Fleetwood Town Cabriolet © Margaret Chute/Getty Images 1935
p.8 Johnny Weissmuller © George Hurrell/John Kobal Foundation/Getty Images c.1935

PLATE SECTION TWO
p.1 Painting by Cheeta
p.2 Top: Johnny and Bobbe Weissmuller swimming © Bettmann/Corbis 1931
Bottom: Beryl Scott with Johnny Weissmuller Jr.
p.3 Top: Johnny Weissmuller marries Allene Gates © Popperfoto/Getty Images 1948
Bottom: Johnny Weissmuller and Maria Bauman
p.4 Top: The *Tarzan* cast sitting in a tree © Getty Images 1939
Bottom: Still from *Tarzan's New York Adventure* © Turner Entertainment Co/Warner Bros 1942
p.5 Top: Johnny Weissmuller as Tarzan is threatened by a leopard woman with a giant claw © Bettmann/Corbis 1946
Bottom: Still from *Doctor Dolittle* © Twentieth Century-Fox 1967
p.6 Top and bottom: Paintings by Cheeta
p.7 Top: Chimpanzee riding a unicycle and holding an American flag © Time & Life Pictures/Getty Images
Bottom: Ham, the first primate to be launched into space © Popperfoto/Getty Images
p.8 Top: Cheeta with Cheeta toys © Frederick Neema/Camera Press 2007
Top middle: Cheeta holding a photograph of Johnny Weissmuller © Frederick Neema/Camera Press 2003
Bottom middle: Cheeta doing a lip flip © Glen Coburn 2008
Bottom: Jeeter © Dan Westfall 2007

# Index